Praise for The Underworld Chronicles Series

"Nielsen cleverly keeps the action and humor flowing from one silly obstacle to the next...Definitely a series to invest in."

—Kirkus

"Oh dear. Funny names (Fudd Fartwick, Tubs Lawless) and unexpected events (almost being scared to death) tumble through the pages, and Nielsen writes about them with tongue in cheek."

—Booklist

"Jen Nielsen invites us into a frightful, funny world...I want to live there. Crown this book King of Goblin comedy and fright."

—Ruth McNally Barshaw, creator of Ellie McDoodle

"A perfect mix of goblin antics, a likable hero, and droll humor!"

—R.L. LaFevers, author of *Theodosia and the Eyes of Horus*

Praise for *The False Prince*

"Sage is deftly characterized through humorous first-person narration...[A]n impressive, promising story with some expertly executed twists."

—Publishers Weekly Starred Review

"A swashbuckling origin story...Sage is a quick wit, and Nielsen showcases it with terrific dialogue...chock-full of alluring details for adventure-loving boys."

—Los Angeles Times

"A surefire mix of adventure, mystery, and suspense."

—Horn Book

"A page turner..."

—The New York Times Book Review

"Sage proves to be a compelling character whose sharp mind and shrewd self-possession will make readers eager to follow him into a sequel."

—The Wall Street Journal

Published by Sourcebooks Jabberwocky, an imprint of Sourcebooks, Inc.
P.O. Box 4410, Naperville, Illinois 60567-4410
(630) 961-3900
Fax: (630) 961-2168
www.jabberwockykids.com

Library of Congress Cataloging-in-Publication data is on file with the publisher.

Source of Production: Worzalla, Stevens Point, WI, USA
Date of Production: June 2014
Run Number: 5001703

Printed and bound in the United States of America.
WOZ 10 9 8 7 6 5 4 3 2 1

The Underworld Chronicles

Includes:

Elliot and the Goblin War

Elliot and the Pixie Plot

Elliot and the Last Underworld War

JENNIFER A. NIELSEN

ILLUSTRATED BY GIDEON KENDALL

sourcebooks
jabberwocky

Table of Contents

Elliot
and the
Goblin War

For Bridger, who can become anything he wants.

Contents

As of today, there are only seven children who have ever read this book and lived to tell about it. Ninety-five children successfully read the first chapter, but upon beginning chapter 2, they started blabbering in some language known only as "Flibberish," which makes it very hard to tell their parents why they can't finish their homework. Thirty-eight children made it halfway through this wretched book before their brains simply shut down and they began sucking their thumbs through their noses.

But these are minor problems compared to what happened to those who read the final chapters of this book. The only thing known for sure is that something in chapter 15 seems to make body parts fall off.

If you're very brave, one of those who would battle a dragon with only a toothpick for a sword, perhaps you are willing to take your chances and turn the page. But before you read even one more sentence, be sure that you have told your family who gets your favorite toys if you do not survive this book. Read it now, if you dare. But don't say you haven't been warned, for this is the story that unfolds the mysteries of the Underworld. Turn the page and begin *Elliot and the Goblin War*.

Chapter 1

Where Elliot Gets a Little Scared

WHEN HE WAS EIGHT YEARS OLD, ELLIOT PENSTER STARTED an interspecies war. Don't blame him. As anyone who has ever started an interspecies war will tell you, it's not that difficult to do.

Elliot had spent the evening trick-or-treating. Everyone thought he was dressed as a hobo, but he wasn't. He didn't have money for a Halloween costume, and so he'd just gone in his everyday clothes.

On that night, his everyday clothes were a pair of his big brother's old jeans with a hole in one knee, a T-shirt that sort of fit if he didn't lift his arms up, and a long-sleeved plaid shirt over it that *did* fit. He also wore two different shoes, which weren't part of his everyday clothes. It's just that he couldn't find their matches.

Either way, he was on his way home with a big sack of candy, which is all that ever really matters on Halloween. He dipped his face into his sack and sniffed up the blend of chocolate, fruit, and sugar smells. And lead? Elliot pulled an orange pencil from his sack and then dropped it back in. Who gives pencils for Halloween? Probably the dentist over on Apple Lane.

Elliot wrapped his sack up tight to keep the smell inside until he got home. He planned to share a few candies with his family and then go wild with the rest in one night of sugar-crazed insanity.

"Help!" a voice cried.

Elliot turned to see a little girl running toward him, dressed as an Elf. Her right arm flailed wildly, and in her left arm she carried a sack almost as big as she was. Every time she screamed, all the dogs in the area howled. Chasing her were two kids about his own size dressed as Goblins.

"Hey!" Elliot yelled at them. "You're not supposed to take someone else's candy!"

Elliot ran toward the kids in the Goblin suits. He tossed his heavy sack of candy over his shoulder then swung it toward them. It hit one Goblin in the shoulder and knocked him into the other. They fell on top of each other on the ground.

"Stay out of this," the Goblin on the bottom snarled. "You're only a human boy."

"Don't make fun of my costume!" Elliot yelled. "Just because you can afford a cool costume doesn't make you cool."

The Goblin on the top rolled to his feet. "We don't want to be cool. We want to be scary."

"My sister cooks dinners that are scarier than you," Elliot said. It wasn't an insult to his sister. She really did.

"You want to see scary?" the Goblin asked. He crouched down on all fours and let out a growling sound that Elliot didn't think any human voice could make.

Then something happened, something Elliot had never seen a costume be able to do before. Not even the expensive ones. It began bubbling, as if it had become a vat of black, boiling oil. Ripples of bubbles started small but gradually grew bigger, almost as if the Goblin itself were growing in size.

Elliot's eyes widened. He'd seen things like this in the movies before. Even if this was only a costume, it was still a lot scarier in person than watching it in a theater with a bucket of popcorn on his lap. He didn't want to watch it, and yet he found it impossible to turn away. Something in his brain yelled at him to run or else he'd be sorry. Elliot agreed with his brain, but his legs didn't obey. He stumbled back a step and then jumped when the Goblin extended a hand—which now looked more like a claw.

"Don't look at him!" the girl in the Elf costume yelled.

Elliot had nearly forgotten about her. Instinct took over, and he swung his sack again at the Goblin, but this time the claw grabbed the sack and tore at it, ripping a big hole. Candy poured out, most of it landing with a *kaplunk* in a big puddle of water that splashed all over the Goblins. The Goblins leapt a foot into the air and screeched as if the water was somehow painful to them. The bubbles melted back into the costumes, though Elliot thought there were holes the size of water droplets in their clothes now.

Without a glance backward, they ran down the street and vanished into the night.

It took a moment for Elliot's heartbeat to return to normal. When he caught his breath, he yelled after them, "Babies!"

If water ruined their costumes so easily, they should've worn something else. He leaned over and picked up a few pieces of candy that weren't too wet. It was the cheap candy, like the kind old women keep in bowls by their TV remotes. There wasn't even enough left to share with his family.

"Sorry about your candy."

Elliot turned to see the girl in the Elf costume speaking to him. She had a small mouth and huge brown eyes. Her hair was thick and hung to her shoulders. Looking at her, Elliot finally understood what a button nose is.

"That's all right," he said. "Someone probably would've stolen it before I got home anyway."

"You have Goblins too?"

He smiled. "Around here we call them bullies."

"Oh." She held out her sack. "Since your candy's ruined, you can have this."

Elliot peeked inside. It was filled with long, green pickles. Dozens of them. Pickle juice leaked from a small hole in her bag and made a smelly puddle on the ground. "Um, no thanks," he said.

"I've got more if you change your mind." She closed her sack and added, "That was really brave, risking your life for me like that."

Maybe that was a bit of an exaggeration, Elliot thought, but he smiled kindly. She was so young, she must've thought the Goblin costumes were real. Poor thing was probably scared half to death. He said, "Nice costume. You're an Elf?"

She puckered her face. "Everyone knows that Elfish ears are short and pointy. I'm a Brownie. My ears are bigger and pointier, see? And Elves are much taller than Brownies. My name is Patches."

"Hi. I'm Elliot." He shifted his feet and found himself staring at her eyes. He'd never seen anyone with eyes that large or that round. "Well, I'd better go home now."

"Okay. Well, thanks for what you did. I won't forget it."

Patches never did forget it, but Elliot's mind was on something entirely different before he even made it home. Maybe he would've remembered if he had known the girl he saved wasn't a human in a Halloween costume, but a real Brownie from her Underworld home.

And as your clever mind also must have guessed, Dear Reader, she was being chased by real Goblins.

Patches went to her Underworld home to tell the other Brownies about her new hero, Elliot Penster. Elliot Penster went home without any Halloween candy. And the Goblins who had ruined his Halloween went home to start a war.

Chapter 2

Where a War Begins

AFTER LEAVING ELLIOT, THE GOBLINS RETURNED TO THEIR Underworld city of Flog. If the name Flog makes you think of a sunny place with green grass and chirping birds, then you are not thinking of the same Flog as where the Goblins live. In the first place, you should have known there's no sun, because Flog is deep underground. Flog gets some light from the glow of the Elves' kingdom, but never quite enough. So it always feels like that hour after the sun goes down but before the moon comes up. Instead of grass and flowers, there are rocks and dirt, and even if a chirping bird somehow finds its way underground, it had better get out quick before it's eaten by a hungry Goblin.

The Goblins weren't hungry at the moment, though. They were busy listening to their two friends describe exactly what Elliot Penster had done to them.

Goblins rarely came face-to-face with a human anymore. That sort of thing used to happen more often a few hundred years ago.

In those days, a Goblin could sneak into a human's home or barn and cause all sorts of wonderful trouble, such as tipping over a lantern or setting the cows loose in the pasture. Meanwhile, the do-good Brownies would work throughout the night repairing holes in shoes or cleaning out fireplaces, always trying to help the humans who did so little for the Brownies in return. It just made the Goblins look even meaner than they actually were.

The Brownies were always careful to leave the home before anyone awakened, but it became quite common for a human to stumble upon a Goblin in the act of causing trouble. When the humans started fighting back, the Goblins had no choice but to join the creatures of the Underworld.

The Goblins still went to the surface now and then, but only if it was really important, such as to chase after a Brownie with a big sackful of pickles. And now that a human had gotten in their way, they crowded into a tight circle to hear the dreadful tale.

If you had actually been sitting with the Goblins in Flog (which I hope is not something you'd ever consider doing, even if you're invited to come; as you've just read, Goblins don't like humans), then you would not have understood what the two Goblins were saying about Elliot. It would have sounded like this: *Arkny flob goopah boohinder human Elliot*, which of course means, "On the surface there is a dangerous human named Elliot" in Flibberish.

All Underworld creatures speak a common language called Flibberish. It is very much like English, except that all the letters to all the words are entirely different. And of course, Flibberish speakers end every conversation by spitting at each other. Many Underworld creatures speak both Flibberish and English, but to make reading easier for you, Dear Reader, whenever the creatures speak in Flibberish, it's been translated to English. If you still can't read it, then you probably don't speak English. Try reading something in Icelandic or pig Latin, and see if one of them is your language instead.

"Tell us about the dangerous human named Elliot!" someone yelled from the crowd.

The larger Goblin, also with the larger vocabulary of at least twenty words, spoke for both of them. "There we were, minding our business"—as they saw it, their business was chasing after an innocent Brownie and her pickles—"when this human ran over to pick a fight with us."

The Flog citizens gasped in horror. Humans were their favorite villains in any story.

"He beat us with a sackful of chocolate candies." More gasping followed this terrible news. "That's right, it was chocolate," the Goblin continued. "We were lucky to escape alive."

The smaller one thrust out his arm, which was covered in welts. "He gave us these too." This had happened when Elliot's sack of candy fell into the water. Water always burns Goblins.

"And he broke all the bones in your face!" a Goblin yelled from the crowd. "You look awful!"

The smaller one rolled his eyes. "No, that's my real face. I always look this way."

There was a slight moment of silence while many Goblins considered that all of them always looked that way. The awkward feeling was soon forgotten as another Goblin in the crowd yelled, "This means war!" It was followed by cheers and plans to go to the surface and begin attacking the humans.

"You'll never win," a Goblin in the back said. His voice sounded like two pieces of sandpaper rubbing against each other. Music to a Goblin's pointy, hairy ears.

Every green Goblin head turned to see the greenest Goblin of all walking to the front of the crowd. His name was Grissel, and he hadn't been seen in public for fifty-five years. He was a decorated hero of the Great Goblin War of the last century, having rescued the entire city of Flog from a human invasion. Goblin children sang songs about him. Goblin females left pickle pies on his doorstep. And Goblin males tried to imitate his fashion sense, although they could never get the rag tied around their waists in just the right way.

By the time Grissel reached the front of the crowd, everyone was silent. He looked the Goblins over for a few moments and then said, "We don't want a war with the humans. There's nothing we want on the surface."

"We want pickles!" a Goblin said.

"And if we kill all the humans, who'll make more pickles for us to steal?" Grissel snarled. "Tell me, what do we like more than pickles?"

"Puppy dogs?" another Goblin said. "Cute little doggies with those sad puppy eyes? They make you just want to hold them and give them a hug."

Grissel stared in disgust and then pointed a finger at the Goblin, who promptly blew up. When the dust settled, Grissel repeated, "I said, what do we like more than pickles?"

This time there was silence, which wasn't a surprise. Nobody likes to get blown up just for giving a wrong answer.

"We like Brownies," Grissel said. "Maybe a human got involved with us on the surface, but we were after the Brownie girl. If you want to go to war, then we go to war against the Brownies."

A cheer rose throughout the crowd.

So it was, on Halloween night while Elliot lay in his bed feeling bad about having lost his candy, that the Goblins declared war on the Brownies. And the Underworld would never be the same again.

Where Elliot Sees the World
a Whole New Way

THERE ARE MANY CAUSES OF FORGETFULNESS, INCLUDING AT least 236 different diseases, most of which you probably can't pronounce. A good way to know that you don't have any of those forgetting diseases is if you remember that the Brownie child, Patches Willimaker, had decided to keep her eye on Elliot in case the Goblins returned again.

(If you don't remember that, then you might have some form of amnesia. You may have forgotten that you have amnesia, because if you do remember having it, then it probably isn't amnesia at all. Maybe you just weren't reading carefully.)

Three years passed from the night Elliot saved Patches from the Goblins, and all that time, she watched him. Elliot lived in the very small town of Sprite's Hollow, which is about a hundred miles away from anywhere you'd want to be. The weather there was usually just about right for the time of year, except for last July when hail the size of golf balls fell all over town and refused to melt afterward. (Or maybe it was the mini-golf tournament they held around town that day. No one really knows for sure.)

Sprite's Hollow was normally a peaceful town, where cows and chickens outnumbered the people, so it was never hard to find Elliot. A person could run from one end of town to the other in less than twenty minutes, even faster if you were Elliot and were being chased by one of the school bullies.

By the time he was eleven years old, Elliot was so skinny that his normal-size head looked too large for his neck. He had blond hair every summer and brown hair every winter and red hair only once, when he fell into a bucket of mashed beets. His legs had grown in the last year, and his great hope was that the rest of his body would soon grow to match.

Sprite's Hollow was also the kind of town where a kid could get into a lot of trouble with only a little effort. Some kids got into trouble by changing road signs so that travelers who thought they were leaving town actually went back the way they had come. Others snuck into barns and added chocolate syrup to the cow's water, hoping the cow would then produce chocolate milk.

Elliot's trouble was named Tubs Lawless, a kid from up the road who was two years older and two heads taller. He was dumber than a Popsicle and so mean that he jumped every time he looked in the mirror.

Patches had helped Elliot escape trouble with Tubs more than once. Of course, Elliot didn't know that, but she figured over the past three years she'd saved him from at least eighteen bruises, two black eyes, and one note taped to Elliot's back telling the rest of the school to kick him.

Today he was in a bit more trouble than usual. Patches watched Tubs chase Elliot behind Elliot's house. She ducked behind a large elm tree as they raced across the grass on the edge of the woods that bordered Elliot's backyard. The woods were mystery territory. No kid had ever explored them all. Even Elliot could get lost in there. It was rumored that a boy named Mavis had been lost in there for the last twenty-eight years.

No sooner had Elliot run into the woods than a rope grabbed him by the leg and yanked his body up in the air, hanging him upside down. As Tubs got closer, Elliot squirmed to get free, but the rope only tightened.

The rope trap was Elliot's father's idea. He figured it was a good way to catch dinner for the family. It had worked only once before, trapping a skunk that sprayed Elliot's father in the face when he let it go. Now the trap had caught Elliot. Elliot wished he had something to spray Tubs with, like extra-strength bully repellent.

Tubs ran up so close that their noses were almost touching, except of course Elliot's nose was upside down.

"Next time I make you do my homework, you'd better put in the right answers," Tubs said.

"I wrote that Tubs Lawless has pudding for brains," Elliot said, smiling. "I thought that *was* the right answer."

"How should I know?" Tubs asked. "But if it was, then why did the teacher mark it wrong?" After a moment, his eyes widened and he said, "Hey! Pudding for brains—that's an insult!"

Tubs backed up and grabbed a handful of rocks, which he began throwing. Even upside down, Elliot did a pretty good job at avoiding the rocks, but Patches knew Tubs would get in a hit soon. She rolled up her sleeves, preparing to do a little magic to get Elliot down.

"I thought we smelled manure back here," a boy behind Elliot said. "Wait, it's only Tubs."

"Hey, Tubs! Look this way!" another boy said.

Patches turned to see Cole and Kyle, Elliot's six-year-old twin brothers, standing in the yard with a long hose kinked in their hands and a naughty spark in their clear blue eyes. The twins released the kink, and a stream of water shot at Tubs, hitting him squarely in the chest. It knocked him to the ground. He crawled backward, cried for his mommy, then ran away.

"Thanks!" Elliot told his brothers. He didn't often use their names, because he couldn't tell them apart. He sometimes wondered if Kyle and Cole even knew who had which name.

"Our pleasure," answered the twins.

Cole and Kyle loved anything with water. They'd been suspended from kindergarten in their first week for putting a water snake in the boys' bathroom toilet, which got into the pipes and ended up flooding the entire nonfiction section of the school library.

"Mom and Dad are going to be home at any minute!" Elliot's fifteen-year-old sister, Wendy, cried as she barreled into the woods. "Look at this mess. Dinner's going to be burned now." She had white flour in her brown ponytail. That meant bad news. She was cooking.

Elliot and his brothers looked at each other. If the family was lucky, burned was the only problem with Wendy's food. The only reason anyone ever came to eat was because she tricked them by putting a yummy-smelling dessert in the oven to call them.

"I'll cut you down, but I'll be late for work," said sixteen-year-old Reed, the oldest of the Penster children. Reed helped the family by sharing his earnings from working in a fast-food restaurant named the Quack Shack. Nobody thought duck burgers had much of a chance in becoming more popular than plain old hamburgers. They were right. Duck nuggets dipped in barbecue sauce weren't too bad, though. Reed also tried to improve his family's meager food supply by bringing home leftover pickle relish each weekend in case anyone wanted some. No one ever did, and Reed's collection now fit in a jar almost as tall as he was.

Elliot was cut down and the family walked back to their home, a two-story wooden box that leaned in whatever direction the wind blew.

Patches crept out from behind her tree and cradled her head in her hands while she watched them go. It would've been nice to rescue Elliot from Tubs, but that wasn't why she had come here. The Brownies weren't doing well in the war against the Goblins. In this case, "not doing well" meant they were losing in every way possible. She knew that one day the Goblins would decide to come after Elliot too. And she was right.

But as you will see, it didn't happen in the way Patches thought. Elliot just wasn't that lucky.

Chapter 4

Where Queen Bipsy's Spleen
Dies. And Everything Else.

D EAR READER, YOU MAY WONDER WHY I HAVEN'T SAID anything yet about a character in this story named Diffle McSnug. The answer is simple. There is no character in this story named Diffle McSnug. As far as I know, nobody named Diffle McSnug has ever existed, so I'm not sure why you'd think I should write about him.

Even if Diffle McSnug existed, he wouldn't have time to sit around in Elliot's story, waiting to do something important. He'd be off on his own adventure, which right about now would involve his diving with sharks to recover some sunken pirate treasure. Only he's almost out of air and the sharks are licking his toes.

I'm sure you'd love to hear how he escapes. It's too bad he never existed, because if he did, I'm sure that would be a fascinating story.

There is someone far more important to write about in this book, and that is the Brownie known as Queen Bipsy. She had just reached the end of her 561st birthday. That would be extremely old for a human, but for a Brownie it was only very old. Her birthday party was the largest in the Brownie Underworld, because she was the queen of the Brownies, and not attending her birthday party was a crime punishable by ten years of hard labor. (Hard labor in the Brownie world is the nonstop eating of chocolate cake...without frosting or a glass of milk, if you can imagine the horror of it.)

Something happened to Bipsy that night as she walked home from her birthday party. From the corner of a cave someone whispered, "Psst, look over here."

Everyone knows that if someone whispers, "Psst, look over here," that definitely means you should *not* look over there. If there were a good reason to look, then they wouldn't have to say "psst" in a whisper.

Queen Bipsy must not have known this, because she did look. From out of the shadows, she saw something bubbling to life. Ripples moved along leathery green skin, and the figure grew in size. Bipsy knew she should run, but all the wiggly juice she had drunk at her party weighed her down. She wanted to run but couldn't move.

Her eyes remained fixed on the monstrous creature, even as it rose above her. The only reason she was still watching it, and not lying dead on the ground from terror, was that she was full up to her eyeballs with wiggly juice, which made her vision blurry.

She could see it well enough to cause her Brownie heart to do a cancan dance inside her chest, though. And she clearly heard the pleasure in the monster's voice as he said, "It took me three years, but I finally got you, Queen Bipsy."

"Queen Bipsy? Are you all right?" A hand touched her shoulder, breaking her trance. The monster that had been in the cave shrank away, and Bipsy turned to face her friend Mr. Willimaker. Even at this late hour and after such a happy party, he still looked morning fresh.

Ordinarily, Brownies don't worry too much about their personal appearance. They usually have a lot of thick hair, which always looks a little gray no matter what color it really is. Their pointy ears often clog with earwax, and their fashion sense stalled a couple of centuries ago. Their only virtue is they bathe often. Just because one lives in the Underworld doesn't mean they have to smell like the Underworld.

Mr. Willimaker was different. His clothes were made by a Pixie tailor and always the latest in Elfish fashion wear. He trimmed his hair and used a bit of magic each morning to get it pointing all the same way. He wore oversize glasses that made his oversized eyes look even bigger and which often slid off his undersized nose.

Most Brownies found it funny that Mr. Willimaker always dressed for success, because success was the last word they would use to describe him. Three years ago, he had run through Burrowsville, the Brownie city, warning everyone to get out while they could. They were being invaded by a strange creature that no doubt planned to kill each and every Brownie in some gruesome way. Mr. Willimaker caused near riots as Brownie families gathered what supplies they could and hurried into the streets.

The mystery was solved by Mr. Willimaker's own daughter, Patches, who recognized the invading creature as a simple field mouse from the surface world. It must have gotten lost and somehow found its way to the Underworld. She scooped the field mouse into her arms and gave it a loving hug. With Queen Bipsy's help they sent it back home.

The Brownies were angry with Mr. Willimaker for several months at the trouble he had caused. After that, he was laughed at wherever he went. Jokes were written about him, and every time something unusual happened in Burrowsville, the Brownies said, "Maybe it's a mouse attack." If it weren't for the fact that Queen Bipsy was still his friend, Mr. Willimaker would have been laughed out of Burrowsville long ago.

"Are you all right, Queen Bipsy?" Mr. Willimaker asked again.

"No," she answered. "I think I've just been scared to death."

"Pardon me for correcting you, Your Highness, but I notice you're still alive."

Queen Bipsy plumped down on a rock and folded her arms. "Scared *half* to death, then. And I think very soon the other half of me will die."

Mr. Willimaker wondered which half of her had died. Both halves of her body looked equally upset with him. "Could you wait to finish dying until tomorrow?" he asked. "Maybe by tomorrow you'll change your mind and be fine."

"I am the queen, and I'll die when I want to," Queen Bipsy insisted. "I've lived a full life, and besides, I'm pretty sure my spleen just died. You don't seriously expect me to continue living with a half-dead body and no spleen, do you?"

Mr. Willimaker didn't answer. He thought maybe it was a trick question.

Queen Bipsy looked around her. "I need to choose the next ruler of the Brownies. Where's my royal scribe?"

Her royal scribe had been killed in a Goblin attack over a year ago. Maybe her spleen had been in charge of remembering that, before it died.

"I can write for you," Mr. Willimaker offered. He patted his pockets. Somewhere he had a pen—ah, there it was. But paper. He didn't have any paper! The future of the Brownie kingdom was at stake. Why couldn't he find one tiny scrap of paper?

"I don't have all day to die," Queen Bipsy muttered. "Could you hurry it up?"

"Go ahead, Your Highness. Oh! I mean, go ahead and speak. Not go ahead and die. I'll find some paper soon." Mr. Willimaker continued looking through his pockets. He didn't need much. An inch of paper would do.

Queen Bipsy's eyes widened and she gasped. "Too late. I think this is it, the end. I believe this may be my last breath before I die."

Mr. Willimaker gave up his search for paper. Then he did what everyone does when they have an emergency need to write something down. He put the pen to the palm of his hand and said, "I'm ready. What is the name?"

"No, it seems I have another breath." She drew in a slow breath and then added, "There, now this one is probably my last."

Mr. Willimaker leaned forward. "If you could please use that breath, then, to tell me the name of the next ruler…"

"The Brownies will have a king this time."

"A king—yes, that's fine. What's his name?"

"There's only one person—" She paused as she sucked in some air. "You must give him everything necessary to succeed. His name is—"

Then Queen Bipsy's head fell forward onto her chest. Mr. Willimaker sadly bowed his head. She had been a good queen, noble and kind. Her death had come too soon for the Brownies who loved her.

"His name is the following," Queen Bipsy said, tapping him on the shoulder and nearly causing him to jump out of his skin. (You, the reader, may also have nearly jumped out of your skin when you realized the queen was not as dead as Mr. Willimaker had suspected. Studies have shown this very thing happened to twenty-three other readers who failed to fit back into their skin after this point and have had to go skinless since.)

Mr. Willimaker put his pen to his palm. "Yes?"

"No time left to say the name," she whispered. "You must choose him."

Mr. Willimaker tried to point out that it would have been faster to say the name than to have ordered him to choose someone, but it was too late. For when she closed her eyes this time, it was certain she had died, because she didn't spit.

Mr. Willimaker stared at his hand, as if the name should magically appear there. How was he to choose the next king? For a brief moment he considered writing in his own name, but then he remembered that most Brownies would rather be ruled by a patch of mold than by him. He thought about writing in the name of Fudd Fartwick, the queen's closest advisor, but remembered that Fartwick was cruel and evil, and also a known cheater in the delightful game of buzzball.

If he chose badly, think of how the Brownies would laugh at him then. They'd ask, "How many Brownies does it take to destroy the kingdom? Only one, if it's Mr. Willimaker." Not a funny joke, but the Brownies would laugh about it anyway. No, there had to be a way for him to obey Queen Bipsy's command but still get the Brownies to choose the next king.

He forced his eyebrows together. *Think, Willimaker, think*. His nervous brain simply answered, *no*, and quite rudely too. *Fine*, Willimaker told his brain, *then I'll make this decision without you*.

Dear Reader, even a rude brain is better than no brain at all. If your brain has been rude to you, then you may punish it by watching an entire day of cartoons. But when it has apologized, you must turn off the television and start using it again.

As often happens when one is not using his or her brain to think, Mr. Willimaker came up with an idea certain to end in disaster. The queen had ordered him to choose a name, and he had to obey her command, no matter how strange it was. But if he chose someone who was also strange, it would be impossible for the Brownies to accept him. They'd ignore her wish and choose their own king.

So he chose a king none of the Brownies had ever heard of. In fact, the king wasn't a Brownie at all.

It was a human. A human whose name he knew only because his daughter, Patches, never stopped talking about him. An eleven-year-old boy named Elliot Penster.

Obviously, the Brownies would never allow a human to become their king. They'd ignore Queen Bipsy's will and call for a general election to choose their next ruler.

The plan was clever, foolproof, and perfect in every way but one: the Brownies never ignored Queen Bipsy's will.

Chapter
5

Where Fudd Becomes
Seriously Disappointed

A T THE NEWS OF QUEEN BIPSY'S DEATH, AN IMMEDIATE assembly of all Brownies was called. It was held in Burrow Cave, the only place large enough for all Brownies to meet together. Despite the hundreds of fireflies that flew above them, it was always a little dark in there. That was fine by most Brownies, since it meant they didn't have to look too closely at the Brownie in charge of the meeting, Fudd Fartwick.

Fudd had been Queen Bipsy's advisor for the past four hundred years. At twenty-eight inches, he was taller than most Brownies. His nose was longer than most Brownies' noses and slightly crooked, too, which was okay since it kept most people from noticing his eyes. Fudd had mean eyes. He didn't look at others; he glared at them. If he smiled, it was probably because one of his evil plans had worked. In those happy moments, his eyes shrunk to tiny slits on his stout face. He was the kind of creature whom you wouldn't want to look at very long for fear your eyeballs would burn.

Don't laugh. It's happened before and it's not pretty.

Fudd had one simple, humble wish for his life, which was to become the most powerful creature in the universe. There was only one position for him of greater power with the Brownies, and that was as king. Now that Queen Bipsy had died, he was ready to take the crown for himself.

Fudd had big plans for the Brownies. No more homes in underground tunnels and caverns. No more life as second-rate creatures behind the Elves and Fairies. No more making their living by doing secret chores for the humans. No, it was time for the humans to begin serving *them*.

It would take the help of the Goblins, though he'd have to keep that a secret. Brownies and Goblins weren't the best of friends, mostly because Goblins had spent the past three years trying to kill the Brownies. But Fudd planned to trick the Goblins. As soon as he convinced the Goblins to join him, he could end the war and become the hero of the Brownies—but even more, he'd become the Goblins' king as well.

Fudd smiled. His pointy teeth peeked through his gray lips. *Careful now*, he thought. *Accept the crown first, and then you can make your plans.*

Mr. Willimaker stood to speak to the group. He coughed several times, because whenever he was nervous, it felt like something was stuck in his throat, like a pumpkin. He hadn't washed his hand with the name of the king on it, although it had become so sweaty that all of the letters had washed together and now said the new king's name was something like "Lnit Prmsln." He didn't know anyone named Lnit Prmsln, so he'd have to go with his first choice.

Dear Reader, if your name happens to be Lnit Prmsln, then in the first place I'm very sorry for you. In the second place, you are not the human Mr. Willimaker intended to become king, so please do not dig a hole hundreds of feet into the earth trying to correct this problem. You'll get very dirty and still won't reach the Underworld. Besides, as you continue reading this story, you'll probably decide that you really don't want to be the king anyway.

Mr. Willimaker cleared his throat again and began to speak, but one of the Brownies yelled out, "Is the scary little mouse coming again, Willimaker? Will the mouse destroy us all this time?"

Mr. Willimaker tried to say that this was not a time for jokes, but everyone was laughing too hard to hear him. His hands sweat even more and blurred the ink so that no one could read it. He was on his own now.

Patches Willimaker walked up to stand beside her father. "Hey!" she yelled. "My dad has something important to say!"

Slowly the noise settled down, and as the eyes of every Brownie in the cave focused on him, Mr. Willimaker was more nervous than ever. With a tremor in his voice, he stated, "Queen Bipsy did many great things for Burrowsville. Except for our troubles with the Goblins, I believe we've always been happy here. Her final wish before she died was to know that our next ruler will bring us the same happiness. Maybe more, if he can end the Goblin war."

A cheer rose in the crowd. Even Fudd cheered, although making the Brownies happy was not in Fudd's secret plans.

Mr. Willimaker continued, "Before she died, Queen Bipsy gave me the name of our next ruler, a king."

Fudd sat taller in his chair. This was his big moment.

"However, those of you who only speak Flibberish may have a problem with this name, because the name is not a Flibberish word."

Fudd shrank in his chair. His name was a Flibberish word, though he didn't like to remind people of that, since it meant "ugly stink face."

Mr. Willimaker continued, "Our next king is a human named Elliot Penster." He paused, waiting for the uproar. At any moment, the Brownies would realize that Queen Bipsy must have made a mistake. Their only action would be to reject Elliot as king and hold an election for their next ruler. Any second now.

There it was! The murmuring began, just as he expected. They were asking each other what the queen might have meant. Maybe she was playing a joke on them and was laughing at them from her grave.

Mr. Willimaker raised a hand, calling for silence. "Now, we all know the queen couldn't really have wanted a human for our king. Therefore, I propose—"

"But the queen knew how Elliot Penster saved me three years ago," said Patches to the entire crowd. "That must be why she chose him. He'll make a great king. I know it!"

Mr. Willimaker stared at his daughter, wondering why he'd ever taught her to speak. She wasn't helping.

"If he's brave enough to save Patches from the Goblins, then maybe he can save all of us," a Brownie in the crowd called out.

"Did I say he's human?" Mr. Willimaker protested. But nobody seemed to hear him.

"I know he can help us," Patches said. "Just yesterday he fought another human that looks like a Troll. A bully named Tubs."

The crowd gasped in shock, although in fact, Brownies think a lot of humans look like Trolls. Patches didn't mention that Elliot almost lost that fight.

Fudd shot from his chair toward Patches. "You mean to tell me that the next king of the Brownies is a human child?" He turned to Mr. Willimaker. "Are you sure that's the name the queen said? Are you sure what she said didn't sound more like Fudd Fartwick?"

Mr. Willimaker coughed nervously. "Er, no, I think I would've heard that clearly." Now that his brain was speaking to him again, he realized what a terrible idea this had been. He wanted to tell the Brownies that he'd chosen the name himself, but it was too late now. Fudd Fartwick would give him hard labor for lying to all the Brownies and would then take over as king. He couldn't let that happen, even if the lie made his ears turn moldy and sprout grass, which sometimes happens to Brownies who tell lies. He said even more loudly to the crowd, "Elliot Penster is our next king. We must go and tell him the news."

"Hail King Elliot!" the Brownies cheered. "Long live King Elliot!"

Mr. Willimaker became so excited by their cheers that he began to believe he'd done the right thing after all. What he failed to notice was the one Brownie in the entire cavern who was not cheering.

Fudd Fartwick sat back on his chair and folded his arms. The cheer was wrong. King Elliot would not live long. He might not even live until the end of the week.

He needed the Goblins for this. They'd be happy to help. As much as they liked killing any Brownie, they'd like to kill the human king of the Brownies most of all.

Chapter 6

Where Elliot Doesn't Sleep Well

ELLIOT WASN'T THE TYPE TO WAKE UP SUDDENLY IN THE middle of the night, bathed in sweat and afraid for his safety. But his room had never been secretly invaded by creatures from the Underworld before.

"Who's there?" he called out into the darkness. His brother Reed, who shared his room, would've normally answered by tossing a pillow at Elliot and telling him to stop asking strange questions in the middle of the night. But Reed was working at the Quack Shack late tonight. And it wasn't a strange question.

"Are you Elliot Penster?" The voice was higher in pitch than he was used to, as if someone had sucked helium from a balloon before speaking.

"That's me. Who are you?" Elliot switched on the light beside his bed and then jumped back. Two small *things* were on his floor staring up at him, a younger girl and a boy *thing* that might have been her dad, if things had fathers. They were dressed like something out of a fairy tale book and stared at him with wide, hopeful eyes. He didn't think they were trying to be scary, but the fact that they were standing in his room was scary enough.

The boy thing stepped forward. He was dressed in a little suit, and his hair stood out in fewer directions than the girl's. A large pair of glasses slid up and down his nose with the movement of his head. He pushed the glasses up and said, "We're Brownies. Not like the dessert that you eat, but Brownies, the creatures that we hope you don't eat."

Elliot shook his head. "The only brownies I've ever eaten don't talk to me."

Mr. Willimaker smiled at that as the girl nudged him and whispered, "See? I told you he wouldn't eat us."

Mr. Willimaker turned back to Elliot. "We were sent here on behalf of all Brownies. We're friends to you. Do you believe in Brownies?"

"I do now." Earlier that night Elliot would've given a different answer, but it's hard to deny the existence of something that's staring you in the face.

"My name is Mr. Willimaker."

"Oh, well, it's nice to meet you," said Elliot.

Mr. Willimaker pointed to the girl beside him. "This is my daughter, Patches."

Elliot squinted as he looked at her. "I remember you. Halloween three years ago, right?"

"Yes!" Patches seemed pleased to be remembered. At least her ears perked up slightly.

"We live in the Underworld, miles and miles below where we now stand. Not just Brownies there, of course, but also Dwarves and Elves and Pixies— many different creatures. Mostly we keep to ourselves, but I can introduce you around if you'd like."

"Oh, uh, thanks." Elliot waited for the Brownies to say something else, but they didn't. So finally he said, "Is there something I can do to help you?"

The Brownies laughed at that. Elliot pinched his lips together, wondering what the joke was. Then he said, "I don't think that was funny. You came to my room in the middle of the night. I think it's fair for me to ask why."

"Oh, yes," Mr. Willimaker said. "You can ask why, and I'm glad you did. We've come to tell you the good news."

Elliot was suspicious. He didn't know much about Brownies. Maybe their idea of good news was, "Congratulations, your life is about to get a whole lot worse!"

That wasn't exactly it. Mr. Willimaker bowed low. "Congratulations, you are the new king of the Brownies."

It was Elliot's turn to laugh. "Me? That's crazy!"

Mr. Willimaker pressed his thick eyebrows together. "Why? Are you already a king for another Underworld race? The Leprechauns maybe? If it's gold you want—"

"I'm not anyone's king! I'm just a kid. I didn't even know there were Underworld races. Why me?"

Patches stepped forward. "All we know is that right before she died, Queen Bipsy gave my father your name."

"Bipsy? Silly name for a queen."

"You can't pronounce her full name without a lot of spitting and a hard slap to your face," Patches said. "Would you like me to show you?"

"Bipsy's fine," Elliot said quickly and then added, "But I don't want to be king. I've got school tomorrow."

"Just consider being king a sort of homework assignment," Mr. Willimaker said. "There's math homework and English homework. Being our king is like Underworld mythical creature homework."

Elliot folded his arms. "What would I have to do?"

"It's simple. You'll solve whatever little problems come up, such as who gets the potato if it grows across two garden patches."

"You'll sentence prisoners to hard time," Patches said.

"And drink all the turnip juice you want," Mr. Willimaker said.

"And end the war with the—" Patches began before her father clamped a hand over her mouth.

Elliot tilted his head. "What's that last one?"

Mr. Willimaker looked at his feet and mumbled, "Oh, nothing, there's just this little…"

"I can't hear you," Elliot said. "Could you speak louder?"

Mr. Willimaker coughed. "There is this small matter of a war, between the Goblins and Brownies. Well, it's not really a war, since we don't know how to fight back. So it's more like we just wait around to get killed. Most of us are tired of waiting around to be killed, so we hope as king you'll help us end all of that trouble."

Elliot looked at Patches. "Those kids in the Goblin suits three years ago—"

She nodded. "Yep. Real Goblins."

"Figures. They ruined all my candy, you know." Elliot scratched his chin and asked, "Aren't Brownies the creatures that have to do nice things for humans, like if we leave you a job to do?"

"We don't *have* to do anything," Patches said. "We choose to help *if* we like the gift the human leaves for us."

"Yes, but if I were your king, you'd have to do a job just because I ordered you to, right?"

The two Brownies looked at each other. "Well, yes. But we only work at night," Mr. Willimaker said.

Elliot looked over at the clock in his room but then remembered there was no clock in his room, because his family had sold it last week to buy bread. So instead he looked out the window. "Night's almost over, so you'll have to hurry. I'll make you a deal. My Uncle Rufus is getting out of jail tomorrow, and we're having a welcome home dinner. If you can have a nice dinner ready for my family, then I'll be your king."

Uncle Rufus was the oldest man in town who still had all his teeth. He stayed young by eating healthy, taking walks along Main Street, and unfortunately, by stealing shiny things. He claimed he always meant to buy the items, but he had memory problems. The police didn't believe that, but Elliot did. After all, Uncle Rufus often forgot Elliot was a boy and brought him shiny earrings every birthday.

The Brownies smiled. Mr. Willimaker said, "That's it? Make your family dinner? But it's so simple."

"You say that now. Wait until you see my family's empty cupboards." Elliot figured he'd win no matter what. Either he'd get a nice meal tomorrow night or else he wouldn't have to be the Brownie king and end a war with the Goblins. And even if he were king, he'd just do what they wanted for a few weeks and then give the job to someone else.

"Your wish is our command," Patches said, bowing.

"There's one more thing," Mr. Willimaker said. "We have one simple but very important rule. You can't tell anyone that we exist. If you do, you'll never see us again."

"Never?"

Patches nodded. "We don't appear to humans who tell our secrets."

"I won't tell," Elliot said. He was pretty good with secrets. His parents still didn't know where he had buried the glass vase he'd accidentally broken over the summer.

After the Brownies left, Elliot lay back on his bed, wondering what would happen tomorrow. Him, a king? He had holes in the knees of most of his pants. The fanciest thing he owned was the rusty horn on his bike (not counting the earrings Uncle Rufus stole for him). And he still had to take orders from his sister when she said to eat his vegetables, no matter what color they were. Somehow he didn't feel like a king. But Mr. Willimaker seemed sure that Queen Bipsy had chosen him, so he fell asleep with a smile on his face.

Most readers of this story agree that Elliot probably wouldn't have fallen asleep if he knew that hiding in the corner was a third Brownie named Fudd Fartwick. And Fudd Fartwick was watching the sleeping boy, deciding it wouldn't be hard at all for a small band of Goblins to kill him.

Chapter 7

Where Fudd Plays with Fire

BY THE TIME THE FIRST MORNING RAYS PEEKED OVER THE horizon, Fudd Fartwick had thought of at least fourteen ways in which he might kill Elliot. Fifteen ways, if he counted making Elliot play out in the warm autumn sunshine for a few hours. On second thought, perhaps that was only deadly to a Brownie. Brownies could tolerate a little sun, but they didn't like it, which is why they did their work at night.

Fudd snapped his fingers to take him back to the Underworld, vanishing from Elliot's bedroom only about twenty seconds before Elliot awoke. Elliot awoke because he smelled something unusual in his home: hot breakfast. Unless his ears were playing a cruel joke on him, that was definitely bacon sizzling downstairs, and he was certain he detected the quiet *thup* of toast popping up. He'd asked the Brownies to provide his family with dinner. Was it possible they would provide food for the entire day? He jumped out of bed and ran from his room so quickly that he didn't notice the tiny dart stuck into his bed, not four inches from where his head had been.

The poison dart had been Fudd's first idea. But Fudd wasn't a good shot, and he'd only brought one poison dart with him. Rule number eight in *The Guidebook to Evil Plans* clearly stated, "Always have a backup plan in case your first try misses (page 24)." Fudd had forgotten that rule tonight, but he wouldn't let himself forget again.

He poofed himself directly to Flog, the Goblin city. Fudd was fully aware that the last Brownie to accidentally poof himself into Flog came home with most of his fingers bitten off, but Fudd was no ordinary Brownie, and he had not come here by accident.

Fudd was—until yesterday—the closest advisor to Queen Bipsy, making him the second most powerful Brownie in the Underworld. By the end of today, he planned to be the closest advisor to Grissel, leader of the Goblins, and the newest secret enemy of King Elliot.

The Goblins stared at him with hunger in their black eyes, and Fudd shuddered. The eyes alone wouldn't be so bad, but combined with their jagged teeth and mossy green skin, Goblins were never a pretty sight. It had been over a thousand years since a Goblin won the Miss Underworld Beauty Pageant. As the story went, the only reason she won was because the other entrants were literally scared to death of her. Being the only living contestant by the end of the show, the crown was hers.

The Goblins were at that moment fighting over bites of an enormous pumpkin. Fudd hoped they would be so full of pumpkin that they wouldn't want to eat him. But he knew better. Goblins were always hungry for Brownies.

Dear Reader, I'm sure you can understand this. While we humans don't eat Underworld creatures, most humans feel there is always room for one more bite of the chocolate cake–like dessert known as a brownie. For Goblins, it's not much different.

Fudd raised an arm, showing them his gold ring, a sign that he was a royal advisor. They wouldn't attack him if they saw it. He hoped. In his most commanding voice, he said, "Take me to Grissel."

No one answered. Even for a Goblin, it's not polite to speak with a full mouth. But they pointed to a crooked, gray house at the top of a crooked, gray hill. Fudd thanked them, kicked at a Goblin child who was at that moment gnawing on his leg, and then made his way up to the house.

As it turned out, Grissel was sitting on a rock in front of the house, as if he'd expected Fudd to come. Over the past few years, he'd grown meaner-looking than when Fudd had last seen him. Like most other Goblins, his clothing was unimaginative and in need of serious repair. Fudd tilted his head toward Grissel, not a deep bow as you'd have to give a royal, but still a show of respect.

"I knew you'd come, Fartwick," Grissel said, licking his lips. "Your smell arrived faster than you did."

Fudd wanted to point out that Goblins—who avoided water because of the welts it left on their skin—were the worst smelling of any Underworld creature (except perhaps for Trolls, who often create their own swimming holes with how much they sweat). But rather than insult someone who had the ability to swallow him whole, he said, "It's an honor to speak with you, Grissel."

Grissel didn't act like he was honored to speak with Fudd. Instead, he looked at Fudd like he wasn't sure whether to eat him headfirst or feet first.

"What do you want with the Goblins?" Grissel finally asked.

Fudd's eyes narrowed. "Maybe you heard about our queen. She died the other night. Something scared her to death."

Grissel couldn't hold back the smile on his face. "I did hear that. I planned to send flowers, but since it was me who scared her to death, I thought flowers would seem insincere."

A shiver ran up Fudd's spine. "Er, yes, good reasoning. Well, shortly before Queen Bipsy's death, she gave the name of our next king."

"And you're mad because it wasn't you."

Fudd shook his head. "No, I'm mad because it's a human boy. His name is Elliot Penster."

"Why should the Goblins care?"

"Because you know this boy. Do you remember Halloween three years ago?"

Most Goblins have trouble remembering anything from three minutes ago, but deep in the cobwebs of Grissel's mind, he did recall the night when a human got between two of his Goblins and their Brownie dessert. Grissel's shriveled heart pounded in his bony chest like it had in the good old days. The war with the Brownies had become boring lately. They never tried to fight back anymore. So there was no challenge, no glory. A human sounded more interesting. Especially a human who had already interfered with the Goblins once before. His pointed ears warmed as he thought of how he'd tell the Goblins about their new enemy.

"And you say this boy is the king of the Brownies now?" Grissel asked.

"If he agrees to be king, he'll be a ruler in the Underworld!" Fudd said. "Do you want that?"

Grissel leaned forward and thought about Fudd's question. It took a very long time, because Goblins aren't that smart, but Fudd waited patiently. Finally, Grissel looked up at him. "No, the Goblins do not want any humans ruling here, but especially not the human named Elliot Penster."

Fudd smiled and took a seat on a smaller rock near Grissel. Like everything else in Flog, the rock was pointy and made sitting very uncomfortable, so he stood again and rubbed his bottom. Then he said, "I'm going to Elliot's home tonight. I'll let him know what dangerous things can happen to an Underworld king. In the meantime, I need you to cause a little trouble down here."

Of all causes that Goblins support, trouble is their favorite. Grissel's face widened into a crooked smile, and he said, "How can we help?"

Chapter 8

Where Patches Gets
Out of School Early

FUDD AND GRISSEL MADE AN UNUSUAL TEAM. IT WAS TRUE they shared a deep, driving thirst for power. It was also true that each had gained his power through a talent for being the scariest of his kind.

But the tales of how they rose to power are very different.

Fudd had been born to the two nicest Brownies in all of Burrowsville. It's true. His parents even received an award for niceness once, although they hid it away so it didn't make other Brownies feel bad. They taught Fudd always to act politely and speak kindly. They taught him so well that through most of his first thirty-eight years of childhood, he didn't know what a mean Brownie was. The first time he heard someone sneeze and not say "excuse me, please," he ran home crying.

Grissel had not been born to the nicest Goblins in all of Flog. In fact, his father tried to eat him for Christmas dinner every year, which sort of ruined the holidays.

One day in school, Fudd kindly asked a Brownie girl if he could have a turn on the swing. He'd waited in line for five whole hours, but every time he got to the front of the line, someone else would push ahead of him. He'd never gotten a turn on the swing, no matter how many times he asked. Not even once.

"You can't make me," the Brownie girl told him with a sneer.

So Fudd pulled out the strongest weapon he had, the one thing his parents said would always work. Very politely, he said, "Please."

His parents were wrong, however. It didn't work. She laughed and kept on swinging.

I'm sure you know, Dear Reader, that Fudd could stand up for himself and still be a kind person. You could probably think of at least three ways in which Fudd could solve this problem. Fudd couldn't even think of one.

Something changed in Fudd that day. The swing didn't matter. Saying "please" didn't matter. All that mattered was power, so that no one, ever again, would tell him that he couldn't make them do what he wanted. One day that girl on the swing would see how powerful he'd become, and then she'd be sorry for not sharing. He would work his way up in power until he was king of Burrowsville. No—king of the Underworld.

Unlike Fudd, Grissel had never gone to school. No schools existed in Flog, because there was nobody smart enough to teach in one. Unless you count the Flog Academy of Fear-Making, in which Goblins practiced the art of causing fear in others. With his natural talents, Grissel quickly growled, attacked, and clawed his way to the top of his class. He was especially good at blowing things up. In fact, for graduation he blew up the Flog Academy of Fear-Making. The academy wanted to give him a medal for having done such a good job at it, but the medal had been inside the school and also blasted to smithereens. Grissel's father was so proud, saying that next Christmas he could eat at the table instead of being eaten on the table.

Not long after that, the humans opened a mining operation that caused them to dig very deep into the earth. Their drills came close to Flog, too close. The Goblins tried everything they could think of to stop the humans, such as kicking in their tunnels and breaking their drills with rocks. Nothing worked. They just made wider tunnels and stronger drills.

One day Grissel decided it was time to stop the humans once and for all. He led a group of Goblins to the surface one night. They blew a giant hole into the earth and drove all the human machines into the hole. With another explosion, Grissel buried the machines. The humans decided the ground wasn't stable enough for mining, and all drilling stopped. Grissel was a hero.

He had lived a quiet life in Flog until three years ago when that human boy, Elliot Penster, stopped the Goblins from catching the Brownie, Patches Willimaker. Then he knew it was time to be the Goblins' hero once again. He had led them in a war against the Brownies ever since.

Fudd wanted to be the Brownies' hero. He had spent his life trying to become the most powerful of all Brownies. It cost all of his gold to buy the only existing copy of *The Guidebook to Evil Plans*, which clearly stated, "Commit to your beliefs. No super villain ever rose to the top by doing things halfway (page 2)." Queen Bipsy had stood in his way before. Now it was King Elliot who kept him down.

But Fudd couldn't kill King Elliot on his own. Very deep inside, Fudd knew that just wasn't nice. And by nature, Brownies are usually peaceful creatures. But now that he and Grissel had joined together, things were different. With Fudd's superior mind and Grissel's ability to create trouble, Fudd was sure that nothing could stop them.

"If we're going to get Elliot, then we need to know more about humans," Fudd said to Grissel. "There's only one Brownie smart enough to help us. Patches Willimaker."

"Where is she now?"

"Probably in school," Fudd said. "Probably in room twelve on the fourth row, probably coming back from lunch right about now." Grissel stared at him, but Fudd just shrugged. "What? It's just a guess. How would I know?"

Oddly enough, that was exactly where Patches was when the Goblins showed up.

Patches was just about to raise her hand and answer the teacher's question about her favorite food when her teacher cried out in fear and pointed to the back of the classroom.

Patches knew what was happening just by the nasty smell that she'd detected. *Goblins.* Luckily, the school had conducted a Goblin drill only last week, and she remembered what to do. She jumped to her feet and yelled to her classmates, "Don't look at them. Just run!"

Despite her own warning, Patches snuck a look behind her. Three Goblins had come. They looked confused by all the Brownies who were frantically running in every direction. Confused and hungry.

The smelliest of them all focused a stare on her, and his eyes narrowed. Patches ran for the fish tank at the back of the room. She scooped the one fish inside into a cup and then pulled the rest of the tank over on its side. Water splashed across the ground, making instant mud. Two of the Goblins backed away from the water. As long as the ground was wet, they wouldn't touch her.

Two Goblins? Wait, where was the third?

"Gotcha!" a voice said, and as she looked up a claw reached down from the ceiling and snatched her off her feet. A Goblin lifted Patches into the air, hanging her by her pants. She squirmed and kicked but could not make him let go.

"Put me down or you'll be sorry," Patches said.

The Goblin laughed as he crawled across the ceiling. "What could a weak Brownie ever do to make a Goblin be sorry?"

Patches had no answer for that. And she had bigger problems right now than coming up with a clever reply. Like staying alive for the next five minutes.

Usually when Brownies are afraid, they get very quiet and worry until they have upset tummies. Sometimes they get loud hiccups and can't stop sneezing. When Patches was afraid, she talked. Even more than usual. "I didn't know Goblins could crawl on the ceiling," Patches said to the Goblin who carried her. "How do you do that?"

"I'm not sure, but it's pretty fun," Grissel replied.

"If I could crawl on the ceiling, then I'd just live there all the time. I'd do everything on the ceiling except drink from a cup, because the water would just spill out onto the floor."

"I wouldn't know," Grissel said. "Goblins don't drink water. Now be quiet, because all this talking makes it harder to steal you." Keeping hold of Patches, he nimbly dropped to the ground. "Let's go," he said to the other Goblins. Then he threw Patches over his shoulder and walked away.

If you've never been carried over a Goblin's shoulder, you should know that it's as uncomfortable as it sounds. Goblin shoulders are made of muscles so hard you might as well be carried by a rock, so even a thick layer of Brownie fat isn't enough to protect against them. And poor Patches didn't have as much fat as the usual Brownie, since her favorite food was carrots.

"Where are we going?" Patches asked.

"Flog. You'll be our guest there for a while. And don't even think about poofing yourself away. I order you not to do it."

Patches frowned. Most Goblins wouldn't have remembered to do that. She tried another idea. "I've got a bad case of burps. If you eat me, you'll get them too."

"I'm not going to eat you. We have some questions for you."

"About what?"

"About how to get rid of your human king."

"He's my friend. I won't help you do that."

Grissel laughed. "Yes, you will. You will, or else I'll stop your burping for good."

Which normally would've been a good thing. But something told Patches that Grissel had meant what he said in the very worst way possible.

Where There Are Pickles, Pie, and Brownies

ELLIOT HAD SPENT THE ENTIRE DAY THINKING ABOUT WHETHER he wanted to become the Brownie king. He thought about it during recess when he should have been watching the ball that smacked him in the face. He thought about it during lunch when he should have told Dorcas, the lunch lady, he most definitely did *not* want lima beans on his tray. And he thought about it during science when the teacher asked what he'd get if he mixed hydrogen and oxygen. Elliot had said, "Brownies." He was given detention on Friday for that.

What Elliot finally decided was that he was no good at making decisions. If he couldn't decide whether to become king, how could he possibly make decisions for the Brownies? And he didn't like the idea of fighting a war with the Goblins.

He remembered the Goblins he'd met on Halloween three years ago, the way their skin had boiled and bubbled. He'd been lucky that the water splashing on them made them leave, because he was sure they were getting ready to do something bad. Ever since that night, Elliot didn't like scary movies so much. He'd already seen the real thing.

But would he really say no to being king just because he was scared? Elliot could handle scary. After all, Tubs Lawless was scary. Even Tubs's parents were afraid of him. They bought him a new toy every single day as a reward for not burning down their house. He usually took the old toys to school and threw them at Elliot.

Elliot was good at dodging the little things, like electronic games and action figures. It was harder to avoid the bigger things, like Tubs's bicycle.

Just thinking of it now gave Elliot a shudder.

But there was more. Elliot knew he could fight back. He remembered the time when Tubs had tried to push him off the bus. Elliot had tripped him, and Tubs fell face first into the mud. It had been one of the best moments of Elliot's life. Maybe winning a war against the Goblins would feel just as good.

King of the Brownies, how hard could it be? They certainly lived up to his order to provide food for the day. Crispy bacon, toast with homemade jelly, and fluffy pancakes were waiting for him when he came downstairs that morning. Mother happily accused Father of making it for the family as a surprise. Father looked confused, but he didn't deny it. And if dinner was as good as breakfast, then from now on he could eat like...well, he could eat like a king.

That night, Elliot stared at his table loaded with roast beef, steamed carrots, and fresh bread. He would be king for anyone who could cook like this.

Beside him, Kyle reached a hand out to take a slice of bread, but Wendy pushed it away. "Not until Mom and Dad get back with Uncle Rufus."

"They wouldn't care if we started eating. Uncle Rufus is used to cold jail food. We're not." Reed leaned closer to the table so he could smell the food better.

"I'll bet jail food is a lot better than Wendy's food," Cole grumbled.

Wendy looked as if she was thinking about getting mad. Then she shrugged and said, "I guess it wouldn't hurt if we started eating. Just eat slowly so it looks like we waited longer."

Reed, Kyle, and Cole dug into the food so quickly that there was no room for Elliot to dish up his plate. He wanted to stand on his chair and tell them the food was really his because the Brownies made it. But even if he did, everyone was so busy eating that they wouldn't have heard him. Finally, he sat back on his chair to wait for a turn.

"We're home!" Father announced as they came through the doorway. He was carrying a big sack full of Uncle Rufus's belongings from jail. Elliot didn't think his uncle would bother to unpack. As soon as he stole again, he'd just need to pack up to go back to jail.

"Come say hello to Uncle Rufus," Mother said as she walked in. Then she stopped and put her hands on her hips. "Don't you think you should have waited for us before eating?"

"I told them to wait," Wendy said with a mouthful of bread.

"I see that Elliot waited," Father said. "Such a polite boy."

Elliot didn't tell his parents that waiting wasn't his choice. If they wanted to think he was polite, then he didn't want to disappoint them.

Uncle Rufus stopped in the doorway and looked around. "Where's my family?" It sounded as if he were really asking. Maybe his eyes were getting worse.

This time, Elliot beat the others to be first in line to hug his uncle. "We're glad you're home," he said.

Uncle Rufus studied Elliot's face. "Something's different about you. You're standing taller."

"Nobody beat me up today," Elliot said.

"Well, isn't that nice," Uncle Rufus said, patting Elliot on the head.

As Elliot's parents helped Uncle Rufus get seated at the table, Mother stared at all the food and asked, "Where did this meal come from?"

"We know Wendy didn't cook it, because she didn't need to trick us with dessert to get us to come," Kyle said.

Cole laughed and added, "And we know Dad didn't cook it, because this is real food, not something Dad trapped with his rope outside."

"Don't be silly," Father said. "I've never gotten that trap to work. Except for that skunk, of course, which I still say would have tasted fine if it didn't smell so skunkish."

"Well, wherever dinner came from, it's the best way to welcome Uncle Rufus home from jail," Mother said.

Uncle Rufus smiled at his family, and the wrinkles around his eyes folded together. "Speaking of jail, I forgot that I brought each of you a gift." He reached into his jacket pocket and pulled out shiny key chains for Father, Reed, Kyle, and Cole, and earrings for Mother, Wendy, and…"Oh dear, Elliot. I forgot you wouldn't want earrings, your being a boy and all."

Elliot didn't want the earrings or the key chains. "Stealing is against the law, Uncle Rufus."

"It still is?" Uncle Rufus sighed. "Well, you never know. Laws are always changing."

Mother held out her hand, and everyone passed their gifts to her to return to the store. "Elliot's right, Rufus. Besides, you can see this wonderful meal, and we have all our family together. There's nothing more we need."

Wendy cleared her throat. "Mom, you have to tell Kyle and Cole to stop playing with the hose in the yard."

"Why?" Mother asked.

"Tattletale," the twins grumbled in unison.

Wendy continued, "They pulled the hose all the way into the woods today and let the water run until it made a swamp back there."

Mother gave Kyle and Cole the "we're going to have a talk about this later" look and then turned to the rest of the family. "Who saved room for dessert?"

Elliot had forgotten to save any room for dessert, but it was his favorite, cherry pie. There was probably room behind his eyeballs. "I want a big piece." He handed his dinner plate to Wendy, who was clearing the table. Then he winced as something kicked his foot.

"Stop it," he said to Kyle. Or Cole. He wasn't sure which one was sitting next to him.

"Stop what?" Kyle or Cole said. Elliot stared at both of them. It was Kyle. Probably.

Something kicked him again. He quickly looked under the table to catch the guilty person and then realized it wasn't a person at all. It was a Brownie…well, two Brownies: Mr. Willimaker and another mean-looking one he hadn't met yet.

Mr. Willimaker bowed at him, and after a very long sigh, so did the other.

"What?" Elliot hissed. "I'm eating."

"This is an emergency," Mr. Willimaker said. "You must come with us."

"Where?"

"To the Brownie Underworld."

"Not before dessert. And I'm not going to anyone's Underworld. My mom doesn't want me out of the house after dark."

"Then where can we talk?"

"Up in my room. Ten minutes."

Elliot glanced up just as his mother set a thick slice of warm cherry pie in front of him. "Who were you talking to under the table?" Mother asked.

"Oh, uh, my feet."

She blinked. "You were talking to your feet?"

"Nothing wrong with that," Father said. "I used to talk to my feet all the time as a boy. They're very good listeners."

"As long as your feet don't talk back," Rufus agreed. "That's when you should worry."

Elliot didn't have time to worry about whether his feet would ever talk to him. He wanted to enjoy every bite of his pie. Now he had to hurry and eat it so he could see what the Brownies wanted.

Ten minutes later he ran to his room and shut the door. Mr. Willimaker and the other Brownie stood on his bed. They bowed again.

"You don't have to do that," Elliot said. "I haven't even agreed to be your king yet."

"You probably won't want to either, when you hear our news," the mean-looking Brownie said. His thin lip curled in a sneer, and his bushy gray eyebrows were pushed so tightly together Elliot could barely see his eyes. Elliot had seen that same expression on Tubs's face plenty of times and knew what it meant. For some reason, this Brownie didn't like him.

"Who are you?" Elliot asked.

Mr. Willimaker bowed. "Forgive me, Your Highness—er, Your Elliot-ness, er, Elliot. This is Fudd Fartwick. He was the closest advisor to Queen Bipsy and will be your advisor now. He came with me to share some terrible news."

Elliot sat on his bed beside the Brownies. "What news?"

"The Goblins are causing trouble again. They came into Burrowsville, the Brownie city."

"Tell me about the Goblins," Elliot said. "Why are they at war with you?"

"At war with *us*," Fudd corrected. "If you're the king, then they're at war with you too."

Elliot sighed. "Okay. Why are they at war with *us*?"

Mr. Willimaker coughed and then muttered, "It seems we taste good."

"Huh?" Elliot asked.

"We taste good. To Goblins. And we're not strong enough to fight back, so it's very easy for them to come get one of us every now and then."

Elliot leaned against his headboard. He would've leaned right into Fartwick's poison dart, except Fartwick had already taken it back when Mr. Willimaker wasn't looking. It was now stuffed into his pants, making it uncomfortable for him to sit. Not to mention sort of dangerous.

"I don't know anything about Goblins," Elliot said. "I don't know how to fight them, and I don't know how to help the Brownies win any war. I can't be your king."

"Good choice," Fudd said, maybe a little too quickly. "You don't want to mess with Goblins. They're nasty creatures."

"Will they hurt humans?"

Fudd shrugged. "The Goblins scared Queen Bipsy to death. I don't know if they can scare humans to death or not, but I'm sure they'll try. There is also perhaps the slightest possibility that they'll blow you up. It's a Goblin specialty. I assume you're against that idea."

Elliot was very much against the idea of being blown up. He liked all his body parts attached to him just the way they were. He wasn't too fond of being scared to death either.

Fudd continued, "Besides, I'm sure we could find someone else who could do a much better job. Maybe a Brownie who's already been a close advisor or something to someone important, like a queen."

"Like you?" Mr. Willimaker said with a scowl.

Fudd angrily folded his arms. "You have to admit it's very odd that Queen

Bipsy chose a human to replace her when she could have picked me. She must have lost her senses before she died."

"Her senses were working fine," Mr. Willimaker insisted.

"I want to know more about the Goblins," Elliot said.

Mr. Willimaker slowly shook his head. "There's something I haven't told you about the Goblins coming to Burrowsville. They took my daughter, Patches, with them. I think it's because she knows more about humans than anyone else in the Underworld. I need your help to get her home."

"Your daughter must have been in the wrong place at the wrong time," Fudd grumbled. "Where was she? Somewhere dangerous, no doubt."

"In school," Mr. Willimaker said.

"Aha!" Fudd exclaimed. "What sort of loving father would send his child to school? You might as well have sent Patches to try her luck in Demon Territory."

"Will the Goblins hurt her?" Elliot asked.

"I sent them a large jar of pickles. Goblins love pickles, the only thing they like more than us. I hope they'll eat the pickles instead of Patches." Mr. Willimaker's lower lip trembled a little, and then he placed his chubby hand on Elliot's arm. "It doesn't matter how you became king. The important thing is that we need you and that if you don't help us, we will lose." He lifted the corner of a blanket to reveal something that looked like a wide and pointy gold bracelet. It was a crown. Several oval jewels were set around the base with a fat ruby in the center. "Will you accept the job?"

Elliot smiled and picked up the crown. It was too small for his head, so he held it between his fingers and nodded. "Yes, Mr. Willimaker. I am Elliot Penster, and as of today, I am king of the Brownies."

Chapter 10

Where Patches Is Tempted by Turnip Juice

Dear Reader, being the smart person you are to have read so far into this book, I'm certain that you enjoy every minute of your day at school. However, you might have one or two friends who sometimes complain that school is boring. You might tell them that even though they get bored at times, it happens to be much better than being carried away from school into the Goblin city of Flog, like Patches Willimaker was.

Patches had spent the rest of her day in a very deep hole that was made of rock, so she could not tunnel through it. The hole had a dirt floor that was so hard she couldn't write her will into it with her finger, and no windows, so the only thing to look at was rock. Although even if there were a window, it would still only show her more rock. Patches had tried to poof away several times, even though Grissel had ordered her not to. Since she was Grissel's prisoner, she should have known poofing wouldn't work.

Patches also knew that at any minute the Goblins would come and try to get information about the human, but Patches had a plan. She wouldn't help them hurt King Elliot, no matter what.

Her stomach growled at her, which she thought was a little rude, because there was nothing she could do to get more food. Before she could ask her stomach to stop complaining, a rope ladder swung down. "It's Grissel," growled a voice from up on top of her hole. "If you want to live, then you'll cooperate with me."

"Actually, you'd better cooperate with me," Patches said. "I've got a big Flibberish test in school next week. If I'm not back to take the test, then my teacher will come here to give it to me, and trust me, you don't want that. She'll make you take it too."

Grissel was quiet for a moment, and Patches wondered if he'd gone away. Then he called down, "In that case, you'd better tell me what I need to know. I have a question for you."

"No, thanks," Patches called up. "I'm pretty busy right now. Can you come back later?"

"If you help me, I'll let you go."

Patches shook her head. "You don't have to let me go. I plan on escaping by myself."

"I have carrots," Grissel said. "Fat, juicy carrots boiled in turnip juice."

Carrots. That changed everything.

Anyone who's ever eaten carrots boiled in turnip juice will understand why Patches's mouth began watering. Close your eyes and imagine the yummiest dessert ever. Now pour turnip juice all over it and let the flavors blend together. Mmmmm. It was a good thing Patches already had a plan to help King Elliot, because who knows what she might have done otherwise.

This wasn't the first time turnip juice had been used to lure a Brownie. Hundreds of years ago, human mothers could leave a bucket of turnip juice outside with a large pile of laundry. By morning, the turnip juice was gone and the laundry was clean and hung to dry on the line. The mothers thought their plan was pretty clever, but the Brownies always knew they had the better end of the bargain.

"Give me the carrot," Patches said. The delicious smell was becoming too much for her. "I'll tell you anything you want to know."

Grissel sent the carrot down tied to a string, but it was just out of reach, even when Patches jumped for it. Her short, chubby legs were usually one of her prettiest features, but what a curse they were at this moment!

"Okay, I give up. What's your question?" Patches finally asked.

"How can the Goblins defeat King Elliot?"

Patches was quiet for a moment. Then she smiled. "You can't," she said.

"Humans aren't like Brownies. Humans don't wait around for something to come and eat them. They fight back. They defend themselves."

"We can scare the human to death," Grissel said. "He can't defend against that."

Patches yawned loudly. "That old trick? I remember the good old days when Goblins were more creative in how they got humans. Do you think humans would've written all those fairy tales about you if you were as boring then as you are now?"

Grissel sighed. Things *had* been a little ordinary lately. "There's a lot more that we can do," he called down to Patches. "We have magic. And really sharp claws."

"He expects you to use your magic and your claws. If you want to get him, you have to do what he doesn't expect." Patches didn't actually think Elliot was expecting anything to happen, especially magic and claws.

"Oh, I have a plan he won't expect," Grissel said. "It's foolproof."

"That's what I've been trying to tell you! He expects the foolproof plan already. That's how humans are. If you really want to get King Elliot, you have to use your *not* foolproof plan."

Grissel sat back and rubbed his meaty hand along his prickly jaw. In a very strange way, that made sense to him. "Our not foolproof plan, yes, that's clever."

Grissel lowered the string to give Patches the carrot and then called to the other Goblins. They came quickly, pushing into a tight circle around Grissel and standing so closely together that it was hard to tell where one green Goblin started and the other ended. Patches pressed her body against the wall of her hole, because if one Goblin fell in, a bunch of them would fall with him, and she didn't want to be crushed.

"I need three of you to come with me right away. We're going to outsmart the king by not outsmarting him at all!"

That didn't make sense to any of the Goblins, but they cheered anyway. After all, Grissel had never led them wrong before.

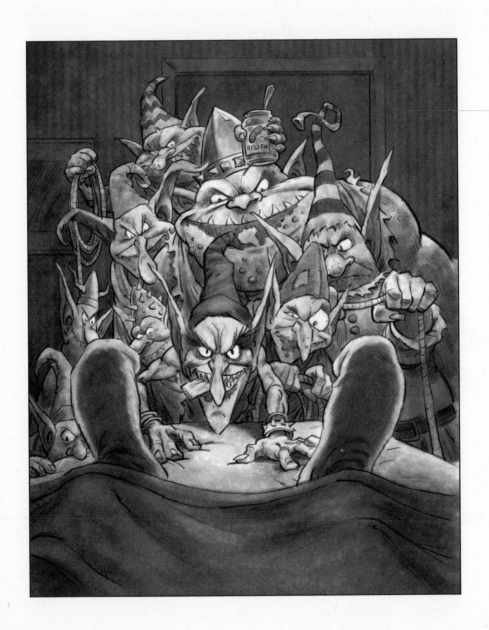

Chapter
11

Where Grissel Tries the Not Foolproof Plan

THE MOON WAS HIGH IN THE SKY WHEN THE GOBLINS poofed themselves into Elliot's room. There were two beds on opposite sides of the room. One bed was empty, but several packets of pickle relish were on top of the blankets. The Goblins fought over them until Grissel won. This was because he knew the other Goblins' ticklish spots, and for a Goblin, getting tickled just isn't funny. He stuffed the packets into his mouth and swallowed them whole.

Then Grissel pointed to the other bed. Something in the shape of a human was underneath the blankets. Dangling on the bedpost was his crown. King Elliot was within their reach.

The Goblins smiled at each other, proud to be a part of the war against the human king. Grissel smiled the widest, unaware of the packet of pickle relish stuck between his pointy front teeth. This was almost too easy for a Goblin of his talents. In just a few minutes, he could return and tell Fudd Fartwick their Brownie king was no more.

Grissel knew exactly what Fudd's next move would be. He'd hurry back to Burrowsville and tell the Brownies the sad news about Elliot. Maybe he'd pretend to cry over Elliot's death for a minute or two, and then he'd wipe away his fake tears and declare himself king. It would be perfect.

Except Fudd wouldn't be able to do any of that, because the hole Grissel had tunneled out for Fudd was even deeper than the one Patches was in. With Fudd out of the way and no Brownie king to lead them, it would be a simple thing to defeat the Brownies once and for all. He smacked his thin lips just thinking about his delicious victory.

Grissel handed some rope to the other Goblins, who climbed up on Elliot's bed. They rolled him around in his blanket, surprised that the human could sleep so deeply. They tied the rope in a double knot, then a triple knot, then finally, in the never-before-untied four-way knot. There was no going back now.

They lifted his body into the air and tossed it toward Grissel, who already had a large trunk at the foot of Elliot's bed open and empty. Elliot could wait in the trunk until they had a chance to get rid of him properly. Most of him landed inside the trunk, except for his legs, which fell limp onto the floor.

Grissel walked over and kicked at Elliot's legs. They rustled softly, something Grissel didn't think human legs normally did. Then his lip curled in anger. He bared his sharp teeth and bit through the knots around the blanket. He pulled the blanket wide and growled. These weren't legs! They were pants stuffed with bags of rice.

"What is the meaning of this?" Grissel yelled. "We've been tricked!"

The Goblins jumped onto the floor beside the trunk and pulled the rope away from the rest of the blanket. They couldn't have been tricked. Not by a human child!

"Aha!" a voice yelled behind them. They turned just in time to be splashed in the face with a bucket of icy water.

The Goblins yelped and screamed and fell backward into the trunk. All except for Grissel, who had escaped the worst of the water by hiding behind the other Goblins. He poofed back to Flog with only three water welts on his arm.

Elliot darted forward and slammed the lid to his trunk closed, locked it, and then sat on it. This was very difficult to do, because the Goblins were beating against the inside of it very angrily. More than once, they nearly tipped Elliot and his trunk sideways onto the floor.

"Quiet down in there, Elliot," his father called from the bedroom down the hall. "You should be sleeping, not playing."

"Sorry," Elliot called back, although none of the playing he'd ever done before involved real Goblins trying to stuff him in a trunk.

The trunk rumbled again. "Are you sure they're stuck in there?" Elliot asked Mr. Willimaker, who had just tiptoed out from his hiding place in the closet.

"You're a king in the Underworld," Mr. Willimaker said. "Command them to stay in there and they must, until you release them."

Elliot's eyes widened. "I just say 'stay in the trunk' and they have to do it?"

Mr. Willimaker shrugged. "You could wave your arm around so it looks fancy, but only if you want to. It doesn't really matter, because as long as you say the words, they have to obey."

"Can I command them to do anything I want?"

"Not with Brownie magic. Possibly you can command them to sing your favorite song in three-part harmony. But unless you want your ears to shatter, I'd recommend against it. All you can do is command them to remain as your prisoners and not poof away. Since you rule in the Underworld, they're bound by your command to stay."

"It's still pretty cool." Elliot waved his arms the way he'd seen a wizard in a movie do it once, then said, "Hey, you Goblins in the trunk. Stay in there."

The pounding got louder, but the trunk stopped banging around as much. "I don't think they liked my command," Elliot said.

"They'll give up after a while and go to sleep," Mr. Willimaker said. "They'll be fine until we figure out what to do with them."

"Was that magic?" Elliot asked. "Can I do magic now?"

"I don't know." Mr. Willimaker stretched out his arms then flicked his fingers apart. In his palm was a small puff of smoke that swirled in the air and disappeared. "Can you do that?"

Elliot stretched his arms and flicked his fingers apart. Mr. Willimaker looked at his palms and said, "Oh, my!"

"What do you see?" Elliot asked.

"Dirty hands. You should've used some of the water you threw on the Goblins for yourself."

Elliot looked at his hands and then shoved them in his pockets.

"You don't have magic," Mr. Willimaker said. "But as long as you are king, your command for a prisoner to remain where he is must be obeyed."

Elliot thought of his younger twin brothers. "I wish I could make Kyle and Cole obey my commands."

Mr. Willimaker coughed. "That'd take a miracle, not magic."

"Very impressive," Fudd Fartwick said, coming forward from the shadows. "I must say the Goblins were no match for you, Your Highness." He raised his voice loudly enough so the Goblins inside the trunk could hear him. "It appears the Goblins didn't realize that Mr. Willimaker would tell you about the water. They should've planned something more foolproof." He turned to Mr. Willimaker. "Go poof somewhere and get King Elliot a glass of water. I'm sure he's thirsty."

Elliot wasn't. Half his room was soaked in water. But Mr. Willimaker was gone before he had a chance to say so. However, he quickly understood that Fudd was only trying to get Mr. Willimaker out of the room.

"Be careful of taking any advice from Mr. Willimaker," Fudd warned. "In Burrowsville he's nothing more than a joke. Not a joke as in, 'Why did the giant cross the road? His foot was already on the other side.' But still a joke."

"Queen Bipsy trusted him enough to give him my name as king."

"Only because nobody else was around at the time. Trust *me* instead. I'll keep you safe."

Elliot nodded. "Thank you, Fudd. I'm sure I'll need your help too. But Mr. Willimaker has given me good advice so far. I don't care what the rest of Burrowsville thinks of him. He's my friend."

"Thank you, Your Highness." Mr. Willimaker stood behind Elliot with a glass of water in his hands. He lowered his eyes and said, "I am a joke in Burrowsville, that's true. I made a big mistake about a field mouse invasion a few years ago, but I've learned a lot since then. If you want me to leave—"

"The Goblins would've gotten me tonight if it hadn't been for you," Elliot said. "No, Mr. Willimaker, I don't want you to leave."

Mr. Willimaker's ears perked up. "Whether they laugh at me in Burrowsville or not, I'll still serve you the best I can."

"Your best isn't good enough for Elliot," Fudd said. He threw up his hands and kicked at the trunk, which bounced again on the floor. Then he looked at Elliot. "So you threw water on a few Goblins. Do you think that makes you prepared to be a king? Do you think you could fight off somebody like Kovol?"

The air in the room seemed to change when Fudd said that name, as if a cold wind of warning was blowing through. Then Elliot looked at the wafting curtains over Reed's bed and shrugged. "Oh, the window's open." He shut it and asked, "Who's Kovol?"

Mr. Willimaker's eyes darted from side to side, and his voice shook when he spoke. "I'm sure Kovol is nothing to worry about, nothing at all. As long as he stays asleep, which I'm sure he will for another thousand years, then we're fine."

Kovol wouldn't sleep for another night if the Brownies visited him as often as they visited Elliot's house, Elliot thought with a yawn.

"Never mind about Kovol," Fudd said. "You have enough trouble with the Goblins. Mr. Willimaker helped you tonight and you got lucky. I don't think you'll be so lucky next time."

"Next time?" Elliot said.

"Oh, yes." Fudd's thin eyes widened until Elliot could almost see what color they were. Almost. "There will be a next time. And the next time will be far worse."

Mr. Willimaker rubbed his hands together nervously. "In the meantime, Your Highness, perhaps I could have the Brownies help out downstairs. There's a squeak on your staircase we could fix. Or how about a delicious breakfast of fried eggs?"

"No, thanks," Elliot mumbled, moving from the trunk to his bed. "I'm not hungry anymore." His trunk full of Goblins rattled again, reminding Elliot that, yes, they would be back. And, no, it wouldn't be so easy the next time.

Chapter 12

Where Patches Finds the Best Hiding Place Ever

Down in her hole, Patches was getting hungry for another carrot. Happily, she didn't have long to wait before another one was lowered to her on a rope, again held just out of her reach. It smelled of turnip juice, and Patches's mouth watered.

Like me, Dear Reader, I'm sure your mouth began watering for some turnip juice when you read that. You should stop reading this book and get yourself some turnip juice right now. If someone in your family just drank the last cupful, then don't be sad. You can make your own.

To make turnip juice, get the biggest pot in your kitchen and fill it with fresh turnips. If you wish to add any of your other favorite vegetables, such as asparagus or Brussels sprouts, that's fine too. Boil until they're tender, and then dump them out on your kitchen floor. Smash the soft turnips with your feet, and gather up any juice that squishes between your toes. It's a treat your whole family will enjoy!

Patches wanted the carrot that had been boiled in turnip juice, but first she was ready to have some fun.

"I don't care what happens to King Elliot anymore," Patches said, trying to sound angry and tired. "Just get rid of him so I can go home."

Actually, she wasn't in too much of a hurry to get home. She had a lot of chores waiting for her there. Cleaning her room was the hardest job, since it was made of dirt and, therefore, was always dirty. Besides, the Goblins made very yummy carrots that she didn't have to share with anyone.

"Tell me how to get rid of the king, then," Grissel said. "The not foolproof plan didn't work."

"I was thinking about chocolate cake. It punishes Brownies, right? So it's certain to punish a human."

"Are you sure?" Grissel asked.

"Last time I was with the humans, I saw a mother put a chocolate cake on the table. She said it was bad for her diet and she shouldn't have any. She finally took some, probably so her children wouldn't have to eat it all. But I heard her say she only wanted a very small piece. It must have been awful for her."

Grissel smugly folded his arms. "Chocolate cake it is. And without the frosting or milk, of course."

"Of course," Patches agreed. "You can call it the Chocolate Cake of Horror."

"Yes," Grissel said. "The Horrifying Chocolate Cake of Horrible Horror."

Patches thought her name was better, but she let it pass.

A short time later, Elliot found a round, double-layer chocolate cake waiting on his doorstep. The Goblins had added extra chocolate to the recipe, just to make his suffering even worse. They also put shaved pieces of chocolate bar on top. When he found it, Elliot showed it to his Uncle Rufus, who happened to have a shiny gold plate under his coat to set it on. Wendy added a few cherries around the outside, and Cole and Kyle even washed their muddy hands before eating it. It made for a beautiful dessert, even without frosting or milk.

Patches was ready the next day for an even better way to trick the Goblins. It was clear that Goblins knew very little about humans, because she could tell them almost anything and they'd try it. As long as she kept this up, King Elliot would be safe. She waited all morning for them to come get her next idea. It had to do with tricking the Goblins into finding some Leprechaun gold to give Elliot. She thought Elliot would like that. But they didn't come. Morning turned to afternoon, and now she really wanted them to come, because she also wanted a carrot.

Patches stared up at the surface. Somewhere up there was a pile of carrots. She could smell them.

Normally, Brownies aren't very good climbers. Their plump bodies are better made for playing on the ground. However, a hungry Brownie is able to do many things a not-so-hungry Brownie wouldn't normally do.

She had to climb the rock wall. And she had to do it now, before anyone came to check on her.

Patches stared up at the rock hole. It was about ten feet to the surface, which is pretty far when you're only two feet tall. There were no branches to hold on to. There was no dirt she could kick at to make a step for her foot.

Patches studied the rock wall. It wasn't smooth and flat. The wall was like a climbing puzzle. Near the bottom was a chunk that stuck out a little. She could fit a toe there. To her right, if she stretched for it, there was a tiny little ledge. She could get a good grip on the rock with her fingers. She really could do this. Or at least she could try.

Patches grabbed some rock and began to climb.

Very slowly and carefully, she found more pieces of the puzzle. There was always another way to move higher. Sometimes it meant moving to the side. Sometimes she had to reach farther than her arm thought it could reach. The effort took all her muscles, some of which she didn't know she had until they began to get tired and almost allowed her to drop off the wall. Patches told her muscles she was sorry for making them work so hard and promised to forget about them once she got home. Her muscles agreed to the deal and continued to help her climb.

Bit by bit, Patches moved closer to the top of the hole.

When she was halfway up, she stole a quick peek below her. She was farther up than she had thought, and the ground looked very far away.

A few Goblins at the top of the rock hole began talking.

Patches froze against the wall. The last thing she needed was to be found out now. The Goblins had kept her alive because they wanted her help in getting King Elliot. But they hadn't come for her help today. Before long, they'd decide that the best help she could give was to sit quietly while they ate her.

The talking at the top of the hole turned to fighting. She couldn't hear everything they said, but she did catch some words like "guard the carrots" and "your turn." It sounded as if one of them had chased the others away from the hole, and pretty soon it was quiet again. Patches continued her tricky climb.

She was so tired by the time she reached the top of the hole that she wanted to curl up and go to sleep right there on the surface. But there was a very good chance that if she did sleep, the next time she woke up it would be inside a Goblin belly. That thought gave her enough energy to crawl behind a pile of rocks and hide.

Patches had never been in Flog before. The city was dark and dirty, and the wind had a smell of rotting fish. No wonder the Goblins were making war against the Brownies. Burrowsville was so beautiful compared to this place. Once the Goblins won the war, they could take over Burrowsville. It wouldn't be long before they ruined it, just as they had ruined Flog. After all, Goblins were the only creatures she knew who had planted their garbage and actually gotten something to grow.

Two voices were coming toward her.

Patches quickly looked around for a better place to hide. These rocks wouldn't keep a Goblin from smelling her. Behind her was a small cave. Her ears tingled. She was sure she *heard* carrots inside. Lots of fat, juicy carrots inviting her to come and hide with them for a while. What polite carrots they were. Such very nice carrots.

Maybe that wasn't actually true. Patches knew she must be very, very hungry if she thought carrots were talking to her. But she had to find somewhere to hide fast and couldn't think of a luckier place. She ran into the cave only seconds before the voices came right up to the rock hole.

"I told you Patches was tricking you," the first voice said. "Humans happen to love chocolate cake!"

Patches's ears perked up. That was Fudd Fartwick's voice! What was Fudd doing in Flog?

"You also told me Patches knows all about humans," the second voice said. "You want to get rid of the human king. I thought maybe Patches did too."

Patches knew that second voice. It belonged to Grissel. If Fudd and Grissel were here together, then Fudd must be helping the Goblins. How could Fudd do such a thing?

Unaware that Patches was hiding only a few feet behind him, Grissel called down into the hole. "Do you hear that, Brownie girl? I'm not using any more of your ideas, and you're not getting any more of our carrots. You're not so smart after all!"

Inside the cave, Patches barely breathed. She was sure the only reason Grissel couldn't smell her in here was because she was surrounded by so many carrots.

"She didn't answer," Grissel said. "Now that's just rude."

But Fudd wasn't interested in Patches's manners at the moment. "I don't know why you have bothered with these simple plans to get King Elliot," he said. "Why not go and scare him to death?"

Grissel sighed as if he were annoyed. "In the first place, scaring someone to death is not as easy as it looks. In the second place, you were the one who said Patches's plans would work. And in the third place, scaring someone to death is not as easy as it looks."

"You already said that one," Fudd said.

Grissel paused and counted on his fingers. "Oh. All right, then, there's only two reasons. So that's what we'll do. The Goblins will scare the human king to death. It's what I wanted in the first place, before Patches talked me out of it."

Fudd clapped his hands together. "This will work. I know it. By tomorrow this will all be over!"

Inside the cave, Patches got ready to run. As soon as Grissel and Fudd left, she had to find a way to warn King Elliot of how much danger he was in.

Fudd and Grissel began to walk away, and then Grissel called to a Goblin who passed by. "Hey, you! Why isn't this carrot cave being guarded? Who's supposed to be here?"

"I dunno," a Goblin with a deep voice answered.

"Then you will stand here and guard these carrots until you can find the Goblin who belongs here!"

"Yes, sir, Grissel. I won't let you down."

Patches sunk onto her pile of carrots. What good was it to be free of the rock hole if she was now trapped inside this cave? Trapped, and the only one who knew the terrible danger that awaited King Elliot.

Chapter 13

Where a Has-Been Hag
Enters the Story

EVEN THOUGH HE WAS NOW KING OF THE BROWNIES, ELLIOT still had to go to school the next day. He was just about to start a spelling test when he suddenly screamed out loud.

"Mr. Penster?" Ms. Blundell, his teacher, stood up from her desk. "Is there a problem?"

As a matter of fact, there was. Elliot had screamed out loud because Mr. Willimaker appeared on his desk. Elliot had nearly written his name and the date on Mr. Willimaker's foot.

"They can't see or hear me," Mr. Willimaker quickly said. "Brownies can be invisible when we need to be. But only for a short time, because it uses a lot of magic. Besides, invisibility makes my head tingle, so it would be helpful if we could talk in private."

"Elliot?" Ms. Blundell prompted.

"There's no problem." Elliot had to tilt his head around Mr. Willimaker to see his teacher's face.

"Are you okay?" Ms. Blundell asked.

"But there is a problem, Your Highness," Mr. Willimaker said.

"Hush," Elliot whispered, but not quietly enough.

Ms. Blundell folded her arms and walked down the aisle, where she stopped at Elliot's desk. "What did you say to me?"

"Er, I meant hush-choo!" Elliot faked a sneeze as he said it. A few kids in class laughed. Ms. Blundell wasn't amused. Harold, the class hamster, wasn't amused either. But, then, nobody expected Harold to be amused. After all, hamsters are known for running on wheels, not for their sense of humor.

Ms. Blundell gave Elliot a warning glance and then walked back to the head of the class. "The first word on your test is 'secret,'" she said. "As in, 'Someone in our class has a really big secret.'"

Elliot looked around. Did anyone suspect he had a secret? "Move," he mumbled as quietly as he could to Mr. Willimaker. "I can't see the teacher."

"Too bad," an annoying, toad-faced girl sitting in front of Elliot said. "I'm not going anywhere."

Elliot rolled his eyes and then stared at Mr. Willimaker. If he wanted something, he'd better say it, because Elliot wasn't going to speak another word.

Mr. Willimaker did have something to say. "Your Highness, you have some official business to attend to."

Elliot shook his head.

"I know that you're in class, but this is very important. We've had a stray wander into Burrowsville. She won't leave, and she's upsetting the Brownies."

"I'm taking a test," he whispered.

"Yes, Mr. Penster, we know," Ms. Blundell snapped. "Now be quiet. The second word on the test is 'annoying,' as in, 'Someone in this class is being annoying.'"

"She said she'll only talk to our king," Mr. Willimaker said.

Elliot huffed. Whoever *she* was, her problem had better be important. He raised his hand and asked, "Can I please go to the bathroom, Ms. Blundell?"

"Can't this wait until the end of the test?"

Elliot glared at Mr. Willimaker. "I guess not."

"You can't make this test up later. If you use the bathroom now, you'll get a zero on the test."

"I've really got to go," Elliot said. The class laughed again, even though he wasn't trying to be funny.

Ms. Blundell pursed her lips. "Then you'll get a zero," she said. "You need to be back in two minutes."

Twelve seconds later, Elliot was in the hall with Mr. Willimaker, running along beside him to keep up. Mr. Willimaker ran so fast that he kept tripping over his own feet, but Elliot didn't slow down. He wanted to get this over with. He had only two minutes, after all.

"I thought we could all talk in the boys' bathroom," Mr. Willimaker huffed, already out of breath from running.

"You brought a girl into the boys' bathroom?"

"Better than making you go into the girls' bathroom."

That was true. Few things could ruin a boy's entire life faster than being caught in a girls' bathroom. He pushed open the door to the boys' bathroom. Luckily, it was empty.

Or was it?

It sounded as if someone was crying in one of the stalls. Specifically, the disabled stall. He glanced at Mr. Willimaker, who nodded that, yes, this was the person whom Elliot had come to see. Great. Not only a girl in the boys' bathroom, but a crying one.

"Hello?" Elliot walked toward the stall. "Are you okay—wah!"

The crying had been so gentle, he had expected to see someone more, well... gentle. He froze, knowing it was rude to look but too horrified to turn away.

The woman in the stall looked a little like Dorcas, the really mean school lunch lady—but only *if* Dorcas had been turned into a zombie, and only *if* Dorcas wanted to serve children for lunch instead of the mystery meat they usually served. Except this woman was way less cool than zombies and, if possible, even uglier.

She was a woman whose face looked like one of those shriveled apple heads. If you could count the age of a tree by its rings, then maybe you could count her age by her wrinkles. If so, then she was at least seven hundred years old. She had wrinkles on top of her wrinkles. Her tattered clothes were wrinkled. Even her white hair was wrinkled.

"Her name is Agatha, Your Highness," Mr. Willimaker said. "Agatha, this is King Elliot."

"Stare if you must," Agatha said, wiping her tears with a fistful of toilet paper. "Few people can turn away from my beauty."

Elliot giggled and then stopped himself by clasping a hand over his mouth. He didn't mean to be rude, but that wasn't what he expected her to say. Beauty was definitely not the word running through his mind.

Her withered skin looked as if it were made of dry oatmeal. Her face had no less than a dozen warts. Her right eye bulged out from her head so far, he wondered why it didn't fall out. Her hands reminded him of the display skeleton in Ms. Blundell's classroom. Her fingers looked twelve inches long.

"What?" she asked. "You don't think I'm beautiful?"

Elliot remembered the rhyme his first-grade class had said every day at the end of school: "I am beautiful because I'm me. I'll be the best that I can be."

He said, "I believe you are the best you can be."

It was the wrong thing to say.

Dear Boy Readers: When any girl asks you if she's beautiful, it's always a good idea to insist quickly that yes, she is, no matter what she looks like. Even if she has worms in her hair and only one tooth (that for some reason is polka-dotted), you should still find something nice to say about her. If you tell her that she is not pretty, then I hope your family has a bomb shelter in your backyard where you can live for several years, because that will be the only safe place you can hide from her and all of her friends.

Agatha pointed a finger at Elliot. "I happen to be the most beautiful woman in all of everywhere. Since you can't see that, I've decided to curse you."

Elliot took a step back. "That's not very nice. Did you know I got a zero on my spelling test just to come help you?"

"Quiet," she hissed. "It's hard to curse you when you're talking. Here is the curse: I am a hag. My beauty is plain. Because you can't see it. You'll soon feel a brain."

Elliot blinked. "Eww. What brain?"

"I think she meant you'll soon feel pain, Your Highness," Mr. Willimaker said. "One moment, Agatha." Mr. Willimaker shut the door to the toilet stall and then pulled Elliot several steps away.

"What's a hag?" Elliot asked. "Why is she here?"

Mr. Willimaker shook his head. "Actually, she's a has-been hag. As you can tell from her curse, she's sort of lost her touch."

"What does this have to do with me?"

"She came to Burrowsville last night looking for a place to stay until she figures out how to get her cursing powers back. She keeps cursing all the Brownies, and it's starting to upset them."

Elliot couldn't believe what he was hearing. He'd agreed to get a zero on a spelling test because of a has-been hag who'd lost her powers of cursing? "Can't you just send her away?" he asked.

Mr. Willimaker bit his lip. "I had this idea, Your Highness. It's probably a terrible one, because my ideas usually aren't very good, but I thought maybe she could help us win the Goblin war."

"How?" Elliot demanded.

"What if she does get her cursing powers back?" Mr. Willimaker asked.

Elliot grinned. "And then she curses the Goblins?"

Mr. Willimaker nodded. "Exactly. But we have to find a place for her to stay in the meantime."

Elliot opened the bathroom stall again and held out a hand for her to shake. "We started out badly, Agatha. My name is Elliot."

She took his hand and shook it and then quickly pulled his hand to her mouth and bit his finger.

"Ow!" Elliot pulled his hand away. "What was that for?"

"I cursed you to feel pain," Agatha said. "Look, it already happened."

Elliot almost smiled. "Only because you bit me. If you make it happen, then it's not a real curse."

"It was a real pain, though." Then tears formed in Agatha's eyes. "Oh, you're right. What kind of a hag am I if I can't even curse a human child?"

"I'm sure you're a very good hag. Maybe you're just tired." Elliot rubbed his bit finger but stopped as he heard a voice in the hallway. Someone was coming into the bathroom. He shoved Mr. Willimaker into Agatha's stall and hissed, "Keep her quiet!"

He slammed the stall door closed.

Tubs! Of course, it had to be Tubs who came in.

Tubs's eyes narrowed. "What are you doing in here, Penster? I told you this was my bathroom."

Elliot shrugged. "I checked for your name on the bathroom door. It said 'boys' bathroom.' Since your name isn't 'boys,' I thought it'd be okay."

Tubs ran that idea through his mind. About halfway through it got lost in empty space, so Tubs let it drop.

"Move," Tubs said. "I want to use that stall."

Elliot kept his back firmly against the stall door. "It's for people who need it. Use a different one."

"I don't want a different one. I like a stall with a lot of space."

Elliot's legs shook, but he held his ground. Behind him, he thought he heard Agatha sniffle.

"What was that?" Tubs asked. "Are you hiding someone in there?"

Elliot smiled. "Like who? A beautiful young woman disguised as a hag who's just waiting to curse you?"

Tubs paused. "Uh, maybe. Now move!"

"You can't have this stall, Tubs."

Tubs darted to Elliot and grabbed his arms, lifting Elliot off the ground. "Ever been flushed down a toilet, Penster?"

Elliot never had. And it didn't sound fun. He kicked and squirmed, but Tubs kept a tight hold on him as he carried Elliot to the other stall.

"What the—" Tubs said.

Elliot looked down. Tubs's pants had fallen down around his ankles. Tubs set Elliot down and pulled his pants up again. They fell again, almost as if someone yanked them down. His underwear had little red hearts on it. Elliot had to bite his tongue hard to keep from giggling. Tubs pulled his pants up, this time keeping his hands on them to hold them in place.

"Tell you what," Tubs said. "If you don't tell anyone about my pants, I won't tell them you're hiding someone in here."

"Deal." Elliot nearly laughed as Tubs ran out of the bathroom. He opened the stall and smiled down at Mr. Willimaker. "Thanks for that."

Mr. Willimaker bowed his head. "My pleasure. Now, what shall we do with Agatha?"

Elliot scratched his chin. "Why don't you come home with me for a few days, Agatha? I'm sure my parents will let you stay, and you can keep my Uncle Rufus company."

Agatha stood. "Okay, but I still may have to curse you again."

That didn't matter to Elliot. The way he figured, ever since he met the Brownies, he'd already been cursed.

Chapter 14

Where the Reader Is Warned

D EAR READER: MAY I SUGGEST THAT BEFORE YOU BECOME too interested in whether Elliot survives the next Goblin attack, that you close this book now. Remember that chapter 15 is coming up next, and that is the very chapter in which several readers lost valuable body parts. It probably won't happen to you, but it might, and many readers who went on to read chapter 15 later regretted it.

Take the example of Libby Frackenflower, a very smart and talented fifth grader who was the captain of her baseball team. She didn't heed this warning. Having decided that if she could outlast the meanest teacher in fourth grade, Mrs. Pinchey, then she could certainly survive a chapter of this book.

Sadly, both of Libby's arms fell off about three paragraphs before the end of chapter 15. Now, do not worry for Libby Frackenflower. She has become very good at swinging a baseball bat with her teeth and catching the ball with her belly button, but we feel certain that if she could go back and un-read chapter 15, she would.

You may be laughing at Libby, which isn't polite. But if you can't help it, then please don't laugh while drinking hot cocoa, or else you might giggle the marshmallows right out of your nose.

Dear Reader, please stop now. Because the start of chapter 15 is going to be so good that you'll find you've reached the end before you know it. And for some of you, it will be too late.

Where Elliot Gets a Lot Scared

THE GOOD NEWS WAS THAT ELLIOT'S FAMILY HAD WARMLY welcomed Agatha the hag into their home. (If you want to call her Hagatha, that's fine. Elliot already thought of it too, even though he didn't dare say it. Don't call her Nagatha or Ragatha, though—no matter how grumpy she is or what her clothes look like—because that's just rude. You can also call her Betsy, but don't expect her to answer, because that's not her name.)

Elliot introduced her as honestly as he could. He told his family that she was a lost woman he met in town who just needed somewhere to stay for a few days.

"She has nothing," Elliot told his parents. "I just feel like we need to help her."

Elliot's father put his arm around Elliot's shoulder. "I agree. We have almost nothing, and that's way better than plain old nothing. So, yes, we have to help her."

"We always have room for one more," Elliot's mother said. "She can stay in Wendy's room."

Wendy's eyes had widened in fear, and a little vein popped out in her forehead, but she wisely said nothing. Elliot hoped her silence would spare her from being cursed. It didn't.

Cursing was the bad news. Reed had dropped his peanut-butter-and-pickle-relish sandwich when she first entered the kitchen, mumbling something about the walking dead. Agatha pointed a spindly finger at Reed and said, "I am a hag. These looks are for show. I curse you with pain when you stuff a crow."

"What was that?" Reed asked. "You want me to stuff a crow?"

"I think she means 'stub a toe,'" Elliot said. "Right, Agatha?"

Reed nodded, a bit confused. "Oh, okay. I didn't know where I was going to find a crow." As he walked past Agatha, she suddenly raised a leg up and then stomped on Reed's foot.

"Ow!" Reed yelped. "What was that for?"

"The curse said you'd stub a toe," Agatha said. "Look, you have."

"You just mashed my toe," Reed said. "That's different! And it hurt!"

"Then you'd better not let yourself get cursed again."

Agatha cursed Wendy as well, telling her she'd soon be quacked on a farm. Then she whacked Wendy on the arm. Agatha cursed the twins that they'd strut past a bear, but they were smart enough to run away before she could cut their hair. Elliot was pretty sure he heard Agatha also whisper a curse against his parents, although he wasn't sure what it was. When his father limped past Elliot that afternoon, he said, "Next time, I get to choose our house guest."

But Agatha poured most of her energy into keeping Elliot fully stocked with fresh curses. By dinnertime, Elliot had already been cursed four times. He stopped paying attention to most of her rhymes. She didn't have any actual cursing power and was only finding a reason to cause everyone a little pain. He'd learned to avoid most of Tubs's hits. He could avoid hers too.

The fifth curse came shortly after dinner when Elliot took his plate to the sink but forgot to take hers. She pointed at him and said, "I am a hag and this curse is your own. The Goblin leader you must face alone."

Hoping she hadn't just exposed his secret, Elliot quickly looked around, but he and Agatha were alone in the room. Then he began to worry. For the first time since he met Agatha, she had used the right word in her cursing rhymes. And facing the Goblin leader alone sounded pretty bad to him.

Fudd knew the Goblins better than anyone. He had spent a lot of time warning Elliot about what terrible things they might try next. Whoever was mean enough to lead the Goblins was someone Elliot preferred to avoid.

But he didn't think he could avoid it now. Agatha had cursed him, and probably with a real curse too.

Or could she be wrong? Maybe another word was supposed to go in there.

Maybe she meant, I am a hag and this curse is your own. The Goblin leader you must call on the phone. Or, The Goblin leader, you must give him a loan? Throw him a bone?

Elliot couldn't even smile. Those ideas sounded good, but he was pretty sure he was doomed.

Uncle Rufus was the only family member who hadn't been cursed so far. He'd been gone when Elliot brought the hag home from school. He had also missed dinner.

But when Rufus walked into the house that night, Agatha was the first thing he saw. He put his hands to his heart, his mouth dropped open, and he shook his head as if he couldn't believe what he was seeing.

"Elliot," he whispered, staring at Agatha as if she were more delicious than a double-decker hot fudge sundae. "Where did you find this angel?"

"Huh?" Elliot said.

Agatha glared at Elliot, probably trying to think of another curse.

"Go on, kind sir," Agatha said with a giggle. In anyone else's voice, her words would have sounded sweet. Coming from Agatha's mouth, the words sounded as if they came from a toad choking on a mushroom.

"I have lived many years all over this world," Uncle Rufus said. "I've seen majestic waterfalls tumbling into glistening lakes. I've seen sunsets that have made me weep. I've seen endless wildflower meadows and laid down in them to count the clouds. But you, my lady, are the most beautiful thing I have ever set eyes upon."

Elliot shook his head. Either Uncle Rufus had gone blind or else he was smarter than the rest of his family at not getting himself cursed.

Uncle Rufus nudged Elliot on the shoulder. "Be a good little girl and get me some of those earrings I gave you last year."

"I'm a boy, Uncle Rufus," Elliot muttered.

"And a fine boy you are. Now go get me some of your earrings. I can't introduce myself to this beautiful woman without a gift to offer her."

Elliot ran to get the earrings, but a gift wasn't necessary. When he got back downstairs, Rufus and Agatha were already sitting on the couch together, laughing as if they were old friends.

He set the earrings on the table and walked outside to sit on his front porch. Maybe Agatha really was a beautiful young woman. Maybe that was part of what it meant to be a hag. If so, why could Uncle Rufus see who she really was, but none of the rest of his family could?

"Psst, look over here," a voice whispered.

(You, the reader, have learned exactly what it means when something whispers, "Psst, look over here." However, Elliot has not read this book, so he doesn't know exactly how Queen Bipsy died.)

Elliot peered into the shadows of his yard, not sure where the *here* was where he was supposed to look.

"Psst, this way," the voice whispered again.

Elliot walked off his porch. To his right was a little clump of bushes. Very slowly, something crawled from them. Elliot's memory flashed to when he was eight years old, facing what he thought were kids dressed in Halloween costumes, but who were actually Goblins. Whatever had happened then was happening again.

Only there were five of them this time.

Five Goblins with boiling, bubbling skin. With each bubble, they grew larger and blacker. Their skin was wet, and in the moonlight Elliot saw bulges form along their back and down their arms and legs.

Run! Elliot's brain screamed it to him, but not loudly enough to get his legs to listen. He could do nothing but stare at the emerging beasts.

His heart beat faster, pounding against the wall of his chest. Pounding in rhythm with the bubbling skin.

The Goblins' faces were changing too. Their jagged teeth, already protruding from their wide mouths, grew into a mouthful of fangs. The ends of their fingers extended into claws long enough to pry a door off its hinges, and their coloring darkened to a sooty dark green. The Goblins banged their teeth together, and the earth shook beneath Elliot's feet. The yard swirled around him. Everything was in a dizzy motion except for the monsters before him. He could see them all too well.

Elliot's breath locked in his throat, and he gasped for air. His lungs must have shut down, because they didn't want to help him breathe anymore. They only wanted to get away from this. His heart knocked unevenly now, like it couldn't keep up with the rhythm from the Goblins' gnashing teeth.

Elliot's eyes rolled back in his head, and he fell to the ground. Someone ran into the yard with a broom. Was it Agatha? She moved fast for a woman her age. She swung the broom at the monsters, and they clawed back at her. She started yelling at them, although he couldn't hear the words...just the pounding rhythm.

It was the rhythm that mattered.

The rhymes. Agatha's curses were in rhyme.

Suddenly, the air filled with light and all went silent. Elliot closed his eyes, and just as quickly, his world went black.

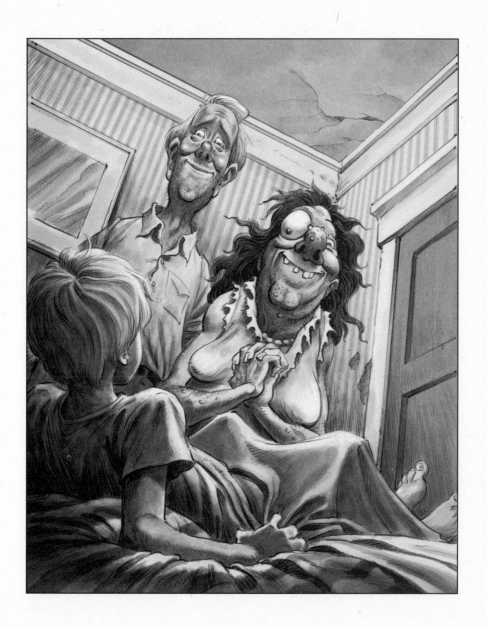

Chapter 16

Where Elliot Might Be a Zombie

THE FIRST THING ELLIOT HEARD WAS GIGGLING. HE DIDN'T expect to hear giggling, because surely he had been scared to death by the Goblins, and whoever thought that being scared to death was funny was just plain rude.

Tubs was rude, and Tubs also might have thought Elliot's death was funny, but Tubs never giggled. So who was it?

Elliot opened one eye, just a peek to see who might be giggling, but he couldn't see anyone. Then he thought maybe he wasn't dead after all. Because if there's one thing dead people can't do, it's open their eyes to peek at the living world.

Elliot did an official test to see if he was alive. He wiggled his toes.

Uncle Rufus once told him a story about a dead person who wiggled their toes. It had something to do with the body's nerves still working for a few hours after death. Elliot gasped. Maybe he was one of those stories! Now all he had to do was figure out how to become a zombie. How cool was that?

Then his brain woke up and told him to stop dreaming. If he was going to become a zombie, then he'd be out on the streets moaning already. Not lying in a bed listening to someone giggle. He was definitely alive, and it was time to wake up.

Uncle Rufus and Agatha stared down at him. Agatha's bulging left eye looked as if it were ready to fall out at any second. Elliot shifted in his bed so it wouldn't land on him, just in case.

"Quiet now," Agatha said. "Don't get up too fast."

"You saved me from those—" Elliot stopped and looked at Uncle Rufus. He knew he couldn't say anything about the Brownies. That probably meant he couldn't talk about the Goblins either.

"He knows," Agatha said.

Elliot sat up on his elbows. "He knows what?"

"I know about Agatha," Uncle Rufus said, smiling. "It wasn't hard to figure out once I realized everyone saw something different than I did."

"Why can you see her and nobody else can?" Elliot asked.

"You'll see her too, in time," Uncle Rufus said.

"Oh." Elliot stole a hopeful glance at Agatha, just in case. It didn't work. She was still the most hideous creature he'd ever seen. He looked back to Uncle Rufus. "Where's my family?"

"Off to work or school, so it's just us to take care of you," he said.

Agatha tapped Uncle Rufus on the arm. "Elliot will be thirsty, dear," she hissed. "Will you get him a drink of water?"

Dear? Just how long had Elliot been asleep?

As soon as Uncle Rufus left, Agatha turned to him. "Your uncle knows about me, but that's all. He thinks the Goblins came to find me and knows nothing about the Brownies. Your secret is safe."

"Can we tell him?"

Agatha shook her head. "If he figures it out, then that's one thing. But the secrets of the Underworld don't belong to you. You can keep their secrets, but it's not your right to tell them."

Elliot lay back on his bed. "Why did you save me from the Goblins? Ever since I met you, all you've done is curse me."

"Yes, and you're still cursed." Agatha stood and brushed her hands together. "But I didn't curse you to die by being scared to death, now, did I? What kind of hag would I be if you died before I'd finished cursing you?"

"Oh," Elliot said. So maybe the fact that Agatha had saved him wasn't such good news after all. "But your curse came true. You told me I'd face the leader of the Goblins, and I think he was there last night."

Agatha shook her finger at him. "You're not getting out of the curse that easily, young man. I didn't curse you to lose—and trust me, you were losing very badly. I cursed you so that you'd face your fears and win."

"Looks like my fears are going to face me, whether I want them to or not." Elliot took a deep breath and then asked, "Do the Brownies know what happened?"

"Yes. Mr. Willimaker has been here several times since last night. He's very worried about you. Fudd visited you too. He didn't stay long, just checked your heartbeat and banged his head on the wall. I'm sure Mr. Willimaker will visit again soon."

"I'm sure he will." Elliot had seen more of Mr. Willimaker lately than his own family. "So that's what it's like, being scared to death, huh?"

"You were only *mostly* scared to death. Trust me, there's a big difference. But the Goblins will be tired after that big show. You're probably safe for the rest of the day."

Probably safe. That also didn't sound like good news. Elliot chewed his lip and then asked, "Agatha, is there someone in the Underworld named Kovol? Fudd said something about him, that he's asleep."

Almost all of the color drained from Agatha's face. All of the color but a strange shade of yellow, which was very unsettling. Elliot was relieved when the color returned and she said, "Kovol. Why would a nice boy like you want to know about him?"

"I just want to know. He's pretty evil, right?"

Agatha frowned. "He's a demon, not a kitty cat. Of course he's evil."

Elliot leaned up on his elbows. "Is he someone so scary that nobody even dares to say his name aloud?"

"Are you kidding? We say his name all the time!" Agatha chuckled. Then her face darkened and she added, "But seriously, though, he is scary. He's the last of the Underworld demons. He's been asleep for the past thousand years, and the last I heard, he was still sleeping peacefully. You don't have to worry about him, Elliot. Just worry about the Goblins. They're trouble enough for one human boy."

Uncle Rufus returned with the water and handed it to Elliot. At about the same time, Mr. Willimaker appeared at the foot of Elliot's bed, scaring Elliot so much he jumped and spilled water all over the room.

"I'll…uh, get you another glass," Uncle Rufus muttered. Obviously, he couldn't see Mr. Willimaker. "This time I'll bring one with a lid."

Agatha winked at Elliot as she followed Rufus out of the room. He wondered if she winked because she could see Mr. Willimaker, or if she were closing her eye to keep her bulging eyeball from falling out of her head.

Elliot turned to Mr. Willimaker, who bowed so low his nose nearly touched the blankets. "Your Highness, I can't believe what happened. Had I known—"

"Had you known, then what?" Elliot interrupted. "Could you have protected me from the Goblins?"

Mr. Willimaker shook his head. "Well, no, I'm afraid not. The Goblins are much stronger than us Brownies. It seems they are stronger than you too."

Elliot stubbornly folded his arms. "No, they're not. I just wasn't ready for them last night. Now I am, and that'll never work on me again."

Mr. Willimaker smiled and sat on Elliot's bed. "I believe you, Your Highness, and admire your bravery. What are your plans now?"

"I dunno. Get better and hope they don't try to kill me again before I go back to school tomorrow? My Uncle Rufus takes good care of Agatha, so I don't have to worry about her being here."

Mr. Willimaker smiled. "Yes, I saw Agatha when I poofed in here. She seems happier."

"She saved me from the Goblins. I think she's going to get her cursing powers back. When that happens, we'll find a way for her to curse them once and for all."

"What if she doesn't?" Mr. Willimaker asked.

Elliot hadn't thought about that. "This war has to end before the Goblins get me," he said. "Better start thinking, Mr. Willimaker, because if Agatha doesn't get her cursing powers back, it'll be up to you and me to solve this problem."

Mr. Willimaker swallowed a lump in his throat. If Elliot needed his help to solve this problem, then they were definitely in trouble.

Chapter 17

Where Fudd Needs Pixie Magic

PATCHES HAD DECIDED THERE WERE WORSE THINGS THAN being stuck in the cave full of carrots. It was better here than at school, where all the other Brownie kids still teased her about her father and the field mouse scare. It was better than being stuck in the rock hole, where she had only gotten a single carrot after she told them an idea to get King Elliot. However, it was *not* better than going on vacation to Underworld World, the happiest place under the earth. But that was an entirely different matter.

For now, all Patches cared about was being stuck. Every time she tried to sneak out, the Goblin guarding the cave peeked inside as if he'd heard—or smelled—her. Trapped with nothing to do but eat carrots left Patches with more than enough time to think about what might have happened to King Elliot. She'd barely slept all night, so anxious for him that she'd only managed to eat 214 carrots.

It was with great worry the next morning that Patches heard Fudd and Grissel return to the rock hole. Their voices were angry. Patches felt a little relief. If they were arguing, then things had probably not gone the way they wanted with Elliot.

The guard quickly ran off when Grissel ordered him to go away. Then Fudd and Grissel began talking right outside the entrance to the carrot cave.

"Your plan to scare King Elliot to death failed!" Fudd said. "How could it fail? You told me you'd use your scariest Goblins!"

Grissel growled. "I did. They were so good they almost scared *me* to death."

"Then what went wrong?"

"It seems your king has a hag. Her beauty forced us away." Grissel threw out his chunky hands. "Why didn't you tell me Elliot had a hag?"

Fudd sounded offended. "They told me that the hag was broken. I didn't think it was important."

"Well, she wasn't broken last night. Maybe her curses don't work as well as usual, but when she transforms, she puts off a lot of light. She burned my eyes!"

"Ouch. That's why they're so red."

Grissel whimpered. "No, that's because after I came back I tried to put some burn cream on them. I guess you can't put the cream right on your eye."

Fudd huffed. Even a river troll knew that. "So what now?" he demanded.

"We're done," Grissel said. "Let the Brownies have a human king if they want. We'll continue our war against the Brownies as we have for the last three years. Pretty soon we'll have eaten every Brownie, and there won't be anyone left for the human boy, Elliot Penster, to rule."

"No!" Fudd said, stamping a foot. "The idea is for you to get revenge against Elliot and for me to become the Brownie king! We had an agreement."

"Whatever happens next, you'll have to do it on your own," Grissel said. "So far we've done all the work. If you want to get Elliot, then it's up to you."

Fudd kicked at a rock. It rolled into the cave, not far from where Patches was carefully listening to every word.

So the Goblin plan hadn't worked! Elliot was alive! For now.

"You tried the *not* foolproof plan, and it failed," Fudd mumbled. "You tried the Chocolate Cake of Horror plan, and it failed. Then last night you tried the foolproof plan, and it also failed. So maybe it's time to try something that isn't either one. Something no one can protect Elliot from, because it's never been done before."

"I like it," Grissel said. "Better yet, I love it. Whatever *it* is, it's got to be great!"

"That's right," Fudd agreed. "If it's never been done, then it's never failed yet. And something that has never failed is certain to succeed! We'll do something final. Something really, really awful." Fudd thought about all the plans he'd formed that first night in Elliot's room. Then he smiled. The last idea was so crazy that it just might work. It was evil, cruel, and only required a bit of black market Pixie magic. Besides, rule number twelve in the *Guidebook to Evil Plans* clearly stated, "Think big. Small plans have never produced great villains (page 33)."

Fudd turned to Grissel, his grin so wide it showed most of his pointy teeth. "Wait until tomorrow," he said. "After tomorrow, Elliot Penster, king of the Brownies, will be no more."

Inside the cave, Patches gasped. They were going to get Elliot this time. And there was nothing she could do about it. She had to make a run for it. Her short Brownie legs weren't made for running really fast, but the Goblins didn't know she had escaped the hole. Hopefully they'd be so surprised that she'd get free before they caught her.

Patches waited until it was quiet outside and then took a deep breath and began running. She ran from the cave as fast as she could—maybe as fast as any Brownie had ever run before. But even a fast-running Brownie is still pretty slow. It was no trouble at all for Grissel to grab on to her hair as she exited the cave and pull her back to him.

"Did you think I couldn't smell you in there?" he snarled at her. "Where were you going in such a hurry?"

"I had to warn King Elliot," she said. "I have to help him."

"You will help him," Grissel said with an evil grin. "You'll help him lose." He tossed Patches to a couple of Goblins waiting nearby. "Tie her up good. I have a feeling we're going to need her help soon."

Chapter 18

Where Reed Misses His Shoelaces

DUE TO BEING ALMOST DEAD, ELLIOT HAD MISSED SCHOOL on Thursday. By late afternoon he was completely alive again. He was so completely alive that the rest of his family decided he must've only had a case of the stomach flu the night before. Wendy baked him another cake to celebrate his getting better. Elliot thought it was chocolate, but it was actually a very burned white cake. He crunched it down anyway. Reed brought him a whole bag of pickle relish from the Quack Shack in case he felt like having any. (He didn't.) And Kyle and Cole flooded the woods behind Elliot's house again. Not really to celebrate Elliot getting better. It's just what they liked to do.

The next day was Friday, and if you remember from chapter 9, Elliot had to stay after school for detention because his teacher thought he'd made a joke during science class. He couldn't explain to his teacher at the time why he had Brownies on his mind. And now he was fairly certain that even if he tried to tell the teacher that he was the king of the Brownies, it would only earn him more detention.

As it turned out, getting detention probably saved Elliot's life, because while he was at school, Fudd used his Pixie magic plan. When Elliot came home later that afternoon, he noticed one very different thing about his house. His room was gone.

It wasn't simply that everything *in* his room had disappeared, although that was true. It was that where he once had four walls, a door, and a window, there was nothing.

Elliot patted on the hallway wall where he used to have a door to enter his room. But it was only solid wall.

He walked outside and stared at the new shape of his home, which now looked as if it were missing a piece, right where his room had been.

"What's wrong?" Wendy said, walking outside.

Elliot pointed at where his room wasn't. "My room is gone."

"Hmm, you used to have a room there. How strange."

"Strange? Do you think?"

Reed came out to join them. "What are you looking at?"

"Our room is gone," Elliot said. "Look."

"Oh, bummer," Reed said. "I had a new pair of shoelaces in there."

Elliot threw up his hands. "Everything was in there!"

"No need to get so angry," Wendy said. "So what if your room disappeared? Did you ever think about the poor kids in this world who never had their own room at all?"

"It doesn't strike you as odd?" Elliot asked.

"I already said it was strange, didn't I?" Wendy said. "But look at Reed. He lost his shoelaces and he's not complaining."

"I'm complaining a little bit," Reed pointed out. "I really liked those shoelaces."

Wendy and Reed entered the house, fighting about who had to call their parents at work and let them know that there was one less bedroom in the house.

"Consider it good news," Cole said. Elliot jumped. He hadn't realized the twins were behind him.

"What's good about this?" Elliot asked.

Kyle shrugged. "We were home when it disappeared. It happened right after you usually get home from school. If you had been in your room when it happened, you would've disappeared too."

"So you saw it?"

Cole shook his head. "I don't know if you can *see* something disappear. It's just that we were in your room looking at that shiny bracelet you had, and then your room started to shake. So we ran out really fast. We shut the door and turned around, and the door was gone."

"Where's Agatha?" Elliot asked. Maybe one of her curses had worked. Could she do that? Did she have that much magic?

"Agatha hasn't been here all day," Cole said. "She said she was tired of cursing our family and wanted to curse some of the other people in town for a while."

Elliot's shoulders slumped. He had hoped this would have been Agatha's doing. Because if it wasn't her, then the Goblins were already trying to kill him again. It was a warm Friday afternoon, the start of what should have been a nice weekend. He'd gotten all of his homework done in detention, and wherever in the universe his room was, he'd already cleaned it this morning... so he was really looking forward to a relaxing weekend.

But as you well know, Dear Reader, nothing ends the fun of a weekend faster than someone trying to kill you all the time.

"Anyway, you're going to be in trouble when Mom comes home," Kyle yelled to Elliot as he and Cole ran away.

"What for?" Elliot yelled back.

"Remember that time we lost our gloves at school? We were grounded for a week. But you went and lost your whole room!"

As soon as his brothers had left, Elliot turned and shouted, "Mr. Willimaker!"

"No need to be so loud, no need for that," said a voice from the trees in Elliot's backyard. "I'm already here."

Elliot trudged into the trees a little ways. He found Mr. Willimaker sitting on a fallen tree stump, his head in his hands and a wide frown on his face.

"I'm so sorry," Mr. Willimaker said. "This is all my fault."

Elliot pressed his eyebrows together, wondering why Mr. Willimaker might need to apologize. After all, he hadn't scared Elliot half to death or made Elliot's room disappear. Elliot didn't know that Mr. Willimaker was actually thinking about how he had written Elliot's name in as king. Queen Bipsy had been one of Mr. Willimaker's last friends in the entire Brownie kingdom. She had believed in him when no one else did. That's why she trusted him to choose the name of the next king. She would be so disappointed now to see that once again, instead of making things better for the Underworld, he had only made them worse.

The future wasn't looking too rosy for Elliot now either.

"I'm sorry, Your Highness," Mr. Willimaker repeated.

"You didn't do this," Elliot said. "Was it the Goblins?"

"It must have been, but I don't understand how they could've done it on their own. Making an entire room disappear needs Pixie magic. But Goblins can't use other creatures' magic. They can only use their own. So they must've had help."

"Whose?"

Mr. Willimaker sighed. "I wish I knew. I hate to say it, but I fear it might be a Brownie who has done this. We don't have a lot of magic of our own, but we are very good at borrowing it from other creatures. If only we had Patches back. She could help us figure this out."

"Can I help to get her back?" Elliot asked.

"I wish you could come with me to the Underworld. The Pixies could poof you there. But since they just helped the Goblins, I don't think they'd help us."

Elliot nodded. "I don't think I'm allowed to go to the Underworld anyway. My parents don't like me to go to new places by myself."

Mr. Willimaker smiled sadly. "King of the Brownies, and you still need permission from your parents."

"But if my parents knew why I was going to the Underworld, they'd probably understand," Elliot said. "We can't trust the Pixies to poof me there, but you could do it, right?"

Mr. Willimaker's eyes widened. "No, sir. I wouldn't dare, not even to rescue Patches. My magic isn't strong enough to poof a human anywhere. I'd probably get your feet into the Underworld and your head and maybe a few of your fingers, but I'd lose the rest of your body. It'd be very hard to rescue Patches with only half of your body."

"Oh," Elliot said. His parents might understand if he had to go to the Underworld to rescue Patches. They definitely would not understand his having only half a body. "Then we have to think of a different way to save her."

"We will." Mr. Willimaker cocked his head. "Where is your crown, Your Highness?"

Elliot turned to where Cole and Kyle were now at the side of the house. "Wait one minute."

He ran to his brothers. They had dug a ditch in a circle, filled it with water, and then had put several ants on the dirt island in the middle.

"What are you doing?" Elliot asked.

"We want to see what the ants will do," Cole said. "They want to get off the island but can't swim."

"Oh. Where's the cr—I mean, the bracelet you took from my room? You didn't leave it in there, did you?"

"No," Kyle said. "Cole, you had it last. Where'd you put it?"

"I left it in the kitchen. But next time I looked it wasn't there. It's pretty shiny. Maybe Uncle Rufus got it."

Elliot ran back and knelt beside Mr. Willimaker. "My uncle won't lose it or anything. He'll just carry it around for a while, and then I can get it back later."

Mr. Willimaker's face went green, like the color of canned peas. Not a good color for either peas or Brownies. "Do you know why your room disappeared?"

"Because the Goblins knew it was my room. They hoped I'd be in it."

"A king always wears his crown, and if your crown was in your room, then they thought you were in your room. Wherever your crown is now, when the Goblins try again, they'll think they're attacking you."

Elliot stood. "What will they do to the crown?"

Mr. Willimaker shook his head. "Goblins don't make things disappear. They blow them up."

Elliot began racing toward his house. "I've got to find Uncle Rufus!"

But there was no time. He fell onto the grass as a rush of wind knocked him flat on his back. It was followed by a boom. Then his entire house exploded.

Chapter 19

Where Elliot's Problems Get Worse

IT TOOK A MOMENT BEFORE ELLIOT REALIZED EXACTLY WHAT had happened. He stood on shaking legs and staggered toward what just ten seconds ago had been his home. Now it was rubble, a heap of wood and broken pipes and chunks of furniture. Shreds of paper and fabric still rained from the sky like confetti, and there was an eerie silence, as if even the breeze didn't dare make any sound.

In the center of where the Penster home had stood, the bathtub had somehow survived. On top of it was a mattress that had fallen from the second story.

"No, no," Elliot whispered. He sat on what had once been a toilet and buried his face in his hands. The kitchen must have blown this way. He saw pieces of his mother's dishes, half of a chair, and Reed's large jar with his collection of leftover pickle relish in it. A crack ran down the jar where it had landed, but amazingly it hadn't shattered.

If he could have chosen the two things to have left in this world, it probably wouldn't have been a bathtub and a jar of pickle relish. But his luck seemed to work that way lately.

Then he heard a sound. It was muffled, but someone was speaking nearby. "Hello? Hello?"

It came from the bathtub. Elliot pushed the mattress off the top and then smiled with relief. Uncle Rufus was lying inside it, fully clothed, with the crown between his fingers.

"I didn't realize we had such a lovely view of the sky from the bathroom," Rufus said.

"The house blew up," Elliot told him.

"Oh." Uncle Rufus sat up and glanced at the mess around him. "So it did."

"Didn't you hear the explosion?"

Blushing, Uncle Rufus said, "I, er, passed gas. I thought that was what I heard."

"Our whole house exploded," Elliot said. "It was very loud."

"Yes, but I don't hear so well anymore. I thought it was me. What a relief."

"That our house blew up?"

"No, that I don't have gas. Although if I did, it would be a good thing that we're out here in the open air." Rufus remembered the crown between his fingers. "I think this is yours. I thought you might allow me to give it as a gift to Agatha. It was just so shiny, and I know she'd like it. But I shouldn't have taken it without asking you."

"I wish I could let you have it, but I can't give this up now, even if I wanted to." Elliot took the crown and then helped Rufus out of the bathtub. "I have to find everyone else."

But everyone else found him. Wendy walked across the rubble holding Cole and Kyle by the ears. "Look what you two did," she said to them.

"We didn't blow the house up," Cole protested.

"That's just what someone who *did* blow up a house would say," Wendy replied.

"We promise," Kyle insisted. "Tell them, Elliot. You saw us outside. Did it look like we were blowing up the house?"

"They didn't blow up the house," Elliot told his sister. "Where's Reed? Is he okay?"

Wendy released Cole and Kyle. "He left for work. Then I saw that he forgot his name tag, so I went running down the street to catch him. I was on my way back to the house when it exploded. What happened?"

Elliot hung his head. "I think the Goblins blew it up."

"Fine time for making jokes." Wendy put her hands on her hips. "Okay, well, let's see if we can get everything cleaned up before Mom and Dad get home from work."

"I didn't make this mess, so I'm not cleaning it up," Cole said.

"I'll clean up my exploded room parts, but that's all," Kyle said.

"I don't think it matters," Elliot said. "Mom and Dad are pretty smart.

I think they're going to notice when they sit down for dinner tonight that THE ENTIRE HOUSE IS GONE!"

"Of course they'll notice," Wendy said. "But we've got to have dinner somewhere, and I think it's better to have it in an organized blown-up house than a messy one. That's all I'm saying."

"Well, you'll have to burn our dinner somewhere else tonight," Elliot said. "I'm not hungry anyway."

He stomped off back into the woods. Wendy called after him, but he had bigger problems than his sister's hurt feelings. Mr. Willimaker waited for him at the edge of the trees, right at the border of sunlight and shadow. "What a waste of a perfectly good house," Mr. Willimaker said. "Well, a somewhat good house anyway."

Elliot turned back to the smoky pile of rubble. "When I said I'd become king, I didn't know things would go this far. I'm just a kid. I can't protect myself from the Goblins. Now it looks as if I can't protect my family. I can't save the Brownies either."

"I have to tell you something," Mr. Willimaker muttered nervously. "Something I should have told you at the very start. The truth is that Queen Bipsy didn't exactly give me your name. She told me to choose the king, and I was the one who wrote in your name, because you saved Patches three Halloweens ago. I never thought the Brownies would let a human become king. I never thought any of this would happen."

"So I'm not really the king?" Elliot asked.

"Not if you don't want to be."

Elliot shrugged. "I'm just not sure if I'm right for the job. But I have to finish what the Goblins started. After that, I'll decide whether I'll stay as king."

"But what are you going to do?" Mr. Willimaker knotted his fingers together. If he twisted his hands any longer, he might never get them apart again.

Elliot pushed his jaw forward. "If I can't go to the Underworld, then I'm bringing the Underworld here. We're going to rescue Patches. Then we'll find out who is helping the Goblins. Then we're going to teach the Goblins a lesson once and for all."

Mr. Willimaker bowed low to Elliot. "At least for now, my friend, I'm very glad that you're our king."

Chapter 20

Where the Family Goes to Jail

ELLIOT'S FATHER WASN'T AS ANGRY AS ELLIOT HAD EXPECTED him to be about their blown-up house. Or maybe he was just in shock.

"The staircase had a squeak in it," he said, staring at where the staircase used to be. "I guess that's not a problem now. But that's all right if we don't have a staircase, since there's no more upstairs. If anyone did try to go up the staircase, they'd just fall off at the top."

On the other hand, Elliot's mother just shook her head and about every ten seconds would mumble, "Oh dear, oh dear." Elliot also noticed she had stopped blinking. That probably wasn't good.

The police had been at the house for three hours trying to figure out why it blew up. Uncle Rufus confessed that maybe his passing gas had somehow blown up the house, but the police said they were sure that wasn't the cause. Passing gas has only been ru-mored to blow up a house one time in Sprite's Hollow, and that was supposedly after the owner gorged on some very spicy chili for an entire year. Elliot knew that unless the police had Goblins on their list of sus-pects, they'd never find the real answer.

Wendy shambled by Elliot with a pitcher of water in her hands. Elliot wondered where she'd found it. "You thirsty?" she asked him.

"Nah. Sorry about what I said before, about you burning our food."

Wendy smiled. "Don't worry about it. I'll be burning

our food again in no time." Then she hurried over to offer their mother a drink.

"I can't believe it!" Agatha said, walking up behind Elliot. "Why, this is unexpected. I don't remember cursing your house."

Elliot sighed. "It wasn't you, Agatha. The Goblins did this."

"Oh. I hoped I had cursed your house to explode. Then I'd know I had my powers back."

"You've always had them," Elliot said. "You just weren't doing your rhymes correctly."

Agatha tilted her head toward Elliot. "What do you mean?"

"The last words in all your curses. They're not the right words. You say 'sung to by a pea' when you mean 'stung by a bee.' Or 'eat something hairy' when you mean 'meet something scary."

Agatha drew back. "I meant something hairy. Like a Yeti."

"Yetis aren't real."

Agatha laughed in a way that made Elliot think maybe she knew something he didn't. A shiver ran down his spine, and he said, "Anyway, the only time you got the rhyme right is when you cursed me to meet the Goblin leader alone. I figure that's still going to happen."

Agatha's voice softened. "Everyone gets cursed at times in their life, Elliot. The trick is, can you look past the cursing? Can you see it for what it is? Take your house, for example. Beyond the exploded pieces, what do you see?"

Elliot shrugged. "I guess I'm really lucky that nobody got blown up inside my house. And it wasn't that great a house anyway, so we haven't lost much." He sat up straight as an idea came to him. "And maybe it'll help me end this war. I know what I have to do!" He turned back to Agatha, and his eyes widened.

She was still Agatha, but her tattered dress was flowing and perfectly white. Her knotted gray hair was gone, replaced by long, silky blonde curls that waved softly in the breeze. Her warty, oatmeal skin was now creamy and soft. He couldn't tell how old she was, because she was ageless. Uncle Rufus was right. She looked like an angel.

"You're beautiful," Elliot whispered.

"I always was," she replied. "You just didn't know it until now."

"I need you to stay with me, please, Agatha. I have to fight the Goblins, and I need your help."

"No, you don't. All you need is the Brownies, and all they need is you. You are their king and you will save them." With that, she clapped her hands together and began to walk away.

"Where are you going?" Elliot asked.

"To say good-bye to your Uncle Rufus. Now that I can curse again, I have places to go."

"Hey, if you happen to see this boy named Tubs Lawless, give him an extra curse for me," he called after her.

Agatha pressed her lips together and then said, "A boy like Tubs doesn't need me to curse him. He has enough problems."

Elliot shook his head. Tubs didn't have problems. He *was* the problem. "Yeah? What problems does he have?"

Agatha turned and her clear, green eyes pierced straight through to Elliot's mind. "His problem is that one day you'll figure out who you are. Then he won't be able to bully you anymore, Your Highness."

Agatha gave Elliot a gentle bow and then walked over and spoke to Rufus. He looked sad for only a moment until she reached up and kissed his cheek. Then his face lit up. He beamed and wished her a warm good-bye.

Reed came to stand beside Elliot as they watched Agatha leave. "I'm glad she's going," Reed whispered. "I know letting her stay with us was the right thing to do, but she was the scariest-looking thing I've ever seen."

"She's not scary," Elliot said. "She's a beautiful young woman. I was lucky to have met her. We all were."

Reed chuckled. "Careful. Whatever's the matter with Uncle Rufus, it looks like you're catching it too."

After Agatha was out of sight, Uncle Rufus ran a hand across his head and then marched over to two policemen and talked with them. A few minutes later, they all walked over to Elliot's parents.

"What did you steal now?" Mother said to Uncle Rufus. "We've got a bigger problem to deal with here."

"No, it's good news this time," Uncle Rufus said. "These nice officers have arrested me so many times we've become quite good friends. They want to help us with our blown-up house. They said the jail is nearly empty tonight, so if we want to stay there for a day or two, they'll let us stay for free."

Mother shook her head, but Rufus added, "The meals are good, and the beds aren't too bad. The only fellow in the jail right now is another friend of mine. Perfectly harmless."

"What's he in jail for?" Father asked.

"He steals the wool off sheep. Sneaks into their pen and shears them in the middle of the night. So as long as we don't bring any sheep into the jail, we'll be fine."

Father shrugged. Mother sighed. Then Rufus smiled and clapped his hands together. "Okay! The Penster family is going to jail!"

"Yay!" Cole and Kyle gave each other high fives.

"Er, I'm going to stay with friends tonight," Elliot said. His friends were the Brownies, but he didn't think his parents needed that detail.

Mother folded her arms the way all moms do when they're not sure something is a good idea. "Do I know these friends?"

"They've been to our house a lot lately," Elliot said, quite truthfully.

Father brushed a hand over Elliot's hair the way dads do when they're trying to get Mom's permission. "Just tell your friends that your family is in jail and to call if there are any problems."

Mother smiled. "Elliot's just an eleven-year-old kid, dear. I don't think he'll have any problems tonight."

Elliot didn't think so either. Not unless the Goblins succeeded in destroying all the Brownies and also got rid of him. That would definitely be considered a problem.

Father said, "Okay, but it sounds as if you'll miss out on quite an adventure with us."

"Don't worry," Elliot said. "I'm sure I'll have an adventure of my own." As soon as his family left, Elliot sat down with Mr. Willimaker in the woods. "How many Brownies can come here?"

Mr. Willimaker sighed. "I can't get them to come. What Fudd told you before was true. I am a joke in Burrowsville. The last time I tried to warn everyone of danger, it turned out to be nothing but a little mouse. They won't listen to me this time."

Elliot leaned in to Mr. Willimaker. "You *have* to make them listen. Maybe you were a joke before, but now you have a message straight from the king. I know you can do this."

Mr. Willimaker smiled. "You're right. I can do it. I will do it." He began counting on his fingers. "A few will need to stay behind and look after the young ones. I suppose we might close the shops early and that will spare some more." He looked up at Elliot. "Would a couple hundred Brownies be enough?"

Elliot smiled. "Yes, but I need them right away. We have a lot to do before dark. Tell everyone to wear work clothes."

Mr. Willimaker straightened his back, making him at least a half-inch taller, which is a lot for a Brownie. He stuck out his chest and said, "Work clothes are a Brownies' only clothes. Even if I lose my voice, I won't stop talking until they agree to come."

"I also need to meet with my royal advisors," Elliot said, then added, "Do I have any royal advisors?"

"Just Fudd Fartwick, I suppose," Mr. Willimaker said. "He was Queen Bipsy's closest advisor."

"I want to speak with him, then," Elliot said. "And you as well. You have been my closest advisor."

Mr. Willimaker bowed very low and then poofed himself gone. While he waited, Elliot sat down on the ground to think about his plan. He hadn't done so much thinking since learning double-digit multiplication. This thinking was so much work that Elliot didn't hear the footsteps creep up behind him.

A hand grabbed Elliot's shoulder. He heard Tubs Lawless snarling at him in his usual mean voice, "Okay, Penster, now you're gonna get what's coming to you!"

Chapter 21

Where Elliot Shares His Lemon Pie

WHEN TUBS LAWLESS TELLS A KID HE'S GOING TO GET what's coming to him, that's usually a sign that the kid will need several bandages. But Elliot's bandages were somewhere in the blown-up house, so all he could do was turn around slowly and hope he didn't end up wishing *he* had been in the blown-up house.

Tubs stretched out his hands toward Elliot, but in them was something Elliot hadn't expected. A lemon pie.

"My mom said that we have to bring this to you, since your house blew up," Tubs said. "I hope you're happy. This was supposed to be my dessert tonight."

"Er, thanks." Elliot kept waiting for Tubs to do whatever he'd really come to do, like push the pie in Elliot's face and laugh, or run away when Elliot reached for it.

"Do you want the pie or not?" Tubs asked.

Elliot shrugged and took it. "Smells good."

"I wouldn't know. I haven't been able to smell anything since I was five years old and shoved a bunch of chocolate candies up my nose."

Maybe the candies had worked their way up to Tubs's brain. It would explain a lot. But Elliot only said, "Well, tell your mom thanks."

Tubs began walking away but then turned back and said, "You know, since you just took my family's dessert, I should probably take something from you too."

Elliot waved his hand toward the pile of his blown-up house. "Take whatever you want." It didn't matter to him.

Tubs kicked around a few wooden boards and then pointed to a trunk. It wasn't just any trunk. This one had been in Elliot's room until the other night when it started making noises again. Elliot had dragged it into the hallway so he could sleep. The trunk was dented from the explosion and one of the handles had come off, but it was still in one piece. "I'm going to take that."

It had been making noise because it still had three Goblins in it. "Not that trunk," Elliot said, jumping up. "I meant you could take anything else."

Tubs held up a fist. Elliot had seen that fist up close plenty of times and stopped in place.

"Don't tell me what I can or can't take of yours," Tubs said. "Enjoy my mom's pie—or else!" With that, he picked up the trunk and dragged it behind him, huffing and puffing.

Elliot started to go after him but was stopped by Mr. Willimaker returning with Fudd Fartwick.

"Will the Goblins hurt Tubs?" Elliot asked.

Mr. Willimaker stared after Tubs. "Hard to say. They'll either be so happy to get out of the trunk that they'll barely hurt him at all. Or they'll be so mad about having been locked in the trunk that they'll chew his arms off." Mr. Willimaker shrugged. "He'll probably be fine."

"I hope so," Elliot said. "Or else everyone will call him Tubs Armless instead. Ha! Now tell me about the Brownies. Did you talk to them?"

Mr. Willimaker nodded. It hadn't gone well at first. It had started with him poofing to the center of Burrowsville and announcing that the Brownies were in danger. The Brownies only laughed at him and asked if it was another field mouse invasion.

Then Mr. Willimaker did something so extreme, so out of his usual character that all the Brownies had to listen: he loosened his bow tie.

He loosened his bow tie to make it easier to jump up and down, which messed up his neatly combed hair. Then he yelled, "Burrowsville needs you! Your king needs you! You will listen to me because for once in our lives the Brownies are going to fight back!"

Now, as he faced Elliot, Mr. Willimaker couldn't help but smile with pride. He bowed low and said, "I did it, Your Highness. The Brownies are coming."

"I knew you could do it." Elliot turned to Fudd. "I'm glad you're here too."

Fudd looked at Elliot, then at the house. Then back at Elliot. Of course, Fudd had known that the Goblins were going to blow up Elliot's house. He didn't realize Elliot would survive the explosion, though.

Fudd's eyes got so wide they almost popped out of his head. "This is crazy! Couldn't they even blow up your house correctly?"

"What?" Elliot and Mr. Willimaker both asked.

Fudd paused and then said, "I meant, the Goblins must've been crazy to blow up your house. I assume you have a plan for revenge. Perhaps to throw that lemon pie you're holding at them."

Elliot set the pie down and shook his head. "Revenge never makes things better. I just want to stop this war." He turned to Mr. Willimaker. "Get all the Brownies to dig a big circle in the clearing in the forest. Leave an island in the center." Mr. Willimaker bowed and scampered off.

"What's the island for?" Fudd asked.

"I'm going to lure all the Goblins to that island." Elliot pointed to a clump of trees at the edge of the woods. "I'll hide alone beside those trees. When the Goblins arrive, I'll trap them."

Fudd nodded. "Very clever. What do you need me to do?"

"I need you to go to the Goblins. Tell them they can surrender now and stop this war against me and the Brownies. If they don't, then I'll stop them myself."

A sly smile crossed Fudd's face. "You'll stop them? Waiting all alone beside those trees?"

"That's right."

"Really? Just sitting there? Like you've got nothing better to do than wait for a bunch of angry Goblins?"

Elliot shrugged. "I don't have anything better to do." He really didn't.

Fudd gave his most evil laugh. He had put a lot of practice into his laugh, so for an evil Brownie, it was very impressive.

"What was that?" Elliot asked.

Fudd coughed. "Er, I meant to laugh like this." Then he gave a little giggle. "What about that one?"

"Your other laugh was better. Use that one with the Goblins and they're sure to give up." Elliot picked up the lemon pie. "By the way, do you want to have this?"

"Your pie?"

"Sure. It's not payment for helping me, because I know Brownies don't like that. So it's a gift. Not from a king to an advisor. Just friend to friend."

Fudd took the pie and sniffed it deeply. "Are you sure? This whole pie for me?"

"It's all yours," Elliot said. "Lemons give me the sniffles anyway."

A tear welled up in Fudd's eye. He thought way back to his childhood, to the girl who had laughed when he had asked for a turn on the swing, even after he said "please." He'd never had a real friend since that day. Now there was someone who did want to be Fudd's friend, and of all the bad luck, it just happened to be someone Fudd was trying to kill. "Look at that. Your pie is giving me the sniffles too." He pushed it toward Elliot. "I can't accept this. You should give it to Mr. Willimaker. He's been a much better friend to you than I have."

"But you're one of the Brownies, which makes you my friend too." Elliot looked back to the woods, then said to Fudd, "You'd better hurry to go talk to the Goblins. I'm almost ready for them here."

"Thank you, King Elliot. I want you to know that if the Goblins ever do succeed in killing you, I'll always feel a little bad about that." With his arms around the pie, Fudd bowed and poofed himself away.

"What else do you need?" Mr. Willimaker said, running up to Elliot. "The circle digging has begun."

Elliot explained the rest of his plan to Mr. Willimaker and then put a hand on his shoulder and said, "I haven't forgotten about Patches. We'll get her back, okay?"

Mr. Willimaker bowed gratefully. "I trust you, King Elliot. But how will you get the Goblins to come here?"

Elliot pointed to Reed's very large jar of pickle relish. "Didn't you tell me that Goblins love pickles?"

"Oh, yes."

"What about pickle relish? I bet they love it too."

Mr. Willimaker grinned. The jar was as tall as he was, a little bit wider, and far more see-through. Somewhere in Flog were hundreds of Goblins who had, in their wildest and craziest dreams, hoped to find a treasure like this one day. Every Goblin in Flog would come to eat as much as they could. They loved pickles more than anything else, and now pickles were going to be their downfall.

Chapter 22

Where Fudd Gets Burned

W HAT'S THAT AROUND YOUR MOUTH?" GRISSEL ASKED Fudd. "It's yellow."

"Lemon pie." Fudd smeared his mouth across his sleeve. He'd stopped before entering Flog to eat the lemon pie King Elliot had given him. He thought he'd feel less guilty about working with the Goblins if he couldn't see the pie anymore, but for some reason, eating it had only made things worse. His stomach growled at him in a rather accusing way. Fudd tapped his foot on the ground and silently ordered his stomach to be quiet. He had bigger worries than an upset tummy.

"So let me make sure I understand," Grissel said. "You're telling me that King Elliot is just going to wait, all by himself, in some trees to catch us Goblins? Doesn't he know how much stronger we are than he is?"

Fudd threw up his hands. "He thinks he can get all of you into his forest and trap you there." He noticed a little lemon pudding on one of his fingers and licked it. Every lick sent a shock of guilt through him. Sweet, delicious guilt.

Grissel knocked Fudd's hands away. "How will he trap us?"

"It doesn't matter, because it won't work," Fudd said. "You and I will poof directly there and capture him, and then you're free to get rid of him."

Grissel smiled. "You said Elliot has the Brownies in those woods?"

"Yes."

"Then I'll bring all my Goblins. Once we've captured Elliot, I'll make sure that my Goblins finally destroy the Brownies!"

Fudd rubbed his hands together nervously. That had not been part of his plan. "But we agreed that I'd become king of the Brownies."

"You can become king of anyone we don't eat."

"And what about Patches?" Fudd cringed as he asked the question, worried about the answer.

A wicked glint crossed Grissel's eyes. "She's fine. For now. But that will probably change tonight."

Panic welled inside Fudd, choking him. "No, Grissel. No, you can't."

"Who's going to stop me? You?" Grissel bared his sharp teeth and let out a low growl. "I'll do whatever I want. Now come with me."

At this point, Fudd had no choice but to follow Grissel, but when they left Grissel's home, he saw Goblins already poofing themselves away. Some of them licked their lips. Some rubbed their hands together in excitement.

Grissel grabbed one of them. "Where's everyone going?"

"Can't you smell the pickles? Hurry before they're all gone!" With that, the Goblin poofed himself away.

Grissel sniffed the air. The sour smell of vinegar and cucumbers filled his nose. It came from the human world. A line of drool ran down Grissel's chin, and he grinned hungrily at Fudd.

"Remember the pickles," Fudd said, waving his hands and taking two steps back. "Goblins should eat more pickles and fewer Brownies."

Grissel watched as the last of his pickle-hungry Goblins poofed themselves to King Elliot's woods.

"It's a good thing I already decided to let them go," Grissel said. "Because otherwise they'd be in a lot of trouble for leaving without me."

Fudd sadly shook his head. He hoped the Goblins would find the pickles before they found any Brownies. He couldn't help but feel a little responsible for what was happening.

Grissel grabbed Fudd by the arm. "Now you and I will teach the human king it's not wise to trick Goblins."

Grissel poofed himself and Fudd to a spot just outside the trees. From there they could see a large pile of pickle relish. Every Goblin from Flog was gathered around the pile, fighting for as many bites as they could get. Several of them were so busy clawing at each other that no Goblin could get any relish.

"They're not trapped here at all," Grissel said happily. "Your king doesn't know as much about Goblins as I thought."

"Maybe they'll fill up on the pickle relish," Fudd whispered. "They won't be hungry for Brownies."

"We're always hungry for Brownies," Grissel said, licking his lips with his crooked blue tongue.

Fudd didn't like the sound of that, but he continued walking toward Elliot's hiding place in the trees. Grissel followed closely behind him. Too close. Fudd walked faster. He thought he heard Grissel smelling him.

When they arrived in the woods, they found Elliot facing them, relaxing with his back against a large oak tree. He didn't seem surprised to see them. He didn't look afraid either, which worried Fudd. This was the point in the plan when Elliot should have begun to look terrified.

"You were the only one who knew where I'd be hiding," Elliot said to Fudd. "And now you've brought the Goblin leader here to me."

Fudd still tasted the lemon pie in his mouth, which was a little sourer now than he remembered. It had been a gift from Elliot, and he repaid that gift by bringing Grissel here. Rule number four in the *Guidebook to Evil Plans* clearly stated, "Never accept a gift of kindness from your mortal enemy" (page 12). Fudd had never really understood the meaning of that rule...until now. He kicked a foot in the dirt, ashamed of himself.

"You've been helping the Goblins try to get me," Elliot added. "Why?"

Fudd's lower lip quivered. Ever since he learned that Grissel would be eating his friends, he'd begun to think working with him wasn't such a good idea.

"This is all my fault. More than anything I wanted to be king, but I know now I was wrong. I'm so sorry."

"Well, I'm not sorry," Grissel snarled, pushing his way past Fudd. "I still want to get rid of you, human. I already scared you half to death. It's time to finish the job."

Elliot smiled. "Better get close enough that I can see you this time."

Grissel growled and took a step toward Elliot. Grissel's foot landed on a rope that instantly went tight around his bony foot and pulled him up into the air. In a panic, Fudd stepped to the side and into another rope that yanked him up beside Grissel. They dangled upside down, their bodies swinging softly in midair. Fudd clasped his hands together and waited until his body turned to face Elliot, then said, "Forgive me, Your Highness."

Elliot marched right up to Grissel and Fudd and said, "These are my dad's traps. I've been in them myself, so I know you can't get yourself free. If you're both very good, I'll let you out before my dad finds out and tries to have you for dinner. I order you both not to poof out of there. I order all Goblins not to poof away from here."

"You think you can defeat me that easily?" Grissel said with a sneer. "Release me now or else."

"Or else what?" Elliot asked.

Grissel pointed high up to a tree that stood over the pile of Goblins and the pickle relish. Two more Goblins had appeared there. Tied up in a rope dangling from their hands was Patches. If they let go of the rope, she would fall right onto the backs of the Goblins.

Grissel showed his jagged teeth as he laughed. "You've lost, little king. Release me now, or else they get your favorite Brownie for dessert!"

Chapter
23

Where Elliot Gets Some Fresh Air

ELLIOT RAN TO WHERE HE COULD GET A BETTER LOOK AT Patches. The Goblins had tied the rope several times around her whole body. She wouldn't be able to wiggle free on her own, and even if she did, there was nowhere she could go but down onto the pile of Goblins. Several had already smelled her and left the pickle pile to stand beneath her with their arms out. When her rope dropped, they wanted to be the first to get her.

"Help!" Patches cried. "Elliot, help me!"

"You have ten seconds before I order them to drop her," Grissel hissed. "Eighteen!"

Elliot turned. "I have eighteen seconds?"

Grissel rolled his eyes. "Didn't you hear me? Ten seconds. I didn't say which ten. Now it's seventeen!"

Mr. Willimaker ran to Elliot's side and tugged on his shirt. "That's my daughter. Please, Your Highness, we have to save her."

"Can't she just poof away?" Elliot asked.

"She's Grissel's prisoner. If he ordered her not to poof away, then she can't. Just like Grissel can't poof away from here until you allow it."

"Sixteen!" Grissel said.

"Let me go up there," Mr. Willimaker said, beginning to flap his hands nervously.

"You're not strong enough to stop them." Elliot took a deep breath. He didn't want to admit that he was sort of scared to say the next part, but there was no choice. "Poof me up there."

The Goblins holding Patches began playing with the rope. They swung her in a little circle so that the Goblins below would have to run to catch her when she fell.

"Stop that!" Patches yelled, wiggling angrily. "I'm not a swing!"

"Fifteen!" Grissel said.

"Poof me up there," Elliot repeated. His heart pounded and his fingers felt numb, but he had made his decision.

Mr. Willimaker shook his head. "I told you before, Brownies don't have enough magic to poof humans. I'd send part of you up there, but the rest of you might not make it."

"Thirteen!" Grissel said.

"You're on number fourteen!" Elliot said.

"Never heard of that number," Grissel yelled back. "Twelve!"

"Poof me now," Elliot said to Mr. Willimaker. "Do it, or else they're going to drop her."

"Even for a Brownie, my magic isn't powerful enough," Mr. Willimaker protested, wringing his hands together. "Maybe a stronger Brownie could do it, but not me."

From behind them, they heard a small and much humbler voice than usual. "I could try," Fudd said.

"What?" Grissel snarled. "Whose side are you on?"

"I'll never be on your side again," Fudd said. "That was my terrible, unforgivable mistake." As his rope swung him again to face Elliot, he added, "Your Highness, I know there's no reason you should trust me. But Mr. Willimaker will tell you that I'm the only Brownie strong enough to attempt poofing you. I don't know if I can do it, but I do know there's no other Brownie strong enough to try."

"Just for that, I'm skipping to ten." Grissel stuck his long, snakelike tongue out at Fudd. "Ha! That'll show you."

Mr. Willimaker tugged on Elliot's shirt again. "Fudd is stronger than me, sir. But this is still too dangerous. Even though she's my daughter, I can't risk the life of our king."

"Nine!" Grissel said. "Release me now, or it'll be too late for Patches."

Elliot closed his eyes, took another deep breath, and then calmly turned to Fudd. "Poof me up there now, Fudd. I know you can do it."

"I'll do my best, King Elliot." Fudd closed his eyes and snapped his fat fingers together.

Dear Reader, generally speaking, poofing is not a bad way to travel. It's quick, painless, and at worst, only a little bit ticklish. But it's always best to be prepared, or else poofing tends to confuse the brain for a moment as it tries to figure out how to keep all the body parts together during the trip.

Since humans aren't used to getting poofed around, they should always start with a creature that has a lot of experience. The Brownies have no experience in poofing other creatures to places. None. Zip. Zero. It would have been better for Fudd to practice this trick a few hundred times with tiny worms who wouldn't mind if they arrived somewhere without their arms or legs, because they have no arms or legs.

However, Fudd had no time to practice. And no second chances. In less than a second, Grissel would order his Goblins to drop Patches. Elliot was the only one who could save her.

To Elliot, getting poofed somewhere by a Brownie felt as if a bunch of invisible hands had grabbed every part of his body and pulled them all in whatever order they wanted to the top of the tree. It didn't exactly hurt, but it wasn't comfortable either. When he opened his eyes (after his eyes were returned to their sockets), he was standing beside two surprised Goblins on a tree branch high above the pile of Goblins below.

One of the Goblins lunged at Elliot, claws out. Elliot ducked and the Goblin flew directly over his head. He flapped his arms as he began to fall. Not being a bird, he continued falling, landing on some Goblins below who had been hoping to catch the far more edible Patches.

Elliot stood again, trying to regain his balance. Then he noticed one very important detail. His left arm was gone. Fudd had gotten most of him here, but not all. He fell onto the thick tree branch and with his right hand grabbed a bunch of leaves to keep from falling. He locked his legs around the branch and steadied himself.

"Where's my arm, Fudd?" he yelled.

"I'm working on it, Your Highness!" Fudd called back.

"Eight!" Grissel screamed from his upside-down trap. "Eight, you idiot. Eight!"

The Goblin holding Patches looked confused for a moment, as if he couldn't figure out the importance of the number eight. Then Grissel yelled, "Drop her!"

"I thought that was on seven," the Goblin called back.

"Do it now!" Grissel yelled again.

The next few seconds passed so fast, Elliot would never be sure exactly how it all happened. He let go of the leaves that were keeping him steady and, while tightening his legs around the branch, swung his weight downward. The Goblin holding Patches released her rope, which fluttered in the air past him. He tried to grab it once, but it slipped through his hand. He tried again, and this time he somehow kept a hold on it, although Patches was so close to the Goblins now they could almost reach her if they jumped high enough.

The weight of catching Patches caused the branch to bow, and then it sprang back up like a rubber band. The Goblin who had been holding Patches hadn't considered the importance of holding on to anything other than the rope, and as the branch rebounded he flew into the air and then fell back to the earth like a Goblin-shaped rocket. He landed on another two Goblins who were trying to jump up and reach Patches.

Still upside down with his legs locked around the branch of the tree, Elliot felt Patches's rope begin to slip. With only one arm, he knew he couldn't hold on to her much longer. But he had no way to pull her up.

"You're not Grissel's prisoner anymore," Mr. Willimaker shouted to Patches. "Elliot has you. Now poof out of there!"

Patches closed her eyes, and Elliot felt the weight of the rope disappear. He looked over to Mr. Willimaker and saw her poof close to her father, who grabbed her in a tight hug.

"Where's my arm?" Elliot called to Fudd. If he fell, he wouldn't last long against the Goblins below.

"Wish me luck." Fudd snapped his fingers, and Elliot's arm returned to his body. But something was still wrong.

"I don't need two arms on my right side!" Elliot said as his left arm appeared just below his right arm. "Fix this!"

"Sorry about that," Fudd said.

With another snap, the arm reappeared where it should be, properly attached to the left side of his body. Elliot wiggled it a few times to make sure it was going to stay in place, then used his arms to pull himself back onto the branch.

"We can poof you down now," Mr. Willimaker said.

"No, thanks." Elliot didn't want to get poofed anywhere ever again. He pulled the rope up with him and tied it around the branch. Holding tightly to the knots on the other end, where Patches had been, he took a running leap into the air.

Okay, so it didn't swing him back to the ground quite as well as he had pictured it. But in a clumsy sort of way, it did get him away from the Goblins where he fell onto the ground not far from Mr. Willimaker. It would have been nice if he could have landed on his feet, because landing on his hands and face didn't seem very king-like. But at least he landed with all of his body parts in one piece and where they should be. Plus, Patches was safe.

She ran to him with a hug that nearly choked him. "Thank you, thank you, thank you!"

"Welcome back," Elliot said, getting to his feet. "But this isn't over yet."

"You're right about that," Grissel said. "Because my Goblins are just about finished eating that pickle relish. And if they can't poof away, then they'll have nothing better to do than attack you."

"I don't think so." Elliot pulled his crown off his wrist and placed it on his head. It was a little small, but still a crown. It was time to end the war.

Chapter 24

Where There's an Island in the Woods

ELLIOT HAD PUT THE PICKLE RELISH IN A VERY SPECIAL PLACE in the woods, on an island. Of course, it didn't look like an island at all. Instead, it looked like pieces of Elliot's exploded home had fallen into the woods and landed in a wide circle around a pile of pickle relish. What the Goblins didn't know was that the Brownies had put the pieces of wood from Elliot's home around the island where the Goblins were able to cross over them like bridges. They were so excited to get to the pickle relish, they never thought about what was beneath that wood.

It was time for them to think about it.

Elliot stepped out from the trees and yelled to the Brownies, "Remove the wood!"

Brownies appeared from their hiding places. There were more of them than the Goblins could count (which isn't saying much, since few Goblins besides Grissel can count higher than eight, their number of fingers). There were boys and girls, young and old, and all of them stood ready to obey their human king.

Each Brownie grabbed a single board and dragged it away from the island. It left the Goblins surrounded by at least a foot of water. The hose that Cole and Kyle played with every day was flooding the trench. A few Goblins tested the water with a toe or finger then pulled it out with a water welt on their green skin.

The Goblins hissed and scowled and shouted insults at the Brownies: "Your mother makes chocolate cake!" and "Pickles and Brownies taste good together!"

Elliot ran up to the island and stood on a large rock so that all the Goblins could see him. "Listen to me," he yelled. "It's time for the war between the Goblins and Brownies to end!"

The Goblins booed, the Brownies cheered, and a little squirrel who had wandered onto the tree branch overhead quickly scampered away. (As nearly everyone knows, squirrels have never been interested in interspecies wars.) Elliot held up a hand for them to be quiet and then proclaimed, "This war has been going on for a long time. You're so used to all this trouble that it seems normal to you. But from now on, friendship will be normal. Peace will be normal. I know Goblins are used to eating Brownies, but now you must learn to only eat things that want to be eaten. Brownies, I know you're used to losing in this war, but it's time to stop thinking of yourself as losers. You're too great to think that way. It's not who we are anymore."

Elliot paused and thought of Tubs. Tubs...who chased Elliot across town, and made Elliot do his homework, and who almost flushed Elliot down the toilet. Agatha had said Tubs's problem was that one day Elliot would figure out who he was. Elliot smiled. It was so wide that his smile almost stretched off his face. Maybe what Agatha had said would happen one day just had happened.

Elliot decided he wasn't going to accept bullying from Tubs anymore either. Just as he was helping the Brownies stand up for themselves, he planned to stand up for himself from now on too. He stood even taller on his rock, like a true king would.

"Here's the deal. Any Goblin who promises to live in peace with the Brownies will get to come off the island. If you make this promise, you can return to Flog. We'll become friends and learn to help each other. If you won't promise to live in peace, then you will have to learn to live on this island."

Elliot watched as several of the Goblins tried to poof themselves off. But he'd already commanded them not to leave, and they were too afraid of the water to cross the island. They truly were trapped.

After a number of failed tries at leaving on his own, a tall Goblin with an extra-long nose stepped forward and raised his hand. "King Elliot? I will promise."

Elliot walked forward so that he stood across the water from the Goblin. "You won't eat any more Brownies?"

The Goblin raised his hand. "May I be forced to eat chocolate cake all the rest of my life if I eat another Brownie."

"Then be a friend to us, and we'll be a friend to you." Elliot nodded his head at several Brownies near him, who lowered their boards and helped the Goblin cross off the island. "You can poof home," Elliot told him.

With a short, respectful bow to Elliot, the Goblin snapped his fingers and left.

In turn, nearly every other Goblin did the same. Some went home right away, some stayed to talk with other Brownies, setting up pickle trades and sharing ideas on Underworld gardening.

Suddenly very tired, Elliot leaned against a tree, watching the Goblins and Brownies as they worked together. Beside him, he felt a tug on his shirt.

"Your Highness, I couldn't wait any longer to thank you," Mr. Willimaker said, holding Patches by the hand. She danced from one foot to the other, clearly excited to be back with her father. Patches scampered over to Elliot, bowed before him, and then leapt into his arms and gave him a hug.

"You saved me from the Goblins," Patches said, punching Elliot lightly on the arm. "That was really cool."

"I think you saved me from the Goblins too," Elliot said. "We're even."

Patches blushed. "I might have helped a little bit." She told Elliot about escaping from the hole and then hiding in the carrot cave where she was captured again.

Elliot didn't know what a carrot cave was. Maybe he'd ask about that later.

"I was pretty mad when they caught me again," Patches said. "I really enjoyed those carrots. Dad says I ate so many I'm going to turn orange for a week!" Patches rubbed her belly with a hand that Elliot thought already looked a little orange, and then she let out a giant-size burp. Nobody who is only two feet tall has ever let out a burp such as this one. Earthquake scientists hundreds of miles away rushed to their monitors to see what happened. Astronauts orbiting the earth saw the entire planet shake just a little. And Mr. Willimaker laughed. He had missed Patches very much.

"We shouldn't ever have trouble with the Goblins again," Elliot said. "The Goblin war is over."

In the end, every single Goblin left the island in the woods. The Brownies cheered again when the last one left. They hugged each other and then bowed together before Elliot.

Elliot raised his hands again for them to be silent. He took the crown off his head and gave it to Mr. Willimaker, then said, "There's something you all should know. Queen Bipsy never gave Mr. Willimaker my name to be king. She told him to choose a name, and he chose mine. If you all want to have someone else as king, a Brownie maybe, I'll understand."

There was silence as the Brownies looked at each other. Then Patches said, "Your Highness, everything is as it should be. My father did exactly what Queen Bipsy told him to do. When he wrote your name, he was following her command."

"That's right," Mr. Willimaker said. "When I chose you, I did obey her."

Patches continued, "We know you're the king, because when you commanded the Goblins not to poof away, they had to obey you. They would only have to obey a real king."

"Hail King Elliot," the Brownies cheered. "Long live King Elliot!"

Mr. Willimaker pushed the crown back into Elliot's hands. "Your Highness, the Brownies need you. Patches was right. You are our king."

Elliot smiled and put the crown back on his head. "Then as your king, I will finish this." He marched over to the ropes where Grissel and Fudd were still hanging. Their upside-down faces had turned slightly purple, but otherwise they were fine.

"Your war is finished," Elliot told Grissel. "There are no more Goblins who'll fight with you."

"I saw them leave, the cowards." Grissel folded his arms. "Fine, I'll make the promise too. Now let me go home."

"He's crossing his fingers," Fudd said. "I can see him from here. Don't believe his promise, Your Highness."

Elliot shook his head at Grissel, disappointed to see he'd try something as sneaky as crossed fingers. "Mr. Willimaker, take Grissel to the Brownie prison. I want him to receive the most chocolaty chocolate cake we have, every single day, without frosting or milk, until he truly agrees to become a friend to the Brownies."

Mr. Willimaker nodded, and then both he and Grissel disappeared.

Elliot turned to Fudd, who wiped a tear from his eye.

"I suppose you'll want me to have chocolate cake now too," Fudd whimpered.

"You helped me save Patches," Elliot said. "If you still wanted me dead, that would've been your chance."

"I've changed," Fudd said. "I hope I can show you that."

"It will take me a long time to trust you again," Elliot said. "If anyone tries to get me, you have to understand that I might wonder if you're involved."

Fudd scrunched up his face. "What do you mean?"

"Let's just say that no one ever blew up my house until I met you." Elliot frowned as he said it, but Fudd thought he might have seen a slight grin as Elliot looked his way.

"It will take me a long time to prove that I can be trusted," Fudd said meekly. "But if you give me the chance, I'll be a much better advisor than before. I'll be a much better Brownie than before. Tell me what I can do to fix things."

Elliot pointed to the mess of his exploded home. "To start, you can get the Brownies to build me another home. I don't need it fancy or new. I don't care if the stairs still squeak. I just want a place for my family to come back to."

For the first time since Elliot had become king, Fudd Fartwick gave him a real bow (which is not easy when one is hanging upside down with a rope around his leg). "Your Highness, it may not be fancy or new, and the stairs might still squeak, but you are a king and the Brownies will build you a castle."

"Then I release you," Elliot said. "You may poof out of that trap."

Fudd snapped his fingers and landed upright on the ground. He bowed to Elliot again and then quickly ducked into the trees as someone behind them yelled, "Penster!"

Elliot turned and saw Tubs Lawless running across his lawn, dragging the trunk he'd taken behind him. Tubs dropped the trunk in the middle of the yard and said, "Penster, it's a good thing your house blew up!"

"Why?" Elliot asked.

"It was probably full of those big green rats I found in this trunk."

"Did they get out?"

"They're back in the trunk now. Finally." Tubs shook a fist at Elliot. "But watch out. I'll get you for letting me steal those things."

"No," Elliot said firmly. "You won't."

Tubs's lip curled in anger. "What did you say?"

"You won't chase me through town. And you won't throw rocks or toys or even your bicycle at me. I'm not going to do your homework for you or let you flush me down the toilet. You are done being a bully."

"Who's gonna make me stop?"

"Me. And those big green rats will help me if I need them. They're my friends now."

Tubs stumbled back a few steps. "Fine. Just keep that trunk away from me!" He turned and ran, revealing long claw marks down the back of his pants.

Elliot smiled as he watched Tubs scramble away. Then, with a happy sigh, he grabbed a hose and walked toward the trunk. A king's work was never done.

Elliot
and the Pixie Plot

JENNIFER A. NIELSEN

ILLUSTRATED BY GIDEON KENDALL

For Sierra, who amazes me every single day.

Contents

No Pixies were harmed in the writing of this book.
Sadly, we cannot say the same for our Shapeshifter,
who badly stubbed his toe during the writing of chapter 7.

Warning!

An entire floor of St. Phobics Hospital for Really Scared Children has been set aside just for readers of this book. If you are about to begin reading, then you may wish to take a minute first and reserve yourself a bed there. St. Phobics Hospital is located right on the Strip in Las Vegas, one of the brightest places on earth. You may not understand why that's important now, but somewhere in chapter 18 you will.

As you read, you may begin to understand myctophobia (mic-to-fo-be-a), or the fear of darkness. However, do not expect this book to help you with arachibutyrophobia (a-rak-i-something-be-a), the fear of peanut butter sticking to the roof of your mouth. There is no peanut butter in this book. Elliot's family is out of peanut butter and probably won't buy any for another month. Nor does this book deal in any way with zemmiphobia (just show the word to your teacher and she'll pronounce it for you), the fear of the great mole rat, although most readers will agree that great mole rats are pretty freaky.

If you can't get yourself to St. Phobics Hospital, then there are things you can do at home to protect yourself. First, get every lamp, flashlight, and lantern you can find, and drag them into your bedroom. Next, turn them all on. Not bright enough? Before we go any further, it is very important, no matter how afraid you are of the dark, that you never, ever light a fire in your bedroom to try to make it brighter. A fire won't give you that much more light, and it will probably burn your house down. A much better idea is to go to a baseball field and ask the owners if you can borrow all of their field lights for your bedroom. You'll need them until you're certain there is nothing in the dark that is going to try to kill you.

At least that's what Elliot wishes he had done.

Chapter 1

Where Elliot Is Hunted

Deep inside, even past his intestines and kidneys and all that yucky stuff, eleven-year-old Elliot Penster wondered if there was something different about him. Like, maybe he was really a magical half-breed or a young wizard.

Usually in these stories, when a kid wonders about things like that, it's because he's right; that's who he is.

But that's not who Elliot is. He can wonder about it until his face turns purple, but it won't matter. The fact is he's just a regular kid.

A kid who happens to be king of the Brownies.

The story of how Elliot became king of the Brownies is pretty good. Some people think it should be in a book or something. The book could be called *Elliot and the Goblin War*, and it would probably be terrific. As a strange coincidence, a book with exactly that title does exist. Maybe it was sitting on the shelf right beside this book. But if you haven't read it, don't worry. Neither has Elliot.

All that's important to know is that he did become the Brownie king. And although it would be nice to tell you more about that now, Elliot happens to be in a bit of trouble, which requires your immediate attention.

For Elliot is being chased. *Hunted* may be a better word, because the hunter is sly and tricky and finally has Elliot square in her sights. She watched for him all week, the way a hungry lion waits in the brush for the antelope to pass by. It stops at the edge of the water hole for a drink. The lion creeps forward, and BAMMO! The antelope is captured.

Now, don't worry. That didn't happen to Elliot, mostly because he never drinks from strange water holes, and there are no lions in his small town of Sprite's Hollow. But something was waiting for him to pass by. The hunter searched everywhere for him at school, sort of like the way your little brother searches your room when he knows you've got candy hidden in there. She looked for him beneath the slide on the playground and under his desk in the classroom. Rumor is she even went into the boys' bathroom to search for him. She found Elliot's twin brothers in there, shooting spit wads onto the ceiling, but no Elliot.

Then, just when Elliot thought it was safe to come out of hiding and hurry home, the hunter spotted him. He only made it halfway home before she threw her weapon of choice, an old jump rope, around his legs and toppled him to the ground.

Elliot rolled onto his back and looked into the leering face of the scariest thing ever to cross his path—Goblins included. She was the curse of the entire fifth-grade class, the plague of Sprite's Hollow, and if the entire planet ever imploded inside a black hole, he knew that somehow she'd have caused it. The hunter, whose real name was Cambria Dawn Wortson, had found him at last.

She leaned over him with her hands on her hips. "Elliot, we have to talk."

"Later. For once, my sister isn't cooking tonight, so this might be my only chance to eat real food all month."

"Always thinking about yourself. Did you ever think that my grade is going to be ruined if we don't do our project?"

He hadn't. Elliot tried very hard never to think about anything related to Cambria Dawn Wortson. Everyone except her mother called her Cami. Elliot preferred his own nickname for her: Toadface. He had called her that once at lunch. She dumped her tray on his head and convinced the lunch lady it was an accident. Now he called her Cami too. Seemed like a good compromise.

She leaned even further over him, and he wondered how she kept her balance. In a bossy voice, she said, "Science fair projects are due next week. You didn't ask to be my partner, and I definitely didn't ask to be yours, but we're stuck with each other, so let's make the best of it, okay?"

As proof that the entire will of the universe was now focused on the single

purpose of destroying Elliot's life, Cami had been assigned as his science project partner. Elliot thought back to when he had nearly been scared to death
by the Goblins. If he'd known then that he would have to do a whole science
project with Cami, he might have let the Goblins finish the job.

Not really. But he definitely would've moved to a different country.

"Elliot, are you listening to me?"

He was now. The way Cami pronounced his name, the last part rhymed with
"Scott." Whatever. Her name rhymed with "Fanny." Almost.

"I said, are you listening?"

"Sure." He began loosening the rope around his legs. "We have to do our
science project."

She huffed. Being a toadface, it was no surprise her breath smelled like a
toad's. Although to be fair, he'd never really smelled toad breath before, so it
was really just his best guess.

"So do you have any ideas?" she asked.

Anti-girl spray? Probably best not to suggest that, so he shrugged. Something
fast and easy. That was all he cared about.

Cami plunked down beside him and pulled a notebook out from her backpack. A pink pen was lodged in the middle of it, and she opened the notebook
to that page, showing him a bunch of writing that was so *girly*. The dots over
her *i*'s were tiny hearts, for Pete's sake.

"Then we'll have to use my idea," she said. "I read on the Internet about a
potion we can make that might turn things invisible."

Elliot snorted. That was close to the stupidest thing he'd ever heard. The
actual stupidest thing was when Tubs Lawless, a boy who used to bully Elliot,
had forgotten his own name. Cami gave Elliot a dirty look, then continued.
"Anyway, my mom got us all the stuff, and I've already mixed it together,
but she doesn't want to store it at our house in case it blows up. I figure your
house already blew up once, so if it happens again it's probably not as big a
deal. Okay?"

"Do I have to do anything but store it?"

"Well, it wouldn't kill you to stir it once in a while—unless stirring makes it
blow up, in which case it really would kill you. My mom thinks it's probably safe

just to keep it somewhere. It has to sit for a while before it can be tested. So what about it? Can I bring it over tomorrow morning?"

Tomorrow was a Saturday. Elliot had always liked the idea of never having to see Cami on the weekends, but for once in her life she was right. The project was due really soon, and if all he had to do was store it, then that didn't sound so bad.

"Fine," he said. "We'll try to turn something invisible. You can bring the potion over in the morning."

She jumped to her feet and offered him a hand up, which he ignored. She kicked her foot on the sidewalk a couple of times, then said, "By the way, I hear you finally stood up to Tubs."

"Oh, yeah." Tubs had bullied Elliot for as far back as either of them could remember. Tubs probably only remembered as far back as last week, but Elliot remembered his preschool years when Tubs used to tie Elliot to the merry-go-round with his blankie and start it spinning. After he won the Goblin war a few weeks ago, Elliot had told Tubs the bullying was going to stop. Tubs had pretty much left him alone since then. In fact, Tubs's parents had even asked if he could sleep over at Elliot's house tonight while they were out of town.

Proof that good deeds do get punished.

Cami shrugged. "Well, I thought it was really brave of you to do that. See you tomorrow!"

She skipped off down the sidewalk away from him, like the tricky hunter he knew she was. All of that being nice to him—it was just her game, her bait to draw him in. But it wouldn't work, because he was no ordinary kid. He was Elliot Penster, king of the Brownies. And he had to hurry home before his dinner was all gone.

"Pssst, Your Highness!"

Elliot jumped back on the sidewalk as his Brownie friend Mr. Willimaker motioned to him from behind a tree. "Oh, it's you. I wondered when I'd see you again."

Mr. Willimaker pressed his bushy gray eyebrows together. "It hasn't been that long, has it?"

"Just a few weeks, I guess—since the Brownies finished rebuilding my family's blown-up house."

Mr. Willimaker nodded as if he had no clue what Elliot was talking about. "Er, yes, naturally I know all about that story, so let's say nothing more of it. I've got to talk to you. It's an emergency."

Elliot sighed and tilted his head in the direction of his home. If he really concentrated, he could almost smell his mother's lasagna from here. And he had the sinking feeling that whatever Mr. Willimaker's emergency was, it meant Elliot might not get any of her delicious dinner.

"Okay," Elliot said, sighing. "Tell me your problem."

Chapter 2

Where Elliot Meets a Triple Scoop of Evil with a Cherry on Top

Elliot followed Mr. Willimaker deeper into the orchard where he'd been hiding. "If you can be invisible to other people, then why do we have to go so far away to talk?" Elliot asked.

Mr. Willimaker frowned. "*I* can talk, but you'll look pretty silly talking back to me. You can only talk to invisible people a few times before people start to wonder about you."

"People already wonder about me." Elliot noticed something new about his friend. "Hey, you've got a white patch of hair on the back of your head. When did that happen?"

"It's always been there. You just didn't notice it," Mr. Willimaker said.

Elliot was sure he would have noticed it, but it didn't seem important to push the matter. So he set his backpack down and knelt on the ground beside Mr. Willimaker. "So what's the problem? Are the Brownies okay?"

"Probably. But we need to talk about Grissel."

Elliot's eyes narrowed. "What about him?"

Elliot wasn't the type of kid to hold grudges, but it was hard to forget that as leader of the Goblins, Grissel had scared Elliot half to death and blown up his house. Elliot finally tricked the Goblins into ending the war and eating things for dinner other than the Brownies. All of the Goblins agreed and have lived quite happily with the Brownies ever since. All of the Goblins, that is, but one.

Their leader, Grissel, is cruel and calculating and entirely unpleasant, and that's when he's in a good mood. He is not in a good mood now. That's because in addition to having lost the war, Elliot also sentenced him to hard time in the Brownie prison.

Doing hard time with the Brownies means eating chocolate cake at every meal without frosting or even a glass of milk. You'd be entirely unpleasant too if you had to eat chocolate cake day after day while surrounded by a bunch of Brownies.

"What's the problem with Grissel?" Elliot asked.

Mr. Willimaker clasped his hands together. "It's, uh, just not working out with him. I feel—er, we Brownies feel it's time to release him. We're sure he'll return peacefully to Flog and never bother anyone again."

"Did he promise that?"

Mr. Willimaker's mouth, which he must have opened to speak, dropped a little wider. "I don't, er, think we need to worry about any promises. Just give the order to release him, Elliot, right here and now, and then he can go free and we'll all return to our happy lives."

Elliot scratched his chin. "Are you all right?"

"What? Yes, of course." Mr. Willimaker tilted his head. "Why do you ask? Don't I seem like my normal self?"

"You're acting really strange."

"Ah, well, this is just how I act when I want you to release a prisoner. You've never seen me act this way, because I've never asked you to release one before."

"Oh. Well, I'm not going to release Grissel."

"What?" Mr. Willimaker threw up his hands in disbelief. "Why not?"

"Because he'll just start eating the Brownies again. Until he promises to stop, he has to stay in jail."

Mr. Willimaker's face darkened. Normally, he was excessively polite, and his tidy gray hair and suit made him look like a gentleman. But something about him was different now, and Elliot was sure he heard an angry growl escape his lips. "But Your Highness," he said between clenched teeth. "If you knew how important this is."

Elliot sat flat on the ground and rested his arms across his legs. "What's going on, Mr. Willimaker?"

Mr. Willimaker's nose began to quiver. Not his entire face. Just the nose. For a brief second it popped out like a long, pink carrot, then he took a deep breath and it flattened itself back to its regular button shape. He said, "I'm asking you for the last time, Your Highness, to release Grissel the Goblin."

Elliot stood. He placed his hands on his hips and then thought maybe that was too much like what Cami had done, so he put his hands to his side. "Who are you? Because you're not Mr. Willimaker."

The creature who was not Mr. Willimaker stared at Elliot with wide eyes while he searched for something to say. He stuttered out a few halfhearted protests, then finally leaned his head back and closed his eyes. He exhaled slowly, and as he did, the body of Mr. Willimaker dissolved, leaving in its place a small white goat.

Elliot stepped back, just to be cautious. Although he had figured whoever this was would give up trying to look like Mr. Willimaker, this was not what he had expected.

With black eyes, the goat looked up at Elliot, bleated loudly, then said, "Release Grissel or else!"

"Or else what?" Elliot asked. "What are you going to do, eat my shirt?"

"I might."

Elliot sighed and picked up his backpack. "If this is the best you can do, then I've got to go."

The goat drew in a large breath of air that seemed to fill its entire body. It stretched and expanded until it was four feet taller than Elliot. The goat's thin white hair turned dark and wild (except for a small patch of white hair on the back of its head). Long, muscular legs formed, leading to a wide, hunched back and the face of a wolf.

With a growl, the creature said, "So you're not afraid of farm animals. What about a werewolf?"

Elliot wondered why the creature hadn't turned into a werewolf to begin with. Goats don't have fangs, or sharp claws. This was much more impressive. In a bad way.

Elliot tried to keep his voice from shaking as he said, "You won't hurt me. I'll bet you're not as bad as you say you are."

"I'll take that bet," the werewolf said. "And I'll win, because I am very bad. I'm like a triple scoop of evil with a cherry on top. A wicked, evil cherry that you'll probably choke on if you don't chew carefully before swallowing."

Elliot tilted his head. "Huh?"

The werewolf leaned in closer. "I'm so evil that my analogies don't even have to make sense. So I win the bet. Never trust anything that can change its shape."

Elliot shrugged. "In my world, the only thing I can think of that changes is a butterfly. It starts as a caterpillar, and then it changes to a butterfly. I trust butterflies. They'd never hurt me. I don't think you would either."

The werewolf raised a claw and growled so loudly that the branches of the tree behind Elliot trembled. Elliot stumbled a few steps backward and said, "Look, if you want to talk to me, then just do it as yourself."

"There is no myself," the werewolf said. "I am a Shapeshifter. I am whatever form I take at the moment."

"So this is your scary form?" Elliot asked.

The werewolf laughed, which sounded more like a pre-hunt howl. Then he asked, "Do you want to be scared?"

Elliot didn't, but it was clearly a rhetorical question. The werewolf wasn't looking for an answer. It retreated into the shadow of a tree and took a deep breath; then its height shrunk by a foot or two. The werewolf's fur blackened to become more like a body of smoke and fire than of flesh and bones. Elliot could feel the heat from the black fire, but there was no light, just the bitter smell of burning. A long, black cloak hung around the creature's shoulders, and when Elliot glanced down, he saw that the creature was only barely touching the ground.

The creature's voice was like a whisper Elliot heard in his head, but not through his ears. It ran a shiver up Elliot's spine as the creature said, "Now I am a Shadow Man. I am your worst nightmare."

Chapter 3

Where Harold Is Also the Name of the Class Hamster

Dear Reader, this may be a good time to think about your worst nightmare. Is it one where you are being chased down a very steep hill by a million hungry white bunny rabbits and you are holding what appears to be the last carrot on earth? Or am I the only one having that dream?

Elliot doesn't remember most of his dreams. However, he felt that if he had dreamt of his Brownie friend turning into a goat, changing to a werewolf, evolving into a Shadow Man, and threatening to do something horrible to him if he didn't release Grissel, who would then turn around and do something horrible to the Brownies, he would certainly remember such a dream. So this was probably not his *worst* nightmare.

It was a pretty scary daymare though, if such a thing existed.

The Shadow Man stared down at Elliot, who felt beads of hot sweat line his forehead. Something inside Elliot stopped working. Something important, like his heart. This was nothing like being scared to death by the Goblins. It was worse. He stumbled backward, tripping on a root and falling to the ground.

"Is this what you are?" Elliot asked, not sure what he was seeing.

The creature's laugh sounded like the powerful hiss of a steam engine pulling into a train station. "Shadow Men are servants of the evil Demon Kovol. Fear them, Elliot, and hope you never cross their path."

Elliot's heart pounded in his chest. Kovol was asleep. His friend Agatha the Hag had told him that. As long as Kovol remained asleep, the Shadow Men would have no reason to bother him. He hoped.

"You're not Mr. Willimaker, and you're not a goat or a werewolf," Elliot whispered. "And you can take the shape of a Shadow Man, but that's not you either."

"I am far more powerful than they are, for I can become them when I want to, or become anything else. I am a Shapeshifter, and you will do what I say."

Elliot shook his head and forced himself to look into the empty black pits that were now the Shapeshifter's eyes. "You're made of shadow. You can't hurt me."

The figure swirled around Elliot, creating a wind that sucked the air from his lungs. Heat from the Shadow Man filled the space where the air had been, and sweat stung Elliot's brow. He collapsed forward and whispered, "Okay, I get it. You're bad."

The swirling stopped, and Elliot was able to breathe again. "I'm not bad actually," the Shapeshifter said. "I just wanted to scare you because you bet me I couldn't."

"You win, okay? Please change."

The Shadow Man shrugged as if it didn't matter to him, then exhaled slowly and dissolved into the shape of a boy about Elliot's age.

The boy was about Elliot's height but with normal legs (Elliot's legs were still too long for his body). Elliot's hair had darkened since summer to the same light brown as the boy's, although streaks of blond still showed in Elliot's sun-bleached hair. And unlike Elliot, the boy's clothes matched. Elliot wondered if he'd change anything about his own body if he were a Shapeshifter. Bigger muscles maybe.

"What's your name?" Elliot asked.

"Harold."

"Harold?"

"All the best Shapeshifter names were taken before I was born. By the time I came along, it was either Morphid or Pupa Boy." He shrugged. "My parents skipped Shapeshifter names and called me Harold instead."

"Harold's good. That's our hamster's name at school."

Harold groaned. "That doesn't make me feel better."

"It should. He's a good hamster. Runs fast on his wheel and everything. I guess you already know my name."

144

"Obviously. Now please, King Elliot, you must release Grissel."

"Why?"

"All I know is that the Pixies want him free. They forced me to come here and try to fool you into releasing them."

"How did they force you?"

Harold threw up his hands. "How many times has your mother told you that rhyme, 'Pixie one, lots of fun. Pixie two, trouble for you. Pixie three, better flee.'"

"Never." Elliot's mother didn't know Pixies exist.

"Well, my mother says it every time the Pixies trick me. She says it a lot. Anyway, they said I wasn't a very good Shapeshifter, because I couldn't turn into anything I wanted. I said I could. They bet me I couldn't." Harold lowered his eyes. "I have this problem with bets. I can't say no to them."

"What did they want you to turn into?" Elliot asked.

Harold's mouth twisted. Then with a sigh he said, "A marshmallow."

Elliot giggled. "Regular or mini?"

"It's not funny," Harold said. "Of course I had to prove that I could do it. Then when I became a marshmallow I couldn't think my way back, because as it turns out, marshmallows don't have brains. The Pixies said they'd change me back but that I had to do what they wanted."

"What was that?"

"They wanted me to pretend to be you and order the Brownies to release Grissel. But even if I looked exactly like you, I still wouldn't be the king, so I couldn't release him. So after they helped me change back, I promised that if they released me, I'd come here pretending to be Mr. Willimaker. The Pixie princess, Fidget Spitfly, agreed, and here I am. So will you release Grissel?"

Elliot wasn't usually a stubborn kid, but he didn't see a lot of room to bargain on the issue of Goblins eating his royal subjects. "You'll have to go back and tell Princess Fidget that I'm not releasing Grissel until he promises to stop eating the Brownies."

Harold shook his head. "Are you crazy? I'm not telling her anything. Do you know how mad she'll be that I failed? Sorry, but you'll have to tell her yourself."

"If she comes after me, I'll just capture her," Elliot said. If he had done that with the Goblins, he could surely do that with her.

"She's not some stupid Goblin, Elliot. When Princess Fidget wants you, you'll be the one coming to her."

Elliot didn't like the sound of that. "How? When?"

"I don't know. But if I were you, I wouldn't go to sleep."

"Tonight?"

"Ever." With that, Harold exhaled slowly, and his human body dissolved into the shape of a brown sparrow. He fluttered into the air, waved a wing at Elliot, and then began to fly away. He circled around and stopped midair in front of Elliot, then tweeted, "Sorry about trying to trick you."

"That's okay," Elliot said.

"Maybe I can make it up to you in some way."

"Yeah, maybe."

"Penster!"

Elliot rolled his eyes and turned. Crashing through the bushes was Tubs Lawless, his least favorite former bully.

"Okay, Penster, now you're going to have to deal with me!"

Where Elliot Has Other Things on His Mind

Not so long ago, if Tubs Lawless had crashed through the bushes and told Elliot, "Now you're going to have to deal with me," what that really would have meant is, "Now you're going to have to deal with a twisted neck." These days what he meant probably wasn't a whole lot better. It meant Elliot would have to deal with Tubs through an entire sleepover that night.

"My stuff's already at your house," Tubs said. "My parents dropped it off before they went out of town. I already ate the rest of your mom's lasagna, because I'm always hungry after school. Wendy said she'd cook you something to eat if you ever decide to come home from school."

"More like she'll burn me something to eat," Elliot said grimly. Maybe he could have real food next year.

"Anyway, I told her that I'd find you and drag you back home."

"I know the way to my own house. I was just talking to someone."

"I saw that. You were talking to a bird." Tubs gave Elliot what was probably meant to be a playful jab in the arm. Elliot wondered if it would leave a bruise. "Who are you, Snow White or something?"

Elliot nodded and slung his backpack over his shoulder. "Yeah, something like that."

Tubs pretty much stopped talking at that point, which was fine by Elliot, who would have preferred to be alone. He wanted to think about everything Harold had said, and what it might mean for him.

The only thing Elliot knew about Pixies was that during the Goblin war, Fudd Fartwick had borrowed some of their magic to make Elliot's bedroom disappear. Fudd had been an advisor to the queen of the Brownies before Elliot took her place. Then Fudd had worked with the Goblins to try to get Elliot killed so that Fudd could become king.

When Elliot won the Goblin war, Fudd had confessed to his crimes and promised to change. No one had worked harder in getting Elliot's blown-up house rebuilt than Fudd Fartwick. He even made it so that the stairway didn't squeak anymore.

If Tubs weren't walking beside him now, Elliot would have called for Fudd to come talk to him and tell him everything he knew about the Pixies and their princess, Fidget Spitfly.

But Tubs had started talking again. Elliot wasn't paying much attention, but it sounded like a story about Tubs last Halloween.

"My mom says I'm too old for trick-or-treating," Tubs was saying, "but I think, who's too old for candy? Not me."

Elliot smiled. Finally he and Tubs had something in common.

Tubs continued, "Did I ever tell you about a few years ago when I saw these kids in Goblin costumes? They looked so cool, I could've sworn they were real."

Elliot shoved his hands into his pockets. "Do you think Goblins exist, then?"

Tubs snorted. "They weren't real Goblins, dork. They were eating all these pickles, and a real Goblin wouldn't eat pickles."

"Right," Elliot muttered, thinking about how the Goblins had started a whole war with the Brownies over a bag of pickles.

Elliot's mind wandered back to his own troubles. If Princess Fidget was so dangerous, why hadn't Mr. Willimaker warned Elliot about her? Mr. Willimaker had told Elliot everything he needed to know about the Goblins during the war. Why hadn't anyone told him about Pixies? Maybe Harold was making Princess Fidget sound worse than she really was. Just because he got himself tricked into becoming a marshmallow didn't mean Elliot was in any danger of being tricked. After all, Elliot couldn't turn himself into a marshmallow, even if he wanted to. Which he didn't, by the way.

He also wondered about the Shadow Men. When Harold had turned into one, everything in Elliot's body froze with fear. And that wasn't even a real Shadow Man. It was just a Shapeshifter pretending to be one. He was glad Kovol remained asleep, because he'd rather face a hundred Goblins trying to scare him to death before he faced a real Shadow Man.

"Hey, Tubs," Elliot said. "Are you afraid of anything?"

Tubs shrugged. "You'd have to be stupid not to be afraid of something."

"But you are—" Elliot stopped. It didn't seem like a good idea to point out the obvious, which was that several important pieces of Tubs's brain seemed to be missing, such as the thinking piece.

"So what are you afraid of?" Elliot asked instead.

"Same thing everyone's afraid of," Tubs said.

"Snakes?"

"No, you wimp. Afraid that the ground beneath us will suddenly turn to quicksand and all of Sprite's Hollow will be swallowed up under the world."

"Why are you talking about the Underworld?" Elliot said quickly. "There's no Underworld."

"Sure there is," Tubs said.

Elliot stopped walking. "How do you know?"

"The clouds are over the world. We're on the world. The dirt is under the world."

Elliot breathed a sigh of relief and kept walking. "Oh, yeah, sure." When he first became king, Mr. Willimaker had told Elliot that if he ever shared the secret of the Underworld with anyone, the Brownies would never be able to return to him again.

When they got home, Wendy met Elliot at the front door. "Why didn't you save me any dinner?" he scowled at her.

Wendy's eyes widened, then she said, "Mom told you to hurry home. But I can make you something else if you want."

"Nah. I can ruin my own food later on."

Wendy frowned, and Elliot knew he had hurt her feelings. But she shrugged it off and said, "You need to go to the backyard. You have a visitor."

"Who?" Elliot asked.

"Oh, just a *special* visitor who wants to see you. Better hurry."

Elliot handed her his backpack, then walked around his house into the backyard. Beyond the grass was the end of Sprite's Hollow and the beginning of a thickly wooded area that went on for miles. Since nobody had ever bothered to think of a name for it, everyone just called it "the woods." When Elliot saw who his visitor was, his eyes flicked to the woods. The idea of hiding there for a couple of years until it was safe to come out again crossed his mind.

Cami was sitting on the ground weaving blades of grass together. She was working on a chain that was now almost as long as her arm.

"Hey," he said, "stop using up all my family's grass."

"Sorry," she said, throwing the grass chain down. "I didn't realize you were down to your last gazillion blades."

"Never mind," he said. "What's going on? I thought you weren't coming here until tomorrow morning."

"Yeah, but when I got home my mom said I have a soccer game in the morning. Are you just getting home from school now? You're slow."

Elliot let Cami's comment pass and followed her to a big white bucket with a black lid on it. "I've added the ingredients already," she said. "I won't tell you everything that's in there, because you really don't want to know. The recipe says it has to sit in the sun for five days, then it's ready."

"Can I look in it?"

"Sure. Just don't smell it too deeply, because it'll probably kill brain cells."

Elliot opened the lid and immediately slammed it closed. "It smells like something died in there."

Cami nodded. "Like I said, you don't want to know about the ingredients."

Elliot cracked the lid open again. The liquid inside was clear and thick like syrup. Every now and then a thick bubble rose to the top and popped, even though it wasn't cooking. Elliot shut the lid. "So what do I have to do?"

"Nothing but let it sit. Stir it if you want." Cami began to walk away but then turned back to him. "Oh, and one more thing, if it starts making noises, then you'd better get everyone out of the house, because that means it's going to blow up."

"What kind of noises?" Elliot asked.

"I dunno," Cami said. "It's a liquid, so it probably shouldn't make any noises at all. Anyway, I'll come back in a day or two and check on it."

As she began to leave, Kyle and Cole, Elliot's six-year-old twin brothers, ran to Cami and Elliot. "Secret lovers, hiding place. Secret lovers, kissy face," they teased.

Elliot picked up a stick and hurled it toward his brothers. "Stop bothering me all the time!" he yelled, although this was in fact the first time they'd bothered him all day.

Cami shrugged. "I have to go anyway."

"You really should go out through the gate on the other side of the house," one of the twins said. It was probably Cole, Elliot thought. He had trouble telling the twins apart.

"But there's no fence in your yard," Cami said. "Why do you have a gate if there's no fence?"

"It's rude to cross the grass where there would be a fence if we had a fence. Use the gate." Kyle winked at Cole as he finished, but Elliot didn't think Cami noticed.

"All right," Cami said and followed the twins to the gate. She waved at Elliot in such a nice way that he couldn't help but wonder what devious tricks she had up her sleeve. Then he noticed she wore a short-sleeved shirt, so she probably didn't have room for any tricks up there. And if she did, they probably weren't very good tricks.

Elliot was so busy wondering about Cami's tricks, he didn't notice how watchful Kyle and Cole were being until it was too late. Kyle and Cole only watched what entertained them, and something about Cami leaving through the gate definitely had their attention.

She stepped on a pile of grass that instantly sunk beneath her feet, leaving Cami knee deep in mud.

Only a few weeks ago, Kyle and Cole had been fascinated with water. It only made sense that by now they had moved on to mud.

Cami's face turned red, the color a face gets when a person is really mad. She tried to pull her legs out but only got more mud on herself. "I'm stuck," she said to the twins. "Help me." They only laughed, which of course made her face even redder.

Elliot didn't wait around to see what happened next. He yelled, "Okay, well, I'll keep an eye on the science project for you," and ran away.

Chapter 5

Where Tubs Is a Deep Sleeper

Those readers who lived near Lake Baikal in Russia on June 30, 1908, will remember the meteor explosion that occurred a few miles up in the sky. Some 80 million trees were knocked over from the force of the explosion, and glass windows shattered as far as a hundred miles away. If there is anyone reading this story who did *not* happen to be living near Lake Baikal over a hundred years ago, then you should know it is considered to be the loudest single event ever to happen on this earth. It was a hundred times louder than a one-ton bomb and was more than three times the sound required to cause hearing loss.

Lying in his room that night, with his ears sandwiched between two pillows, Elliot was sure he had discovered the second loudest sound in history.

Tubs was snoring.

Tubs snorted in air, and Elliot thought this must be what it's like inside a tornado.

Then Tubs exhaled, and Elliot imagined a million tiny Tubs germs being sent as far away as the jungles of Africa, all riding on a single breath.

Mother had insisted that Elliot let Tubs use his bed for the night. "He doesn't have things as good as you," she told Elliot. "Be nice and let him have the bed."

Tubs could literally have his bed now, Elliot thought. He didn't think he ever wanted it back again.

When Tubs took Elliot's bed, Elliot took his older brother Reed's bed and made Reed sleep on the floor. It had seemed fair at the time, although now Elliot wasn't so sure. Reed didn't stay on the floor for long. He had finally left about an hour ago, saying he was going in to work at the Quack Shack, his fast-food duck burgers job, either on the really late night shift or on the really early morning shift, whichever was closer. Elliot rolled over in Reed's bed and tried to plug his ears with Reed's pillow.

Tubs drew in another breath. It sounded like a train running through Elliot's room.

Elliot threw off his covers and shoved his feet into a pair of slippers beside his bed. They were Reed's, but he'd only borrow them for a minute. Elliot trudged downstairs and into the kitchen to get a drink of water. Maybe he could take some of that water upstairs and throw it on Tubs. That'd get him to stop snoring.

Elliot was halfway through his glass of water when he heard heavy footsteps clomping down the stairs. Tubs must've woken up for a drink too.

"Snoring must make you thirsty," Elliot said, but as Tubs entered the kitchen he didn't answer. He didn't even really seem to be awake.

"Tubs?" Elliot asked.

"Pretty mist," Tubs mumbled, reaching out his hand.

Elliot squinted. The kitchen was dark enough that he hadn't noticed it, but in a beam of moonlight through the window, he did see what appeared to be a silver mist. His first thought was of the Shadow Men, but theirs was a dense, black smoke. This was lighter, and it was pretty in a spooky sort of way.

But what was it?

Elliot flipped on the kitchen light, and the mist sparkled to life, as though it were made of thousands of mirrors. Its shape folded and curved like a fast-moving cloud.

Elliot ran his hand through the mist, then pulled it away when it stung him. "Okay, sorry," he muttered. The mist clearly had touch issues.

It moved toward the back door with Tubs following obediently behind. Elliot grabbed his arm, but he might as well have tried to slow down an elephant for all the good it did him. Tubs put a hand on Elliot's face and shoved him to the ground without breaking his stride.

"Tubs!" Elliot called. "What are you doing?"

"Pretty mist," Tubs said again.

Elliot thought Tubs was sleepwalking, but he couldn't be sure. Tubs said a lot of strange things while he was fully awake too.

Elliot leapt to his feet and tried to block Tubs from opening the door, but Tubs pushed past Elliot as if he were made of feathers. The mist expanded once it reached open air and continued to lure Tubs away.

"Wake up, Tubs!" Elliot cried. He considered running upstairs to get his dad's help, but Tubs would be gone before Elliot could get back. He grabbed a rock and threw it at Tubs's back. It hit with a klunk but bounced off without Tubs reacting.

Elliot was a little relieved about that. If Tubs had reacted, Elliot would have a bloody nose already.

He ran up to Tubs and began punching his arm, yelling at him to stop, and kicking at his legs. In any other situation, Elliot might have considered this a golden opportunity. But the mist was beginning to worry him. It was clearly something magical, but why did it want Tubs?

Elliot decided to appeal directly to the mist. "Hey!" he yelled. He swatted his hand through the mist, even though it felt like he was being bitten each time. "Where are you taking him?"

The mist didn't answer, which wasn't surprising considering that it had no mouth. It led Tubs across Elliot's backyard grass, all the while folding and dancing in the air. It was taking him into the woods behind Elliot's house. Elliot barely liked going there during the day. And as dark as it was out here in Elliot's yard, it was even darker in the woods.

"Wake up, Tubs!" Elliot called again. "Come back to my house. We have candy in there! Remember, you like candy!"

Tubs hesitated, just for a moment, and then continued to follow the mist.

Elliot ran back to his house and grabbed the hose that had been Kyle and Cole's favorite toy for the last several months. He turned it on full blast and shot a stream of water at Tubs, who kept walking as if unaware. So Elliot shot the water toward the mist. It created some sort of barrier that turned the water back on Elliot and soaked him with what felt like an entire lake of water splashing down on his head.

Elliot turned the hose off and sloshed back to Tubs, now at the edge of the woods. Obviously there was nothing he could do to wake Tubs up, but he could speak again to the mist.

"Whatever you are, you don't want him," Elliot yelled. "Trust me, you really don't! Just take me instead. I'll go with you, but leave him out of this!"

"Like, you're totally in the way, human," a girl's voice said.

It didn't come from the mist. Elliot swung around and saw a bright light a little deeper into the woods, like a small star had landed there.

"Who are you?" Elliot walked toward the light. Whoever had spoken was hidden behind a row of fallen trees. He climbed over the trees, now with Tubs only a few steps behind him. In front of him was a...a...a—he didn't know exactly what.

She was a foot high and didn't look any older than he was, but she sounded like one of those teenagers who thought she was cooler than everyone else. She had round wings; long, thin ears; and a bunch of curly, yellow hair. Her dress was bright red, purple, and yellow, and looked like something a little girl would dance around in, just to watch the skirt twirl. Around her neck were several loops of the grass chain that Cami had woven in his backyard earlier that day.

"Are you a Fairy?" he asked.

The girl shot a furious look at him and aimed her wand in his direction. Instantly a tree grabbed Elliot's right leg and yanked him upside down high into the air.

"I so totally don't need to be insulted right now," she said. "If I didn't have more important things to do, I'd just hurl you into space or something."

Okay, she wasn't a Fairy. But how was he supposed to know?

Elliot watched the mist approach her. It swirled in a wide circle and then settled at her feet. Slowly the particles of mist revealed themselves to be other similar creatures, each one bowing to her first. They all wore brightly colored dresses too, like a rainbow had exploded all over them.

Tubs stood in front of them. His eyes were open, but he didn't appear to be seeing anything. "No more pretty mist?" he mumbled.

The not-a-Fairy who had spoken before said to the others with her, "Wow, humans are so lame-brained. Grissel should've told me."

Grissel? Was this the Pixie princess, Fidget Spitfly? He wondered if she liked to spit on flies.

And she talked funny. He knew it wasn't Flibberish, the language of the Underworld, but he didn't know any humans who talked like her either. Not even his sister Wendy's giggly friends.

Fidget stood and fluttered into the air so that she was directly in front of Tubs. "So, dude, it would be totally awesome if you released Grissel from the Brownie jail," she said, tossing her pile of curly blond hair behind her shoulders.

"Sure," Tubs mumbled, clearly still asleep. "He's released."

Above them, Elliot kept silent. Tubs had been sleeping in Elliot's bed, so they must have thought Tubs was king of the Brownies. Elliot hoped the Pixies would think Grissel had been released and would leave long enough for him to get Tubs safely back to the house.

But it didn't happen that way. A Pixie poofed beside Fidget a moment later and whispered something in her ear. Fidget angrily sliced her wand through the air. Responding to her magic, hundreds of fall leaves lifted into the air and began swirling like a tornado around Tubs. The wind it created rushed up into Elliot's face.

"Not awesome!" she said with a shrill, high-pitched voice. "You totally tried to trick me!"

"Totally uncool," Tubs agreed.

Her voice got even higher and angrier. "You want to keep Grissel in jail? Then I'll keep *you* in jail!"

The tornado tightened around Tubs until in a flash of light he was gone.

"No!" Elliot cried. "Bring him back!"

Fidget seemed to have forgotten about Elliot until then. She fluttered up beside him, then said, "Human, you totally have to look at me so I can do this little forgetting spell on you. What you saw was just between the Pixies and Brownies. Way not any of your business."

"I'm afraid it is," Elliot said.

Her eyes narrowed. "Like, why?"

"Bring him back, and I'll tell you."

With a wave of her wand, the tree dangled Elliot higher. It had loosened its grip, and Elliot felt sure if he wiggled too much he'd go crashing to the ground. Even if his head was still attached after he fell, he would probably get one monster headache.

"That human has no power to release Grissel," Elliot said. "Only the Brownie king can do that."

Fidget's eyes darted to where Tubs had stood, then back at Elliot. "What's your name?" she asked.

"I'm Elliot Penster, king of the Brownies. I'm the one you want."

"Oh, fruit rot!" Fidget scowled. "You're the king and not him? Okay, so you heard the whole speech before. Are you going to release Grissel or not?"

"Not," Elliot said.

"What-ever." Fidget flicked her wand and the tree released Elliot. Wind blew up at him as the dark ground rushed to greet his fall. The last thing he remembered was the ground about two inches from his face.

Chapter 6

Where *Surfer Teen* Is the Awesomest

Some kids wake up to the sun shining through their bedroom windows. Others wake to an alarm clock on their bedside table. For some kids, their mother sings some annoying good-morning song while bacon sizzles on a pan in the kitchen.

Elliot Penster woke up to Tubs punching his arm.

"What?" he scowled, swatting Tubs away. "Stop that, I'm awake!"

"Where are we?" Tubs asked. "How'd we get here?"

Elliot slowly sat up and absorbed their surroundings. They were deep underground, in the Underworld obviously, and in a small cave with thick tree roots serving as the bars of their jail cell. This must be a Pixie jail.

"When you said I couldn't bully you anymore, I told myself fine, there's plenty of other kids to beat on," Tubs said. "And I haven't touched you for weeks, even when you did something so stupid that I should have beat you up at least a little. But I know that our being here is somehow your fault, Penster, and I'm going to get you for it."

"Will you be quiet?" Elliot hissed. "First we've got to get out of here, then you can beat me up."

"Yeah, but if you save us, then I'll feel bad about beating you up," Tubs said. "I'd rather do it now."

Elliot scratched his foot across the ground toward Tubs, hoping to kick dirt in his face, but he was still wearing Reed's slippers, which were soaking wet, so he only ended up smearing mud across his leg.

"I'm hungry," Tubs said. "And really, really confused."

Elliot crept to the bars, hoping to see more of where they were. The cave that trapped them seemed to be at the top of a tall hill. Far below them was what appeared to be a thick patch of woods. Bass drums beat a soft rhythm somewhere inside them, and colored sparks of light constantly jetted into the air in various places. Those woods were probably the Pixies' home.

He wondered how far away the Brownies' home of Burrowsville was. Did they know he was here? If so, was there anything they could do to get him out?

"Mr. Willimaker," Elliot hissed. "Mr. Willimaker!" There was no other Brownie who Elliot trusted more. If anyone could help, it was Mr. Willimaker.

"What are you doing?" Tubs asked.

Elliot turned back to Tubs, who looked so relaxed leaning against the dirt wall that he might as easily have been sunbathing. "I'm working on getting us out of here," Elliot said.

"Okay, you do that, and I'll work on my thing," Tubs said.

"What's your thing?" Elliot asked.

"Taking a nap. I didn't sleep so well last night."

"That's because you were wandering all over my yard and got us here in the first place!" Elliot said.

"Yeah? Well, you should've tried to stop me," Tubs said.

Elliot scowled and turned back to the bars. "Mr. Willimaker?" he called more loudly.

He jumped away from the bars as a figure poofed in front of him. Not Mr. Willimaker, but Fidget Spitfly. Her hair was in a high ponytail on the side of her head. She had so much hair, he wondered why it didn't make her tip over sideways. She wore a bright purple dress today. Really bright and really purple. Elliot felt a headache coming on just looking at her.

"Do you really think anyone can hear you calling while you're my prisoner?" she asked. "How clueless would I have to be if I made it that easy? As if!"

Elliot lifted his eyebrows. "Where did you learn my language? You talk... different."

"Only on the best human television show ever, *Surfer Teen*. It's so totally the awesomest show of the whole universe!"

Dear Reader, *Surfer Teen* so totally is not the awesomest show in the universe. In the first place, *awesomest* is not even a word, but the actors in *Surfer Teen* don't seem to know that, since they use the word in almost every sentence. And in the second place, the show was only on for one season, because it so totally was the stupidest show in the history of television, which is quite an accomplishment. But it is Fidget Spitfly's favorite show, and she has watched every episode at least 458 times. She has watched the episode where the awesomest boy first kisses the hottest-to-the-max girl at least 873 times. Totally.

Elliot rolled his eyes. His sister, Wendy, used to watch *Surfer Teen*. Now he felt like he was talking to one of the characters on the show. "Listen," he said to Fidget, "I'm the one you want. This other human here with me can't do anything for you. Send him home, and then you and I can talk."

"Just wait one minute," Tubs said, getting to his feet. "Let me understand something first. Am I having the weirdest dream ever or not?" Then he punched himself in the eye. "Ow! I hate it when I do that."

"Why did you?" Elliot asked.

Tubs glared at him. "It proved that I'm awake, didn't it?"

"You are awake," Elliot said. "We're being held by the Pixies in the Underworld."

"Oh," Tubs said, as if that sort of thing happened all the time.

Fidget eyed Tubs, who was now busy picking his nose. "I'm just hungry," Tubs muttered. "My parents are out of town anyway, so if you get me something to eat, I don't care if you send me back or not."

Fidget smiled and said to Tubs, "Like, get your friend to release Grissel, and I'll give you anything to eat that you want."

"Anything?" Tubs asked. At the moment, all he had to eat was whatever he'd pulled from his nose, so he seemed to like this idea. "Anything, like a big bowl of hot fudge topping for breakfast?"

"Totally," Fidget whispered.

Tubs grabbed Elliot by the neck and shoved his face into the tree root bars. "Tell her you'll do what she wants, jerk."

Elliot kicked his foot out behind him and sank it into Tubs's chubby stomach. Tubs released him with a gasp, and Elliot fell to the ground. He rubbed his neck, then said to Fidget, "Before I can do anything, I have to talk to Mr. Willimaker. If I can't call him, then will you send someone to let him know I'm here?"

"You can't call him," Fidget said, "but I can."

She flicked her wand, and immediately Mr. Willimaker appeared beside her. Unfortunately, he seemed to be just getting out of his bath. He had a towel around his waist, and his gray hair was still wet and sticking up in all directions. Most Brownies liked the just-stepped-out-of-a-tornado look, but Mr. Willimaker always tried to keep his hair neatly combed.

"Another Pixie?" Tubs asked.

"Brownie," Elliot said.

"He looks like a gopher with hands," Tubs whispered. Luckily, Mr. Willimaker was so confused, Elliot didn't think he heard.

"What—" Mr. Willimaker gasped, then he saw Elliot. "Oh, Your Highness." He tightened the towel around himself and then turned to Fidget. "Princess Fidget, I demand an explanation."

"Like, chill out," she said. "You release Grissel, and I'll let you have your king back."

"Elliot's a king? But he's such a dork!" Tubs started laughing so hard that tears rolled down his face.

"He happens to be a very good king," Mr. Willimaker said. Then to Fidget, he added, "You know I can't release him without King Elliot's orders."

"Duh! So make him give the order."

"I won't," Elliot said.

"Is there someplace he and I can talk?" Mr. Willimaker asked Fidget. "Somewhere private?"

Fidget waved her wand again. In an instant, Elliot and Mr. Willimaker found themselves perched at the top of a lofty tree. They were so high up that

Elliot couldn't see the ground. He only assumed it was somewhere far down below him. He grabbed the branch beneath him and held on tightly. Mr. Willimaker seemed more concerned about keeping his towel wrapped around himself than with falling.

"I'm so sorry, Your Highness," Mr. Willimaker began. "I knew she was talking to Grissel in the prison, but I didn't know they were planning something like this."

"Grissel never said anything?"

"A few days ago Grissel told his guards that the Pixies were forming a plot for his escape. I just didn't know it would be something like *this*."

Elliot rolled his eyes. "And you didn't think you should've told me about that?"

"Yes, obviously I should have told you. Forgive me."

"It's too late to worry about that now. Can you help me escape?"

"Pixie magic is more powerful than mine. I can't stop her from keeping you here." He twisted his hands together. "What are we going to do?"

Elliot grabbed Mr. Willimaker's hands and untwisted them, then said, "I'll figure a way out of this mess, but I'm not going to release Grissel."

"I think you have to, Your Highness."

"Why?"

Mr. Willimaker looked up at Elliot with a frown. "If you don't, she'll kill you."

Chapter
7

Where Harold Offers
the Worst Kind of Help

Mr. Willimaker finally left Elliot with the agreement that he would speak
to Grissel to find out what he knew about the Pixies' plot. As soon as Mr.
Willimaker poofed away, Elliot was poofed back into the jail. Princess
Fidget wasn't there anymore. In her place was another Pixie girl, also
with blond hair but with bright blue eyes.

"Who are you?" Elliot asked.

"Claire. Princess Fidget's advisor. She asked me to tell you that she is
'so totally tired of waiting around' that I could 'gag her with a spoon.'"

Elliot smiled. "So did you?"

"What?"

"Gag her with a spoon?"

Claire shook her head. "There's a pretty strict no-gag-
ging-the-princess-with-a-spoon rule here. Even when she
deserves it."

Elliot glanced behind him where Tubs was sleeping
peacefully, his thumb in his mouth.

"What'd you do to him?" Elliot asked.

"Nothing," Claire said. "He just got tired of waiting too. He said his brain
hurt from trying to figure everything out." Claire used a tiny hand to
push some hair off her forehead, revealing a thin streak of white hair
underneath the rest.

"You don't talk like the princess," Elliot said, eyeing the Pixie suspiciously.

"I bet you think all Pixies talk the same," Claire said. "Wanna bet they don't?"

Elliot stared carefully at Claire. "Harold, is that you?"

Harold the Pixie looked around to be sure nobody else was there and then flew in closer to Elliot. "I don't have long, but I wanted to come see you. Because if you really think about it, this could be a little bit my fault."

"A little bit?"

"Okay, a lot. I feel guilty. But I'll try to help you now."

Elliot pushed at the tree root bars of the jail. "Can you get me out of here?"

"I can imitate the Pixie look, but not their magic. Elliot, you have to release Grissel."

"Why does Fidget want Grissel released anyway? Are they friends?"

"As Fidget would say, 'That's so grody.' No, you've heard of the Totally Tubular Turf War, right?"

Elliot shook his head.

Harold folded his short Pixie arms. "I don't mean to lecture, because I'll only sound like my mother, but if you're going to be king of the Brownies, you should at least take ten minutes to learn about the Underworld."

"Sorry," Elliot said. "I've been busy with this science fair project."

Claire—or Harold—continued. "Ever since creatures entered the Underworld, Fairies and Pixies have battled over the land known as the Glimmering Forest. Woodland is hard to find down here, and this is the best in all the Underworld. Streams and rivers flow from beautiful waterfalls. Flowers of every color and variety grow wild. And the trees live forever in the Glimmering Forest."

"Sounds nice," Elliot said.

"Nice? That's like saying turnip juice is only pretty good. The Fairies want Glimmering Forest, and the Pixies want it too, but neither of them will share the land. Grissel promised Fidget that if she gets him free from Brownie prison, he'll blow up all the Fairy settlements that border the Glimmering Forest. Then the Pixies think they can take the rest of the forest for themselves."

"I can't help Fidget get a bunch of Fairies hurt. Do her parents know about this?"

"The king and queen of the Pixies are on vacation. They told Fidget if she solved the Fairy problem before they came back, they'd let her take surfing lessons."

"Mr. Willimaker says that if I don't release Grissel, the Pixies will kill me," Elliot said.

"Probably." Harold fluttered down on a rock and rested his head on his hands. "I love flying, but it's tiring."

"Can we get back to fixing my problem?" Elliot asked.

"Huh? Oh, I can't fix your problem. I'm a Shapeshifter, not a miracle maker. But I can do one thing for you. It'll be morning soon at your house. Until you get this all worked out, I'll go to the surface and pretend to be you."

"No thanks," Elliot said.

"It'll be fine," Harold said. "I've imitated humans plenty of times before. No one will even notice a difference."

"Don't," Elliot said.

"You'd rather your mom wakes up and finds you missing?"

"My family might not care. I wasn't very nice to them before I left."

Harold grabbed a root to get closer to Elliot in his jail. "You want the whole town of Sprite's Hollow out looking for you, your picture in the paper? All that homework you'd miss?"

Elliot sighed. "Okay, fine. But you can't change things or do anything different from what I would do. Just stay in my room as much as you can, and don't talk to anyone unless you have to."

"No problem," Harold said.

Elliot gestured at Tubs, who was still sleeping. "What about him?"

Harold shrugged. "I already put his clothes over a bucket and mop in the corner of your kitchen. So far nobody's noticed that it's not him. Just do what the Pixies want, and you'll both be home soon."

With that, Harold snapped his fingers and poofed away. Tubs was taking up the entire space on the ground of their cell, so there was no room to sit. Elliot leaned against the wall at the edge of the jail and closed his eyes to think. He didn't know what worried him most—that the Pixies were going to kill him, or that Harold the Shapeshifter was going to take his place at home.

Chapter
8

Where Elliot Wants a Time-Out

Dear Reader, in this chapter, you're going to hear about Elliot's next visitor to his jail. You may wonder if his next visitor is Diffle McSnug, who has recently returned from an exciting trip to the Far East, where his hot air balloon became tangled in a flock of migrating geese. Of course, as you should well know, there is no character in this book named Diffle McSnug. Don't you think Elliot would be confused if a character who doesn't exist in this book suddenly showed up at his Pixie prison with a story about hot air balloons and migrating geese? It's too bad Diffle's not a character, though. You would bite off your fingernails with fright hearing how Diffle fell to the earth after the angry geese chewed through the ropes of his basket. And you'd be shocked to know the amazing way he survived. You wouldn't believe it, even if you heard the story.

Which of course, you won't, because this is Elliot's story. Diffle needs to get his own book.

Elliot only had to wait about twenty minutes before his next visitor (not Diffle McSnug) poofed in to see him.

Mr. Willimaker's daughter, Patches, ran forward, trying to hug Elliot through the thick tree root bars of his prison. This really meant that she hugged the bars more than she hugged Elliot, but, Dear Reader, you should not take this to mean that Patches loved the prison more than she loved Elliot. She just couldn't reach him, that's all.

Elliot had saved Patches from the Goblins twice. In her opinion, that made

Elliot at least as cool as her great-great grandfather Willimaker, who had fought in the Demon wars a thousand years ago.

"Here," she said, pushing a wrapped-up bundle to Elliot.

"What's this?" he asked.

"Food. Carrots and beets and some turnip juice. And a couple of pickles."

Elliot already knew about the pickles. Pickle juice was leaking from the bundle onto his brother Reed's slippers, which were pretty much ruined by now.

"Thanks," Elliot said, although ever since he'd learned the Pixies planned to kill him, he hadn't felt very hungry, not even for pickles. He set the bundle on the ground for when Tubs woke up. Tubs would be hungry no matter who wanted to kill him. Elliot had once seen Tubs so hungry at the Quack Shack that he ate his entire duck burger without taking the paper wrapping off it first. And rumor had it that Tubs had once buttered his lunch tray at school. He'd broken off a tooth trying to take a bite from it.

"Nice clothes," Patches said with a giggle.

Elliot glanced down at his checkered pajamas. "I didn't have time to change into clothes before we were kidnapped."

"Pixie led."

"Huh?"

"You were Pixie led, not kidnapped exactly. Did you see a mist last night?"

"Yeah."

"That was the Pixies leading you to their snare."

Elliot folded his arms. "Tubs was Pixie led. I was Tubs led."

Patches frowned. "Humans know how to escape being Pixie led, right?"

Obviously, Elliot didn't know. "How?" he asked.

"Just turn your clothes inside out. It confuses them."

"I wasn't going to turn my clothes inside out in front of a bunch of Pixie girls," Elliot said.

"Don't worry. Princess Fidget would've gotten you here one way or another," Patches said, as if that should have made him feel better. "She always gets what she wants. What we must do now is figure out how to fix this."

"Do you think I should release Grissel?" Elliot asked.

"No!" Patches said. "Before long, he'd get the Goblins to start eating us again."

Which, Elliot agreed, would be bad. No matter what, releasing Grissel was not an option. "Any advice?" he asked.

Patches shrugged. "I don't know about them, but in school my teacher told us that hundreds of years ago, if two Pixies couldn't settle an argument, they took a 'time-out.' The winner won the argument, and it was done."

"Time-out," Elliot mumbled. "I know about those. So I guess to win, I just have to stay in time-out the longest?"

At just that moment, Mr. Willimaker appeared. His bushy gray eyebrows were pressed close together, telling Elliot he had not made any progress with Grissel. Princess Fidget poofed in immediately after. On either side of her were two larger Pixies with sour looks on their faces.

"Like, get rid of the Brownie king first," Fidget said to the Pixies with her. "Mind wipe the other boy if you can, and totally return him to the surface. If you can't, then get rid of him too."

The Pixies pulled out their wands and pointed them at Elliot, who backed up and stumbled over Tubs on the ground. He said, "Wait! Princess Fidget, I demand a time-out."

Her eyes narrowed. "A time-out?"

"Yeah. Me and Grissel together. If I win, you set me free. If he wins, I'll set him free."

"No, Your Highness," Mr. Willimaker cried, but it was too late.

Stretching her hand to study her nails, Fidget said, "Under the terms of a time-out, if you lose, Grissel goes free. And if he decides to leave you alive, which he probably won't, then you must remain here as my servant for, like, forever."

Elliot glared at Patches. She might have mentioned that. Still, it was better than being killed in here. "Okay," Elliot said. "I want a time-out."

Fidget clasped her tiny hands together. "What-ever. I'll prepare the battle zone. If you somehow survive the time-out with Grissel, which you probably won't, I'll totally have you for a servant, human."

"It looks like the rules are in Grissel's favor," Elliot said.

"Nobody ever said time-outs were fair," Fidget said, and then with a mischievous shrug added, "especially when I get to make the rules!"

When she poofed away, Elliot rushed to the bars. "Mr. Willimaker, what happens in a time-out?"

"It's a fight. When the time runs out, someone's usually dead. Isn't that what time-out means in your language?"

"No," Elliot said, slumping to the ground. "No, it isn't."

Chapter
9

Where Elliot Gets a Song
Stuck in His Head

Elliot's twin brothers had spent most of their first six years of life either in time-out or doing something that deserved a time-out. Elliot had done his share of time-outs too. Something told him, however, that this time-out would be very different from sitting alone on a stool in the corner.

For one thing, no one had ever tried to kill him in time-out before, and Elliot's parents were very strict about not letting Elliot kill anyone, whether in time-out or not.

For another thing, time-outs were usually done alone, and Elliot was pretty sure every Pixie, Brownie, and Goblin in the Underworld had gathered around the Battle Zone to watch.

The Battle Zone was about as big as Elliot's schoolroom, but it was round and fenced in with thorny tree branches and had a dirt floor. Elliot had removed Reed's slippers for the fight. He'd never seen anyone win a battle to the death while wearing house slippers. He'd never seen anyone win a battle in red-checkered pajamas either, but he couldn't do anything about that.

Directly across from Elliot, Grissel paced in preparation for the fight. He hadn't changed much since Elliot had last seen him. A little rounder around the middle, maybe, due to his eating a lot of chocolate cake lately. But still the same shade of green skin, same bony face, same hatred of humans reflected in his eyes. He'd barely looked at Elliot since he was poofed here, but he was already drooling, hungry for revenge. The Goblins cheered loudly for him. The Brownies sat behind Elliot, cheering for him. The Pixies seemed to be cheering for a long battle, no matter who won. Then from somewhere nearby, Elliot heard, "You can take this one, Penster. Win it for the humans!"

Elliot turned. Even Tubs was cheering for him. Then Tubs yelled, "Besides, if you die, how will I get home?"

That was less helpful. Although just before Elliot was poofed to the Battle Zone, Tubs had given him some good advice: "If you can't beat him, just move around a lot until he gets tired of chasing you. I always hated it when you did that to me."

"Grissel doesn't need to chase me. Goblins scare you to death."

"But that only works if you're scared, right? Just think funny things and you'll be fine."

"Wow, Tubs," Elliot had said. "That's actually a good idea."

Tubs had stuck out his chest. "I'm smarter than all the kids in the whole first grade."

"But you're a seventh-grader."

"Duh." Tubs snorted. "I didn't say I was in their grade, I just said I'm smarter than them. And it *is* a good idea, so use it or else!"

Now Elliot waved at Tubs, who shook a fist back at him. Threatening to beat Elliot up if he didn't win was Tubs's style of cheering him on.

Fidget fluttered in from above them and landed in the center of the Battle Zone. For the time-out, she had chosen a bright yellow shirt with a hot pink skirt. She looked like she was dressed for a disco party. "Like, welcome to all Pixies, Goblins, and everyone else," she began, clearly forgetting that other than Tubs, "everyone else" was the Brownies. "We are so blown away by having a time-out today, which has totally not happened for over a hundred years."

A cheer rose from the Pixies. Not sure whether they should be celebrating this or not, the Goblins clapped a little, then lowered their hands when Grissel turned to glare at them. The Brownies remained silent.

Fidget continued, "So here are the rules. The time-out will last for ten minutes, because the awesomest stylist ever is coming to do my hair. If Grissel kills Elliot faster than that, it would be so radical, because then I'll have time to get my nails done too. If Elliot's still alive after the ten-minute time-out, he'll totally be my servant. Either way, Grissel goes free, and then he keeps his promise to me, and we'll, like, totally blow the Fairies to dust!" She forgot to mention what happened if Elliot survived. Maybe she didn't think there was any chance he would.

Both the Pixies and Goblins cheered loudly. The Brownies squirmed in their seats. Even they didn't expect Elliot to win.

"Happy thoughts, happy thoughts," Elliot mumbled. But his brain was in a fuzz. For some reason, all he could remember was the awful theme song to Fidget's favorite show, *Surfer Teen*.

> *Surfer Teen,*
> *Awesomest kid on the scene.*
> *Rockin' muscles lean and mean.*
> *You're Surfer Teen.*

"Like, when I say 'Time in,' then the battle begins," Fidget said.

"Happy thoughts," Elliot mumbled to the tune from *Surfer Teen*.

"Time in!" Fidget sliced her wand through the air, and sparks shot out from the end of it. The crowd cheered as she flew away and the battle began.

Grissel ran toward Elliot, but stopped in the center of the ring where Fidget had stood. With a low growl, he crouched on all fours. Elliot knew what was happening. He was preparing to scare Elliot to death.

> *Rockin' muscles lean and mean.*

Grissel's bony skin began to bubble in rhythm.

Oddly, he bubbled to the rhythm of the lyrics stuck in Elliot's head.

Elliot started singing them: *"You're Surfer Teen..."*

As he sang, Elliot pictured Grissel as a surfer teen. Grissel on all fours on a surfboard. But Goblins hate water, so he'd have to balance on the surfboard so that no water splashed on him.

Maybe just because he was so tired, that the pictures he imagined seemed really funny. Funnier than Grissel was scary, and Elliot was laughing hard before he even finished the lyrics.

Grissel growled at Elliot, arching his back even higher. It should have been scary, but for some reason it wasn't. Maybe Elliot was laughing too hard to be scared. Now he was picturing Grissel wearing a swimsuit with tropical flowers. And sunglasses—he'd have to wear sunglasses! Pink ones that matched his swimsuit. If a green-skinned Goblin gets a suntan, does he turn olive green? What color is a sunburn? Mud color?

Tears came to Elliot's eyes as he laughed. His stomach ached from laughter.

"Nobody laughs at me," Grissel said, rising up to his full height. He lunged at Elliot with bare teeth. Elliot used the only weapon he had available to him. Spit. He spit on Grissel while Grissel was still in midair. The spit landed in Grissel's eye, and he fell to the ground, screaming and writhing in pain.

"Oh, that's so totally time out," Fidget said, fluttering into the ring from above. She stared down at Grissel, who was still helpless on the ground. "This is, like, such a bummer."

Elliot jumped into the air in celebration. So Grissel had not killed him, and the time-out was over. "That's it?" he said. "Then I won."

"Wrong," Grissel said. "I scared you to death. You're just slow at dying."

Elliot folded his arms. "Am not. I'll bet I could die really fast if you were any good at scaring me."

"I've been scary longer than you've been alive," Grissel said. "Just admit you've lost and die already, then I'll go free."

"Like, that's totally enough." Fidget flicked her wand at the crowd. "All of you just go away."

And with that, the entire audience disappeared. Elliot wasn't sure where they'd all gone. Somewhere safe, he hoped.

Grissel smiled wickedly at Elliot. "Now it's just you and me, little king."

But Fidget flew between them. "You had your chance, Goblin. You're so yesterday, and I'm already on tomorrow. Back you go to the Brownie jail."

Grissel's protest was only half spoken when Fidget poofed him away with her wand.

Elliot held up his hands, the way bad guys do when the cops say to freeze. Fidget sighed. "Don't be so lame, human. If I wanted to kill you, I'd have just done it already."

"You're letting me go home?"

"Hello?" Fidget rapped Elliot's head with her wand, then she pointed it at the Glimmering Forest. "Does it look like we've beaten the Fairies? You're not going home yet."

"I know you've got a Fairy problem," Elliot said, "but I've got a problem too, one named Cami Wortson. If you think Goblins are scary, you should see this girl when she gets a bad grade."

"Can Cami Wortson turn you inside out with a wave of her wand?"

Elliot clutched his stomach. Maybe if she had a wand she could. She'd probably enjoy doing it too.

Fidget folded her arms. "Let's get this straight, human. Even if this Cami Wortson has snakes for hair and spikes for teeth, I'm still the scariest girl you know. And if you want to go home, then you'll have to solve my problem first."

"You think I can get the Fairies out of Glimmering Forest? I can't even get my sister out of the bathroom in the morning."

"I'll take care of the Fairies. All I need from you is one little hair."

"My hair?" Elliot would shave himself bald if that's all it took to go home. It'd be hard to explain the baldness to his family, but it would be worth it.

Fidget sighed in a way that reminded Elliot of how stupid his question was. "Eww, gag me! I so totally don't want human hair. To keep the Fairies out of Glimmering Forest, all I need is one hair from their worst enemy—the Demon Kovol."

Chapter 10

Where Elliot Gets a Neck Ache

Dear Reader, if you've recently traveled to Greenland, you probably noticed the musk ox grazing nearby. The musk ox has two layers of hair, so even when it loses the outside layer, it still has plenty of hair left. The hair can be two to three feet long and sometimes drags on the ground. So if Fidget had ordered Elliot to steal a hair from a musk ox, as long as Elliot was nice about it, the musk ox probably wouldn't have cared.

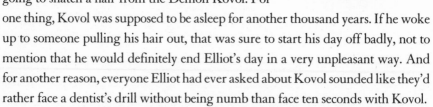

But that's not what Fidget ordered.

She wanted a hair from a very different creature.

Elliot had about a hundred reasons why he wasn't going to snatch a hair from the Demon Kovol. For one thing, Kovol was supposed to be asleep for another thousand years. If he woke up to someone pulling his hair out, that was sure to start his day off badly, not to mention that he would definitely end Elliot's day in a very unpleasant way. And for another reason, everyone Elliot had ever asked about Kovol sounded like they'd rather face a dentist's drill without being numb than face ten seconds with Kovol.

Agatha the Hag had told Elliot that Kovol was the last of the Underworld Demons. He didn't know why Kovol was the last, and he didn't know why Kovol was sleeping. But Agatha had seemed certain that asleep was the way everyone in the Underworld wanted Kovol to remain.

Elliot didn't have time to tell Fidget why he wasn't going to snatch a hair from Kovol. She apparently had bigger problems to deal with. Fidget stamped her foot and whined, "Oh, fruit rot. I'm late for my hair stylist. Now it'll be wash and go. Not awesome!"

Elliot tried to say something before she fluttered away, but she cut him off and said, "Oh, and that other human with you—Tubs—he's staying here until you bring me the hair. Better hurry before I get bored and put him in time-out with a Troll." With that, she poofed Elliot away. He decided that he didn't like being poofed places. It made his stomach feel upside down. For all he knew, maybe it was.

But the question for now was where Fidget had sent him. He was standing on some grass near a small town set on a hill, where it looked as if little homes had been made from caves in the hillside. A maze of dirt paths went from one house to another, so it would be nearly impossible to travel anywhere without stopping at a dozen homes along the way. Wherever he was, Elliot decided he liked this place. He wouldn't fit inside any of the homes, but it was a friendly looking town. All it needed was a good ice cream store and it would have been perfect.

"Elliot?" Patches came running up from behind him. "I mean, Your Highness. You're free?"

"Is this Burrowsville?" Despite the serious task that lay ahead of him, Elliot couldn't help but feel excited about seeing the land where he was king.

"This is Burrowsville. Your home away from home, I hope. You can come to our cave for dinner. My mother really wants to meet you. She just made a fresh batch of turnip juice this morning. Squished it with her own toes."

"Yum." Elliot smiled grimly. "Maybe another time. I need to—"

"Your Highness?" Fudd came running over a hill and bowed low before Elliot. Back when Fudd was a bad Brownie trying to get Elliot killed, it made sense that he should also be mean-looking. His long, crooked nose and thin slits for eyes seemed a little unusual for a good Brownie, who was most definitely not trying to kill Elliot. But nothing could be done about Fudd's face, so Elliot had gotten used to it. Fudd clasped his hands together and added, "How did—oh, Princess Fidget must have sent you here."

"I need to meet with you and Mr. Willimaker," Elliot said. "Privately."

Fudd nodded, and then said to Patches, "Take the king to Burrow Cave. He should fit comfortably in there."

Ten minutes later, Elliot disagreed with Fudd. He did *not* fit comfortably inside the cave. It was easily wide enough, but he had to tilt his head in order to sit up. He could lie down for the meeting, but that didn't seem very king-like. Mr. Willimaker and Fudd had offered to bring in some Brownies to dig the floor lower for him, but there was no time.

With his head tilted almost down to his shoulder, Elliot explained what Fidget wanted him to do.

"Get a hair from Kovol?" Mr. Willimaker exclaimed. "You can't."

"I have to," Elliot said. "She still has Tubs in the jail."

Mr. Willimaker shook his head. "No, I really meant that you can't. Humans aren't allowed in Demon Territory. We don't get many human visitors, of course, but it's still the rule. There's even Elfish guards and a big sign telling humans to stay out."

Fudd clamped a hand on Mr. Willimaker's shoulder and said, "A Brownie could do it." Mr. Willimaker frowned at Fudd. He didn't look convinced.

"How dangerous is Demon Territory if the Demon is asleep?" Elliot asked.

"How dangerous is a lion's den if the lion's asleep?" Mr. Willimaker responded. "And if the lion's really hungry because he hasn't eaten for a thousand years? And then you go up and ask him for just one little hair? You think he'll just smile and hand it over?"

"Then I'm not sending you there for a job I have to do," Elliot said. "If you'll come with me as far as the border of Demon Territory, I'll do the rest."

"Your Highness," Mr. Willimaker said, "it's not worth it, not for Tubs Lawless."

"Tubs is only here because of me," Elliot said, sitting up straight and banging his ear on the roof of the cave. He tilted his head a bit more and then said, "I have to do this."

"Then we'll leave first thing in the morning," Fudd said. "First, Your Highness, I believe you need a good sleep, and you look hungry. Your subjects, the Brownies, would like to honor you with a royal feast tonight."

The closest thing to a royal feast Elliot had ever had was when the power went out before Wendy had finished burning dinner and the food came out about right. And he was hungry now.

Fudd stood. "I'll take care of dinner plans." With that, he poofed away.

Mr. Willimaker stood as well. "And please don't be offended, Your Highness, but checkered pajamas aren't the best way to meet your subjects. May I suggest we have a tailor prepare some clothes for you?"

Elliot looked down at his pajamas. "Yes, please."

Mr. Willimaker bowed to Elliot, then said, "Sir, don't worry about Kovol's hair. With Fudd and me by your side, nothing can go wrong."

He poofed away, leaving Elliot alone in the cave. Somehow, Mr. Willimaker's words didn't make Elliot feel better. If he'd learned anything since becoming king of the Brownies, it was that something could always go wrong.

Chapter
11

Where Elliot Gets an Itch
and a Flashlight

"Your tailors haven't sewn for kids lately," Elliot said to Mr. Willimaker as he faced a mirror. It was the largest mirror in Burrowsville, but Elliot could still see only part of himself in it at a time. And he'd had to dress behind some bushes. He wasn't positive someone saw him, but he had definitely heard giggling nearby.

Mr. Willimaker agreed. "It seems human fashion has changed over the last century or two."

For pants, Elliot wore breeches that gathered at his calf. He had a pullover shirt with full sleeves that gathered at his wrists and a vest that buttoned up the front. "I look like a pirate," he said.

"Don't be silly," Mr. Willimaker said. "Pirates never wore vests like that. You look like a pioneer."

The only things Elliot didn't hate were his shoes. They fit him perfectly and were very comfortable. Elliot tugged at his shirt. Maybe if he didn't tuck it in, it wouldn't look so much like something his great-great-great-great-grandpa would've worn while picking up cow pies on the plains.

"I'm sorry, Your Highness," Mr. Willimaker said. "We'll find some patterns for modern-day boys so that next time you're kidnapped—"

"Next time?" Elliot asked. "Thanks for the clothes, but next time I'd like to come to the Underworld on my own."

Fudd entered the room. "King Elliot? Dinner is ready. We're eating outside, where you'll be most comfortable."

Elliot nodded. If he was half starved before, then he was all the way starved by now. He forgot all about his clothes and followed Fudd outside. He expected most of the Brownies to be at the royal feast, but he had no idea how many Brownies there were. When he had used the Brownies to help end the Goblin war, the stronger ones had come, but the rest had stayed back.

"Is this all of them?" Elliot whispered to Mr. Willimaker.

"We know you'd rather be home," Mr. Willimaker said, "but for us Brownies, the king has come and today is a holiday. Everyone wants to see you."

A cheer rose through the crowd when they saw Elliot enter. Long rows of tables lined a large grassy field. Hundreds of Brownies of every size and age stood near the tables. Babies sat on their fathers' shoulders. Younger Brownie children stood on chairs to get a better look at their king. The only thing the Brownies all had in common was their various shades of gray hair, sticking up in wild directions. Together, they looked like a field of unmowed gray grass. Elliot had never guessed there would be so many of them.

At the head of the crowd, a table had been specially built for Elliot. Fudd pulled at Elliot's bulky sleeve and said, "We tried to have a throne made for you, but there just wasn't time. We did find a giant toadstool that was about your size."

The royal toadstool was in front of Elliot's seat at the table. A red satin cloth lay over the top for him to sit on, and blue flower petals surrounded the base of it. "Looks comfortable," Elliot said, grinning. "This is a great throne."

He went to sit, but Mr. Willimaker touched his arm. "Aren't you going to say anything to the Brownies?"

"Huh? Oh, sure." Elliot faced the Brownies, who all fell to their knees when they saw he was about to speak. "You don't have to do that," he said. Slowly they rose again, and he continued, "Um, so thanks for letting me be your king. I'll try to do a good job."

The Brownies cheered again and a cry rose up of "Long live King Elliot!"

"That was quite a speech," Mr. Willimaker said. "Very inspirational and, uh, easy to remember."

"Now it's time to eat," Fudd said. "I hope you're hungry."

Elliot was so hungry that he was almost ready to eat his shirt (which might be one good way to get rid of it). Back at home, if there was ever any decent food, you had to grab it fast before someone else got it. But here, Elliot noticed, the Brownies were waiting for him to eat first. The only time Elliot's family had waited for him to eat first was last April Fool's Day, when the twins had switched the sugar and salt. Elliot was three bites into his cold cereal before he realized that wasn't sugar on his flakes.

When Elliot was seated on his royal toadstool, then the Brownies sat. Immediately a Brownie woman put a plate of food in front of him. It was full of bread, a yellowish fruit, and a lot of green vegetables Elliot didn't recognize. All the Brownies were watching him, including the woman who had just served him.

"Yum." Elliot picked up his fork and took a bite of the green vegetables. They tasted like Kyle and Cole's mud pies, only with the unexpected aftertaste of peppermint. "Mmmmm," he said, doing his best to convince the woman that he liked the strange food. "Really good."

There probably weren't any Quack Shacks in the Underworld. Too bad. French fries sounded great right now.

"Have you tried the turnip juice yet?" Mr. Willimaker asked.

It looked like apple juice, but it was more syrupy, and Elliot thought he saw a turnip root floating on top of his juice. But he put on a smile, lifted his cup, and said, "Cheers!"

Mr. Willimaker toasted Elliot in return, and they both drank. Elliot's plan was to finish the whole thing in one awful gulp, but he was surprised at his first taste that it wasn't bad. Not that he'd want to replace chocolate milk with turnip juice or anything, but he wouldn't mind it so much if they gave him some more.

"That turnip juice is sort of like me," said a woman walking up to him. "We're both better than we first appear."

Elliot looked up. "Agatha!"

The first time Elliot had met Agatha, she was a has-been Hag who couldn't quite get her curses to work. She was also the closest thing to what Elliot imagined a real witch might look like. After a few days, Agatha had remembered how to curse again, and eventually Elliot saw what a truly beautiful woman she was.

Beside Elliot, Mr. Willimaker stood and greeted her with a polite bow. "Agatha, we weren't expecting you."

"The king of the Brownies finally comes to the Underworld. I wouldn't miss this moment," she said, then pointed a crooked finger at Mr. Willimaker. "But for forgetting to invite me, this curse I leave with you today: I am a Hag and here's what I think. You'll find some trouble when you take a drink."

Mr. Willimaker looked at his cup of turnip juice, frowned, and then pushed it aside, just to be safe.

Fudd jumped up and pulled out his chair on the other side of Elliot. "Take my chair, please, my lady."

"I can't stay," Agatha said. "I just need to speak to Elliot for a moment."

Elliot stood. All the Brownies were still watching him, and he had a sudden itch on his backside. He wondered what kings were supposed to do when they needed to scratch in an embarrassing place and everyone was watching them.

"Pay attention, Elliot," Agatha said.

Elliot turned to her, hoping that whatever she had to say was so important it would help him forget the itch.

"I have a gift for you," she said, rummaging through a bag hanging from her arm.

A gift? Maybe it was a bottom scratcher.

"I heard a rumor that you have agreed to help the Pixies," she continued. "I have a guess at what they've asked you to do, but I'm not going to say what I think it is because I can't do anything more to help you. Do you understand?"

"Sure," Elliot said, although he really didn't understand at all.

"Ahh, here it is." She pulled a flashlight from her bag.

"Oh," he said, reaching for it. "Thanks."

Agatha yanked the flashlight away from him and added, "This isn't a human flashlight. It's not for seeing *in* the dark. It will see *through* the dark."

Same thing, Elliot thought, but he said nothing.

Agatha continued. "It can be turned on only once, so you don't want to use it until you're sure you need it."

Fudd tapped Elliot's arm. "Like when it's light outside. Whatever you do, don't turn it on in the light."

"Right." Elliot figured that was obvious.

"If it's a little light and a little dark, don't turn it on then either," Fudd added. "Or if it's mostly dark but you can still see."

"Got it," Elliot said.

Agatha continued, "This flashlight doesn't run on batteries. It runs on the sun."

"There's no sun in the Underworld," Elliot said.

"But the flashlight doesn't know that," Agatha said with a sigh. "Honestly, Elliot, I thought you were a smart boy. The flashlight doesn't know why it works, it just does. Why would you think the flashlight knows anything at all?"

Elliot shrugged, still confused.

"Once you turn the flashlight on, it gets its power from the sun at the surface of the earth. It will remain on until the sun is blocked by a solar eclipse. Then the light goes out and the flashlight is used up."

With that, Agatha handed Elliot the flashlight. It was heavier than it looked and made of a shiny silver metal that was a bit greasy.

"The grease isn't from the metal," Agatha explained. "I had fried chicken before coming here and forgot to wash my fingers. Sorry about that."

"Oh, no problem," Elliot said, wiping the flashlight with his shirt. He really didn't care if he ruined the shirt. "Thanks for this."

"I owed you one. You helped me when I was in your world. I'll help you now that you're in mine. Now, sit back down and finish your dinner. You have a long trip ahead of you tomorrow."

Agatha disappeared in a puff of smoke (sometimes called "poofed in a puff," but Elliot doesn't like to think of it that way, because it sounds like something one might do in a toilet). He smiled. The itch was gone. Maybe good luck was finally turning his way.

Where Fudd Stays Home

Elliot slept in Burrow Cave that night. Mr. Willimaker apologized that his own home wasn't large enough for Elliot, but added that it was probably a good thing, since Patches would only keep him up all night with questions.

Elliot was glad for the chance to be alone. He'd been awake most of the previous night, either from Tubs's snoring or with the whole kidnapped-to-the-Underworld thing. And tonight the Brownies had kept him awake very late trying to feed him, or wanting to ask him questions about life on the surface, or thanking him for ending the Goblin war.

Elliot was glad for the time alone, because he really wanted to think about how he was going to sneak into Demon Territory and pluck a hair off the head of the most dangerous Demon of all time.

He wanted to think about it, but he was too tired. He soon fell asleep between thoughts of Kovol and whether Harold the Shapeshifter had been able to fool his family that day pretending to be Elliot. Harold might be able to fool his sister and brothers, and maybe even his dad. But not his mom. One time, Elliot hadn't wanted to worry her about the black eye he got when Tubs pushed him into a door. So Elliot wore sunglasses to dinner. Didn't fool his mom one bit. Could Harold fool her?

The next morning, Fudd and Mr. Willimaker met Elliot at the mouth of Burrow Cave. Mr. Willimaker was kneeling in front of a large sack, making sure he had packed everything he thought they should bring on their journey.

"Squash greens, turnip juice, branberries—" Mr. Willimaker looked up at Elliot. "Is there anything else you'd like me to bring, Your Highness?"

"Is there any bread left over from last night?" Elliot asked. The bread had been good.

"I'll check." Mr. Willimaker bowed slightly at Elliot and then poofed away.

Fudd tapped Elliot on the shoulder, then handed Elliot a cup with a cream-colored, foamy drink inside. It looked like a vanilla shake. "Breakfast, Your Highness."

Elliot took a small first swallow—just in case it tasted like squash greens or turnip juice, which he hadn't quite decided to like. But this was delicious. A perfect drink, really. It was different from a vanilla shake, maybe even better. He drank the rest in only a few swallows.

"That was great," he told Fudd. "What do you call it?"

"Mushroom Surprise," Fudd said.

Elliot coughed. He was surprised, all right.

"This is a favorite breakfast for Brownies," Fudd added. "I always feel it's wise to drink your daily dose of mushrooms."

"Sure," Elliot agreed. "Why not?"

"Just so you know, this wasn't made with poisonous mushrooms," Fudd said, holding up his own cup. "I made the same drink for myself."

"I know. I trust you." Elliot handed his cup back to Fudd, who held on to it with Elliot for a moment and whispered, "Thank you, sir," before poofing the cups away.

Next, Fudd folded his short, chubby arms, then unfolded them, and finally sort of held them halfway folded. "King Elliot, please don't go."

"Don't worry," Elliot said. "I'll come back. Kovol won't wake up." Elliot hoped if he said the words enough, they would come true.

"But what if the Fairies find out you're helping the Pixies? They won't like it."

"Even if they did find out, what could the Fairies do to me that the Pixies haven't already done?"

Fudd shook his head. "King Elliot, I have to tell you something." Then he fell silent.

"What?" Elliot finally asked.

Fudd coughed. "I own this book, *The Guidebook to Evil Plans.* It clearly states, 'Choose your friendships carefully. Good friends might weaken your evil plans. On the other hand, evil friends might destroy you so that they can take over your plans (page 16)."

Elliot waited for Fudd to explain why he was saying this. Finally, Fudd shrugged and said, "There's nothing else. I was just quoting."

Elliot asked, "Fudd, do you support me as king?"

Fudd's beady eyes shifted. "I wish you didn't have to ask, Your Highness. My point is that you need to be careful out there. The Fairies want Glimmering Woods just as much as the Pixies do. They won't be happy about this."

"They can join the club," Elliot said. "*I'm* not happy about this either." Then he jumped a bit as Mr. Willimaker poofed back on his right side and Patches appeared on his left.

"I found bread," Mr. Willimaker said.

"No, *I* found it," Patches corrected him. She held a large bundle in her arms. "Actually, I put together a whole bunch of human food. Sorry for my dad, Elliot. He doesn't know all the food humans like."

"I just drank Mushroom Surprise," Elliot said. "I liked that."

Patches made a face. "Don't you know what the surprise is?"

"No."

She grinned. "You will."

Elliot took the bundle from Patches. Whatever she'd put in there, it smelled

190

good. And Elliot had the flashlight from Agatha tucked in his belt. Maybe this trip wouldn't be such a big deal after all.

"Are we ready then?" Fudd asked. "Ready to go to our deaths, no doubt, but we'll see some nice sights along the way."

"Only Mr. Willimaker and I are going," Elliot said.

"But Your Highness," Fudd protested. "I owe this to you."

"You can owe it to me later. I need Mr. Willimaker to show me the way, but if I don't come back, then someone will need to stay here as king."

Fudd shook his head. "I don't want to become king that way. Not anymore."

Elliot smiled and tapped Agatha's flashlight. "Don't worry. I have the flashlight, and Kovol is asleep. I'm sure it won't be as hard as everyone thinks."

"Let me come with you," Patches said.

"No," Mr. Willimaker and Elliot said together. Mr. Willimaker added, "Besides, you have school tomorrow, and no Shapeshifter is available to take your place."

Elliot and Patches both groaned, although for very different reasons. Then Patches slumped to the ground and folded her arms. "Fine, but I could've helped."

To his right, Elliot noticed a winding road paved in yellow bricks. "Oh. A yellow brick road. I suppose we should follow it out of Burrowsville, right?"

Mr. Willimaker grabbed his arm to hold him back. "Are you crazy? Don't you know where that leads?"

Elliot shook his head. "No. Where?"

Mr. Willimaker shuddered. "No Brownie who's walked that path has ever returned. We call it the Yellow Brick Road of Doom." He pointed to a hill leading in the opposite direction. "We go that way, Your Highness."

"Then let's go." Elliot took his first steps, and Mr. Willimaker quickly caught up to walk beside him. "How long will it take for us to get there?"

Mr. Willimaker pulled a map out of his pocket. "If we don't stop to see any sights along the way and we keep up a good pace, maybe a week."

"A week?" Elliot asked. "That long?"

"I said *maybe,*" Mr. Willimaker said. "I could be wrong. It might take us much, much longer than that."

Chapter 13

Where Elliot Thinks about the Number Fifty

Before Elliot had become king of the Brownies, he'd done a lot of running. Mostly running away from Tubs, who would have left bruises on any part of Elliot's body he could catch. Reasons like that help a kid run away fast.

But Tubs hadn't chased Elliot since the end of the Goblin war, and Elliot was a little out of shape. Now he was thinking that Burrowsville had a lot of hills. Going down them wasn't bad, except the next hill up always seemed to be a little taller than the one before it. At least the bright colors of the Underworld trees and flowers kept things interesting. Obviously there was no sun above them, but everything was warm and light, and the sky had a cool, pastel yellow glow.

It took them a while to get out of Burrowsville. As they walked the winding road through the town, Brownies came out to greet Elliot and to thank him for what he'd done in ending the Goblin war. Mr. Willimaker pointed out that many of the younger Brownies had never seen a human up close before. After a few hours they left the border of Burrowsville and entered what Mr. Willimaker called the "Underworlderness."

There weren't a lot of trees here, but the narrow trail was lined with blueberry bushes even taller than Elliot. For nearly a mile, the thick bushes marked the trail. Elliot and Mr. Willimaker ate a lunch of them as they walked.

Mr. Willimaker tried to talk with Elliot that afternoon, but Elliot was deep in thought. It was cool to have seen Burrowsville, and Elliot was proud of the fact that he'd beaten Grissel in the time-out—not that he could tell any of his family that—but he still wished he were home. He wondered whether the twins had dug any more mud pits, or whether his Uncle Rufus had returned to his habit of stealing shiny things, or what Wendy had burned for dinner last night. Funny that he missed her burned food. Maybe she'd messed up his taste buds, and burned food was starting to taste normal to him.

And something in his stomach had been rumbling for a while, as though his own personal volcano were trapped inside. He took two more steps, and then the volcano erupted in the form of a gigantic burp. Mr. Willimaker ducked, and the burped-out air hit a large blueberry bush that promptly wilted and died.

"Did I do that?" Elliot asked.

"More correctly, your Mushroom Surprise drink did that. Better a bush than me, I always say." Mr. Willimaker brushed off his clothes and continued walking. "Warn me the next time you feel that coming, please."

"Sorry," Elliot said, although he secretly thought his toxic burp was pretty cool.

"Your Highness, if I may—" Mr. Willimaker began.

"We've got a long walk ahead of us," Elliot said. "You don't have to call me that. Just use my name."

"Yes, Your Highness. Anyway, if I may ask, I'm a little unclear about your plan to get the hair from Kovol's head."

"I don't have a plan," Elliot said. "I think I'll just have to figure it out when we get there."

"Understood. But if you did have a plan, what would it be?"

Elliot sighed. "The thing is, I've never been to Demon Territory. I've never seen Kovol before, and I really don't know anything about him other than that he's supposed to be asleep. And to be honest, I've never tried to pull a hair out of anyone's head before, especially while they're asleep."

"Ah," Mr. Willimaker said. "To be honest, I haven't done that before either. Not the sort of thing a polite creature does, is it?"

Elliot smiled. "No." Tubs had pulled a chunk of his hair out once, in kindergarten. Actually, Tubs had put a whole glob of superglue on his own hand. When Elliot teased him about it, Tubs smacked Elliot in the head, and his hand stuck to Elliot's hair. Then when he tore his hand away, a lot of Elliot's hair had come with it. Later that day, Elliot's mom had shaved the rest of his hair really short to cover up how many bald patches there were.

They continued to walk, with Mr. Willimaker pointing out some of the sights in the Underworld. "If we went south tomorrow, we'd come to a lake where the Mermaids like to swim. You can't fish there, though. Turns out the Mermaids don't like to be fished." A couple of hours later, Mr. Willimaker pointed in another direction. "See those mountains in the distance? The Dwarves live there."

"Are there any Mermaids or Dwarves on the surface world?" Elliot asked.

"A Mermaid finds her way to the surface every now and then, but not in the numbers there used to be. You'll find Dwarves anywhere there's enough treasure to be found, though the Underworld is still rich in valuable stones. If humans knew how many diamonds were down here, they'd have found a way into our land ages ago."

"I have a question," Elliot said. "How is there light so far under the earth, and air I can breathe? This is a lot like the surface world, but with no humans."

"It's the combined magic of all Underworld creatures," Mr. Willimaker said. "Everyone gives a little, and together we have a much nicer life than most humans would expect. If they knew we had a life down here, of course."

"Does it bother you about humans?" Elliot asked. "I mean, that most humans don't believe you exist?"

"It's a good thing, actually," Mr. Willimaker said. "Hundreds of years ago when humans did believe in us, life was far more difficult. Now our only problem is the way your books and movies talk about us. You'd be surprised how wrong you are most of the time. To be fair, I suppose our books and movies get a few things wrong about humans too. For example, I don't suppose humans can leap over tall buildings in a single jump?"

Elliot smiled. "Maybe super humans. But I don't think they're real."

Mr. Willimaker shrugged. "Not long ago, you didn't think Brownies were real either." He checked his map. "What say we stop here for supper?"

"Sure." Elliot dropped his bag to the ground and untied the knot holding it together. Inside were apples, blueberries, cucumbers, and carrots. Naturally, Patches had also snuck in a large bag of pickles. Elliot pulled one out and began munching on it. "Mr. Willimaker," he asked, "what do you know about Shadow Men?"

Mr. Willimaker, who was eating something that looked like an orange artichoke, stopped chewing. He swallowed hard, then in a low voice said, "They're Kovol's army. They guard him in his sleep, which means they haven't left Demon Territory in over a thousand years. Few creatures live through an encounter with the Shadow Men, so most of what we know is from the old writings. My own great-grandfather was killed trying to fight them."

"Sorry," Elliot mumbled.

"It happened a thousand years ago, so it's an old memory now. There was a great war in which all Underworld creatures united against the Demons. They would've lost too, if not for an agreement Kovol made that put him to sleep."

"What agreement?" Elliot asked.

"A human sorcerer named Minthred got involved in the war. I don't know the terms of the agreement, I'm afraid, just that Kovol went to sleep, and the Shadow Men have watched over him ever since." Mr. Willimaker paused to finish his artichoke. Then he added, "How will we get past the Shadow Men, Your Highness?"

Elliot shrugged. "We'll go in the daytime. I figure Shadow Men are probably night creatures, since in the daytime there aren't as many shadows where they can hide."

"How do you know about Shadow Men?"

"Harold the Shapeshifter turned into one when I was still on the surface. He was scary, but I beat Grissel trying to scare me to death. I can beat the Shadow Men too, if I have to."

"Even in the form of a Shadow Man, he was still just a Shapeshifter," Mr. Willimaker warned. "And there was only one of him. Kovol's army is probably much larger."

"How much larger?"

Mr. Willimaker held out his hands. "I don't know. It's been a thousand years since anybody's seen one. I'm sure their numbers are smaller than before, but you could face an army of fifty or more."

Fifty was a lot. Elliot sighed and tried not to think about that. Because if he did, he would have to admit that he didn't know how an eleven-year-old kid and a Brownie had any chance against fifty of the scariest creatures he'd ever met.

Chapter 14

Where Elliot Doesn't Get His Drink of Water

Mr. Willimaker finished his supper at about the same time Elliot decided he might have lost his appetite for good.

"Didn't you like the food Patches packed for you?" Mr. Willimaker asked. "I tried to tell her."

"No, the food was good," Elliot said. "I'm just not hungry."

"You have Shadow Men on your mind?"

"A little." Elliot pressed his lips together. "All we have to do is sneak past them, get a hair from Kovol, and sneak out."

Mr. Willimaker smiled. "I wish it were going to be as easy as you make it sound. But if we do survive, it'll make a grand story for the Brownies." He stood and brushed off his clothes. "It's getting dark. Are you cold?"

Elliot wasn't. If anything, the clothes the Brownies had made for him locked heat in. "Did you want to make a fire?"

Mr. Willimaker shook his head. "It's usually warm in the Underworld, but a little light would be nice."

"I have the flashlight from Agatha," Elliot said. "Though with my luck, the next eclipse will happen five minutes after I turn it on, so let's wait until we really need it."

Mr. Willimaker snapped his fingers together. When he did, a spark of light remained on his thumb. He pressed his thumb to a stick, and it lit. Then Mr. Willimaker gathered a few other sticks together in a pile, and the light passed to them as well.

"Is that a magic fire?" Elliot asked.

"It's only light." Mr. Willimaker passed his hand through the center of the light. "There's no heat, and it won't burn anything. The light won't last long, but it'll do until we fall asleep."

"Can you make another fire?" Elliot wanted one to play with.

"Not for a few minutes. I need to recharge."

Elliot ran his hand through the center of the light as well. It was no warmer than the air, and yet it flickered on the sticks as a fire would. "Cool," he whispered. "I wish I had magic."

"All Underworld creatures have their own kinds of magic," Mr. Willimaker said. "Brownies aren't that powerful compared to Pixies or Fairies, or even Goblins. Elves have only a little magic but are more powerful in other ways. Same with the Dwarves. A Leprechaun has quite a bit of magic, and yet a human could easily overcome one if he knew how."

"How many Underworld creatures exist?" Elliot asked. "Are all the myths true?"

"There are creatures down here that humans know nothing about and some creatures that you know more about than you think." Mr. Willimaker shrugged. "I'm not sure how many of us there are. The Underworld is very big and not very well explored. Most of us keep to ourselves."

Elliot used his bundle as a pillow and laid back on it. Had he been sleeping on the surface, he would have expected to see stars, but the sky here was only black.

"I miss the moon," he said.

Mr. Willimaker lay on his own bundle near Elliot. "Wait for it to get a bit darker. The Star Dancers, creatures of the night, provide us with the night sky. I think you'll like it."

And he was right. After about a half hour, the Underworld became dark enough that Mr. Willimaker's cool fire was the only light around. Elliot stared at the sky again, but now it became painted in streaks of thin neon colors. Bright lines of blue, green, and orange raced across the sky, slowly fading as new colors were drawn over the top of them.

"Those are Star Dancers?" Elliot asked. "I don't think I've ever heard of them."

"They never go to the surface world," Mr. Willimaker said. "Why would they when they can have this much fun down here?"

"I like the Underworld," Elliot said. "If I survive Kovol, I might come back again one day. Fudd said the Brownies would build me a home here that's my size."

Mr. Willimaker was quiet for a moment, and then he said, "Your Highness, I want to talk to you about Fudd."

Elliot leaned up on his elbows. "What's the matter?"

"I hope it's nothing. Ever since the Goblin war ended, I believe Fudd has been sincere in trying to earn back your trust. But last night, after the royal feast, I overheard something that worries me. I believe the Fairies had a meeting with Fudd. He worked with them for years under Queen Bipsy, you know."

"I didn't know," Elliot said. That wasn't a question he had even thought about asking.

"Yes, well, the Fairies know you're down here. They asked Fudd why."

"What did he say?" Elliot asked.

"He said he couldn't tell them anything, but then they said they already knew the Pixies brought you here and they weren't happy about it. You see, the Fairies want the Glimmering Woods too. If they think you're helping the Pixies, they'll be upset."

"But I don't have a choice," Elliot said. "The Pixies have Tubs."

"I know, but the Fairies might not understand that," Mr. Willimaker said. "Fairies aren't the most forgiving creatures. They reminded Fudd about an old treaty the Brownies have with both the Pixies and Fairies, promising not to get involved in any fights between them. They told Fudd to stop you, or else they would."

Elliot groaned. "And what did Fudd say?"

Mr. Willimaker shrugged. "He told them he'd think about it. I don't know what he's decided."

"Doesn't sound good," Elliot said.

"No, it doesn't," Mr. Willimaker agreed.

They stared at the streaks for a while longer, although now that Elliot wondered whether Fudd had betrayed him again, the streaks didn't seem so bright and colorful. He sighed and said, "I don't think I'll get much sleep tonight."

"Cheer up, Your Highness," Mr. Willimaker said. "Other than the Brownies, I can think of at least five Underworld creatures who aren't trying to kill you right now."

"Great."

"Try to get some sleep," Mr. Willimaker mumbled. "I'll have breakfast ready when you wake up, and sn…"

Whatever "sn…" meant, Elliot wasn't going to find out. Mr. Willimaker was asleep before he finished the word.

Elliot slept better that night than he thought he would. He woke up to a cheery sunrise, or whatever it was in the Underworld that provided light. Morning magic, perhaps. He would have liked another cup of Fudd's Mushroom Surprise, although if Mr. Willimaker was right and Fudd couldn't be trusted, he probably shouldn't take anything else Fudd offered him.

Mr. Willimaker greeted Elliot when he sat up. "Awake, Your Highness? My apologies, I expected you to sleep awhile longer."

"Hard to sleep when you're hunting a Demon," Elliot said.

"Ah, yes." Mr. Willimaker said. "My cousin once said the same thing about hunting for delicious burbleberries. Although to be fair, burbleberries won't rip your arms off if you get close to them."

Elliot turned to Mr. Willimaker, who was finishing getting dressed. He looked as fresh and clean as ever. Elliot, on the other hand, thought he could smell his own body odor, and something sticky was on his cheek.

Mr. Willimaker hurried over to unwrap his bundle. "I saw a stream a little ways back. Maybe I can heat some water for a warm mint broth." As Mr. Willimaker pulled two cups from his bag, his ears suddenly perked up at the side of his head, the way a dog's might when it hears something.

"I don't mean to alarm you," Mr. Willimaker whispered, "but is there any chance that noise came from you?"

Elliot hadn't heard anything. "What noise?"

"That rustling noise. I was hoping that perhaps it was you over in those bushes."

"It's not me," Elliot said.

"Are you sure?" Mr. Willimaker's ears were at full attention now, then they relaxed and he added, "It was probably nothing. A rodent or a snake perhaps."

Elliot pulled his feet in close to him. He didn't like snakes. He didn't trust anything that could move on the ground without legs.

Mr. Willimaker tapped the cups. "I'll get some water. Won't be long." Then he walked away toward the stream.

Only a minute later, Elliot heard a "Hamph!" and a loud "No!" Then a small puff of smoke rose in the air and everything went silent. Elliot hoped it wasn't a snake that had gotten to Mr. Willimaker, because that would have to be some freaky large snake. He ran in the direction Mr. Willimaker had gone, calling his name, but there was no answer. Then he ran to the stream, but it didn't look as if Mr. Willimaker had gotten this far. At least, no footprints were in the mud other than Elliot's.

Elliot turned back the way he had come. Under a bush he saw the two cups Mr. Willimaker must have dropped.

"Mr. Willimaker?" Elliot called again. What had happened to him?

He picked up the cups and then saw a small note hanging from a branch of the bush. He plucked it off and read:

To the king of the Brownies—

By helping the Pixies, you are in violation of a treaty agreeing to stay out of any fighting over Glimmering Woods. Therefore, we have taken the Brownie, Mr. Willimaker, and will hold him as our captive until you also do something for the Fairies. We want a sock off the foot of the

Demon Kovol. It shouldn't be a problem for you. We hear you're going to see him anyway.

Refuse to help us and you will never see Mr. Willimaker again. Should you fail with the Demon Kovol, no one will ever see you again.

Cheers!

The Fairies

Elliot crumpled the note into his pocket and yelled again, "Mr. Willimaker!" Then he yelled, "Fairies! I want to talk to you!"

But there was no answer.

He was alone in the Underworld, with no map either back to Burrowsville or ahead to Demon Territory. And he thought he heard a sound nearby. Something was coming toward him.

Chapter 15

Where Elliot Is Clever Enough to Find Gripping Mud

Elliot hurried back to camp and gathered up both his and Mr. Willimaker's bundles. With his arms full, he began racing in the direction they'd been walking yesterday. He didn't know if he was still walking toward Demon Territory or not. But he did know he was moving away from whatever was following him.

Maybe it was Goblins, who knew he was alone and wanted revenge for his ending the Goblin war.

Maybe it was Fairies, coming to capture him before he could find Kovol.

Maybe it was the ice cream man on his secret Underworld route. That'd be cool, but he sort of doubted it. Elliot didn't have money for ice cream anyway.

Elliot ran so quickly through the bushes that he lost track of where he was going. All that mattered was getting away. Then he burst into a small clearing and took a step onto something that wasn't hard ground.

It was a kind of mud, but no ordinary mud. His foot sank into the mud almost up to his knee. His second foot landed in the mud before he had time to stop, and he went in up to his thigh.

He didn't think he was in quicksand. Elliot had never been caught in quicksand before, due to the fact that there was no quicksand in Sprite's Hollow. But this wasn't sand at all. It was mud, and the mud seemed to be holding him in. The more he struggled, the more tightly the mud held on.

"King Elliot? It's me. Where are you?"

Elliot turned his head toward the sound. It wasn't Goblins or Fairies chasing him. It was Patches, who had disobeyed both him and her father to follow them into the Underworlderness. But she was about to save his life, so he decided to ignore her rule-breaking.

"I'm here," he called. "I need help!"

Patches poofed from wherever she was to stand on solid ground near Elliot. "Oh," she said. "Gripping mud."

"That's what this is?"

She giggled. "In case you didn't know, you're not supposed to walk on it."

"Now you tell me. How do I get out?"

Patches giggled again. "You can't. Well, I mean you can't get out by yourself. The more you try, the more you'll get stuck."

"So can you get me out?"

"If I get you out, then you can't get mad at me for following you, okay?"

Elliot smiled. "If you hadn't followed me, I'd be stuck here forever."

Patches knelt on the ground. "Okay, so here's how it works. I'm going to hand you a branch. You have to let me pull you out by myself. Don't help me at all. Anything you do will only make the mud hold you tighter."

"I'm pretty heavy for you," Elliot said.

"I'm pretty strong for me too." Patches snapped off a branch of a nearby tree and held it out to Elliot. "Just hold on."

Elliot held to the branch. Once Patches started to loosen him from the mud, he wiggled his legs to work his body upward. Instantly, the gripping mud pulled him down again.

"You might be a king, but now you have to obey me," Patches grumbled. "Don't help."

"Right," Elliot said. "Sorry."

This time he relaxed his body and did nothing to free himself, no matter how hard Patches groaned to pull him out. Even when it was only his toes remaining in the mud, he still let her drag him forward until he was entirely on solid ground.

"No one can get out of gripping mud on their own," Patches said between breaths. "Sometimes the Brownies call it friendship mud. If you don't have any friends, you stay stuck."

"Thanks for being my friend," Elliot said. "You saved me."

"You're welcome, but don't hug me," she said. "You're dirty."

Elliot heard a river nearby. "Give me a minute, and I'll be back." He ran to the river, this time being more careful to watch for any signs of gripping mud, then waded in. The water was cool but clean, and he splashed around until all the mud had washed away.

When he got back to Patches, she had caught her breath and was gathering up what little remained from his and Mr. Willimaker's food bundles. "Don't try to hug me now either," she said. "You're all wet."

"That gripping mud is pretty nasty stuff," Elliot said. "Is there a lot of it in the Underworld?"

"No, but you see it from time to time. You can sometimes see a brown glow around it. That's how you know it's there before you run into it."

"So why'd you come?" Elliot asked. "It's dangerous out here."

"I know," Patches said. "But I remembered a few things after you left. Some really important things."

"Like what?"

"Well, I wanted to tell you about the Shapeshifter in case he comes back and tries to trick you again."

Elliot shook his head. "He's on the surface, pretending to be me. That'll keep him busy until I get home."

"But if he does come," she said, "there's a way to keep him from changing forms. Just pinch his ear."

Elliot pinched two fingers against his own ear. "Like this?"

"The tighter, the better."

"Anything else?" Elliot asked.

"Yes. I'm worried about your helping the Pixies. I was thinking about a treaty the Brownies have. A really long time ago, Queen Bipsy agreed not to help either the Fairies or the Pixies while they were fighting over Glimmering Forest. I think the Fairies are going to be mad if they find out."

Elliot nodded. "Your dad told me the same thing last night."

Patches looked around. "Where is he?"

"The Fairies got mad," Elliot said. "They just took him."

Patches groaned. "My mom won't like that. After the Goblins took me, she made it a family rule that nobody else can get kidnapped."

"I don't think it was your dad's choice," Elliot said.

"My mom won't see it that way. She'll think he's trying to get out of weeding the garden."

Elliot shook his head. "He's fine for now, but the Fairies left me a note that said to get him back, I need one of Kovol's socks for the Fairies. I have to get to Demon Territory, but your dad had the map. Do you know how to get there?"

"Of course," Patches said. "Let's go."

"I don't want you to take me there," Elliot said. "Just point me in the right direction."

Patches put her hands on her hips. "It's still a long way, Elliot, and without me you'll be lost. Do you want my help or not?"

"Fine," Elliot said. "Let's go."

He followed Patches across a wide field of tiny white flowers that made him sneeze. And every time he sneezed, it blew the flower apart into bits that created new flowers where they landed. By the time they left the field, there were hundreds more flowers than when he began. He followed her up a tall, sandy hill where with every footstep he slid almost as far down as where he began. Patches was lighter and climbed it much faster but waited for him while he heaved his way to the top.

"That wasn't much fun," he said once he arrived.

"Yeah, but going down makes the climb worth it." She turned and leapt into the air, landing on the soft sand and rolling the rest of the way down the long hill.

Elliot followed, laughing as he rolled until he got a mouthful of sand and wisely kept his mouth closed the rest of the way. Once he reached the bottom, he and Patches lay on the sand and laughed a little longer.

"My dad would've taken you around the hill instead of over it," Patches said. "Now aren't you glad I'm here?"

Elliot nodded. "You have to go home soon, though. You can't come into Demon Territory with me."

"Oh, I forgot," Patches said, sitting up. "That's the other thing I had to tell you!"

But she never got a chance to tell him because at the last moment—

Dear Reader, don't you hate it when a character is about to say something really important, but they never get a chance to say it, because they're interrupted by something else? Maybe someday you'll have something really important to say, such as, "Mom, did you know the house is on fire?" Even if someone tries to interrupt you, like your little brother asking for a drink of water, you should still tell your mother about the fire. Not only was it rude for your little brother to interrupt and you have to teach him good manners, but your mother will probably also want to use that glass of water for the fire.

In this case, Patches never got a chance to finish what she was going to say, because Harold the Shapeshifter poofed in right in front of Elliot. He was still in Elliot's form, and the only reason she could tell them apart was that Harold had a small patch of white hair on the back of his head.

It took Elliot a moment to realize that it was not a mirror that had suddenly poofed in, but it was actually Harold, who looked exactly like him.

Elliot tried to say hello, but Harold spoke first. "I'm very sorry to tell you this," he said to Elliot, "but you'll have to stay in the Underworld forever. I won't let you go home ever again."

Chapter 16

Where Ears Become Important

Except for the Pixie prison, Elliot quite liked the Underworld and thought if he ever did get home, he might want to return for a nice visit one day. But he didn't want to stay in the Underworld forever. For one thing, his family was on the surface, and he missed them. For another, Underworld creatures thought chocolate was about the worst thing since liver and onions. Elliot couldn't see himself living anywhere without chocolate.

And he didn't at all like Harold the Shapeshifter telling him he couldn't go home again.

Elliot dropped his bundle just as Harold was drawing in a large breath of air to change into something, probably a scary something. He grabbed Harold's ear and held on tight.

"Stop that!" Harold said. "I've got to change into something that can kill you."

"I'm sick of everyone in the Underworld trying to kill me lately," Elliot said. "So it's bad timing on your part. I'm not letting go."

Harold grabbed Elliot's shoulders and started kicking his shins. In turn, Elliot kicked him back, all the time keeping hold of Harold's ear.

"That really hurts," Harold said.

"It's my ear I'm pinching anyway," Elliot said. "You're just borrowing it."

"It's your ear, but it's on my body, and it hurts. Want to see what it's like?" With that, Harold grabbed Elliot's ear.

"Ow!" Elliot yelped. "You're pinching harder than I am." So he pinched Harold's ear harder. In return, Harold began stomping on his feet.

"You can't stomp on a king's foot," Patches said. She rolled up her sleeves and flung some magic toward Harold, who suddenly sank to the ground like all the bones had gone out of his body. Elliot, who had been holding tightly to Harold's ear, also dropped to the ground, but he knew he still had bones, because they cracked against a rock as he landed.

"What did you do to him?" Elliot asked.

"I just zapped his energy for a couple of seconds," Patches said. "An Elf taught me that trick a while ago."

"Cool." Elliot leaned in to Harold and asked, "So why do you want to kill me?"

"I'm in love," Harold said. "We Shapeshifters sometimes do crazy things when we're in love."

"That's stupid," Elliot said. "Who are you in love with? My sister, Wendy? Because I've got news for you. You're up there pretending to be me, so if you go and fall in love with your sister, that's just creepy."

"It's not your sister," Harold said, "though I must say it's been nice to eat real human food after all this time. I've eaten so much of her food, it's really surprised her. She says I've never been as nice to her as I have this week."

Elliot groaned and Harold continued, "But, no, the girl I love is that beautiful human Cami Wortson."

For a moment, Elliot's brain went numb. He thought his heart had just stopped beating and that he'd faint and fall back into the gripping mud and sink to the center of the earth. And that would be fine, because not him or anyone who looked like him was ever supposed to even like Cami, much less claim to love her!

"No," he finally said. "No, you can't love her, because she's out to destroy my life. Which means as long as you look like me, she's out to destroy your life too. And if she finds out that you like her, she'll use that as a weapon that may or may not involve her reaching down your throat and ripping out your guts and feeding them to a crocodile!"

Harold sat up on his elbows. "That seems a little extreme for the love of my life."

Elliot shuddered. "Cami Wortson is not the love of your life. You'd have an easier time loving a toad. Trust me."

"And she has a nice smile," Harold said. "I don't think toads can smile."

Elliot had to give him that. He'd never seen a toad smile either. "Okay, listen," he said. "I have to let go of your ear now, because this is getting really weird. But don't try to change into anything that's going to kill me, because Patches will just zap your energy again."

"I can really only do that once," Patches whispered to Elliot, but he shushed her and hoped Harold hadn't heard.

Harold sat up. "I won't change into anything that can kill you. But I can't let you return to the surface again either. I've decided to remain as you for the rest of your life."

Elliot shook his head. "No."

"Why not? For your information, I've been a very good Elliot Penster. I'm probably better at it than you are."

"You can't be me, because nobody else knows the combination to my piggy bank. I've got my whole life's savings in there, and you'll never get it, because you don't know the combination."

"I broke the safe with a hammer and used the money to buy Cami some flowers," Harold said.

"Oh." That had been Elliot's best argument. "But did you have to buy flowers? Why didn't you just go ahead and propose marriage?"

Harold's eyes lit up. "Do you think—"

"No!" Elliot cried. "Listen, I'm not going to be here much longer. I just have to get a couple of things from Kovol, and then I'm going home, so you'd better get back up there and make enemies with Cami again."

"You're going to make Kovol mad," Harold said.

"Not if I don't wake him up," Elliot said.

Harold chewed on his bottom lip for a minute and then said, "How about this? I can change into a large bird and fly you to the border of Demon Territory in just a few minutes. It'll save you days of travel."

"No, thanks," Patches said.

"Wait!" Elliot said to Patches. "I lost most of our food in the gripping mud, and I'd rather get this over with."

"You shouldn't trust a Shapeshifter," Patches said.

Elliot turned to Harold. "Are you only flying me there so that Kovol can kill me faster and then you can be me forever?"

"Yeah, pretty much," Harold said.

Elliot looked back at Patches. "See? There's no reason not to trust him. He's telling the truth."

"About wanting you gone."

"Yeah, but it's still the truth."

"Okay," Patches sighed. "Fine."

Harold stood and drew in a deep breath. As the air moved inside him, he stretched his arms out wide. They expanded and grew into wings covered with long, brown feathers. His legs thinned and grew talons where his toes would have been. Finally, his nose stretched into a sharp orange beak, and his hair became smooth white feathers that covered his eagle head.

Harold looked at Elliot and cawed to get on his back. Elliot climbed on, then turned to Patches. "Listen, he's going to take me all the way to Demon Territory. I want you to go back home. I'll come back with your father in another day or two."

"No, wait!" Patches said, but it was too late.

Elliot had already climbed onto Harold the Eagle's back. As Harold lifted off the ground, Patches leapt into the air and tried to grab hold of Harold's tail, but Harold shook her off and back to the ground.

"Hey!" Elliot looked down. Patches was standing and trying to yell at him, but they were already too far away for him to hear her. He knew she'd be angry about his leaving so fast, but at least she was okay.

The view of the Underworld from the air was better than anything Elliot could have imagined. He could easily see back to Burrowsville, which from here looked like it was made of small mounds in the ground that served as the Brownies' homes. Then he stopped himself. The Brownies' homes *were* small mounds in the ground. Far in the distance he could see the Glimmering Forest. He wondered if Mr. Willimaker was being held somewhere near there by the Fairies.

Elliot was pretty mad at the Fairies and still mad at the Pixies. He was mad at Harold too, for wanting to take over his life, even though Harold was doing him a big favor right now. Of course, Harold was only doing him the favor so that Elliot could get killed faster. Then Harold, pretending to be Elliot, could declare his love to Elliot's worst enemy.

On second thought, Elliot seemed to have a lot of enemies lately. If he included Tubs, Grissel, the Fairies, and the Pixies, Cami was only his second or third worst enemy.

Harold cawed again and aimed a wing ahead of them. Elliot looked down at what appeared to be a long, black hole. Although it was late in the morning, it looked blacker than midnight in that spot.

That was Demon Territory. Somewhere in the middle of the blackness was the worst Demon in the history of time. And Elliot had to take a hair from his head. And now, one of his socks too.

They neared the territory and Harold flew lower to the ground, preparing to land. By now, Elliot couldn't see Burrowsville anymore. He couldn't see anyplace he recognized. The thought occurred to him that even if he somehow survived in Demon Territory, how was he going to get back to Burrowsville again?

He put his mouth close to where he thought Harold's ear would be, if giant birds had ears. "Will you wait around to fly me home when I come out?"

Harold shook his head so roughly that a few feathers fell free. Elliot didn't blame him. He wouldn't want to wait around either.

They landed in a clearing not far from the entrance to Demon Territory. Elliot slid off Harold's back, and soon Harold changed into the human boy he'd talked to on the surface.

"Okay, listen," Elliot said. "I had time to think up there, and I'll make you a deal. If I don't come back, then it's okay with me if you want to live out the rest of my life. Just promise never to tell my parents. My parents can be old-fashioned, and hearing that their son is really a Shapeshifter named Harold—well, they'd have a hard time with that."

"Yes, I've noticed that human parents are very strange about Shapeshifters taking over their children's lives."

"They love me," Elliot said. "But as long as they think you're me, I guess they'll love you too."

Harold kicked at the ground. "Now, why did you have to go and be nice to me when I'm clearly trying to help you get killed?" His eyes narrowed. "But in a way, being nice only makes me feel guilty for wanting you killed. It's not at all nice to make someone feel guilty."

Elliot shoved his hands into his pockets. "I have to go in there now, with or without your help. So don't feel guilty. Just go back and be a good me. Be a better me. I wasn't very nice to my family before I left them."

"It'll be hard to be better than the Elliot Penster I know," Harold said, "but I'll try. I'll be the kind of boy Cambria Dawn Wortson can love in return."

That pretty much ruined the moment for Elliot. He rolled his eyes and said, "Don't get too comfortable, though, because I am planning on coming back."

Coming back? Crazy thing to say, considering he didn't even know how to get in there first.

Elliot started to walk off, then with a smile turned to look back at the Shapeshifter. "I bet you can't get me inside Demon Territory."

"Bet I—" Harold stopped. "You're trying to trick me, aren't you?"

"Who, me?" Elliot raised his hands to show his innocence. "I just think it'll be too hard for you to get me into Demon Territory. I bet you're not that clever."

"Bet I am," Harold said, walking up to Elliot. "And I know you're tricking me, but I don't care, because it just so happens that I want to take the bet. I'll show you just how clever I am."

Elliot turned to look at Harold, but Harold had changed again. He was now an Elf. Probably. Based upon the Elves Elliot had seen in a lot of movies, Harold was not how he figured Elves would look.

Elliot had always thought Elves would be smaller than him, like most Underworld creatures seemed to be. But Harold was tall, very slim, and very handsome. He had pointed ears on the side of his head, and his skin was pale in color.

"You're an Elf now?" Elliot asked.

"Elves are the caretakers of Demon Territory," Harold said. "No humans can get through."

"That's fine for you, but how do I get in?" Elliot asked.

Harold sighed. "Do I have to do everything? Honestly, you'd think I was

215

the only one who wanted to see you killed today." He rubbed his hands together, then ran them along the edges of Elliot's ears. Elliot felt a tickling sensation in his head. When Harold removed his hands, Elliot touched his ears. They were pointed, like Harold's.

"You can change my shape?" he asked.

"I can only change a few small things, and those won't last more than five or ten minutes, so we've got to hurry. Are you ready for this, Elliot? Because after the next step you take, it'll be too late to turn back."

Elliot held his breath, closed his eyes, and took the next step.

Chapter
17

Where Elliot Has
an Embarrassing Secret

Harold and Elliot hurried to the entrance of Demon Territory, which was very clearly marked with a large sign, just as Fudd had described to Elliot. The sign said, WARNING: YOU ARE NOW ENTERING DEMON TERRITORY. ALL CREATURES MUST ENTER AT THEIR OWN RISK. HUMANS MAY NOT ENTER FOR ANY REASON.

Dear Reader, it's important to pay attention to signs. For example, if you ever see a sign telling you not to swim because there are alligators in the water, then you should definitely obey the sign. Sometimes alligators will pretend to be friendly, hoping to trick you into coming into the water. Then they'll eat you. However, if you ever see a sign telling you that it's okay to swim in a place where you know alligators live, you still shouldn't go in. It's possible that the alligators got a marker and changed the sign. Alligators are a lot trickier than most people think.

A female Elf as tall as Harold the Elf, but with long, golden hair, stood in front of the sign. Elliot thought she looked very bored. There probably weren't many creatures who came this way, so she probably didn't have much to do.

She straightened up as Harold and Elliot came closer. "You wish to enter Demon Territory?"

"We're on a long trip, and it's a shortcut," Harold said.

"I don't recognize you, Elf," she said. "What is your name?"

"We're southern hemisphere Elves," Harold answered. "We're here on a journey of discovery."

"Demon Territory is dangerous, even to Elves," she said. "I suggest you take the longer path."

"This is our path," Harold said. "You have no right to stop us, so allow us to pass."

"It's true I have no right to stop you," the Elf said. "I can only stop humans."

Elliot laughed like that was ridiculous. "Humans down here?" he said, slapping at his leg. "What is the Underworld coming to?"

The Elf looked at Elliot. "You don't look like an Elf to me."

"He's a young one," Harold said. "And notice the long legs. The rest of him will grow soon."

"No, it's in the face. It doesn't have the smooth beauty of Elfish skin. The eyes, there's too much fear in them for an Elf."

Elliot tried to get rid of the fear in his eyes, but that's not as easy as it sounds. The harder he tried, the more afraid he got that he couldn't get rid of the fear.

"Of course I'm an Elf," he said, then his eyes widened. "In fact, I'm so much an Elf that it's the initials of my name."

"Oh? What's your name?"

Elliot looked around. Suddenly he didn't want to say his full name. Not with Harold listening anyway. He leaned in close to the Elf female and whispered, "Elliot Louise Penster."

Dear Reader, clever as you are, you no doubt picked up on Elliot's middle name: Louise. And, yes, it is a girl's name. Here's how it happened. When Elliot was born, his middle name was supposed to be Louis. He would be named after his grandfather, Louis Penster, who was a war hero, a fighter pilot, and, lately, the slowest driver in the fast lane of the highway. The nurse who wrote down Elliot's name was very smart at nursing, but she was a terrible speller. This is because as a child, she played nurse on her dolls when she was supposed to be studying her spelling words. So when she wrote the birth certificate, she put an *e* on the end of Elliot's middle name, thus making him Elliot Louise Penster for life. His parents were saving up the money to get his birth certificate changed, but the money always seemed to go to other needs, like dinner.

"Elliot Louise Penster?" the Elf said. "Your initials spell ELP." (Apparently, the Elf was better at spelling than Elliot's nurse.) "And it sounds like a human name."

Elliot laughed. "Human name, yes, my parents—who are Elves, of course—are big fans of humans. In fact, that's the rest of my name. Elliot Louise Penster Human. E-L-P-H. That spells Elph."

Elliot was very good at spelling. And you have to agree, Dear Reader, that sometimes he is a very good thinker.

"Elph," the Elf said. "Let me see your ears."

Elliot turned his head so that she could inspect his ears. She tugged on them and twisted them until he said, "Ouch." That was the second time today someone had pulled on his ears.

"Very well," the Elf said. "You may proceed through Demon Territory. I advise you to be careful and stay on the path."

"Of course," Harold said.

They walked past the sign, then Elliot turned back and asked the Elf, "By the way, can you tell me where Kovol is? We'll have an easier time avoiding him if we know where he is."

"When the air around you is so black that you cannot see your hand in front of your face, then you have found Kovol," she said.

"So stay away from the pitch black. Good advice." Elliot thanked her and then ran to catch up to Harold. "Thanks for coming with me. I feel a lot better not being here alone."

"You are alone, because I'm leaving," Harold said. "But I must admit, I feel a little bad about helping you get killed. That doesn't seem right somehow. If you do die in here, I'll never be able to look at my face in the mirror again, which, of course, will be your face. Listen, I hate to do this, because I really love Cami, but I'm going to help you."

"You're coming with me to find Kovol?" Elliot asked.

"No way. I feel bad, but I'm not stupid." Harold withdrew a small bottle from his pocket. "This is some of that invisibility potion from my—I mean you and Cami's science fair project. I snuck it away because I wanted to test it when nobody else was around. You can rub this on you. It'll make you invisible while you pass through Demon Territory. You could move right past a Shadow Man, and he wouldn't even know it."

Elliot took the bottle. "How long does it last?"

"I don't know, but I tried some on myself and I stayed invisible until I shapeshifted again."

"Are you sure it works? Maybe you just shapeshifted yourself invisible."

Harold laughed. "I think I'd know if I were making myself invisible. Just use the potion, and if you hurry, you might get all the way to Kovol and out of Demon Territory before it wears off."

Elliot started to thank Harold, but he disappeared before Elliot got the words out. Elliot stared at the bottle, then put it in his back pocket. He decided to wait as long as possible before using it. It was still a little light here, so he doubted he'd run into any Shadow Men yet.

"Elliot?" Patches was in the middle of saying his name even as she poofed in front of him. She wrung her hands together, and her eyes darted around. She didn't seem to like where she was, but then, who would? (Other than evil Demon armies, of course.) "I'm glad I found you. It's very hard to poof in here, since it's so dark."

"Patches, I want you to go home," Elliot said. "It's dangerous here."

"If it's dangerous for me, then it's dangerous for you too."

"If your dad finds out I let you come with me to find Kovol, *he'll* be more dangerous to me than Kovol could ever be."

Patches frowned. "Yeah, that's probably true. But I tried to tell you something before you came here. I read a story a while back about why humans can't enter Demon Territory. The story said what keeps Kovol asleep is an agreement that no human will ever disturb the peace of his territory." Her eyes widened. "Elliot, I think you're disturbing the peace of his territory!"

Elliot paused a moment, then whispered. "Is the story fiction or nonfiction?"

Patches wound up her face. "Which is which?"

Elliot shrugged. "Can't remember. I thought you'd know. Was the story about Kovol sleeping a real one or made up?"

"I don't know. But what if it's real, Elliot? What if you've already woken him up?"

Once, Elliot had woken up Reed for breakfast without knowing he had already been up all night on a double shift at the Quack Shack. Reed had said a few words that would've made their mother's ears melt, then threw his Quack Shack cap at Elliot. Elliot had been more careful about waking up sleeping people since then.

Waking up evil Demons was probably worse.

Elliot put his hand on Agatha's flashlight and forced a smile onto his face. "I don't think the story is real. But even if it is, I'm not disturbing his peace. Just getting what I need and leaving."

Patches wrapped her arms around Elliot's waist. "You're the best king the Brownies have ever had," she whispered. "Hurry and get the hair and the sock, then get out."

"I will," Elliot said. "Now go home and be safe." Patches poofed away as Elliot took his next step deeper into Demon Territory.

He was certain it was already getting darker.

Where Elliot Tests
the Invisibility Potion

N ear the Philippine Islands is an underwater canyon known as the Mariana Trench, which goes down almost seven miles beneath the surface of the ocean. It's deeper there than Mount Everest is tall. Light can't break through all the water to reach the bottom, so if you want to ask how dark it is, the answer, in scientific terms, is "super dark."

Elliot has never been to the bottom of the Mariana Trench (which is probably good, since the pressure of being in water that deep would crush him like a bulldozer running over a soda can). But Elliot didn't need to go to the Mariana Trench to understand true darkness.

All he had to do is look at the trail leading deeper into Demon Territory. Even from where he stood, the air was so dark he couldn't see the colors of things anymore. Everything around him was in shades of gray and brown. Or maybe everything in Demon Territory really was gray and brown. It would be silly to call it Demon Territory if it were all happy pastels.

But the trail narrowed ahead and looked like the kind of darkness where he could put his hand in front of his face and, if he was lucky, maybe see his fingers. But Elliot didn't care too much about seeing his fingers. His fingers weren't going to try to kill him.

The Shadow Men might. And they were somewhere ahead of him on the trail.

Elliot felt for the bottle of invisibility potion Harold had given him. It was still in his back pocket. How dumb, he thought, snorting in the air. Invisibility potion. What a stupid idea for a science project. If there was a potion that could turn people invisible, some company would already be selling it for fifty dollars a bottle.

Or maybe nobody knew about the potion yet. Harold said he had tried it and that it had worked on him. Maybe Elliot could sell it and make fifty dollars a bottle. Or more likely, Harold had accidentally turned himself invisible just because he wanted Cami's project to work.

Either way, Elliot wasn't going to use it on himself yet. Not until he had to.

He wondered again what his family was doing right now. Uncle Rufus hadn't stolen anything since he'd met Agatha. But had anything shiny caught his eye since Elliot had been gone? Had Reed gotten any more pickle relish from the Quack Shack? Whatever Wendy was burning for dinner tonight, Harold got to eat it, not him.

Sometimes when Kyle and Cole were flooding things, Wendy was burning things, and Uncle Rufus was stealing things, Elliot had wondered what it'd be like to live with another, more normal family.

He'd only been gone a few days, and yet he missed them—flooded, burned, stolen things, and all. Odd or not, they were his family.

It was time to finish this job and go home.

Elliot took several long steps forward, then stopped. The sky had darkened. He felt for the flashlight at his side. *Not yet,* a voice inside him said.

Dear Reader, we all have a voice inside our head. It keeps us safe and helps us remember things we have to do. Usually when Elliot listens to the voice, he's very glad he did. You should listen to the voice inside your head too, unless the voice tells you to cut your sister's hair while she's asleep. If that happens, it might not be your own voice inside your head. Instead, it's probably an evil spell that a wizard put on you as his idea of a joke.

If you have an evil spell on you, dump all of your mother's salt on your bedroom floor, then stand on your head and kick your feet in the air. Your mother might be mad at first, but if you explain that you're just getting rid of an evil spell, she'll probably understand.

So Elliot walked deeper into Demon Territory, but after only a short distance, something changed. He heard a whisper in the air, a breath, a hiss.

Elliot looked at the tree beside him, with claw-like branches and long, spiny, gray leaves. The leaves were perfectly still. There was no wind here.

Then something moved on his right. Elliot's heart pounded. Cold sweat licked his palms. He had an itch in the middle of his back too, but that wasn't from fear. It just itched sometimes.

Elliot swung to his left at another sound. The trees beside him shivered as if something terrible was hiding there.

The Shadow Men had come.

With trembling fingers, Elliot grabbed the bottle of invisibility potion. That voice inside him said to test it on his finger first, but Elliot told the voice to be quiet. It was one thing for the voice to be sitting safely inside Elliot's head giving him orders, and a whole other thing for Elliot to be alone in Demon Territory with Shadow Men coming toward him.

Elliot pulled out the cork stopper and dumped the potion all over him. It tingled on his skin, like extra-fizzy soda pop. As quickly as he could, he rubbed it in, on his clothes, his skin, in his hair, everywhere but his eyes. For a brief moment he wondered if the potion would make his eyes go invisible, or if the Shadow Men would see nothing but a pair of eyes floating in midair. Maybe that would scare *them* for a change.

The tingling slowly faded, but the potion left his skin feeling greasy, even slippery. He didn't care. If Harold was right, he'd soon see himself start to become invisible, then he could slip right past the Shadow Men and get to Kovol.

Elliot raised a hand in front of his face. It was so dark, it was hard to tell whether he actually was fading, but he thought he could still see himself.

Maybe that was how invisibility potions worked. Maybe he could always see himself, but nobody else could.

He decided to continue walking, conducting a little science experiment of his own. If the Shadow Men reached out and grabbed him in a few minutes, then, no, he was not invisible at all.

Experiments like this were why Elliot didn't like science projects.

There was more shuffling in the trees ahead. Something was definitely in there, watching, waiting for him to come closer.

Elliot walked a little farther, but he must have been moving away from Kovol now, because the area around Elliot seemed to be getting lighter, almost like he was carrying a soft yellow lamp.

Elliot was not carrying a soft yellow lamp. In fact, he wasn't carrying anything either soft or yellow. He had Agatha's flashlight strapped to his side like a sword, but it was turned off.

So what was causing the glow?

Elliot raised his hand in front of his face and gasped in horror. The invisibility potion was supposed to make him invisible, supposed to make it possible for him to slip past the Shadow Men without them being able to see him.

But somehow it had done just the opposite. The soft yellow glow was coming from him. Every part of his body that was covered in the potion was glowing. Elliot was the lantern!

And instead of being invisible to the Shadow Men, he was a beacon of light in the darkness. They could all find him now.

Chapter 19

Where Elliot Is Stuck Again

He was homesick, tired, and so scared that he could barely move a muscle. But mostly Elliot felt stupid. Harold probably did believe the potion would turn Elliot invisible. So even though Harold was trying to help, maybe that annoying voice inside Elliot's head was right. Elliot should have tested the potion on his finger before pouring the entire bottle all over himself.

Dumb voice, being right all the time.

There was nothing for Elliot to do now but run. He ran the way he used to when Tubs would chase him across Sprite's Hollow. No, he ran faster, the way he did that time he'd run from Cami when a game of kissing tag broke out during recess.

He was lightning. He was a cheetah. He was—Elliot groaned as his foot landed in something familiar—he was stuck in gripping mud again.

Elliot struggled to pull his feet out, which only got him stuck deeper. Patches had told him before that he couldn't get out of gripping mud on his own. She was right all the time too.

Around him, Elliot saw the dark outlines of dozens of Shadow Men swarm in a circle around the gripping mud. He could feel the heat of their anger that he'd invaded their territory. Or maybe it really was heat. It was a warm night, after all, and he was beginning to sweat. They hissed at him and held out shadowy hands to pull him free. Yeah, they'd love to help him get out. Help him get out so they could finish him off.

These Shadow Men were far more frightening than the one Harold had turned into back at Sprite's Hollow. He could see into their eyes, or the empty holes that served as their eyes. They were without souls, just smoke and fire without light, whose only order was to serve Kovol. And serving Kovol meant killing any human who dared enter Kovol's territory.

Elliot braced himself for the worst. There was nothing he could do to fight them from here, and obviously his attempt at running away from them had failed. Would they get stuck in the gripping mud too? They didn't seem to touch the ground, so probably not.

They were trying to reach him, but Elliot noticed it didn't seem to be working. A Shadow Man would almost touch Elliot, but about the time he reached the glow on Elliot's skin, he'd stop and back off, then hiss in anger.

Elliot didn't like the hissing. It was different than a snake's hiss—which he didn't like too much either—but instead was a whispered screech. It made the hairs stand up on his arms and neck. Even in the warm night, goose bumps crawled down his spine.

They were angry. But they weren't coming any closer.

Another Shadow Man tried. He pushed just inside Elliot's glow with a shadowy hand, then Elliot noticed the hand disappeared. The Shadow Man yanked his hand back into the darkness with a different sort of hiss. This one was of panic, of pain.

Elliot raised his hand to his face again. He was putting off light. Light makes shadows disappear. Which means light makes Shadow Men disappear.

The glow from the invisibility potion may have called all the Shadow Men in Demon Territory to him, but as long as he glowed, they couldn't touch him. In a really strange way, he was safe.

Except, of course, that he was still sinking in gripping mud.

Someone needed to poof here to help him. Not Mr. Willimaker, who was currently locked in a Fairy prison. Not Patches. She'd come if he called her, but Elliot refused to put her in danger.

The only one he could think of was Fudd.

But was Fudd working with the Fairies? Mr. Willimaker had thought there was a chance that Fudd was helping the Fairies stop Elliot. Then the Fairies had taken Mr. Willimaker away, leaving Elliot alone against Kovol. If

Kovol succeeded in getting rid of him, Elliot had already asked Fudd to be the Brownie king.

Elliot didn't want to believe that Fudd was betraying him again. And lately everything about Fudd told him that the Brownie could be trusted. But if he was wrong, asking Fudd to help him get free of the gripping mud might be the very worst plan possible.

Elliot sank a little deeper into the gripping mud. Whether it was a good plan or not, it was his only choice.

Elliot cupped his hands around his mouth and yelled, "Fudd, I need you!"

The Shadow Men didn't like that. They began spinning in a circle around the mud. The air around Elliot thinned as the Shadow Men sucked it away from him. He wanted to call Fudd a second time but couldn't get a deep enough breath. He had to hope Fudd heard him the first time.

Elliot wanted to push his hand into the mud and find Agatha's flashlight. He could turn it on and chase all the Shadow Men away. But he knew that once he put his hand in the mud, it would be stuck in there too.

"Fudd!" he called, more softly.

Although the Shadow Men were removing the air, if anything, the heat around Elliot was building. He wiped a bead of sweat off his forehead and then groaned as drips of light fell from his hand. Elliot was alone, surrounded by Shadow Men, stuck in gripping mud, and the one thing keeping the Shadow Men from reaching him was slowly sweating away.

Chapter
20

Where Fudd Gives an Order

Elliot was about to move to plan B in his hope of escaping the Shadow Men. Plan B was to cry like a baby and hope the Shadow Men became so embarrassed at being around him that they would decide he wasn't worth it. It wasn't a perfect plan, because Elliot knew that if he did it, he'd never be able to show his face in the Underworld again, but he was out of options.

And there was no plan C.

"Fudd," he breathed one last time.

"Your High—" Fudd said as he poofed in front of Elliot. His feet were at the very edge of the gripping mud, and he teetered forward as if he was about to fall in.

The Shadow Men advanced on Fudd, so Elliot stuck his arm as close to Fudd as he could reach, spreading barely enough light to protect him.

Fudd flapped his arms wildly to balance himself away from the mud, but it did no good, and he fell forward. A half second before he landed, however, he poofed himself away, poofing back almost instantly at a safer distance from the mud, though still within Elliot's light.

"My apologies for the delay," Fudd said. "It's very hard to find you in this darkness." He glanced back at the Shadow Men. "So this isn't going well."

"Stay as close to me as you can," Elliot said. "We're surrounded, but they can't touch me in this light. The more I sweat, the more the light is gone, though. I need your help to get out of here."

Fudd inched closer to Elliot. "I assume the gripping mud wasn't part of your plan."

"Of course not."

"Oh, good, because I couldn't help but think what a terrible plan that would have been. Like a rabbit hiding in the trap to escape the hunter."

"Just get me out of here!" Elliot scowled.

"Right away, Your Highness. Give me your hand." After a few grunts and several groans, Fudd pulled Elliot from the mud. Then he asked, "What do we do next?"

"Stay close and let me think," Elliot said. Warm mud dripped from his clothes, pulling the glowing potion off him with every drop.

Fudd didn't need to be reminded to stay close. He pushed so close to Elliot that there was no room for air between them.

Fudd tapped Elliot's shoulder to get his attention. "Back in Burrowsville, I've been reading about Kovol. Patches reminded me about the story with Kovol. She's right. Either Kovol is awake, or he soon will be."

"Kovol's awake?" Elliot shuddered. "That sounds bad."

Fudd shrugged. "If you think it'd be bad for the entire human race to collapse and be ruled by an army of the undead, then, yes, I suppose it is bad." He paused for a moment, then added, "I can help."

"I might not want any more of your help," Elliot said. "I'm not sure I can trust you."

Fudd looked at Elliot as if he'd been slapped. "Your Highness?"

"Mr. Willimaker is gone. The Fairies took him until I get Kovol's"—Elliot paused and wondered if the Shadow Men were listening—"until I do something for them too. Did the Fairies contact you?"

Fudd's eyes widened and he drew his hands together. "Can we talk about this when we're not surrounded by hundreds of creepy Demon servants?"

"Hundreds? Mr. Willimaker told me there'd only be fifty."

Fudd shook his head. "Based on the numbers here, I suspect there's closer to fifty thousand Shadow Men in Demon Territory."

A trickle of sweat rolled down Elliot's cheek. He wiped it free and saw the light so dim around his body that the Shadow Men could now get within inches of him. He began backing away with Fudd on his toes at every step.

"The flashlight," Elliot whispered.

"Not yet. It's for the darkest of dark places." Fudd's voice shook as he spoke. "I'm afraid there are darker places ahead of you."

"It's dark enough. I can't see where we're going."

"Your light is almost gone," Fudd said. "But I can't poof you away. My magic is too weak right now."

"Last night, Mr. Willimaker made a cold fire in his hand. Are you strong enough to do that?"

"Yes, but it's not enough light for the two of us." Fudd glanced up at Elliot. "The Fairies did ask for my help, but I told them no. After the Goblin war, when I said I'd never again betray you, I meant it. You are my king." Fudd flattened his palm, and instantly a spark of fire appeared on it. He placed it onto Elliot's hand, who thought it was surprisingly cool amid all the heat created by the Shadow Men. It gave off enough light to surround Elliot, but the light wasn't enough for Fudd. "This will only burn for a few minutes," Fudd said. "Run fast."

Elliot shook his head. "What about you? Make more fire."

"I can't. Not yet. I'll run in the other direction. Without a light, the Shadow Men will follow me instead of you. I'll run for as long as I can and then poof away."

"Don't get caught," Elliot said. "That's a king's order."

"There won't be much time, so don't you get caught either. That's a friend's order." After a short bow, Fudd poofed himself away. He must have reappeared at a close distance from the Shadow Men, because Elliot heard him yell, "Hey, Shadow Men! You can't catch Brownies or Goblins or Elves. You're so slow, you can't catch yourselves!"

Almost instantly the Shadow Men turned from Elliot and swarmed toward Fudd. Elliot took off in the direction where Demon Territory looked darkest, although he didn't dare run too fast. Not only was he afraid the breeze would blow out the small, cold flame that danced on his hand, but it also didn't throw light very far ahead of him. The last thing he needed was to run into more gripping mud.

He ran until his lungs ached and then ran until worry made his lungs do little flips in his chest (which can really hurt, if you think about it). Fudd had said he wouldn't be able to give Elliot a lot of time to get away. But it had been a long time and Elliot still hadn't seen any more Shadow Men. Did that mean Fudd hadn't been able to poof away before they caught him?

Elliot made a promise to himself. If he, Fudd, Mr. Willimaker, and, yes, even Tubs, made it out of this alive, Elliot would never enter Demon Territory again. Not even if they put up the best theme park ever and let him come for free. Not even if they had the fastest, tallest roller coaster and no long lines. But…what if they also gave free cotton candy?

Elliot shook that thought out of his head. Now was not the time to think about cotton candy. That soft, sticky, sweet, chewy sugar rush. It was a good thing he wasn't thinking about it, because otherwise he wouldn't have noticed that his fire had burned out. And that the air around him was so black, it would have even put out a firefly's light (if a firefly were stupid enough to come in here).

Elliot froze, not sure where he was or where he should go next. About the only thing he was sure of was that the snores he now heard could only be coming from the most evil tonsils in the Underworld.

Somehow, Elliot had found Kovol.

Chapter 21

Where the Flashlight Is Turned On

Kovol wasn't awake. Or at least Elliot was pretty sure he wasn't awake *yet*. He'd never heard anyone snore when they were awake, and that was definitely snoring.

He thought back to the night when all of this had started, when Tubs's snoring had kept Elliot awake half the night. He sort of wished he hadn't complained about that snoring, because this was much, much worse.

Elliot figured he must be in some kind of cave, because the air moved whenever Kovol breathed. When he snorted air in, a cold wind blew from behind Elliot's back toward Kovol. And when Kovol exhaled, the foulest smell rushed at Elliot's face, like rotting, decomposing eggs.

Demon morning breath.

So Kovol was asleep, but he seemed to be rolling around a lot, as if he was restless. As if he knew a human was in this cave with him. He could wake up at any second.

Elliot kept one hand by his flashlight, ready to flip it on as soon as he had to. He knew he'd have to use it soon, because he couldn't find a sock and a hair without it, not in this darkness. But he didn't want to turn it on too early and have the light wake up Kovol. He crept forward on tiptoes, testing every footstep before he put his full weight down. Snails moved faster than him, but he didn't care. He had only one chance at this.

With every step, he was closer to Kovol. He stopped every time the snoring stopped and it sounded as if Kovol rolled over. Then the snoring would begin again, and he'd continue forward. Once or twice it sounded as if Kovol had stopped breathing entirely for a second or two, but he always started again with his next snore.

Dear Reader, there is a condition known as sleep apnea in which a creature might stop breathing entirely for a second or two. This is not just for evil Demons. Several humans have it too. If you have this condition, you are lucky, because a doctor can treat it, and you'll be fine. Sadly, no doctor can help Kovol, mostly because Kovol would likely rip the doctor's arms off first. If you have a condition where you stop breathing for an hour or two rather than just a second or two, this is not sleep apnea. This means you're dead, and you should go see a doctor right away, even before you finish reading this book, no matter how exciting this chapter is.

After twenty steps, the snoring was so loud that Elliot was sure Kovol was within an arm's reach of him. He silently pulled out his flashlight and then put the lens inside his shirt so that when he turned it on, it would give off only dim light.

He flipped it on, then immediately turned the light toward his body. It was very bright. Bright like a miniature sun were inside it. Of course, Agatha had said it got its light from the sun. Elliot didn't understand how this flashlight worked, but magical tool design was hardly his biggest concern right now.

Even with the lens pressed against his skin, Elliot had enough light to see the dim outlines of Kovol's body. He was asleep but kept stretching and rolling over like he was trying to wake up. It must be hard to wake up when you've been asleep for a thousand years.

Kovol slept on a flat rock that seemed to have molded to his body while he slept. Like memory foam, but less comfortable. He was very tall, at least twice Elliot's height, maybe more. He was dressed with only a cloth around his waist and had leathery purple skin. His ears were long and pointed, and the horns on his head were gray, sharp, and twisted. His hands were gnarled with long fingers and fingernails that ended in spiked points. The skull of something that once might have been human was cuddled under his arm, like the Demon version of a teddy bear.

Elliot aimed the reflection of his light toward Kovol's feet. How could the Fairies possibly have wanted a sock? Anyone who looked like this, dressed like this, wasn't going to wear—oh, there they were. His socks.

Maybe sleeping in a cave for a thousand years gives a creature cold feet. Kovol's socks were long and thick, made of the skins of some animal Elliot didn't recognize.

Elliot stood as close as he dared to Kovol's feet and tried to ignore the stink that came from them. Maybe this was why his mother always told Elliot to sleep with his socks off, so he didn't have foot sweat at night.

Demon foot sweat was pretty awful. Like sticking your head into a garbage can full of old, rotten fruit that's been baking in the sun for a week.

Elliot stuffed the flashlight into his pants so that he could free both hands. He put his fingers on the sock closest to him and very slowly rolled it down Kovol's meaty leg, then over his shin, then—Kovol yawned, a wide yawn that reeked of moldy fish, and he turned over. His movement trapped the sock Elliot had been unrolling under Kovol's other leg.

Elliot made a "why me?" gesture with his hands. He'd made it this far with more problems than anyone deserved. Couldn't he get a break for once?

He pinched the new sock between his fingers. This one was already resting at Kovol's ankle, so he decided to pull it off from the evil Demon's toes, like pulling off a glove.

He pulled very slowly, pausing every time Kovol twitched or stopped snoring. After what seemed like hours, Elliot finally pulled the last of the sock off his foot. Even while asleep, Kovol must not have liked the feel of only one sock, because he pushed the remaining sock off with his big Demon toe.

Elliot picked it up and put both socks in his pocket. That way, if he lost one he'd have a spare. Elliot took a deep breath. Halfway there. This wouldn't be so bad.

Then Elliot crept up to the top of Kovol's body, standing beside his head. The Demon yawned, revealing a long row of spiky teeth.

He tilted the flashlight just enough to see Kovol's head. All he needed was one hair, so he'd pull it, then get out.

But Elliot hadn't expected this.

There was no hair. Whatever Kovol had looked like when the Pixies last saw him, he was very different now. He was a bald Demon.

Elliot leaned in closer to Kovol. There was no hair on the rock slab, although the way Kovol created a wind with every snore, he'd probably scattered his fallen hair all over Demon Territory.

One hair, surely Kovol had one hair left.

Elliot needed a little more of the light from the flashlight, and he worried because Kovol's snoring had turned to softer breathing. The light probably bothered him.

There! Right on the center of his head. One long, coal black hair that had been lost in the shadows. One hair. That's all Kovol had left and all Elliot needed.

He rubbed his fingers together to get rid of any sweat on them and then pinched the hair between his thumb and forefinger. Elliot held his breath and closed his eyes tight as he plucked the hair.

He had it! Kovol's socks and Kovol's hair. Elliot shoved the hair into his pocket and then raised his arm again to steady the flashlight.

Only something grabbed his arm with a grip so tight that Elliot wondered if it would pinch his hand off.

Elliot looked up and found himself staring directly into eyes as black as the deepest darkness and full of anger that could only belong to something truly terrible.

Kovol was awake.

Jennifer A. Nielsen

Chapter
22

Where Elliot Had Better Run Fast

Kovol yanked Elliot into the air, hanging him by his arm. He yelled out something in words Elliot couldn't understand. They probably weren't words at all, unless there's a word in Demon language that sounds like "Arrroooowwagh!"

If there is a word in Demon language that sounds like "Arrroooowwagh," then it probably means, "It's not polite to pull my hair out when I'm sleeping. Now I have to kill you."

Elliot screamed back at him. Not *at* him, really, because who'd be stupid enough to scream in a Demon's face? But Elliot did scream something that sounded like, "Waaahh," which, as all humans know, means, "I have to use the bathroom really bad."

The Demon dropped him to the ground and growled, "What have you done?" His voice sounded like the roar of a rockslide down a mountain.

"I needed a hair," Elliot tried to explain. "For the Pixies."

Kovol ran his hand over his scalp. His eyes widened and went from shock to anger to rage. "You made me go bald, human."

"I only took one hair," Elliot said.

"And before you took it, I had hair. Now I'm bald."

If this had been a less serious moment, Elliot would have pictured Kovol in a wig. But it was a very serious moment, not the time for Demons in wigs.

"I'm sorry," Elliot said. "Please let me go."

Kovol laughed. Not in a funny, ha-ha sort of way, but in an evil, prepare-to-die sort of way. "No human goes free from Kovol. And because of you, I will now destroy every human on the face of this planet!"

Well, that's all Elliot needed. To be forever branded as the kid who got Earth destroyed. Who'd want to be his friend now?

"I'll start with you," Kovol said. "It will take a hundred years to fully finish you off, and I will enjoy every moment of it. Where to start? I think with your legs."

Elliot fell to his back. As Kovol reached for him, Elliot fumbled with the flashlight, pulled it out of his pants, and shone it directly into the evil Demon's eyes.

Kovol made a new scream this time. Not of anger or revenge, but of pain. He clutched at his eyes and stumbled backward onto the stone slab.

Elliot scrambled to his feet and raced out of the cave. This time, with the help of the flashlight, he could see exactly where he was going. It was a good thing he hadn't seen the cave before. It was creepier than he had imagined, with moss and giant spider webs, and rats running along the sides of the walls. Something was hanging in a corner of the cave, but he didn't have time to figure out what. And there were bound to be snakes here too. Giant ones with ten heads that had big poisonous fangs.

Elliot heard Kovol running behind him. The Demon's feet shook the ground, and rocks tumbled to the ground beside Elliot with each of Kovol's steps. Elliot cleared the cave and paused briefly to decide which direction to run in to leave Demon Territory. Which way were the Shadow Men? Which way was the closest border?

As if he knew.

So he chose the easiest path, where there was a sort of trail between thorny bushes and dense, overgrown trees. Kovol crashed through the trees behind him and emitted a howl that Elliot instinctively knew was calling the Shadow Men to him.

Elliot kept running. His heart pounded so fiercely inside him that he could barely breathe, but as he found out, you don't really have to breathe to run, not if you're running to keep from having your legs ripped off.

The air warmed around Elliot, which normally he would have thought was because he was running so fast. But this was hardly a normal time, so he knew it was warming because the Shadow Men were getting closer. In the light from the flashlight he saw smoke rising like black vapor from their bodies. They were coming to serve Kovol. They were coming for Elliot.

It sounded like the Shadow Men were coming from the right, so Elliot darted to the left. He almost darted into an area with a brown glow hanging over it, but this time he stopped himself, barely avoiding landing in the very same patch of gripping mud where he had fallen last time.

Elliot tiptoed around the gripping mud, but he had to hurry. With the flashlight on, it was easy for both Kovol and his army to know where Elliot was. He had to get away.

Or did he?

A plan formed in Elliot's mind. It was dangerous, and his mother would have killed him if she had known what he was about to try. But not getting killed was the whole idea of his plan.

"Help!" Elliot cried. It wasn't hard to make his voice sound panicked. Even with a plan in mind, he was still in a pretty good panic.

Somewhere behind him, Kovol adjusted his path to run more directly toward Elliot. He heard Kovol's laugh as he sent another howl into the air. Elliot could feel the Shadow Men getting closer. He hoped Kovol would reach him first.

He crouched low in some thick, prickly weeds beside the patch of gripping mud. Within seconds, Kovol crashed through, and just as Elliot had almost done, Kovol ran straight into the gripping mud.

Kovol thrashed around violently, which of course made him stuck even worse. Elliot shook his head. When Kovol had time to think about this moment later on—and Elliot intended to make sure he had a long time to think about it later on—he was going to feel pretty stupid about the thrashing.

Elliot stuck the handle of the flashlight into the dirt, too far away for Kovol to reach it, but at such an angle that it threw light all around the Demon's body.

The Shadow Men swarmed in to the sound of Kovol's angry screeches. They seemed to have forgotten all about Elliot. They kept trying to push into the light to reach their master, but each time any part of the light touched them, they vanished within it. They hissed in anger and frustration. Trapped inside the mud, Kovol gnashed his teeth and cursed his army for their failures.

Kovol turned to Elliot. In a voice that was so calm it sent a chill up Elliot's spine, he said, "One day a solar eclipse will put out that flashlight. When it does, my army will free me. Watch for me that night, human, because I will come for you and destroy everything. You will regret the day you awoke me."

If Elliot had any ability to speak right then, he might have told Kovol that he already regretted this day. But it seemed a little too late for apologies. Kovol didn't seem like the forgiving type.

So he pushed out his chest and forced himself to sound brave as he said, "I'll be ready for you, Kovol. If you're smart, when you get out of this gripping mud you'll just go back to sleep. I've defeated you once, and I can do it again."

He wasn't sure that was true, but he liked the way it sounded. And it really made Kovol angry. Kovol began slapping at the gripping mud again, trying to reach Elliot.

Elliot stood as far from Kovol as he dared, but as close to the flashlight as he could. Here was an interesting problem. As soon as he left the light, the Shadow Men would get him. In trapping Kovol, he'd trapped himself.

Chapter 23

Where Elliot Likes Eagles

Elliot was in the middle of what he called half of a perfect plan. This must be why his father always said to never do a job halfway. Although Kovol was stuck and the Shadow Men couldn't reach him, Elliot was stuck too.

Above Elliot came a familiar squawk. He looked up and his eyes went as wide as manhole covers (well, almost as wide. Eyes can only stretch so far). "Harold!"

Harold the Eagle circled in the air over Elliot. The Shadow Men leapt up, trying to reach him, but Harold could always fly higher than they could leap.

"Your Highness!" Fudd called from Harold's back. "We're here to rescue you! Hold out your arms."

Elliot obeyed. Immediately Harold soared down, moving faster than the Shadow Men had time to react, darting between them like a fly that can't be swatted. He picked up Elliot with a giant talon and yanked him back into the air.

As they lifted off, a Shadow Man leaped forward and grabbed hold of Elliot's leg. Elliot felt the burn of his grip and yelled, but he could not shake him off.

"I'll save you, sir!" Fudd jumped off Harold's back and landed on the Shadow Man, holding him by the shoulders. The Shadow Man hissed and spat something into Fudd's eyes. Fudd reared back, yelping in pain. In his flailing around, Fudd kicked the Shadow Man, who released Elliot's leg. Both the Shadow Man and Fudd started to fall, but Elliot grabbed Fudd by the back of his pants, and Harold lifted them higher into the air.

The Shadow Man tumbled to the ground, landing in a burst of smoke and flame. Other Shadow Men hovered beneath them as they flew, hoping for a chance at Fudd or Elliot.

"I can't see!" Fudd cried. "He blinded me."

"You'll be okay," Elliot said, although he wasn't sure that was true.

"Let me go," Fudd said. "I'm slowing you down!"

"Just stop wiggling," Elliot said. "I can hold you."

Harold cawed that he was flying as fast as he could. And he was flying really fast. Elliot wasn't sure how he knew which way to go, because even up here Demon Territory was very, very dark.

Slowly, the Underworld light began to get brighter like an airplane moving down through clouds to reveal the city below. There are no clouds in the Underworld, Dear Reader, and certainly no airplanes, but you probably get the idea.

Soft pastel light filled the horizon in front of Elliot, a sunrise that could only happen in a mythological world. He described it to Fudd, who said, "It's the last painting of the Star Dancers each night. How I shall miss seeing it."

Every color of the rainbow found its way into the morning light, except pastel black, because there's no such thing. It was warm in a comforting sort of way, and Elliot felt his body relax just to cross into it.

He'd been in Demon Territory all night. In a place that never saw sun and never felt any sort of warmth that didn't burn.

Harold paused on the ground long enough for both Fudd and Elliot to climb onto his back, and then Elliot ordered Harold to take them directly to Glimmering Woods.

"Wouldn't you rather go to Burrowsville and rest first?" Fudd asked. "We've made you some new clothes. Better clothes."

The clothes Elliot wore were now muddy, burned, and soaked in sweat. He didn't mind that he had ruined them. It saved him the trouble of telling the Brownies there was no way he could wear them back to his home.

"Patches can bring the clothes to Glimmering Woods," Elliot said. "I want to see what can be done about your injury. And I want to get Tubs and Mr. Willimaker back."

"Don't worry about me," Fudd said. "But, Your Highness, I'm concerned about you giving the hair and sock to the Pixies and Fairies. We've had a treaty agreeing to stay out of their battle for the Glimmering Woods. Whatever you do may change that."

"That's okay," Elliot said. "I have a plan for that too." Then he asked, "When did Harold come back from the surface world?"

"When I ran from the Shadow Men, they were a little slow to follow, because it was really you they wanted. But they couldn't get you with the light, so they finally came for me. I ran and ran and bumped straight into Harold. He came back to tell you that he had tested the invisibility potion again and not to use it. So I bet Harold that he couldn't save both me and you without getting caught by the Shadow Men."

Elliot laughed and patted Harold on what he thought was an eagle's shoulder. "You took this bet. What did you win?"

Harold shrieked, then said, "I get full rights to your life whenever you're not using it anymore."

Elliot smiled. "Okay, but for the record, I can hardly wait to get back to my life. You'll have a while to wait."

Harold did whatever an eagle would do if it could shrug. Elliot lay on his back as they flew and just closed his eyes for a little rest.

Chapter 24

Where the Fairies and Pixies Find Something They Can Agree On

It didn't take long after Elliot arrived in Glimmering Woods for the Fairies to gather. It would take the Pixies longer, Harold explained. They were doing their hair.

Elliot hadn't really met the Fairies before. They hadn't bothered to say hi while they were stealing Mr. Willimaker.

They looked young, but not childish the way Pixies did. They were very beautiful, with flawless skin and elegant pastel clothes. They were a little larger than the Pixies and could also fly, although they had no wings.

A female Fairy flew up to Elliot and introduced herself as Aphid Flutterby. It was too bad he couldn't tell his brother Reed about the Fairies, because he would instantly fall in love with her long, coal-black hair and eyes as bright as a summer sky. "So, like, we have no royalty," Aphid said. "But I can totally speak for the Fairies."

Elliot smiled. "You speak like Fidget."

Aphid's mouth dropped open. "Fidget Spitfly, the Pixie princess? Like, gag me! I so totally don't. I speak like the humans on the totally awesomest show ever, *Surfer Teen*. Do you know the show?"

"I so totally do," Elliot said.

This seemed to make Aphid happy. "Do you have the sock?"

"Do you have Mr. Willimaker?"

Aphid nodded. "Totally. He's been chilling with us. If you ever want to enjoy captivity, Fairies are way nicer than those lame Pixies."

"I'll keep that in mind," Elliot said. "Now I want to see him."

Aphid nodded her head, and in a flash of light Mr. Willimaker appeared beside them. He fell to his knees and with tears in his eyes said, "King Elliot, I thought I'd never see you again. And no offense, but you look awful."

Elliot could hardly be offended at that. He knew how bad he looked.

"Like, you couldn't have come back at a worse time," a voice behind Elliot said. He turned and saw Fidget fluttering in the air behind him. "I was totally about to get my nails done." Then Fidget pointed at the Fairies. "What are *they* doing here?"

"Since you forced the human to help you, we decided to do the same," Aphid said, cocking her head in anger.

"That's so not awesome," Fidget scowled. "My daddy is going to be totally mad at me!" She turned to Elliot. "So did you get the hair or not?"

"And we want the sock," Aphid demanded.

"Where's Tubs?" Elliot asked.

Fidget groaned. "Like, give me the hair, and I'll return him to the surface. We're totally tired of him anyway. He never stops eating. I'm so grossed out."

"You have to return him with no memory of the Underworld," Elliot said.

"Duh! Do you think we want a grody human like that knowing about us? When he goes back, he won't remember any of this. Now, where's the hair?"

"Where's the sock?" Aphid said.

Elliot pulled a sock from each pocket.

"Two of them?" Aphid said, eyeing Fidget. "That's so awesome! Twice the power against Pixies."

"I can smell them from here," Fidget said. "They're, like, totally gagging me. You'd better have gotten two hairs then."

"Kovol had only one left," Elliot said. "But watch this." He pulled the hair from his pocket and tore it in half. Fidget's smile of triumph quickly faded as Elliot stuffed one hair in each sock. Then he held them out to Aphid and Fidget.

"I am so not touching that sock," Fidget said. "Even to get the hair."

"It's making me gag," Aphid said. "I totally won't take the sock as long as it has a hair inside."

"Suit yourselves," Elliot said, laying the socks on the ground. "But I did what

249

you each told me I had to do to get Tubs and Mr. Willimaker back. The Fairies have their sock, and the Pixies have their hair. It's not my problem if you don't want them now. But you have to keep your promises."

Fidget stamped her foot. "What-ever. " She waved her wand and then with a glare at Elliot said, "Pixies don't like to be tricked. Anyway, that human, Tubs, is home now. If there's any good news, it's that he's out of my hair. My beautiful, beautiful hair."

"The Fairies don't like to be tricked either," Aphid said. "And for the record, we have way better hair. But all we really wanted was to stop the Pixies, so at least after all this, nothing has changed."

"Actually, a lot has changed," Elliot said. "What you did got me to wake up Kovol, which means the entire Underworld will have to defend against him one day. My friend Fudd Fartwick was blinded in saving me from the Shadow Men. And I used to think Pixies and Fairies were pretty cool, but I don't think so anymore. If you want the Brownies to help you when Kovol does attack the Underworld, you'd better start being a lot nicer to me."

Aphid and Fidget glared at each other. "Gag me," Aphid said at the same time as Fidget said, "Totally gross." Then their eyes widened and they looked back at each other.

"*Surfer Teen?*" Fidget said.

"*Awesomest kid on the scene?*" Aphid added.

The Pixie and Fairy squealed in some high pitch that probably caused a lot of dogs on the surface world to howl.

"So whatever about the war, that's so my dad's thing anyway," Fidget said. "We can at least hang out to watch the show, right?"

Aphid nodded, then turned to Elliot. "Like, I totally thought you'd be killed in Demon Territory, human. No creature has ever come back from there. So I guess when Kovol attacks the Underworld, the Fairies will fight with you in battle."

"The Pixies too," Fidget said softly. "You were awesome. Totally."

"And you saved my dad," Patches said. Elliot wondered how long she'd been there. She handed Elliot some clothes. "I helped our tailor with the design. I think you'll like them."

"We'll take care of Fudd," Mr. Willimaker said.

"Can you fix his eyes?" Elliot asked.

Fudd shook his head. "We don't have that kind of magic or medicine. But you shouldn't worry about me. I'll be fine."

"And I'll be there to help you." Mr. Willimaker clapped a hand on Fudd's shoulder. "Sorry I lost trust in you, old friend."

Fudd smiled. "We're friends? But I don't even know your first name."

Minutes later, Elliot had cleaned up and changed into a T-shirt and brown cotton pants. The pants were a little goofy, but at least they were from the right century. He wasn't sure about the T-shirt, which read, BROWNIES ARE FOR HUGGING, NOT EATING, but it would have to do until he got home.

Harold had changed back into an Elf to say good-bye to Elliot. "I admit that I'm not totally sad you survived and get to go home," he said. "On the one hand, there's Cami and she's wonderful, but on the other hand, Kyle and Cole are very naughty twins. They dumped a big bucket of ice water on me yesterday while I was outside talking to her."

Elliot chuckled. "Yeah, they do things like that. I never thought I'd miss it."

"So your science project is due today," Harold said. "I've done your share of the work for it. The problem is that Cami never found anyone willing to test it, so she's not sure if it works."

"It doesn't," Elliot said. "I lit up like a glow stick."

"I know. But I couldn't tell her I'd tried it on myself. Obviously I made myself go invisible just to let her be right about the experiment."

"Will I see you around?" Elliot asked.

"I guess if you ever see yourself walking down the street, it's probably me."

"Don't do that," Elliot said. "One of me on the surface gets into plenty of trouble. Two of me would be too much."

"Hmm, we'll see." Harold changed himself to a sparrow. He began to fly away, then fluttered back and tweeted, "By the way, I'm really sorry about your bed."

"What about my bed?" Elliot asked, but it was too late. Harold was gone.

Where Fidget Does Elliot a Favor

Elliot wasn't sure what things would be like when the Pixies poofed him home. He'd been gone for days. He'd been a prisoner to the Pixies and survived a Goblin's attempt to scare him to death. He'd been trapped in gripping mud—twice, fought off Shadow Men, and defeated Kovol. So it would make sense if things were a little crazy on the surface too.

However, his family didn't know about any of that. Tubs wouldn't even know it, since the Pixies had wiped Tubs's memory of the entire Underworld.

The last thing Fidget had said before she waved her wand to poof him away was, "Okay, so like, I'm sorry about the whole kidnapping thing. I know just how to make it up to you."

He didn't like the sound of that, but she poofed him away before he could ask what she meant.

He returned to the surface just outside his home. It was a cool, crisp autumn morning, and Elliot enjoyed the feeling of sun on his face. Although the Underworld had plenty of light, he had missed the sun. The large bucket of invisibility potion was nearby. It was bubbling more than ever, and Elliot was glad that at least it had not blown up his home while he was gone.

Strange, the things that made him happy ever since he had become king.

Harold had said the science project was due today. Did that mean Elliot had to somehow get the potion to school? His parents were probably already at work, so getting the potion there would be Cami's problem.

"Elli-ot!"

Elliot cringed. There was only one person who said his name that way. If getting the potion to school was Cami's problem, then Cami was his problem.

She began talking even before she rounded the corner to his backyard. "If we can't prove the potion works, then we're not going to get a good grade. So what—" She stopped and stared at Elliot. Her eyes widened, and then she let out a high-pitched scream like Aphid and Fidget had done. Why did girls always do that? More specifically, why was Cami screaming right now?

"Just wait there. I'll take a picture." The words tumbled out of her mouth so quickly, he wondered how she could pronounce them all.

"A picture of what?" he asked.

She began digging through her backpack. "Your legs, silly. I can't believe it worked!"

Elliot looked down at his legs. Or where his legs were supposed to be. He was standing on them, so he knew they still existed, but they were invisible. He sighed loudly enough for her to know he was bothered. This wasn't the potion. It was Fidget's way of making up for having kidnapped him.

"Don't fuss, it's just a photo," Cami said, finding the camera. "Now smile!" She snapped a picture, then said, "I guess you don't have to smile, because the photo is really just of your legs."

She took three or four other pictures and then gave Elliot a big hug (he promised himself to shower as soon as possible so that her girl germs didn't stick to him).

"I can't believe you tried the potion on yourself," she said. "Nobody else dared to do it. You are so brave."

Elliot wanted to say, "Well, I did battle an evil Demon." But all he did was shrug and wonder how long Fidget was going to keep his legs invisible. He didn't want to go to school like this.

As Cami put her camera into her backpack, she said, "You know, Elliot, I always thought you were a pretty cool kid, but I thought you hated me."

Elliot didn't know what to say to that. Calling her Toadface wasn't exactly a sign of burning love. But Cami continued, "Anyway, you've been extra nice to me these past few days, and I wanted to tell you thanks. Sometimes I feel a little out of place, and, well, it was just a good week."

Elliot frowned. He felt pretty bad now for calling her Toadface.

Cami put a hand on the potion. "So my mom's waiting out front in our car. I can get the potion to school, and I'll see you there, okay?"

"Are you sure you can carry that by yourself?" he asked.

She grinned at him. "Will you help me?"

Anyone who battled Demons and Shadow Men could surely defend himself against girl germs. Elliot went to the far side of the potion and after a "one—two—three" from Cami, they lifted it up.

"It's gotten heavier," Cami said. "Like it all turned to syrup or something."

It was heavy for Elliot too. He couldn't catch enough breath to say anything. They made it only four steps before Cami grunted a "wah," Elliot spat out a "whoa," and the entire bucket of invisibility potion tumbled to the ground. It spilled out like floodwater breaking free of the dam and quickly soaked into the dry autumn grass.

Cami and Elliot stood beside each other for several seconds. Cami made a small sniffling sound, and Elliot took a step away from her, certain she was going to cry floodwater tears as well.

But she didn't. She began laughing. Then she did start crying, but it was only from laughing so hard. "This is terrible," she said, still laughing. "What's going to happen to our grades now?"

"We still have the pictures on your camera," he said, laughing too. "And my legs."

"I can see your legs now," she said. "The potion probably splashed on them and turned them back."

He looked down and saw that she was right. Fidget had returned his legs to him. She probably had made the potion spill too, just so Cami couldn't try it on anyone else.

"Oh, well," Cami said, wiping a last happy tear from her eye. "We had fun doing the project, and I have the picture of your legs, so we'll get a good enough grade." She paused then added, "And I guess we're friends now, right?"

"Uh, right." Elliot scratched his chin, then said, "Hey, a few days ago when you were stuck in that mud my little brothers made, sorry I didn't help you get out."

"I finally made it out on my own," she said. "Good thing it wasn't quicksand."

"Or gripping mud," Elliot said under his breath.

He gave an awkward wave as Cami skipped out of his yard, calling back, "See you at school!"

"Look at this mess!" Wendy said, opening the back door to the house. "Elliot, what are you doing out here? I thought you left early for school."

"Nope. Just finishing up my science project," he said.

"Oh. Hey, that white patch in your hair is gone."

Elliot reached up to the back of his head. "Oh, yeah."

"I guess that bleach you spilled on it must have worn off or something."

Elliot didn't think bleach worked that way, but if Wendy believed it, he wasn't going to argue the point.

"Hey, did something happen with my bed?" he asked.

"Since you gave it to Tubs?" Wendy asked.

Elliot's jaw dropped. "I did *what?*"

"Don't you remember when Tubs's parents came to pick him up?"

Elliot's muscles tightened. "Obviously not."

"You told his parents he could stay for another night or two. They thought that was great, because he didn't have a bed, because he'd broken it last week. So you said Tubs could have your bed. We all thought it was really nice. Sort of strange, though."

"That is strange," Elliot agreed. "Doesn't sound like something I'd normally do." He planned to talk to Harold about that very soon.

"I think you did it to impress Cami," Wendy added. "Interesting clothes, by the way. Where did they come from?"

"A friend gave them to me."

"Oh." Wendy brushed some flour off her hands. "You might want to change into something more normal if you don't want Tubs to start beating you up again. Luckily, he's been really quiet these past few days, barely even moved off his chair in the corner. While you're changing clothes, I'll dish you up some breakfast. The eggs are a little burned, but the toast isn't too bad if I scrape it first." Then she frowned. "I know I'm not a good cook, Elliot, but I'm doing the best I can since Mom and Dad are so busy. So thanks for being really nice about it this week."

Elliot walked up to Wendy and wrapped his arms around her waist for the best brother hug he could give. "Sorry I haven't been nice about it before this week. I'll be better. I don't know what our family would do without you."

"Our family wouldn't know what to do without you either," Wendy said, walking back into their home. "I mean, it's not like we could just go find another Elliot somewhere, right?"

Elliot smiled. Not if he could help it.

Elliot
and the Last
Underworld
War

For Chase, who has the heart of a king.

Contents

Unless you already know how to save planet Earth from total destruction, read the next sentence of this book! Actually, this second sentence won't be all that helpful. Obviously not this third one either. Let's be honest, you'll probably need to read the entire book if you hope to learn anything useful.

In the first two books of Elliot's story, children were warned to stop reading as soon as possible. Recent scientific studies have shown that one in five readers obeyed the warning and put their books down right away. They have hidden in fear under their beds ever since, gratefully living off whatever crumbs were left behind by their kind mice friends.

Those readers who ignored the warning stepped into dangers they could not have foreseen. For example, at least twenty children read about Elliot while walking to school and accidentally stepped into potholes. This might not seem dangerous now, but if you continue reading this book, you will understand that holes of all sizes should be taken very seriously.

Even if you dared to read the other books about Elliot, this book's warning should not be ignored. In fact, if you care at all for planet Earth, you will pay very close attention to the lessons inside these pages. In past books, you were urged to close the book and run away. But now you are warned to turn the pages as fast as you can read them. You must know what happens inside this book to learn whether Earth gets destroyed. Because let's face it—that would be a bad thing.

If you cannot wait until the end of the book to find out if Earth has been destroyed, then here are a few tips to help you figure it out for yourself.

First, you should go to your kitchen cupboards and see if you have some peanut butter to make a sandwich. If you have no peanut butter, no cupboards, and for that matter, no kitchen, then it's possible that Earth was destroyed.

Second, you should ask your teacher when your homework is due. If she says it's not due until Friday because Earth was destroyed, then you will have your answer. Also, you won't have to worry about your grades anymore.

The final way to know if Earth has been destroyed is to look out your bedroom window. If you see planets and cosmos instead of plants and cars, then you are flying through space. This will mean that Elliot lost the war, and you will have to find a new planet to live on.

Hint: Choose a planet that has ice cream. You won't regret it.

Chapter 1

Where Mr. Beary-Boo Is Not Happy

It was a day Elliot Penster would remember for the rest of his life. Oddly, up until exactly 11:14 a.m., it was a day Elliot would very much have liked to forget.

Because in all of his eleven years of life, Elliot had never had a day like this one. He had experienced some pretty unusual things, especially beginning last fall when he was made king of the Brownies. Since then, he'd been scared half to death by Goblins, had his house blown up, and had been kidnapped to the Underworld, where he ended up on an adventure that could change the course of world history. More about that later. Much, much more, in fact.

But as unusual as Elliot's recent life had been, somehow nothing was stranger than his being paired for a game of Capture the Flag with the scariest girl in the fifth grade, Cambria Dawn Wortson, aka Cami with Warts On, aka Toadface.

For a long time, Elliot had felt that Cami must have inherited her looks from a toad somewhere in her family. But over the past winter she had gotten rid of her thick glasses that made her eyes look like melons with pupils, and she had stopped wearing clothes that made her look like a prison guard. Elliot's mother even commented that she thought Cami had become quite pretty over the winter. Elliot's sister, Wendy, said the only reason Elliot insisted he didn't like Cami was because he secretly *did* like her. That was ridiculous, of course. But at least he had stopped peeking at Cami's hands to see if the fingers were webbed like a toad's.

Over the past few months, Cami had decided that she and Elliot should do stuff together. Maybe even have fun at the same time. So apparently, they were friends now. Despite that, Elliot still considered Cami his number one arch nemesis.

Many readers of this book will be surprised to learn that Elliot's arch nemesis is Cami and not Kovol, the most evil Demon of all time.

Battling evil Demons wasn't Elliot's favorite thing about being king of the Brownies. He would have much preferred to drink Mushroom Surprise and sit on his royal toadstool in Burrowsville, where the Brownies lived. But nearly four months ago, he had awoken Kovol from his thousand-year nap. It was an accident, and the last thing Elliot had wanted to do, but he'd had no choice. Going to Kovol's cave in Demon Territory had been the only way to save his ex-bully, Tubs Lawless, from the Pixies, and his Brownie friend, Mr. Willimaker, from the Fairies. In revenge for what Elliot had done, Kovol had promised revenge on the entire human race. Good grief, Elliot thought. That had to be about the biggest overreaction of all time.

But one thing still kept Kovol from being Elliot's arch nemesis. For the past four months, Kovol had been stuck in a pit of gripping mud deep in the Underworld. He wouldn't be able to escape until there was a total eclipse of the sun. At that point, Kovol would probably move up to the number one position on Elliot's list of enemies.

Then Cami would have to slide down to number two, because, after all, she isn't trying to kill Elliot. She just really annoys him.

And she was especially annoying him today. Because when he showed up that morning to play a game of Capture the Flag in the woods behind his house, Cami had already picked him for her teammate. The other team wasn't much better. On that side was Tubs, who often got confused if he ever had to say more than two sentences in a row. Tubs was playing alone, because even he couldn't bully someone into being on his team.

"That's okay if I'm alone." Tubs pulled a stuffed teddy bear from his shirt. "Mr. Beary-Boo will guard our flag."

"Why do you have a teddy bear in your shirt?" Elliot asked.

"He's my best friend!" Tubs snarled. "Besides, there's two of you, so I need his help."

"We'll make you a deal," Cami said. "You let Mr. Beary-Boo guard your flag, and then we'll find something to guard ours. Then all of us will go out and try to steal the other team's flag."

And so the game began. Cami and Elliot found a small clearing surrounded by tall trees and thick bushes. They hid their flag in the dense branches of a maple tree while Tubs hid his flag somewhere farther away. "You start looking for the other flag," Cami told Elliot. "I'll get the guard for ours."

"Like what? Mr. Beary-Boo's long-lost teddy bear brother?" Elliot said. "You could have a dumb rock as guard for all it matters, because in case you didn't notice, Mr. Beary-Boo isn't real!"

Cami laughed. "You'd probably say Leprechauns aren't real either."

Elliot only shrugged. If Goblins and Elves and Pixies were real, then Leprechauns probably were too.

"Let's go!" Cami said. "Try to find his flag. I'll be back in a minute with our"—she stopped to giggle—"our guard!"

Elliot rolled his eyes and then began running. He used to think these woods behind his house were sort of scary, so he'd always tried to avoid them. But then he had come face-to-face with Kovol, and nothing could ever be as scary as that.

He explored different areas where he was sure Tubs might have hidden the flag and listened carefully for any sounds that would tell him where Tubs was searching for his and Cami's flag. But all he heard was the wind brushing through the springtime leaves and the occasional chirp of a bird.

Then Elliot squinted in the distance. It was hard to know because of the shadows ahead, but he was pretty sure he saw Tubs's flag—an old green pillowcase—hanging from a tree.

Just hanging from a tree? Not hidden or disguised or anything?

Elliot smiled as he got closer. Tubs had put it near a clump of leaves. He probably hoped Elliot would think the pillowcase was just a really, really, really big leaf.

On the tree branch beside the pillowcase was Mr. Beary-Boo. Up close the teddy bear looked really old, and one of his button eyes was missing. No wonder he hadn't seen Elliot coming.

Laughing at his own joke, Elliot plucked the pillowcase off the tree. Now he had to get it back to his home base without being caught.

He turned to go and immediately ran right into Tubs's wide chest. Elliot bounced off it and landed on the ground.

"Mr. Beary-Boo thought you'd try something like this," Tubs said in a voice that reminded Elliot of the days when Tubs used to bully him. "Give me that pillowcase, or else."

Elliot swallowed hard. When Tubs talked like that, it always meant trouble. And trouble was the last thing Elliot wanted today.

Chapter 2

Where the Sun Goes Dark

Tubs was the closest thing to a brick wall Elliot had ever run into (other than the brick wall he had run into a week ago when he forgot to watch where he was going). Now Elliot sat on the ground with the pillowcase flag in his hand.

"I said give me the flag, or else," Tubs snarled.

Elliot gripped the flag tighter. He wouldn't back down, no matter what Tubs threatened. "Or else what?" he asked.

Tubs frowned. "Or else I'll lose. Duh!"

Elliot rolled his eyes and got ready to run again. Tubs reached for the flag, but Elliot crawled between his widespread legs. Tubs kept bending lower to catch Elliot but ended up with his head behind his knees, then rolled into a somersault that left him flat on the ground.

Elliot leapt to his feet and ran toward his and Cami's base. "I've got it!" he yelled. "I've got it!"

Tubs crashed through the woods behind him, calling Elliot's name. At first he had laughed as he yelled for Elliot to slow down. Then his voice became angrier as he said, "Seriously. Give me the flag. I hate losing!"

"Me too!" Elliot answered. He wasn't far from

their base now. He was easily going to win, and Cami hadn't done one thing to help. So he had beaten Tubs on his own!

Elliot ran into the clearing where their flag was still hidden. Then he stopped.

Cami had told him at least 120 million times over the winter that she had taken up paper-mache as a hobby. (Okay, maybe not quite that many times. But it was at least twice.) She had explained that this craft was as simple as dipping strips of paper in watered-down glue and putting them on a frame in whatever shapes she wanted. Then she had invited him over to her house to try it. "When it dries, you can paint it however you want!" she had said.

But Elliot had never wanted to try it. And he couldn't think of a single reason why he might ever want to in the future. Even if his life depended on it, he wouldn't have anything to do with Cami's paper-mache. So she told him that was fine, she would do her project without him.

And right now, beneath their hidden flag was their "guard." It was Cami's paper-mache project and was almost guaranteed to ruin his life once and for all.

It was a life-size version of him.

The worst part was that she had done a pretty good job. He had to get right up to its paper-mached face to know it wasn't really him.

"What do you think?" Cami bounced on her heels excitedly.

"Um." That was all he could think of to say. If he had ever known any other words, he couldn't think of even one.

"It's cool, right? I worked on it all winter and just finished it a week ago. I've been waiting for the perfect time to show it to you."

How could she possibly think *this* was the perfect time? And why did she have to carry that thing out in public? Everyone who saw it would know it was supposed to be him.

Behind Elliot, Tubs crashed into the clearing. He stopped right beside Elliot when he saw the paper-mache doll.

"You've got to be kidding," Tubs said.

Elliot closed his eyes. This was it. The beginning of the end (or the end of the beginning). The point when he wouldn't mind so much if the entire universe folded in half and squished him flat. Now Tubs would tease him and

Cami about liking each other. Or sing rhymes using their names. Or make kissing noises when they walked by.

"I really don't believe it," Tubs added, walking closer.

"Do you like it?" Cami asked.

"It's so cool!" Tubs said. "I mean, whatever makes Elliot such a dork all the time, you really understood that when you made this. Great job!"

Elliot frowned. That might've been a compliment to Cami, but it wasn't to him.

Cami gestured at the doll. "What do you think?"

"It doesn't look anything like me," he said. "My hair is dark blond, not light brown, and my eyes aren't purple."

She giggled. "Yeah, but they're cooler that way."

"And I don't have a goofy, crooked smile," he continued.

"Sure you do," Cami said. "But this is my first try with life-size humans. Mostly I've been doing creature crafts."

Elliot's ears perked up. "What sort of creatures?" As king of the Brownies, he had to guard very carefully against anyone learning of the existence of mythological creatures. The Brownies were very sensitive about that.

"Oh, you'd love it! I just finished a model of a Goblin. He's tiny, and I painted him light pink. He's so cute!"

Elliot rolled his eyes. Goblins were not tiny or any shade of pink, and they definitely were not cute! If their leader, Grissel, ever saw the model, he'd blow it up. And probably Cami's house along with it.

Seeing that Elliot was not impressed, Cami frowned and said, "I thought if you saw how cool this model was, you'd want to make some paper-mache creatures with me sometime."

"Um, no," Elliot said. Which was a very ordinary thing to say considering the very extraordinary thing that happened next.

Exactly when Elliot's watch turned to 11:14, the sunlight dimmed. It had been high in the sky when they started this game not too long ago.

Elliot forgot the flag in his hand and dropped it on the ground. It was as if night had suddenly decided to come all at once, even though it was still the middle of the day. "What's going on?" he asked.

"Oh, I forgot!" Cami rummaged through a bag slung over her shoulder. "There's a total eclipse of the sun today! I made a pinhole viewer so that we could watch it. Now, where—ah!" She pulled the pinhole viewer from her bag and showed it to Tubs and Elliot. "This is the only safe way to watch a solar eclipse."

As far as Elliot was concerned, there was nothing safe about a solar eclipse. Or at least, not *this* solar eclipse. Because as soon as the moon fully crossed in front of the sun, Kovol would be free.

Kovol had promised to destroy Earth once he escaped the gripping mud. Part of Elliot hoped that Kovol might have changed his mind while he was stuck in the mud. Maybe instead of getting revenge on Elliot, Kovol would celebrate his release by ordering some pizza. But the rest of Elliot understood that probably wouldn't happen. At least he couldn't think of any pizza places that delivered to the Underworld.

The eclipse created a strange light in the air. It wasn't true darkness, but more like everything had fallen into shadow. And with Elliot's mind on Kovol, the unusual light became even eerier.

A moment later the sun and moon had passed each other, and everything became normal again. It would've been an exciting moment if Elliot hadn't understood exactly what was now happening in the Underworld.

"Where are you going?" Cami asked him. "If you leave, we're gonna lose the game!"

"Mr. Beary-Boo will be so happy when I tell him we won!" Tubs said.

Elliot didn't care about the game or what Mr. Beary-Boo thought about anything. He was already sprinting home as fast as his long legs would carry him.

Kovol was free. And about to seek his revenge.

Where the Earth Sinks

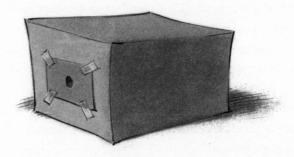

The door to Elliot's home banged open as he ran through it. His sixteen-year-old brother, Reed, and fifteen-year-old sister, Wendy, were sitting with their eyes glued to the television. (They weren't actually *glued*, of course, because think of how painful that would be! They were just watching it very carefully.)

"You were supposed to tell me if a solar eclipse was coming," Elliot said to them. "You promised to warn me!"

Wendy turned to him. "Sorry, I forgot."

Sorry? Wendy would be plenty sorry when the entire world was destroyed.

Reed shrugged. "So you missed the eclipse. I missed free popcorn day at the zoo once. But you don't hear me complaining."

"That's not even close to the same thing!" Elliot said.

"You can see the next one," Wendy said. "It's no big deal."

"It is a big deal," Elliot insisted. "It happens to be about the biggest deal ever. Like the kind of big deal that means you won't cook dinner ever again!"

"It just so happens that I don't mind cooking anymore," Wendy said. "I haven't burned a single dinner in eight days."

"You burned the chicken nuggets last night," Reed said.

"I meant the eight days *before* last night," Wendy said. "My cooking is getting better lately."

This was mostly true. Her dinners still tasted like they were made of cornstarch and glue. But except for last night, at least it was unburned cornstarch and glue.

"Anyway, there's a much bigger deal than your missing the eclipse." Reed pointed to the television. "Look! About five minutes after the eclipse, this happened!"

Elliot walked closer to the TV screen. A reporter was standing in front of a road that had caved into the earth, as if it had been built on top of a giant sinkhole. It looked like Elliot's entire house could fit into that hole.

"Nobody knows what caused this unusual event," the reporter was saying. "And it's not the only one."

Other pictures of caved-in roads were shown on the screen. A few had cars at the bottom of them, and helicopters were being flown in to help pull the people out of the sinkholes.

The reporter continued, "Right now, every road into the town of Sprite's Hollow has caved in. Until they can be repaired, it will be very difficult for anyone to either come or go."

"What about Mom and Dad?" Wendy said. "They won't be able to get home from work!"

Reed shrugged. "They'll find a way home as soon as they can. But this is weird, right?"

It's not weird, Elliot wanted to shout. This was obviously Kovol's way of letting Elliot know he was free, and he was making sure Elliot had no way to leave Sprite's Hollow. But of course Wendy and Reed didn't know about Kovol or any part of the Underworld. So in a voice not too different from a shout, he asked, "Where are the twins? They shouldn't be outside right now."

Elliot's six-year-old twin brothers, Kyle and Cole, had a talent for getting themselves into trouble. Elliot figured that if sinkholes were appearing in Sprite's Hollow, his brothers were probably very near one. They'd love to fill a sinkhole with water to create a giant mud pit to play in.

"They're out gathering extra hoses," Wendy said. "They want to make a super hose as long as Sprite's Hollow. But you're right. Come on, Reed. Help me find them."

As soon as they had left, another reporter came on the screen again. "More sinkholes have begun appearing outside of Sprite's Hollow," he said. "Dozens of new ones are being reported, some appearing as far away as China."

Dear Reader, if the reporter had said a sinkhole had appeared in Guatemala, this would not be much of a surprise, because they already have a giant sinkhole right in their capital city. It's over a hundred feet deep and big enough that it swallowed a three-story building. Nobody is sure exactly what caused that sinkhole, although scientists did eliminate the possibility of caved-in tunnels from freak-sized worms larger than rockets. Apparently, freak-sized worms don't exist. Besides, the reporter was very clear that this sinkhole was happening in China, not Guatemala. He pointed out that their fortune cookies would have to change to say, "Beware of walking into any holes larger than your house." Elliot thought most people would know that even without a fortune cookie's help. Except for maybe Tubs.

Once he made sure he was alone, Elliot ran up to his bedroom and closed the door. He put his hands around his mouth and shouted, "Mr. Willimaker!"

Mr. Willimaker was one of Elliot's closest Brownie friends and also his trusted advisor. Although it was true that most of Mr. Willimaker's advice was not very helpful, Elliot also knew that nobody had tried harder to help him be a good king.

But after two long minutes of waiting, no one appeared. Elliot shook his head. Mr. Willimaker usually came very quickly. He called again, but before he finished calling, Mr. Willimaker's daughter, Patches, poofed in.

Despite being half Elliot's size, Patches's brown eyes were twice as big as human eyes. She had a small mouth and thick hair that went in all directions.

Patches had made it clear on every possible occasion that she thought Elliot was the greatest king the Brownies had ever had, and that he was about the greatest human in the history of the world. Elliot thought that last part was a bit of an exaggeration, but he was okay with letting her believe it.

As soon as she poofed in, Patches said, "I took a peek at your television news downstairs. Is that what it looks like on the surface?"

"I guess so. How does it look in the Underworld?"

"Worse. So far he's left Burrowsville alone, so the Brownies are fine. But it won't be long before he attacks us too." Patches widened her eyes. "Kovol's free now, Elliot."

"I know," he said. "But why is he making sinkholes?"

Patches bit her lip, and it looked as if she was trying hard not to cry. "He's collapsing the Underworld. He's going to destroy everything."

Chapter 4

Where Cami Walks In

C ollapsing the Underworld," Elliot whispered. "Why would Kovol do that?"

"Because he's evil!" Patches replied, as if that was the only explanation needed.

Elliot shook his head. "I think that must be only part of the reason. With the Underworld in chaos, none of the good creatures will be able to help fight him. And those sinkholes will create a bunch of problems here on the surface. Because that's what Kovol really wants. To destroy the surface world."

Patches groaned and sat on Elliot's bed, her tiny legs dangling in midair. "This is bad. Worse than bad."

"Yeah." Elliot sat beside her and put his head in his hands. "Even though I knew he'd escape one day, I didn't think he'd act so fast."

He looked up at the sound of a poof, and Mr. Willimaker appeared, along with one of Elliot's other advisors, Fudd Fartwick. Never one to forget his manners, Mr. Willimaker bowed to Elliot. However, Fudd didn't bow. He'd been blinded when he helped to save Elliot from Kovol's army, the Shadow Men, four months ago. He didn't appear to have any clue where he was now.

"King Elliot," Mr. Willimaker said (and at that moment, Fudd did bow). "Sorry I'm late. There's a lot of trouble down below. You've heard the news, I assume."

"Do you mean the news that Kovol has escaped and is now collapsing the Underworld?" Elliot asked. "Or something else?"

Mr. Willimaker blinked. "Um, yes, that news."

"Just checking to be sure. Yeah, I heard. But I have another question first." Elliot turned to Fudd. "How are you doing?"

"Blindness is a bit of a challenge," Fudd said. "But at least I don't have to see my face in the mirror each morning!" He smiled as if he had tried to make a joke, but his voice still sounded sad.

"I'm sorry, Fudd," Elliot said. "It's my fault that happened."

Fudd looked directly at Elliot, or where he thought Elliot was, which meant he was actually looking at a bedpost. "King Elliot, sacrificing my eyesight was the least I could do in return for all you've done for me."

"Isn't there any way to fix your eyes?" Elliot asked. "I'd think with all the magic in the Underworld, healing an injury like this would be easy."

"That's just it," Mr. Willimaker said. "Fudd's eyes weren't injured that day. They were cursed. The only way to undo a curse like that and heal Fudd is for a creature to give away all his magic."

"And I'd never let anyone to do that," Fudd said. "It's just too big a sacrifice."

They fell silent for only a moment before Wendy called from downstairs, "Elliot! Your friend Cami is here. She wants to apologize about some doll!"

"Tell her everything's fine and to go away!" Elliot yelled back.

"Can I send her up to see you?" Wendy asked.

It was hard to hear her because of the noise of the twins running around downstairs. Elliot was glad they had not fallen into some giant sinkhole, but now he had to yell back to his sister even louder.

"No way, no chance, never!" he answered.

"Okay!"

Elliot turned back to the Brownies. "All right, I need some ideas about how we can stop Kovol."

Suddenly, Patches and Mr. Willimaker disappeared. In the same instant, Elliot heard the creak of his door behind him.

Fudd must not have heard the door creak. Still looking at the bedpost, he said, "Your Highness, I think—"

He had spoken about four words too many and failed to disappear about four seconds too late.

"What is that?" someone asked.

Elliot turned and saw Cami in the doorway of his room. Her mouth hung open and her eyes were wide as she stared at Fudd. For a moment, Fudd looked as if he wanted to poof away, but then he must have decided there was really no point in that now.

Elliot groaned. What did Wendy think "no way, no chance, never" meant anyway: "Sure, send Cami right up"? With the noise the twins were making downstairs, she might not have heard him.

"Elliot, what is that?" Cami repeated, pointing at Fudd. "It's looking at me."

"*It* is a *he*, and he's my friend," Elliot said. "And he's blind, so he isn't actually looking at you, but he can hear you just fine and you're being rude."

"Oh. Sorry," Cami said. "But you still haven't told me what it—what...*he* is."

Elliot sighed. "Come back, Mr. Willimaker and Patches. I guess you can show yourselves now." Then he turned to Cami. "I've got a sort of big secret. Sit down and I'll tell you everything."

Chapter 5

Where Something Grabs Elliot's Gut

Cami's eyes got wider and wider while Elliot told her all about the existence of Pixies, Goblins, and other mythical creatures, and about how he had come to be the king of the Brownies.

"This explains a lot," Cami said. "Like why you've been such an odd kid for so many years."

Elliot arched his head. "I've only been the Brownie king since last fall."

"Oh," Cami said. "Well, this explains why you've been odder than usual since last fall."

She crouched down to Mr. Willimaker and shook his hand. "So Elliot's your king, huh?"

"He's been a great king," Mr. Willimaker said.

"The best," Fudd agreed.

Cami leaned over to get closer to Patches. "How old are you, little girl?"

Patches made a face. "Little? Are you saying I'm short?"

"Oh! Um, no! I'm sure you'll grow up to be a very big girl one day. Well… as big as Brownies ever get, which I guess is still little."

Elliot tried hard not to laugh. Cami probably didn't realize that Brownies live a lot longer than humans. Maybe Patches was the smallest in the room, but she wasn't the youngest—at least not in human years.

"So why are you here?" Elliot asked Cami.

"Well, you left the woods so fast that I was worried about you. And then my mom called, and she can't get home from work because of all the sinkholes." She shrugged. "I guess I was scared being there alone."

"Okay, but why would you come *here?*" Elliot repeated.

"Because we're friends. And friends help each other."

Oh, *that.* "My parents can't get home either, but I guess you can stay with us until your mom gets back," Elliot said. "In exchange, I need your help too."

"Sure."

He took a deep breath. "I'm going to the Underworld, at least to make sure the Brownies are okay, and then I'll decide what to do about Kovol."

"Thank you, King Elliot," Mr. Willimaker said softly.

Elliot continued, "I'm not sure how long I'll be gone, but until I get back you've got to cover for me with my family."

Cami clapped her hands together. "Oh, the Underworld? Fun! Can I come?"

And this was why Elliot didn't trust having girls for friends. First he had let her stay over because she was scared. Now she wanted to visit the Underworld with him. Next she'd decide they were best friends or something even worse. He wasn't falling into that trap! No way. He knew her tricks.

And besides, even if he wanted to bring her to the Underworld (which he definitely didn't), he needed her help up here.

"Who'll cover for me if you come with us?" he asked. "If my sister or brothers wonder where I am, I need you here to make an excuse for me so that they won't worry."

"Oh. Okay."

Cami looked so disappointed that he finally added, "You wouldn't want to come anyway. I might end up having to battle this evil Demon who wants to destroy Earth."

"Yeah, that old excuse," she said, waving her hand. "Fine, go battle your evil Demon. I'll just stay here and be bored."

"That's really why I'm going there," Elliot protested.

"Whatever. You didn't have time to make paper-mache animals, but you do have time to save the world."

Patches folded her arms and said, "He always has time for us."

Elliot looked at Mr. Willimaker as if to ask him why Patches was acting jealous. But Mr. Willimaker only shrugged and suggested they should leave. Quickly.

Looking at Elliot's bedpost again, Fudd said, "Your Highness, are you really coming to the Underworld with us?"

"It'll be dangerous," Mr. Willimaker warned.

"I know," Elliot said. "But I'm the one who woke Kovol up. If I can help anyone stop him, I will."

"Hold my hand," Fudd said to the bedpost. "That will be the safest way to poof."

Since the bedpost had no hands, and in fact had not answered Fudd even once, Elliot took Fudd's hand in his, then closed his eyes in dread of the next moment. He didn't like being poofed.

Then he cracked one eye open as Cami said, "Be safe, Elliot. If anyone can stop that Demon, you can."

Elliot started to thank her, but it was too late. The poofing magic grabbed on to his gut and yanked him away from his room. He was headed to the Underworld.

Chapter 6

Where It Begins

The last time Elliot had been in Burrowsville, he had loved the quiet, peaceful feel there. It had been so nice he could hardly wait to come back for a visit. But things had changed. The small town was still quiet—too quiet, in fact. Not because it was peaceful, but because the fear was so thick in the air that nothing dared move. Even the usually gurgling stream through Burrowsville ran silently today.

Fudd, Patches, and Mr. Willimaker all stood beside Elliot at the top of a hill overlooking the town. In the distance of the Underworld, Elliot saw smoke and haze. The light down here was provided by the combined magic of all the Underworld creatures. But now it was dim and flickered on and off, as if the creatures were using their magic for hiding from Kovol rather than for lighting the Underworld.

"We're glad you came," Mr. Willimaker said as they began walking toward the center of Burrowsville.

"I wish I didn't have to come because of Kovol," Elliot said. "But I'm glad I'm here."

"You need to know about a power Kovol has," Fudd said. "A dangerous one. If he spreads his hands out wide"—Fudd demonstrated by holding his own hands apart—"like this, he's gathering his magic into that little space. It can hit you with the force of lightning."

"And that would be bad," Patches said.

"Don't get hit with a ball of lightning," Elliot said. "Good advice." He did a quick glance over the town. "It looks like Kovol's left Burrowsville alone."

"So far," Mr. Willimaker said.

The tiny mounds of homes with the paths between them were all in place, and their yards were as neat and orderly as always. But there were no Brownies working in their gardens or walking the winding paths of Burrowsville to visit with friends as they passed by. Now the town looked completely deserted.

Dear Reader, a deserted town is one where everyone has gone away and left it empty. Sometimes these are called ghost towns. A name like that can mean only one thing: ghosts must have chased everyone away.

If you have a ghost living in your town, there's no need for you to run away. There are ways for you and the ghost to become friends. You should start by doing things the ghost enjoys, such as floating around in attics. And moaning. Lots and lots of moaning.

Later you can invite the ghost to do fun things with you. Remember that some things will be tough for him, such as catching a baseball or swimming. And if you run a race, he'll probably win unless you can also fly to the finish line. But it'd be nice to let him win. After all, he's dead and you're not.

Finally, you should introduce the ghost to your friends. If you really want to have fun, suggest playing the game Ghosts in the Graveyard. When you bring the ghost out to play, everyone who doesn't faint with shock will enjoy a good laugh.

Elliot enjoyed playing games, but he definitely didn't feel like laughing right now. Besides, it didn't look like anyone was around to play with. He turned to Mr. Willimaker. "Where is everyone?"

"Hiding in their homes. We think it's only a matter of time before Kovol comes here to collapse Burrowsville."

"And if he does, then the Brownies will be trapped inside!" Elliot said. "Get them out to help me. We have to stop Kovol before he does anything to Burrowsville."

Mr. Willimaker and Patches bowed to Elliot and then poofed away to start gathering the other Brownies.

"He'll send the Shadow Men first," Fudd said. "Nobody knows how to fight them."

"I know how," Elliot said. "And you do too. We've already fought them once."

"I learned one thing," Fudd said. "Don't let a Shadow Man spit in your eyes and make you go blind."

"Definitely not," Elliot agreed. Actually, he didn't want anyone to spit in his eyes, no matter who they were.

Then Fudd snapped his fat fingers. "Light!"

"Exactly." Shadow Men couldn't touch direct light or they'd disappear in it. Elliot pressed his mouth tight and then opened it and said, "The Pixies promised to help us when Kovol escaped. It's time for their help. Fudd, I need you to bring the Pixie princess, Fidget Spitfly, here."

Fudd bowed to him and poofed away. At the same time, Elliot saw several Brownies already leaving their homes. They came out timidly at first, checking the sky to make sure it wasn't about to fall in on them (which is good advice for everyone, even if you're not being attacked by evil Demons, don't you think?). Then as more and more Brownies came out from their homes, they moved together in a big clump into the center of Burrowsville.

Elliot ran to the top of the hill near his toadstool throne. He could see hundreds of Brownies gathering, from tiny newborn Brownies all the way up to Brownies who were several hundred years old. All were dressed in simple, earth-colored clothes. Their wild gray hair was sticking up so much, it made them look even more frightened than they probably already were. Elliot still didn't know most of their names, but he thought of each one as his friend.

He waved his hands to get everyone's attention and said, "I know you're scared. You might be thinking that we have no chance. When I first became king, I wasn't sure we could stop the Goblins either. The Brownies had been losing that war for so long, we forgot that we are strong and clever and that we never give up! We won the Goblin war, and now we will fight Kovol and his Shadow Men. Whatever else happens, Kovol will *not* collapse Burrowsville while I'm king!"

Then he looked up as small bits of dirt landed on his head.

"What—" He jumped back as a large chunk of dirt fell on the ground, barely missing him.

"It's starting!" yelled a Brownie in front of the crowd.

"Burrowsville is collapsing!" another cried.

"Wait!" Elliot called. "I know about a kind of magic that all Brownies can do. You can make a cold fire in your hand. Get anything you have to hold that fire. Sticks or papers or anything made of wood! Surround Burrowsville with it, and then light the wood with the fire. The Shadow Men won't be able to cross it!"

"They can still collapse the town," a third Brownie cried.

"I'm taking care of that. Now move!" Elliot ordered.

Still in a panic, Brownies scurried in all directions. Elliot turned his back on them and called, "Fudd! What's taking so long?"

"Like, I had to do my hair!" a voice behind him said. "Totally chill out."

Elliot turned again. Fluttering in the air in front of him was the Pixie princess, Fidget Spitfly.

Chapter 7

Where Elliot Steps into Shadow

Fidget was a foot high and looked about the same age as Elliot. Except she dressed like every flavor of fruit candy and had learned to speak Elliot's language by watching the totally awesomest television show ever, *Surfer Teen*. Her tiny wings were round, her ears were long and thin, and she had an explosion of curly yellow hair.

She and Elliot weren't exactly friends. But since it was Fidget's fault he had awoken Kovol, they had always known they'd have to work together one day to stop him.

Fidget held her hand out to examine her nails. "Oh, fruit rot! I had to dodge a falling piece of the Underworld and broke a nail. Kovol's totally going to pay for this!"

"The Brownies need your help," Elliot said. "I need the Pixies to spread light all over Burrowsville so that we can keep the Shadow Men out. And if they try to collapse it, have the Pixies poof the chunks away before they fall."

"But what if the Shadow Men attack the Glimmering Forest while we're gone?" Fidget said. "My daddy wouldn't like that."

"We're testing this plan to see if it works," Elliot said. "Better to test it here than on your own home, right?"

Fidget tossed her hair back. "Totally!" She snapped her fingers and instantly hundreds of Pixies appeared. Then she announced, "We're going to make the awesomest ever dome of light to cover Burrowsville! For some strange reason, the Brownies actually like this place and want to keep it. Also, I'm making a scrapbook all about me. So if anyone takes my picture while I'm poofing away some collapsing pieces of the Underworld, that would be, like, totally and completely awesome!"

Together the Pixies flew up into the air. They separated until they were as wide apart as the distance they could spread their light. Once Fidget gave the order ("Okay, so like totally, y'know!"), within seconds a ceiling of light widened across all of Burrowsville.

Elliot kept an eye on the smoke as it continued moving closer to Burrowsville. The Shadow Men were almost here. He hurried over to where the Brownies were building up kindling for their cold fires. They were working hard, but there was still too much to be done. Elliot joined the Brownies in piling up kindling, making sure there were no gaps.

"Hurry!" he said.

"Elliot!"

Surprised, Elliot jumped a little, then turned. When he saw who had come, he jumped again. He wasn't *surprised*, really. *Startled* might be a better word.

Dear Reader, even though the two words mean nearly the same thing, there is a very big difference between being surprised and being startled. Surprised is when it's your birthday and you get a large gift from your brother that you had not been expecting. Startled is when that gift turns out to be a giant python. It's a good thing that it's not necessary to explain what the word *horrified* means, because otherwise we would have to discuss that giant python swallowing your birthday party guests whole. The good news is there will be lots of birthday cake left for you. Surprise!

Unfortunately, it was not Elliot's birthday. And his brother probably wouldn't give him a giant python anyway, mostly because it wouldn't hold still long enough for Reed to wrap it. So when Elliot was startled, it was because Agatha the Hag had just appeared beside him.

Elliot had first met Agatha very soon after he became the Brownie king. In most ways she was the exact opposite of Fidget the Pixie. Fidget was young, fashionable, and beautiful. Agatha was older than dust and wore ragged clothes that were held together by little more than cobwebs. Her skin was dry and wrinkled, and she was dotted with warts. Worst of all, her left eye bulged out so far from her head, it seemed likely to fall out and land on him at any minute.

"I came to help," Agatha said. "It's about time the Underworld started fighting back."

"The Underworld has some powerful magical creatures," Elliot said. "Why aren't they fighting?"

"Nobody knows what to do. Kovol is stronger than any one of us. And we haven't had to work together for a thousand years."

"Not since the first Underworld war." Elliot remembered what the Brownies had taught him about the war that happened a thousand years ago when all the creatures of the Underworld had stood up to Kovol and the Shadow Men. "They worked together then, and now it's time we do that again."

As the last of the kindling was put into place, the Brownies used their magic to light cold fires on their hands and quickly set them on the kindling. Elliot had first seen Mr. Willimaker light a cold fire while they were on their way to Demon Territory one night. It was bright and gave off a little warmth, but it wouldn't burn on its own. As long as the Brownies used their magic to keep the fire alive and the Pixies kept the light above them, they could keep the Shadow Men out of Burrowsville.

Patches ran to Elliot. "We're ready. Are you sure this will work?"

"If everyone does their part, it'll work." Elliot started walking, keeping his eyes open for any dark holes in the dome. Agatha hobbled beside him on her cane.

"You don't have to be here," he said, thinking of how much older she looked and acted than when he'd last seen her. "You should rest somewhere."

"You forget that I'm really a beautiful young woman," Agatha said.

"Oh, right." Elliot hadn't really forgotten, but it was tough to look at her deep layers of wrinkles and remember that a woman even more beautiful than an angel was hiding inside.

"Besides, you might need me," Agatha added.

Before Elliot could answer, a Brownie far from them shouted, "They're here! The Shadow Men have come!"

Elliot ran toward the Brownie who had cried out. It was hard to see through the Pixies' light and the Brownies' fire, but sure enough, an entire army of Shadow Men was on the other side, ready to attack.

Elliot's gut did a belly flop as he stood frozen for a moment. He'd faced Grissel the Goblin and a Shapeshifter posing as a werewolf, and even Cami Wortson when she was mad at him. But he feared the Shadow Men most of all.

Shadow Men were made of smoke and a black fire that burned but gave off no light. They wore long black cloaks that held the fire in, but thick smoke poured out from beneath the cloak in every direction and could choke a person who got too close. They smelled of charcoal and cinders and spoke with a hissing sound that made Elliot's skin crawl.

A Shadow Man in front tried to push through the dome of light but screeched as it stung his hand, and he pulled back. Another two or three tried to get past the Brownies' fire, but they failed too.

"It's working!" one of the Brownies said.

"Keep your guard up," Elliot said as the Shadow Men grouped together and flew to another area of the dome. "They'll keep testing us and trying to find a way in."

"They're over here," several Brownies a long way from Elliot called. "King Elliot, please come!"

Elliot took a breath, then began running. It would be a very long, very tiring war if he had to run everywhere all the time.

He turned to tell Agatha that, but she had already poofed herself there. By the time Elliot came, the Shadow Men were trying to break through the light dome again. Luckily, the Pixies held their magic strong, and no Shadow Man could push through it.

Elliot bent over to catch his breath, but other Brownies from even farther away cried, "Now they're over here!"

Between breaths, Elliot wondered why the Shadow Men had to fly so far away each time. Couldn't they just test the light dome all in one place so that it wasn't so tiring? It was like they wanted to make this war tough on him or something.

"I'll be right there," Elliot panted. He started to run, then leaned over with his hands on his knees and said to Agatha, "Will you go tell them to stay strong?"

Agatha nodded and poofed away. When his breath slowed, Elliot hurried toward the latest cry for help.

Then he stopped as his foot stepped into a shadow.

Shadow? There couldn't be shadows in here. The entire town was bathed in light from all directions. A shadow was bad.

High above him he saw a small gap of darkness. A Pixie fluttered in the center of it. He wasn't sure what she was doing, but her hands were moving behind her head.

"Get your light back," he called up to her.

"In a minute. But I have to tie my hair back first," she said. "You won't believe how much wind the Shadow Men are making out here."

"Light!" Elliot cried.

"Fine!" She lowered her hands and shook her hair out. "But if I get a tangle in my beautiful hair, it's all your fault."

"Light!" Elliot repeated. She huffed and spread her light again, but it was too late. Five cloaked shadows made it through the gap just in time. A sixth one made it halfway through, but the light cut him off and he disappeared.

The five Shadow Men swept down through the air in a flight that reminded Elliot of a hawk diving for its prey. Smoke trailed from their cloaks like a damaged airplane about to crash land. But these creatures weren't damaged and weren't going to crash. In fact, the closer they flew to Elliot, the darker the fire inside their cloaks burned. Then at once, all five of them looked at Elliot and flew even faster. They were arrows, and he was their target. All he could see was the smoke of their bodies and the raging black fire inside their cloaks.

They were coming straight for Elliot.

Chapter 8

Where Fire Burns

Elliot stumbled back a step and looked around for anything he might use to defend himself from the approaching Shadow Men. But there was nothing. Everything that could hold light had been carried to the borders.

The Shadow Men stopped directly in front of him and spoke: "King Elliot of the Brownies." He couldn't see their faces, so it wasn't clear exactly which of them was talking. It sounded like they were all speaking at the same time. If they weren't his enemies who were about to attack him, he'd have asked how they all knew what the others wanted to say. Because the answer was probably pretty cool.

"Get out of here while you still can," Elliot warned. He had tried to sound brave, but it felt like something inside his belly was doing somersaults.

They took a step forward and all said, "You will serve Kovol forever or else pay the price of doom."

Elliot snorted, not sure exactly what the going price for doom was these days. "No way! I'll already be in trouble if my mom finds out I'm down here fighting an Underworld war without permission. Can you imagine if she found out I promised to serve some ugly super villain?"

They laughed, all of them with the exact same laugh. Which would have been fine if Elliot had told a joke. But he hadn't. So it was actually sort of creepy.

"Then you will be the first human Kovol destroys," they said. "Leave with us now, and save this place from doom."

Sheesh, Elliot thought. The Shadow Men really had a thing for doom.

Although he very much liked the idea of their leaving, no way was he going with them. His family had a very strict rule about never going anywhere with strangers. And even if they didn't have the rule, Elliot knew that leaving with the Shadow Men was a terrible idea.

Elliot's hands folded into fists. "I said to leave while you still can."

"We'll only leave with you as our prisoner."

Elliot shook his head. "You're trapped inside this dome of light. I think that *you* are *my* prisoners."

Another laugh, even creepier this time. Then the Shadow Men spread out, surrounding him. They flew to their left, faster and faster, swirling around Elliot. He sank to the ground as they pulled air away from him, sucking it from his lungs. He was really scared but also sort of annoyed. They were supposed to be his prisoners, yet he was the one who was trapped. This wasn't fair!

Elliot should have been used to things in his life not being fair. It wasn't fair that when he was five, Tubs stole his sandwich every day for a whole month and he had to eat napkins for lunch. It wasn't fair that his house had been blown up by the Goblins, or that day when Wendy had accidentally shaved the middle of his head and given him a backward Mohawk. But somehow this not-fair moment seemed worse than all the others combined.

Just as Elliot felt the last of his air being sucked away from him, the Shadow Men let out a pained screech as in their swirling three of them crashed into a wall of light. Air filled Elliot's lungs again and he looked up. Agatha had transformed into her angel self and, with her hands held high, created a light so white it hurt his eyes.

Her wobbly cane was still in her hands, but now it was as bright as the sun. It created a line above her head that seemed to give the Shadow Men pain if they came anywhere close to it.

Elliot stood and ran to where the Shadow Men could hear him. "Tell Kovol to go back to Demon Territory and stop this war," he warned. "If he doesn't, we will defeat him."

"You're only a human," the last two Shadow Men said. "We'll tell Kovol nothing for you."

"Fine! Then he'll find out on his own!" Elliot threw up his hands and began walking away. Add stubbornness to the list of things he didn't like about Shadow Men.

"Elliot, look out!" Agatha cried.

Before Elliot turned, he felt the hot claw of a Shadow Man grab his shoulder. Even through his shirt he felt its burn.

"Catch this!" Agatha tossed her cane at him, and Elliot ripped free and dove for it. As soon as it was in his hands, he swerved around and struck the Shadow Man in the chest. It screeched for only an instant before its cloak dissolved and fell like ashes at his feet.

"This is over for now, but we'll be back," the remaining Shadow Man said. "And next time it won't be so easy for you."

He fled up in the air toward the light dome. He tried to push through it but disappeared, as shadows will. Nothing came through on the other side. Seeing what had happened inside the dome, the Shadow Men on the outside quickly flew away.

Suddenly tired, Elliot fell to his knees. Agatha crouched beside him. "Are you okay?"

"Sure," he mumbled. The shoulder of his shirt was burned off, and the skin below it was hot and red, but he couldn't worry about that right now. "What happened to that Shadow Man I hit?"

"Kovol cursed the fire to create an army from the flames," Agatha said. "That Shadow Man was nothing but smoke and ash."

"They said it won't be as easy next time," Elliot said. "Did they think this was easy?"

"There will be more battles," Agatha said. "And the next one will get much worse."

Chapter 9

Where Everyone Arrives

Whendthe last of the Shadow Men had flown away, a cheer rose up from the Brownies. Mr. Willimaker ran toward Elliot, then stopped and bowed before he said, "You did it, Your Highness! You saved us!"

"Only for now," Elliot said.

Fidget fluttered down from above them. Her thick mass of hair looked wind-tossed and wasn't nearly as bouncy as usual.

"I hope you know that was a lot harder than it looked," Fidget said. "They were, like, so totally mean!"

"But you were…um…awesome," Elliot said. "We couldn't have done this without the Pixies."

Fidget arched her head in pride. "Totally. But now we're even, right? We don't owe each other anything more."

"It's not about being even," Elliot said. "It's about stopping Kovol."

Fidget frowned. "Oh, fruit rot! If I have to fight in a war to save the world, then I'm totally going to miss *Surfer Teen* on TV tonight." She punched a fist into her palm. "If Kovol wants to destroy the Underworld, then that's totally rude. But now he's ruining the awesomest TV show ever, and the Pixies will not allow that!"

Elliot stood and said to Fidget, "I'll help whoever wants to lead this war. But I need some time to think of ideas about how to fight it. Meet me back here later and we'll talk about it."

"What if anyone else wants to come?" she asked.

"If they're willing to fight against Kovol and save the Underworld, then I want them to come!"

After Fidget left, Elliot asked for a place where he could think in private. Mr. Willimaker suggested Burrow Cave, and then Patches offered to walk Elliot there.

"I think I can find it," Elliot said. Burrowsville wasn't that big, and they only had one cave large enough for all the Brownies.

"I know," Patches said. "But I thought you'd want some company."

She was right. He did.

"How's your shoulder?" Patches asked.

"It hurts a little." Actually it hurt a lot. The Shadow Man had been so angry when he grabbed Elliot that his fire had been very hot.

"Kneel down," Patches said.

As he did, Patches walked behind him and rubbed her hands together. "Are you going to heal it with magic?" Elliot asked.

"Not everything is magic," Patches said with a giggle. Then she peeked over his shoulder and began pasting it with something bright green and sticky that smelled like the inside of Reed's old shoes.

"What's that?" Elliot turned his head and quickly faced forward again. Coming too close to that stuff made his nose hurt.

"Pumpkin guts and tree moss and that stuff that sometimes collects on the edges of ponds. It makes a great burn paste." Patches shrugged. "I figured we'd need it, seeing as we were fighting fire and all."

"Thanks, Patches." Elliot gently touched the burn. The pain was already going away. "You really are smart."

"Not just ordinary smart," she said. "I'm super smart!"

Elliot chuckled. "Maybe you're smart enough to figure out how to beat Kovol."

She shook her head. "Nobody's *that* smart." Then she stopped, realizing what she had said. "Oh! I mean except you, right?" She pointed ahead to Burrow Cave. "Here we are! Go in and be super smart too."

"Thanks." The cave wasn't quite big enough for him, but it was the biggest private place the Brownies had. Being the super-smart king of the Brownies that he was, he tripped over a root at the entrance. Then he picked himself up and, without looking back to see if anyone was laughing, walked the rest of the way into the cave.

By the time Fudd called for him a while later, Elliot had decided for sure that Kovol needed to be defeated, and he was double sure he didn't want Earth destroyed. But the details of how someone might stop Kovol were still a little fuzzy. All in all, he hadn't gotten nearly as much thinking done as he had hoped for, and he certainly didn't feel super smart.

"Everyone's waiting for you," Fudd said, walking beside Elliot.

"Everyone?" That sounded like a lot.

It *was* a lot. Maybe five times what he had expected. Crowded into the small open space of Burrowsville were hundreds of creatures of every kind. He thought Fidget was inviting only *some* of her friends.

Near the front were the Dwarves, the full-grown ones about Elliot's own height. They had long, thick beards and strong bodies. Most of them had picks or axes or other mining tools slung across their backs. Behind them stood a herd of half-human, half-horse Centaurs. They were large and muscular with bare chests and hair hanging past their shoulders. Their ears were slightly pointed and high on their head, as if unable to decide whether to be human or horselike, so they settled on something in between. Behind the Centaurs were several Trolls, including one who had half of his fist shoved up his nose in search of something there. Elliot recognized the Fairies up in the air, along with a couple of other flying creatures he didn't know. There were also Elves and a few Yetis, and Satyrs, and even some Mermaids near the banks of the river running through Burrowsville. All waiting for him.

"There are so many," Elliot whispered.

"They came to hear your plan," Fudd replied. "They came to fight Kovol."

The crowd quieted when they saw Elliot. He sat on his toadstool throne and looked them over. These were magical creatures who were smarter than him—and mostly bigger than him.

"Why me?" Elliot asked no one in particular. "I said I would help. But am I supposed to lead this battle?"

"You are our king, and they've chosen you as their leader," Fudd said. "You've defeated the Goblins and gotten past Kovol and his army once before. You're the only one who can help us win this."

Elliot took a deep breath. As he looked around the crowd, he wondered how that could be true. Maybe it wasn't about who was most capable of winning but who was most willing to try. He stood again and shoved his hands into his pockets. He knew that didn't look very kinglike, but he didn't care about looking like a king right then.

"Um, I don't know what to say," Elliot began. "I guess I'm open to any ideas."

A murmur spread through the crowd. Several creatures turned their backs on him, ready to leave.

"Your Highness, they need more than that," Fudd said. "They're here to follow you, but you must show them that you can lead this."

"But I'm not sure that I *can* lead this," Elliot said. "I'm just a kid."

"I know you can, because you're our king," Fudd said. "It's okay if you don't believe that yet. But make *them* believe it."

"I'll try." Elliot raised his hands and started over. "A thousand years ago, Kovol was defeated the first time. It was your parents and grandparents and great-grandparents who fought him before, who made the Underworld safe for us. Now it's our turn. We will beat him again, *if* we are willing to fight him together."

This time the crowd cheered, but Elliot didn't feel much better. That speech had been the easy part. Now he was supposed to tell them how it would happen.

"What are you really good at?" Elliot continued. "Look at your strengths. Figure out how you can use them against Kovol."

"We're good at light," Fidget said, fluttering to the front of the crowd. "But nobody knows where Kovol will go next. We can't build a light dome over the whole Underworld."

A Dwarf stepped forward. "The Shadow Men could grab us before our short arms will ever reach them. But we can build defenses for others to use in their fights."

The Troll with the finger up his nose ambled forward as if he wanted to say something. But then he blinked as if his finger had pushed into his brain, and he stepped back into place.

Don't worry about his brain, Dear Reader. He'll barely notice a difference.

"Anyone else?" Elliot asked.

A large bird that had been in the air landed on the ground, spun around, and turned into a human boy Elliot recognized. This was his friend Harold, a Shapeshifter who had helped save Elliot on the night he woke up Kovol.

"You know my strengths," Harold said. "Just tell me what you want, and I'll do it."

"And me," said a Centaur in the back of the crowd.

"And me," added a Mermaid from the river.

"Okay." Elliot looked around. His mind raced as he looked the crowd over. He started with the Fairies. "We need everyone we can get on our side. Will you gather as many creatures as you can? Tell them we must fight together, or we'll each face the collapse of the Underworld alone."

The Fairies nodded, then vanished. Elliot next turned to Fudd. "You've worked with the Goblins once before. If anyone can convince them to help us, it's you."

"The Goblins only promised not to hurt us," Fudd said. "But they won't help us unless their leader, Grissel, agrees. And he's still in our Brownie prison, having to eat that horrible chocolate cake." He shivered just thinking of it.

"No more chocolate cake," Elliot said. "Bring him the biggest jar of pickles you can find, and tell him I want his help. He still has to promise not to hurt the Brownies, but there's nobody as good at blowing things up as Grissel."

Fudd dipped his head at his king. "Yes, Your Highness." Then he poofed away.

Harold stepped forward. "And what about me? Can I help?"

Elliot took a deep breath, then nodded at the Shapeshifter. "I need you for one of the biggest jobs of all. I need you to turn into me again and let Kovol see you down here. When he does, he'll chase you. If he gets too close, change into a butterfly, or a bumblebee, or something he won't suspect and can't catch. Keep him confused but busy and distracted. And whatever you do, keep him far, far away from Demon Territory. Can you do that?"

Harold paled a little, as if he were already shapeshifting into a white snowman. Then slowly he returned to his normal color. He swallowed hard, then nodded. With a squeak, he said, "I thought you'd ask me to bring chips and dip for the battle, or do something simple. But I said I would help, and I will."

He closed his eyes and shapeshifted into a bird again. Before he flew off, he tweeted back to Elliot, "If I don't come back, make sure to tell the love of my life, the beautiful Cami Wortson, that I was a hero."

"Of course you'll come back," Elliot said. "And for the last time, she's not the love of your life!"

When Harold had flown away, Mr. Willimaker stepped forward from the crowd and asked, "What good will it do to send Kovol away from Demon Territory? None of us are there, so neither is he. We have to defend our homes out here instead."

Elliot smiled. "We're not going to defend ourselves from Kovol. We're going to attack."

Chapter 10

Where Elliot Meets Slimy Toe Jam

Dear Reader, at one time or another, you have probably played a sport such as tennis or basketball, or Limburger soccer. (It's pretty much the same as regular soccer, except that you kick around a chunk of stinky Limburger cheese instead of a ball. The only downside is that it smells so bad, nobody really wants to get anywhere near it.) If you have, then you know it's very important to have a strong defense, or the other team will score points and win the game. But it's even more important to have a good offense, or plan of attack. Because if you don't, you'll never earn any points for your team. A defense only stops you from losing. To win, you have to attack.

And Elliot understood this. His family had played an exciting game of Limburger soccer only one week before. His twin brothers had won the game, in part because they didn't mind bad smells. And also because they cheated.

The rest of the mythical creatures didn't understand the reasons for attacking Kovol quite as well as Elliot did. (Limburger cheese is very hard to find in the Underworld—and that's a good thing.)

When Elliot announced his plan to the group, everyone got very quiet. The Troll in the back did jump up and say "Yay!" but Elliot soon realized it was because he had finally found what he'd been reaching for in his nose, not because he liked the idea of attacking Kovol.

"Why would we go to Demon Territory?" a Fairy asked. "That's Kovol's land."

"Exactly," Elliot said. "If we fight him in our own lands, then he will destroy them. But if we can beat him in Demon Territory, then we'll win this war."

"If Kovol catches us in his territory, he can make us his prisoner," an Elf said.

"I doubt that, because he's not a king," Elliot said. "And besides, he won't know we're there until we're already winning."

The moans continued, but Elliot said, "Everyone go home and gather the rest of your kind. Come as soon as you can to Demon Territory."

There were a handful of grumbles, at least twenty-two growls, and one rather high-pitched whine. But they had chosen Elliot to lead this war and intended to obey him. One by one the various groups poofed themselves away.

Except for the Elves. They waited until everyone had left before one came forward. He was a tall and handsome Elf with long white hair that fell like silk down his back.

"I am Slimmy Tojam," he said.

Elliot blinked. Had that elf just said he had slimy toe jam? If a Dwarf or a Troll or a Goblin had said that, then he could understand. But he wouldn't have thought any type of slime would be a problem for an Elf.

"You're slimy?" Elliot asked.

"It's Slimmy. Like Timmy or Jimmy. And it's my name, not a description of my feet."

"Toe Jam?"

The elf looked annoyed. "Tojam. Not 'jam,' like one spreads on toast, but 'jum,' that rhymes with 'come.'"

The fact that his name sounded like foot fungus made Elliot giggle. However, Mr. Tojam was a very serious-looking Elf and didn't seem to think

302

his name was nearly as funny as Elliot did. So Elliot apologized. He hadn't meant to be rude. It's what he really thought the Elf had said.

"I am a teacher among the Elves," Mr. Tojam said.

Elliot wondered what the kids at his school would say if someone named Slimy Toe Jam started teaching there. They once had a teacher whose name was Mrs. Popzitt. She left after only three weeks to teach on an island where the natives all spoke in sign language, and she hadn't been seen since. Nobody blamed her for leaving.

"You've been thinking about my name for a long time," Mr. Tojam said. "Can we move on?"

"Oh, yeah, sure."

Mr. Tojam held up a book for Elliot to see. It looked very old and dusty, and the pages were wrinkled. "Now, what do you know about Kovol?"

Elliot shrugged. "I know he's the most evil Demon of all time. I know that a thousand years ago, in the first Underworld War, a wizard named Minthred cast a spell that put Kovol to sleep." Elliot also knew from having once been very close to Kovol's wide-open mouth that he had really bad breath. Or maybe that was only Kovol's morning breath. Probably not worth mentioning.

"The Elves believe the only way to defeat Kovol now is to understand how he was defeated the first time." Mr. Tojam held out his arm, inviting Elliot to walk with him. "Is there a private place we can talk?"

Elliot glanced over at Mr. Willimaker, who suggested they return to Burrow Cave. Then Patches reminded her father that Elliot could only barely sit up in the cave, and Mr. Tojam was even taller than him.

"Allow me." Mr. Tojam touched Elliot on his shoulder and then closed his eyes. Elliot felt the tug on his gut poofing him away, but the Elf was a much better poofer than either the Brownies or the Pixies, and Elliot barely felt a thing. They arrived on a thick tree branch very high above the ground, but Elliot was so comfortable in that spot that he didn't worry a bit about falling. Besides, he had much bigger worries on his mind. Such as accidentally calling Mr. Tojam by the wrong name again. Or the end of the world, for example.

Mr. Tojam handed Elliot the book and opened it to the first page. It was an old and faded drawing of Kovol as he would have looked a thousand years ago.

Sure enough, he had a full head of Demon hair. No wonder he had been upset when Elliot pulled out the last hair, making him bald. But as everyone knows, baldness is just one of the risks when taking thousand-year naps. Also, your favorite show might not be on television anymore (if television even exists still!).

In the picture, Kovol was facing an army of mythical creatures that were not too different from those Elliot had just spoken to. In fact, right at the front was a Brownie who looked a lot like Mr. Willimaker. Elliot knew Mr. Willimaker's great-grandfather had fought Kovol before. He wondered if the Brownie in the picture was him.

"It was a terrible war," Mr. Tojam said. "Nobody had ever faced a creature such as this, and nobody had any idea of what to do."

"What made Kovol so much worse than any other Demon?" Elliot asked. "And why is he the last of them?"

"That was Kovol's plan," Mr. Tojam said. "All Demons have a certain amount of bad inside, but it had never been difficult for any of the good creatures to keep control of them. One day Kovol got into a fight with another Demon about who would get the last slice of dessert."

"Seems harmless enough." Elliot and his brothers often fought for that same reason. Unless Wendy had cooked it. Then they fought over who would have to choke it down and not hurt her feelings.

Mr. Tojam shook his head. "It should have been harmless, except that the other Demon ate the dessert first. In a rage, Kovol then picked up the Demon and ate him."

"Eww." There had not been a single fight in Elliot's home in which he had ever considered eating his brothers. Seriously. Not even once.

"As soon as Kovol ate him, he realized that he had taken the Demon's powers into his own body. In that moment, Kovol became stronger. And far more greedy. He wanted more and more power, and so he continued eating others of his own kind. With each meal, he grew stronger and more wicked. One by one, he destroyed every other Demon of the Underworld. Until he was the last."

As he spoke, Mr. Tojam turned the pages of the book, each picture showing Kovol becoming larger and stronger. Then he turned the page again, which showed Kovol in front of a wall of black fire.

"Kovol then turned his eyes upon the rest of the Underworld," Mr. Tojam continued. "For although he had the strength of all the Demons, he did not have the power of other magical creatures. Not the wisdom of the Fairies, or the grit of the Dwarves, or any of the special gifts the rest of the Underworld creatures have. So began the first war of the Underworld."

"You had to fight it," Elliot whispered. "Because he wouldn't stop until everyone was destroyed."

"But Kovol needed an army." Mr. Tojam tapped the picture again. "He couldn't have an army of living creatures, because he knew he'd end up eating them too, to take their power. So he cursed the fire, and from it came the Shadow Men. They are nothing but smoke and flame, and they have no thought other than to obey Kovol's will."

Elliot went to turn the next page and learn more, but Mr. Tojam stopped him. "The last page of this book is for your eyes only," the Elf said. "This is the wizard Minthred's own journal. He knew that one day Kovol would awake, and when he did, someone would have to lead the fight against him. He asked that the last page be read only by that person—by you. The Elves believe that everything you must know to defeat Kovol will be on that page. Call to me when you're finished, and I'll return you to the Brownies."

Mr. Tojam closed his eyes and poofed away, leaving Elliot alone at the top of the tree. This was great news. If the secret to winning the war was in this book, he could have it ended by dinner. Feeling very happy, Elliot blew out a puff of air and then turned the page.

The very first words he read were, "My name is Minthred, but I'm no wizard. And I don't know how I defeated Kovol."

Chapter 11

Where Minthred Likes Goats

If Elliot had not been delicately balanced at the top of a very tall tree, he might have stood up and banged Minthred's journal as hard as he could against the branches. What did Minthred mean by saying he wasn't a wizard? From the very first moment Elliot had heard about Kovol, it was that the *wizard* Minthred had defeated him. And how could Minthred not know how he had done it?

However, since Elliot didn't want to lose his balance by beating up the journal, he only took another deep breath and then read further.

"I'm a poor goat herder," Minthred wrote.

"Oh, good grief," Elliot mumbled. Of course he was.

"Goat herding is a simple life and sometimes a very lonely life. (Which you can probably understand, Dear Reader. Goats rarely have anything interesting to say.) One day, large craters appeared in my field, as if the earth had sunk.

In some places they were as large as an entire row of homes. While I was out studying them, thousands of creatures suddenly appeared, most of which I had thought were nothing but the inventions of storytellers. Yet here they were, standing in my field, and not only standing, but fighting an army of smoke and fire. At the center of it all was the terrible beast I now know is named Kovol."

Elliot closed his eyes and tried to picture what that must have looked like to Minthred. He remembered how surprised he had been when he first saw the Brownies standing in his bedroom, and there were only three of them. Minthred's surprise must have been a lot bigger. And a lot worse.

"I hid in my bed for a while," Minthred wrote. "But one cannot hide from anything so awful for long. Besides, my goats were afraid too, and we couldn't all fit under the blanket."

Elliot scrunched up his face. He wouldn't invite a whole herd of goats to share his bed, whether they'd fit in there or not. No matter how scared they were.

Minthred continued, "I was finally forced to leave the safety of my bed, mostly because my goats ate the blanket. I knew that to face the war I needed the courage that would only come from a tall cup of turnip juice with just a bit of goat spit in it."

Elliot smiled. The Brownies also loved turnip juice, although he didn't think they added any goat spit to theirs. At least, he *hoped* not. Ick! Then he kept reading.

"But when I came to the battle, the Demon Kovol saw my drink. He smelled the turnip juice and roared that he was thirsty. His roar was so loud that all the earwax popped from my ears and fell into the cup. I dropped it and ran for my life. Kovol picked up the cup and drank it. All I know is that after drinking, he fell to the ground, fast asleep. The creatures cheered for me and said that I must be the finest of all wizards. They were so happy, I couldn't tell them I was only a simple goat herder, and that I had no idea why Kovol fell asleep."

And that was it. The last of the entry. The secret page that the Elves believed contained some all-powerful plan to defeat Kovol. What would they think if they knew that page had been written by some goat herder whose only magical power seemed to be the gift of producing an extreme amount of earwax?

Elliot slammed the book shut and then called for—how did he pronounce that again? Not Toe Jam. Maybe he could just call the Elf by his first name. Was it Slimy? Elliot groaned. If he couldn't remember the Elf's name, how could he possibly call him to come back and return Elliot to Burrowsville?

Chapter 12

Where Elliot Stops

Elliot waited in the tree for a moment before someone finally poofed up to see him. Only it wasn't the Elf.

It was Fidget, carrying a mirror in one hand and her wand in the other. She briefly glanced at him before returning to study herself in the mirror. "We're about to fight a war, and you're up here reading?" she asked.

He looked at the book. "The Elves gave it to me. But it wasn't very helpful."

"I could've told you that!" Fidget said.

"Why? Have you read it?"

Fidget scrunched up her nose. "Hello? Does it look like I read totally boring, thousand-year-old books?"

"I didn't think you read any books at all," Elliot said.

Fidget rapped him on the head with her wand for that, then said, "I happen to read the awesome magazine *Totally Awesome Teen*, and it is totally awesome. Your book is obviously a waste of time, because if it had anything important to say, Minthred would have covered it in pink glitter!"

She touched her wand to the book, which disappeared from his hands. "Hey!" he said.

"I sent it safely under your pillow at home. If you want to be bored, then read it there." Her eyes flicked up and down Elliot's body in disapproval. "You totally don't look like someone ready to lead an Underworld war," she said. "I mean, half your shirt is burned. And there's stuff on your shoulder that turned your skin green."

It was the paste that Patches had put on his burn from the Shadow Man. But Elliot wasn't in the mood to explain that to a Pixie princess. Actually, he didn't want to explain to anyone why his skin was green.

"Go away," he said. "I'm waiting for that Elf who brought me here. Do... do you remember his name?"

"It's Slimmy Tojam." Fidget closed one eye to magically dab a little color on the lid with her wand. Then a draft of wind tossed her up in the air, and she poked herself in the eye. Her eye turned pink, the color she had planned to put on her lid. "Ow!" she said. Then she did a quick check in the mirror. "Oh, groovy! I look so awesome."

"What about Mr. Tojam?" Elliot said.

"Oh. He's not coming back."

"Why not?"

She sighed. "Obviously, I sent him away. You'll have to get back to Burrowsville on your own."

"I can't—"

"Sure you can." Fidget lowered her mirror. "Do I have to explain everything to you, human?"

Elliot rolled his eyes. "You haven't explained *anything* to me."

"Oh, that's right." Fidget giggled and turned almost as pink as her eye. "How totally embarrassing! Well, here's the TBNN—totally brand-new news. It's the awesomest news you've probably ever had." Her tiny nose wrinkled. "Well, let's be honest. You probably don't get a lot of awesome news. I mean, your family doesn't even have enough money to give you a shirt without a hole in the armpit. And you've had a bully for almost as long as you've been alive. And you're king of the Brownies, who are, like, the lamest creatures ever when it comes to styling their hair. So I could probably tell you anything, and it would still be better than your usual news."

Elliot was tired of this. "What's the news, Fidget?"

She huffed. "Well, if you *are* going to lead us through this Underworld war, then the Pixies will help. And we thought, what is the awesomest thing we could do for you?" Her face brightened. "I'm the one who thought of this idea! I'm so proud of me." Then for no clear reason, she playfully punched Elliot in the arm, which hurt a lot, considering that her whole body was only the size of his arm. "How lucky are you that we're friends?"

"Obviously, the luckiest kid in the universe," Elliot muttered. "Now, what's the news?"

Fidget waved her wand and glitter poured all over him. It tingled and even tickled wherever it landed. He tried to brush it off, but that only rubbed it into his skin.

"Yay!" Fidget exclaimed.

"That's your big surprise?" Elliot asked. Whatever the glitter was for, it had come from the Pixies. Which meant he didn't like it, or trust it, even one bit.

Fidget frowned, clearly disappointed that he was not impressed. "Fine. If you don't care about it now, then maybe this will make you care."

His eyes narrowed. "What will make me care?"

She smiled and then aimed her wand at him. "Bye-bye."

With a slight *pop*, the branch beneath Elliot disappeared, and he found himself hurtling toward the ground. He knew he'd been high up before, but at the speed he was falling, the hard ground was only seconds away.

"Fid...get!" he yelled. "Help me!"

"Help yourself," she said, calmly flying beside him.

"What?"

"Just think about stopping, and you will."

"I can't!"

"Try it."

He flapped his arms and tried to think about stopping. But mostly all he could think about was panicking. And as everyone who has ever panicked before knows, it's not helpful for any kind of thinking.

Elliot looked down and saw the ground rushing up toward him. "Fidget! Help!"

"Think about stopping!" she insisted. "It's really important for you to do that. Right now!"

Elliot shut his eyes and whispered, "Stop, stop, stop," and then he yelled, "Stop!"

And everything stopped.

Elliot peeked with one eye, just to be sure he hadn't splattered onto the ground. Because if he had, he really didn't want to see what he looked like now.

Nope, he was still in one piece, and, oddly, he wasn't on the ground at all. Using both eyes now, he saw that the ground was in fact an inch or two below him. He had stopped in midair.

He blew out a heavy puff of air and landed on his face. Still lying flat on the ground, Elliot said, "Thank you, Fidget."

She landed gently on the ground beside him and sat on a small rock. "I didn't do that," she said. "You totally did it."

He lifted his head to look at her. A leaf was stuck to his forehead, but he left it there. "I did that? How?"

Fidget smiled. "Our gift to you is Pixie magic. You probably won't know how to use most of it, but you'll figure things out as you go. Totally awesome, right?"

"Totally." Elliot sat up and studied his hands. "I've got magic?" To test it, he raised his burned shoulder and thought the words, *Fix it*.

Answering his magical call, the threads of the shirt regained their color and wove themselves back together. The paste disappeared too, although Elliot noticed his skin was still a little green.

"Cool!" Elliot said.

"Lame," Fidget said. "I just gave you Pixie magic, and you use it to fix a shirt that doesn't even match my dress!"

"Okay. I can do better." Elliot stood and rubbed his hands together. Then he looked around for something bigger to test his magic on. He spotted Fidget's wand and wondered why she needed one and he didn't. Remembering the old cops-and-robbers games he used to play years ago, he closed one eye and pointed a finger at Fidget. "This is a stickup, so drop it!"

Just as he had hoped for, a spark of light shot from Elliot's finger and hit the wand, knocking it to the ground. But then a tall stick flew up from nearby and grabbed the back of Fidget's dress, carrying her high up into the air. Fidget screamed something about what she planned to do to him once she got down from there.

"Let her go, let her go!" Elliot cried. The stick immediately released her, and after a brief fall, Fidget's wings fluttered in the air. Her wand flew back into her hand, and she jetted angry sparks toward Elliot. He ducked, but the ends of his hair still got a little singed.

"That was so not awesome!" Fidget said. "What were you trying to do? Make me break a nail?"

"I thought it would only make you drop your wand," Elliot said. "I wondered if Pixie magic was strong enough to do that."

"Our magic isn't strong," Fidget said. "It's tricky. So be careful when using words like 'stickup.'"

"Sorry." Elliot scratched his head. "I bet it's strong enough for any reason I'd need it, though." It would've been cool to have this magic a year ago when Tubs Lawless was bullying him. But after Elliot won the Goblin war, he'd stood up to Tubs and hadn't been bullied since. Maybe he could ask Tubs to hit him one more time, just for the memories. Then *zapowie!* Pixie magic revenge!

Of course, with Elliot's luck, the Pixies would play a joke and take away his magic. Then it would just be *za-nothing* and a sore arm for Elliot where Tubs punched him.

"Our magic only helps you with tricks, not strength," Fidget said, still annoyed. "So stop playing around. It's time to fight Kovol."

"Can I fly?"

"We gave you magic, not wings."

Elliot didn't want wings anyway. He'd have to put holes in all of his shirts to fit them. Also, it would be hard to hide the wings from his mom. She would notice something like that.

"How do I poof?" Elliot asked. "I can do that, right?"

"Of course. That's like preschool magic. As clearly as you can, think of the place where you want to go, and then send yourself there." She tossed her hair behind her. "So where are we going?"

"*I'm* going home to check on my family," Elliot said. "*You're* going back to Burrowsville. I want everyone who can do battle to meet me in Demon Territory in one hour. Then we start to fight back."

For the first time, Fidget didn't seem to care how she looked or sounded. Her shoulders slumped and she said, "We gave you the best gift we could, Elliot. You have to help us win this war or everything will be destroyed."

Elliot smiled. "I will help. Totally."

Chapter 13

Where Kovol Knows Elliot's Name

Elliot's first ever experience of poofing himself somewhere wasn't as smooth as he had expected it to be. Finally he understood why the Brownies had so much difficulty poofing humans and why the Pixies made it such a rough trip. It was hard to take yourself out of one place and put yourself back together in another. There was a lot more to it than just thinking about where you wanted to go. The trip had happened in less than a second, and yet in some ways it felt more like an hour. At one point Elliot forgot to bring his feet along (and as you can probably understand, Dear Reader, his feet were very upset about being left behind—feet are picky about things like that), but when he opened his eyes, he was inside the bedroom of his house, feet and all.

The first thing Elliot did was to look under his pillow for Minthred's book. It was there, exactly as Fidget told him it would be. He retrieved it, then slid the book under his bed, far from where anyone might find it. Then he pulled off his shirt and shoved that under his bed too. He studied his green shoulder. The color had faded a little, but the burn seemed to have gone away. At least it didn't sting anymore.

He went to his closet for another shirt. The first one he reached for had a small ketchup stain on the sleeve. The second one was comfortable and in good condition, but it was a strange shade of blue. Fidget would say it didn't look like the sort of thing the leader of an Underworld war would wear.

"Argh!" Elliot said in frustration, then pulled the blue shirt from his closet. If he was going to fight an Underworld war, then he should at least be comfortable while doing it.

Next he went downstairs to find something to eat. Wendy might not be the best cook ever, but he was pretty sure her food was better than whatever he might find in Demon Territory.

Or, wait—he had magical powers now. He could have any food he wanted. He could magic himself up a thick hamburger with all the toppings and a whole plate of fries. Or a big bowl of spaghetti. Or even a tray of doughnuts… with their holes. This magic thing was great!

"There you are," Wendy said when she saw him coming down the stairs. "I made you a sandwich an hour ago. It's been sitting for a while, so it's probably all dried out, but we can't waste the food."

Elliot's image of the doughnuts popped in his head like someone had put a pin to a balloon. He still wanted to use some magic to make himself lunch, but Wendy was sure to notice. He couldn't figure out any way to convince her that the doughnuts had just been left on the front porch by the mailman, or any other excuse.

Wendy was sitting on the couch still watching the news stories about the sinkholes. He grabbed the sandwich and took a bite, which promptly stuck in his throat. It took three swallows to get it down, and then it sat like a lump in his empty stomach. It was dry all right, like eating a piece of the Sahara Desert.

Dear Reader, if you are looking for a fun place to spend your summer vacation, consider the Sahara Desert. It's as large as the entire United States, so you'll have plenty of room to play. Many different nomadic groups live there, so you're sure to meet lots of interesting people. And if you aren't attacked by sand vipers, scorpions, or the Saharan cheetah, you should be just fine. Unless there's a sandstorm. Or if you run out of water and can't find even one drop for hundreds of miles around you. Or if you forget to bring an extension cord long enough to charge your video game player. Also, you should know that you won't find many swimming pools in the Sahara Desert, so don't worry about packing a swimsuit. You won't need it.

While thinking of the hamburger he could be eating right now, Elliot choked down the rest of the Sahara Desert sandwich and then sat beside his sister.

She pointed to the television screen. "Look at this! Some new sinkholes started appearing on Main Street about ten minutes ago. Luckily nobody was hurt, but a lot of parked cars fell in."

Elliot looked around the room. "Where is everyone?"

"The twins went to make sure Uncle Rufus's jail hasn't sunk," Wendy said. Uncle Rufus had the unfortunate habit of stealing shiny things. Every time he got caught, he claimed he was too old to remember that it was still against the law to steal things. That trick had only worked the first ten times. Elliot wished Wendy hadn't let the twins go, but at least the jail wasn't anywhere near Main Street.

"What about Reed?" he asked.

"He had to work at the Quack Shack," Wendy said. "I told him not to go, but Reed says he'll get fired if he doesn't have a good reason for not showing up."

"The Quack Shack is in the middle of all those sinkholes," Elliot said. "I think he has a really good reason not to go!"

"Reed didn't know about the holes when he left. But when they started happening, Cami said she'd go try to stop him. I'm sure they'll be back soon. Shh, the reporter's talking."

The cameras went live on Main Street, where the reporter explained that although most sinkholes are round, these new ones on Main Street had different shapes to them. "It's as if someone below the earth collapsed them to look just this way," he explained.

Then the camera cut to an overhead shot from a helicopter. At the angle the cameraman was shooting from, the shapes didn't appear to mean anything. The one at the top looked like a square *M*. Down from that shape were two sideways lines, and then there was a third, shorter line with a dot beside it. Next was a perfectly round hole, and finally, another sideways line at the bottom.

"What could these symbols mean?" the reporter asked. "Is it some message from aliens to Earth? A warning perhaps?"

"It's not aliens," Elliot mumbled. But it definitely was a warning.

"I guess we'll never know what it means," Wendy said. "I'll bet scientists will study this for years."

Elliot tilted his head to the side and looked at the Main Street sinkholes differently. "It's my name," he said. Looked at sideways, the square *M* was an *E*. The two lines were lowercase *L*s. Then the rest of the letters in his name followed.

Wendy laughed. "What? No." She tilted her head too, and said, "Your name has a *T* at the end. That last sinkhole shape just looks like another low-ercase *L*. Your name isn't Elliol."

"I'm telling you, that's my name," Elliot said.

"You're being ridiculous!"

Then the camera shook and the reporter yelled, "It's happening again!" A puff of dirt rose in the air. When it cleared, the camera focused in on the newest sinkhole. Elliot sighed. Kovol had crossed the *T*.

"Oh, well, now I see your name," Wendy said. "That's weird."

"Not as weird as you might think," Elliot said. "I've got to go."

"Still working on that secret paper-mache project?"

"Huh?"

Wendy smiled. "You don't have to be embarrassed. Cami told us that you were working on a paper-mache doll of her and that you didn't want anyone to bother you in your room."

Elliot rolled his eyes. "That's what she said I was doing?" Couldn't she have picked something better? Like maybe he was lifting weights all morning or rescuing pets from burning houses? Then he sighed. A part of him wished Cami would have told Wendy the truth. It would have helped to talk to his sister about the Brownies and the Underworld war and about why there was a sinkhole on Main Street in the shape of his name. He was tired of keeping so many secrets from his family.

But it was not his secret to tell. The knowledge of the Underworld belonged to the creatures who lived there, not to him.

"Yeah, whatever Cami said, I have to go back and do that," Elliot said. "I'll be busy for a while, maybe a really long time."

"Okay." Wendy shrugged, then returned to watching the television.

Elliot ran back upstairs. As soon as he was out of sight, he closed his eyes, pictured the scene on Main Street, and poofed himself there.

Chapter 14

Where Kovol Wants a Duck Burger

Elliot might have thought about the shops and stores on Main Street, but he never could have pictured all the people running in the streets, pushing one another to get as far from the sinkholes as possible. He had tried to poof into a quiet part of the street, but when he got there it was obvious that nothing on this street was quiet today.

The sinkholes were in the middle of the road. From here, Elliot couldn't see his name, but he knew that hundreds of feet below this very spot, Kovol was sending Elliot the message that he was angry. Well, duh. Did he think Elliot hadn't figured that out yet?

"Excuse me," a woman said, nearly running him over.

He moved for her, which put him in the way of a man who only looked down at Elliot long enough to tell him to go home before he also hurried away.

Elliot wanted to get to the Quack Shack, but it was a little farther up the road. Elliot hoped Reed had seen the sinkholes and gotten away before he came into work. Elliot pushed past people who were pushing past him even harder. At first he had tried getting through politely by saying things like "Excuse me," or "Can I get by?" But now he just yelled "Move!" at anyone in his way.

"Elliot?"

He turned as Cami grabbed his arm. "I thought you were in the Underground," she said.

"The Underworld," he said. "I came back to check on my family."

"Thank goodness. Reed needs help."

"Reed? Where is he?"

For the first time ever, Elliot didn't care that Cami took his hand while she led him forward through the crowd. She was good at dodging people, and in no time they had made it to the front door of the Quack Shack. Through the main window they saw Reed on the floor, unconscious.

Elliot pushed on the door, but it wouldn't open.

"It's stuck," Cami said. "It jammed when the last sinkhole collapsed."

"Reed!" Elliot pounded on the window to wake up his brother, but Reed didn't move.

"We need to get some help." Cami stepped forward in the crowd. "Excuse me, please—" But everyone passed her by, in their own hurry to leave Main Street.

While her head was turned, Elliot closed his eyes and pictured the door opening. He didn't think "un-jam" was a word, but he couldn't think of any other word to describe what he wanted the door to do. He whispered that to himself, then checked the door again. Something dark purple began oozing from the door near its handle. He leaned low and sniffed. It was sweet and fruity. On a guess, Elliot put a finger to the stuff and tasted it. Sure enough—grape jam! It was sort of gross, but the jam got into the lock and loosened the door enough for Elliot to inch it open.

"We're in," he called to Cami. "C'mon!"

She ran to help him with the door but then pulled her hand back. "Is that jam?"

"Don't ask," he said.

They rushed inside the Quack Shack and called again for help, but nobody answered. Reed was there alone, clearly because he was the only employee who thought the Quack Shack would be serving duck burgers while the entire city was collapsing.

Elliot dropped to his knees and shook his brother's arm. "Reed!"

Cami pressed her fingers to the side of Reed's neck to feel a pulse. "He's alive," she said. "But we've got to get him out of here."

"Help me lift him up." Elliot stood and tugged on Reed's arms, pulling him into a sitting position, and then saw two giant footprints in the floor beneath where Reed had lain. Not *on* the floor, but *in* it, smashed into the tiles.

"What could have done that?" Cami asked.

"Kovol," Elliot breathed. "Kovol was here. On the surface."

He quickly looked around them, then said to Cami, "I've got to try something that might feel weird to you. But you have to trust me, okay?"

She shrugged. "Okay. I trust you."

He put one hand on Reed's shoulder and took Cami's hand again. "It's better if you close your eyes," he said.

Elliot next closed his own eyes and pictured his bedroom as clearly as he possibly could. And poofed them all home.

It was harder than he had imagined. Instead of keeping one person's body parts together, now he had to do that for three people. And from the first second she had felt her gut being pulled away from the Quack Shack, Cami had started to do the girl-squeal thing. Even if poofing only lasts a single second, it can seem like hours if the girl next to you is squealing.

Then she stopped and they landed in Elliot's room. Somewhere during the trip, Reed had lost his Quack Shack apron, but Elliot hadn't worked very hard to keep track of that. All the important body parts seemed to have come back together and in their correct places.

"How did we get here?" Cami asked. "Did you do it?"

"I'm sort of new at magic, so I didn't do it very well." Elliot patted Reed's cheek. "Wake up. Please."

Slowly, Reed shook his head, then let out a long moan. His eyelids fluttered while he thought about waking up, and he raised a hand to his head.

"Ow," he mumbled.

"Are you okay?" Elliot asked.

Reed opened one eye and then the other. "Where are we?"

"Home."

"How did I get here?"

Cami began, "Elliot did some—"

"Really heavy lifting to get you here," Elliot finished.

"I had this horrible dream," Reed said. "I was in the Quack Shack, and this huge purple beast appeared. He asked if I was Penster. I said that I was Reed Penster and asked if he was hungry, because I figured even if he was a horrible beast, he'd probably order a lot of duck burgers. Then he roared and charged toward me. Then you appeared out of nowhere, Elliot, and dared the beast to come back and chase after you. He picked me up and threw me against the wall. The next thing I remember is waking up here."

Beside Elliot, Cami's mouth was hanging open almost to the floor. Elliot could only stare at Reed, relieved things hadn't been worse. Kovol must have lost Harold, who was shapeshifted as Elliot, so he came looking for Elliot in Sprite's Hollow. Luckily, Harold had arrived just in time to save Reed and got Kovol to chase after him again. But the chase could not last much longer. And Elliot could not let Kovol come back to the surface.

He quietly poofed the family's broom into his own closet, then stood and said to Cami, "Wendy will help you take care of Reed. And tell her to get the twins home and make them stay here."

"Where are you going?" she asked.

"You know where."

Then he grabbed the broom from his closet, walked into the hallway, and immediately poofed himself to the darkest part of the entire Underworld.

Chapter 15

Where Grissel Returns

Harold the Shapeshifter had been given only one job that day, which was to turn into Elliot and lead Kovol on a chase anywhere away from Demon Territory. Elliot hoped Harold had led Kovol and all of his army far away by now. Because if Harold made any mistakes, poofing into Demon Territory wasn't a good idea.

He was kidding himself, of course. It would *never* be a good idea to poof into Demon Territory.

But Elliot already had a plan in mind. If Kovol was there, he'd just put up a magical shield or something. The only problem with this plan was that he had no idea how to create a magical shield, and he was pretty sure Kovol wouldn't give him any second chances to figure it out. So it wasn't a perfect plan.

It had been a bit of a trick for Elliot to poof himself into Demon Territory, because he had a hard time picturing exactly where he wanted to go. The only places he remembered there were dark enough to make him want to poof anywhere else. Finally he decided to go to the area right outside Kovol's cave.

It was very dark there, but better there than inside the cave. On a scale of 1 to 10, with 10 being the creepiest place in the known universe, Elliot figured that spot was an easy 10. But it was way better than inside the cave, which was at least a 789.

Once he arrived, Elliot hunched down to the ground. He wasn't sure exactly why he did that, but it seemed like a good idea. Everything was as eerily quiet as it had been four months ago when he had first entered Demon Territory.

Not far from him was a puddle of mud with a brown glow around it. Elliot recognized it as gripping mud. He'd been stuck in it twice and had kept Kovol trapped in some until the solar eclipse earlier that day.

Elliot looked around carefully for any sign of smoke, which would indicate that the Shadow Men were nearby. But he saw nothing and hadn't really expected to. Kovol thought he was chasing Elliot across the Underworld, so he had likely called his army of Shadow Men to help him there.

Or most of his army anyway. There were thousands of Shadow Men. It wouldn't take long before some of them sensed that Elliot was in Demon Territory. If they told Kovol, he'd be all kinds of angry. Especially the bad kinds.

"Mr. Willimaker!" Elliot called.

Mr. Willimaker immediately appeared, holding his hands over his ears. "Your Highness, when you called just now, it was so loud, so different from before. How did you—"

"I've got magic," Elliot said, "from the Pixies."

"Ah. Well, then, you don't have to yell anymore to call us. We'll hear you fine." Mr. Willimaker pressed his thick eyebrows together. "Be careful about Pixie magic, Elliot. Like Pixies themselves, their magic will sometimes trick you."

Trick magic was still better than no magic, Elliot figured. But he only said, "I think so far we're alone here. When other creatures start appearing, I want us to use Kovol's cave as our defense. It's the closest thing Kovol has to a home, so I don't think he'd collapse it, even to fight us. I'll wait on top of his cave, watching for any sign of trouble. When everyone is ready down there, let me know. We're going to fight as many Shadow Men as we can before Kovol comes."

Mr. Willimaker bowed and poofed away. Then Elliot closed his eyes and poofed with the broom to the top of Kovol's cave. It was higher off the ground than he had expected, but that only gave him a better view. Not that there was much to see. It was as black as midnight in all directions.

That didn't last for long, though. As the different creatures poofed into Demon Territory, they created enough light to help them see and to help Elliot see them. The Satyrs arrived first. They were as tall as the Elves, each of them with thick fur on the bottom half of their body, the hooves of goats, and a man's body on top. They had horns on their head and long ears that stuck out sideways. Then several Leprechauns flew in, each on the back of a Pegasus so white it almost created its own light. Elliot wasn't sure how he could use the Leprechauns (although he had plenty of ideas for how his family could use their gold), but he liked the flying horses. He wondered if the Underworld had any Dragons, because that would be cool too. Then he figured maybe it was better not to ask. Being creatures of fire, they probably had more in common with the Shadow Men than with him.

The Elves arrived next, and near the front of them was Slimmy Tojam. He nodded at Elliot, who only wanted to yell down to him that Minthred's book had been a huge waste of time. But if a goat herder could defeat Kovol, then surely Elliot could. He was only in fifth grade, but he was positive that was more education than Minthred had ever got.

He realized that several creatures hadn't come. Agatha wasn't there. There were several Fairies, but no Pixies. Many Brownies had come, but not the women or children, and Elliot was glad for that. He didn't want to risk anything happening to Patches.

Then Elliot saw Fudd poof in with a group of familiar creatures. The Goblins had arrived.

Elliot closed his eyes to poof himself down there. The Goblins looked surprised to see him use magic, but not Fudd, who obviously had not seen Elliot do anything at all.

"Well, well. Look at how the human king has grown," a voice sneered.

Behind all the other Goblins was Grissel. He was the strongest and boniest of all Goblins, and the meanest too. Every other Goblin was literally green with envy at the exact shade of Grissel's skin, for it was the closest in color to their favorite food, pickles. Grissel was plumper now than he used to be, due to the amount of chocolate cake he had eaten over his last several months inside Brownie jail. He was probably meaner too. "It looks like you've learned a few tricks since we last met," Grissel added.

When they had last met, Grissel and Elliot had tied in a battle to the death. It wasn't the first time they had fought. In fact, every time Elliot and Grissel met, it always seemed that Grissel was trying to finish him off.

"You'll fight for me?" Elliot asked Grissel.

Grissel's eyes narrowed. "I'll fight for the Underworld. I'll even fight for the Brownies, if necessary, to defeat Kovol. But I'd never fight for a human."

As if Elliot cared about a detail like that. "Then fight for the Underworld," he said. "I need the Goblins in front when the Shadow Men come. Slow them down by blowing things up. We can't fight all of them at once, but we can fight back if only a few get through at a time."

With that, Elliot turned to everyone else. He told his magic to make his voice louder, and when he spoke, it was as if he was speaking through a powerful microphone. "The Shadow Men are nothing but fire and darkness that Kovol has cursed. You can't fight them like a normal army, because they're not alive or dead. They're just a curse that will move until it's stopped. They will act like fire. If they surround you, they will suck air away from you. If they touch you, it will burn." Elliot looked over at Fudd. "And if they spit on you, it'll curse you too. But if you can suck the air away from them, you'll put out their fire. I bet it's the same if you get water on them."

"But how do we do that?" an Elf near Elliot said. "Only a few creatures have that power."

"It was a mistake to come," a Gnome grumbled. Several creatures muttered their agreement.

Elliot ran to a rock and stood higher up on it. He remembered his broom and held it up. "No, wait! If we try to fight this separately, then we will lose separately. The Underworld must stand together now."

"What's the broom for?" a Goblin asked. "Sweeping the Shadow Men out of here?"

"I can use this," Elliot said. "For when I fight the Shadow Men."

"What do you know about our fight?" a Centaur said. "You're not from our world."

"I'm not," Elliot agreed. "But I'm a part of it now. I always will be. I'll help save your world, and you'll help save mine. If you don't have power to control the air or water, then you still have something to offer. Light."

The creatures pressed closer, curious about Elliot's plan. He continued, "When the Shadow Men attacked Burrowsville earlier today, they couldn't push through the light. If they tried, they disappeared. So light is your weapon. Get a stick or a wand or whatever you have, and make it as light as you can. A Shadow Man is not only fire, he's also darkness. But your light is stronger than him. Dark cannot exist in light places. And we claim Demon Territory as a place of light now."

From his place on the rock, Elliot saw smoke in the distance, but coming closer. "They're early," he mumbled. He had hoped they wouldn't come so soon.

"Everyone find a place to hide," he called. "Goblins, you go to the border to slow them down. Get ready! The Shadow Men are here!"

Chapter 16

Where Harold Makes a Mistake

The battle of Demon Territory began with an explosion so big it rattled the entire ground. The wind it created rushed across the dark land, shaking the few trees and bushes that had dared to grow there.

Fudd stood on one side of Elliot and said, "That was Grissel. Nobody can blow things up the way he can." There was a hint of admiration in his voice, and even Elliot was impressed.

Elliot, Fudd, and Mr. Willimaker had returned to their places on top of Kovol's cave, but even from high up they couldn't see the Goblins.

The explosion created so much smoke near the border that it was impossible to see the difference between dust from the explosions and the Shadow Men moving deeper into Demon Territory. Elliot planned to keep everyone hidden for as long as possible. He didn't want the Shadow Men to have any warning in this battle.

But the Shadow Men must have already known something was wrong. Because as they flew close enough to be seen, their flight was swift and direct. They were coming to the cave and coming for a fight. If the heat of their black fire was any clue, this battle wouldn't be easy.

"Steady," Elliot whispered, more to himself than to anyone else. "Not yet. Not yet."

In the darkness, and with the speed of their flight, it was hard to tell how many were coming. Beside him, Elliot heard Mr. Willimaker trying to count them anyway. Fudd wiped sweat from his brow and looked nervous. Elliot wondered what it must feel like to sense the approach of the enemy but not be able to see them. Probably not great.

"How many do you think there are?" Elliot asked.

"At least fifty in the air." Then Mr. Willimaker pointed to the horizon. "And more are coming. Many more."

When the first of the Shadow Men was close enough that Elliot saw the fire in his cloak, he stood and yelled, "Underworld creatures, FIGHT!"

Immediately the territory came to life. The creatures focused any light they could into sticks, wands, and some even lit up their shoes for the fight. The Shadow Men swarmed in, and the battle began.

From where Elliot stood, he could see everything. The Brownies and Dwarves were doing their best with water. Their arms were too short to fight the Shadow Men alone, but the Brownies poofed in bucket after bucket of water for the Dwarves to throw on the Shadow Men, who quickly fell like drops of gray mud to the ground.

The Fairies and Pixies were working together to operate a giant fan that seemed to have the exact opposite effect of normal fans. Instead of blowing out cool air, it sucked in hot air. The Shadow Men who had ignored the fan at first were now too close and tried to fly away. But the fan continued pulling them in, and when it did, only ashes came out the other side.

Each Shadow Man destroyed took out another piece of Kovol's curse. Everything was going exactly the way Elliot had hoped it would.

The rest of Elliot's army fought one to one. They held off the remaining Shadow Men with their light sticks. None of the Shadow Men wanted to touch those sticks, which was fine with Elliot's creatures who really didn't want to get any closer than they had to.

In the distance, the Goblins continued to blow things up as new waves of Shadow Men approached. Every time Elliot heard an explosion, he knew that some had been slowed down and some had gotten through.

Yet so far, Elliot's side was holding its own.

"We're winning!" Elliot said excitedly to Fudd and Mr. Willimaker. "I think we're going to win this!"

Elliot may have spoken too soon. He heard a popping sound beside him and turned. In his human form, Harold was sitting beside Elliot, out of breath and with a very worried look on his face.

"I tried," Harold panted. "I tried, Elliot."

"Why are you here?" Elliot asked. "Where's Kovol?"

"I'm sorry. I made a mistake."

Elliot shook his head. "Harold, you were supposed to keep him far away from here!"

"I know." Harold took a deep breath. "I let him chase me everywhere. At one point he got bored and went up to the surface to look for you, but I got him back. But I got confused." Then his eyebrows pressed together. "I had to run so fast, and I forgot where I was. I led him back here."

Elliot gestured around them. "Here? You brought Kovol here?"

A deafening screech roared from the edge of Demon Territory. Hearing it, all the Shadow Men left Kovol's cave and flew away.

"That's Kovol calling his army back now," Harold said, burying his face in his hands. "We're in a lot of trouble, and it's all my fault."

Down on the dark ground, the Underworld creatures looked around at one another, confused and alarmed. They had heard the screech too.

"What's happening?" a Centaur said. "Something's wrong."

"Everyone poof away from here!" Elliot cried. "Back to Burrowsville. Hurry!"

A few of the creatures obeyed, but most of them stared toward the border of Demon Territory, where smoke was gathering into the shape of a cone. It quickly twisted into a circle, slowly moving at the top, where it was widest, and spinning faster and tighter at the bottom.

"What is that?" Mr. Willimaker asked. "I've never seen anything like that before."

"We have those on the surface," Elliot said. "If that's what I think it is."

Elliot knew no one could stop what was coming. They weren't protected beside Kovol's cave. They were trapped there!

"That's a tornado!" he said. But unlike the tornadoes on the surface world, this one was made of smoke and fire. "Everyone hurry!" he yelled. "Poof out of here now!"

Chapter 17

Where Grissel Goes Free...Sort Of

We have to leave now!" Fudd called to Elliot. Already, the wind created by the Shadow Men was so loud it sounded as if a train was running through Demon Territory.

Mr. Willimaker held tightly to his hat with one hand and to his glasses with the other. "It's too late," he said. "With wind this powerful, nobody could hold themselves together to safely poof away."

"Everyone go inside the cave!" Elliot ordered. "There's less wind. You can poof away there!"

Nobody needed to be told. Creatures were already rushing into the cave. Above the noise of the wind, Elliot yelled to both Fudd and Mr. Willimaker to leave. They couldn't poof themselves, but Elliot helped them shimmy down the roof, then he used his broomstick to lower them into the arms of some nearby Trolls.

"You must come too," Fudd said.

"I'll wait until everyone else is safely inside, and then I'll come," Elliot said. Sure, that was the kind of thing a good leader did, but mostly Elliot still hadn't decided which was worse: Kovol's creepy cave or a huge tornado.

When the last of the creatures was inside, Elliot sat on the edge of the cave, preparing to jump to the ground.

Then suddenly he held his ears as a voice boomed inside his head. It was louder than the oncoming tornado and made his brain vibrate.

"Underworld creatures, you are in my territory, so you are my prisoners now!"

Elliot recognized Kovol's voice. Every word felt like fingernails scratching on a chalkboard.

But Kovol wasn't a ruler. Or was he? Could he order prisoners not to poof away? Elliot had been sure he couldn't, or else he wouldn't have brought everyone here.

Then Elliot asked himself why he had believed that Kovol couldn't take prisoners. Nobody had told him so. He hadn't asked anyone about it. Maybe he had convinced himself he was right because he wanted to be right, not because it was true. He had made a huge mistake!

"Nobody leaves this place," Kovol ordered. "I am coming! And I will destroy you all!"

When the voice had gone, Elliot slid the rest of the way down the cave and then ran inside. He tried not to look at the dark walls and wonder what crawled there. Or to peek in the direction where Kovol had slept for a thousand years.

The first thing he tried was to poof himself away. Maybe Kovol was wrong and couldn't make such an order. Or maybe this was like the movies. Since Kovol was the bad guy, then the good guys could find a way to ignore Kovol's order. But no matter how hard he concentrated on Burrowsville or his bedroom at home, or anywhere else, he couldn't leave. Along with every other creature still inside this cave, he was trapped.

"How many of us got away?" he asked. "Before Kovol made us prisoners."

Mr. Willimaker shrugged. "Not many. Maybe only a hundred or so. But hundreds more are still in here. There's nothing we can do but wait like trapped prey!"

"The Goblins are coming!" someone up front called. "Everyone scoot back, or we won't all fit!"

It was easy to smell when they entered. Elliot had thought the cave smelled bad before, but the Goblins brought it to a whole new level of stink.

"Where's Grissel?" Elliot asked a Goblin with a thin and bony face. But the Goblin shrugged and hurried away. So Elliot called out, "Does anyone know where Grissel is?"

Several of the Goblins pointed outside, and a tall one up front said, "The Shadow Men know that Grissel was blowing up Demon Territory. They have him trapped."

Elliot grabbed his broom and ran toward the mouth of Kovol's cave. He felt a tug on his arm and turned to see Mr. Willimaker with Fudd standing beside him.

"No, Your Highness. It's too dangerous," Mr. Willimaker said.

"Kovol will be here any moment," Fudd added. "You can't go out there."

Mr. Willimaker nodded in agreement. "Besides, think of everything that Grissel has done to you. He's not worth it."

Elliot said, "Every creature is worth it. I've got to help him." From here, Elliot felt a little of the wind created by the Shadow Men. It would be worse outside. He held his broom in front of him and thought the word "light," but when he peeked at the broom, it was only about as bright as a light bulb. That wasn't good enough. So he thought of the sunlight, of his family, and of everything good he had ever known, and he poured all of those thoughts into his broom.

Immediately the stick lit with a glow that spread light into every corner of the cave. Elliot held the broom high, then walked back into the storm.

There had to be hundreds of Shadow Men forming the tornado. It was taller than he could see and loud enough to make vibrations in his head. Somewhere in the middle of it all was Grissel. Elliot knew how it felt to be trapped as the Shadow Men sucked out all the air. He wouldn't let that happen to anyone, not even his Goblin enemy.

He tried pushing forward through the wind, but even with all of his concentration, there wasn't enough Pixie magic inside him to keep from being blown away. If he couldn't move forward, he couldn't save Grissel. The wind was so much stronger than he was. Then Elliot felt a sudden surge in his strength and slowly forced himself ahead. He took a quick glance behind him and saw many of the creatures at the entrance, their hands held out to him. It took a minute to understand what they were doing, and then he knew. He was moving forward by their power, not his own. They were using their magic to help him walk into a tornado.

When Elliot got close to it, he stretched out his arms with the lit broomstick. One by one, the Shadow Men crashed into the light, and one by one they fell to ashes. Elliot's arms shook from being so tired, but he held on. He *had* to hold on, because plan B (hoping the Shadow Men got dizzy and fell down on their own) was terrible. Gradually the wind died down as the Shadow Men either flew away or crashed into his broom and disappeared. He had fought a tornado and won!

When the last of them had gone, Elliot fell to the ground, exhausted. After only a minute he felt a bony hand on his arm, helping him to sit up.

"You're not such a bad human after all," Grissel said, smiling. "King Elliot, I promise never to harm your Brownies ever again."

"Then you're free to leave my jail," Elliot whispered.

"I don't think that matters," Grissel said. "You got rid of the Shadow Men for now. But all of us are trapped here in Demon Territory. And Kovol is coming."

Chapter
18

Where the Plan Fails

Elliot might have stopped the tornado of Shadow Men, but it didn't take them long to figure out where everyone was hiding. Elliot and Grissel had barely made it back into the cave before the Shadow Men returned.

"Quick!" Elliot said to the Goblins. "Blow up the entrance."

"But that will leave us trapped inside," an Elf said.

The Dwarves were the only ones who cheered at that idea. They often made their homes underground and, in fact, preferred living there. Everyone else started arguing.

"Better that we're trapped in here than to let the Shadow Men come and get us," Elliot said.

Grissel nodded his agreement with Elliot's order, and the Goblins raised their hands to blow up the cave entrance.

But it was too late.

Hundreds of Shadow Men flew inside the cave with so much speed, all that could be seen was their trail of black smoke, which quickly filled the air. Everyone began coughing and sputtering.

"Change into a stick," Elliot said to Harold between coughs. "Or a rock. Something that doesn't need to breathe."

"If it doesn't breathe, it doesn't think," Harold said. "I won't be able to think myself back."

"Do it!" Elliot said. There wasn't time for arguing.

He heard a small pop and saw a bright orange rock on the ground. "The idea was to be less obvious," Elliot muttered to Harold the Rock. Harold the Rock didn't answer. No big surprise. Rocks are not known for their skills at conversation. Even shapeshifted ones.

Elliot watched the remaining creatures try fighting back with their sticks of light, but without enough air they had no strength to hold on to them. The sticks lost their light and clattered to the ground. Even Elliot found he couldn't hold on to his broom. It was hard enough just to breathe.

One by one the dark claws of the Shadow Men reached out and touched several creatures on their heads. As they did, the creatures froze in place.

Elliot looked up from the ground where he sat, still coughing and choking on smoke. "What's happening to them?"

Beside him, Mr. Willimaker said, "They've turned to stone. It's a curse. As long as the Shadow Men move, our friends will not."

Using the last bit of energy he had, Elliot wrote a message in the dirt. It said, "Orange rock."

Then as loudly as he could, he said, "The only one you want is me. If you leave these creatures alone, I'll let you take me to Kovol."

The Shadow Men stopped in midair. Only a few hundred creatures remained uncursed.

"No, Your Highness." Fudd stood and yelled to the Shadow Men, "Take me!"

"Or me!" Mr. Willimaker said.

They were joined in chorus by dozens of other creatures, each volunteering himself in place of Elliot.

Smoke instantly filled the room, making it even darker than pitch black. (Who knew that was even possible?) Elliot heard the thuds of bodies falling to the ground around him, and everything went silent. As the air gradually cleared, Elliot looked around the cave. Every other creature who had escaped being turned to stone had fallen on the ground. It looked like they were asleep, but they were moaning and shivering.

"What did you do?" Elliot yelled at the Shadow Men.

"A cold coma," the Shadow Men said in unison. "We pulled all the heat from their bodies."

"Well, give it back! I said I would go to Kovol *if* you left everyone alone."

Every Shadow Man in the cave, hundreds of them, laughed with one single laugh. Then together, all of them said, "Oh, but you will go to Kovol. He's ready for you now."

They began swirling around Elliot, choking off his air again. But this time there was no one to save him. His second-to-last thought was how tired he was of Kovol's army doing this, as if they didn't know any other tricks. It was like being a great pianist but knowing only one song. Elliot's last thought was that he was about to pass out, and that when he awoke again, he'd be facing Kovol as his prisoner.

Chapter 19

Where Elliot's Feet Complain

Oddly, when Elliot woke up, he was *not* facing Kovol, or even the Shadow Men. He was facing a tree, which as everyone knows is much less dangerous than an evil Demon and his army. He was also tied up and hanging upside down, which was a bigger problem. It was the sort of thing Tubs had done to him plenty of times. Elliot felt all the blood in his body rushing from his feet to his head, which he hoped would be a good thing. He figured since blood was important for living, it was probably just as important for thinking. And thinking was exactly what Elliot wanted to do right now. Besides, as long as he was tied up this way, he really had nothing better to do other than think.

As nice as the tree was to look at, Elliot twisted his body around to get a different view. He couldn't be certain, because things always look different when you're upside down, but he was pretty sure he was somewhere in the woods behind his house. Which meant Kovol was also here, or he would be soon.

Elliot thought about calling for help, but nobody would be this deep into the woods, especially not this late in the day. And he didn't know how he would explain what was happening, even if he did get someone to come.

Dear Reader, as one of the great coincidences of all time, the great adventurer Diffle McSnug was in these very woods only five minutes before Elliot arrived. Although Diffle has had many wonderful adventures, including his most recent trip down the rapids of the Nile River while balanced on a crocodile's back, Diffle has read the books of Elliot's earlier adventures and was very distressed to realize he was not a character anywhere in them!

So in the effort to make himself a character once and for all, Diffle came to the woods behind Elliot's house, sure that if he looked hard enough, he would find Elliot in great need of help. Once he rescued Elliot, he was sure to finally be made a character.

Unfortunately, Elliot was still in the Underworld at the time. Diffle forgot to look for him there, perhaps because he didn't know *how* to check the Underworld. Diffle can do many great things, but, alas, he cannot poof. Nor can he curl his tongue, but that's really not important right now. Diffle had left the woods only five minutes before Kovol brought Elliot here as his prisoner. Sadly, Elliot was, in fact, very much in need of help.

Since Diffle missed his chance to help Elliot, the decision by the Committee on Character Placement is that Diffle will not be admitted as a character in this or any other book about Elliot. After all his troubles, Diffle still needs to get his own book. Poor Diffle.

And poor Elliot! He just had to wait through an entire story about someone who isn't even a character in this book. Still upside down, and still all alone, with no chance for escape.

Or could he?

Because Elliot remembered he had Pixie magic. Most readers might think if they had Pixie magic, it wouldn't be the sort of thing they'd forget, whether they were hanging upside down or not. But Elliot had a good excuse. After all, he was facing the end of the world, which was partly his own fault since he did wake up Kovol. And if you recall, he'd only had the Sahara Desert sandwich for lunch, so he was also a little hungry. In other words, he'd had a hard day. Also, all the blood in his body was rushing to his head, so his thoughts were starting to get really crowded, and the thought about Pixie magic was stuck way in the back, where it had almost been forgotten.

With Pixie magic, escaping would be simple. All he had to do was poof away. Then maybe hide in the bushes until Kovol came and saw that his trap was empty. Elliot thought he'd love to see the expression on Kovol's face. He'd be so angry, he'd start ripping whole bushes right out of the ground…wait, now that Elliot had a chance to think about it, hiding in a bush was a terrible idea.

Elliot closed his eyes and told his body to poof out of the ropes. But nothing happened. He closed his eyes even tighter, and this time he ordered—no, he *demanded* that his body poof away. Again nothing happened.

"It's because I'm Kovol's prisoner," Elliot muttered. "Well, that's dumb."

But he wasn't finished yet. Maybe he couldn't poof away, but that didn't mean he had to stay here, tied up and helpless. He closed his eyes and imagined he was tied up with licorice ropes. Elliot planned to eat his way free—and get a yummy snack too! It was a perfect escape plan.

But as hard as he tried to make it happen, his ropes remained as they were, and Elliot remained stuck. However, he was able to poof in a piece of licorice to snack on while he thought of a new plan. So his Pixie magic wasn't completely useless.

Then Elliot's eyes widened. He might be trapped here, unable to use magic to free himself, but there were still things he could do.

"Patches!" he hissed. "Patches, I need you!"

Instantly, Patches appeared and hugged his face, the only part of him she could reach. "There you are! Kovol must have found some way to block us from finding you." She frowned. "Are you okay? Your face is really red."

"All my blood is in my head right now. But that's okay. It's helping me think…or I think it's helping me think."

With a shrug, she said, "If you say so. And where's everyone else? They haven't come back from Demon Territory yet. The creatures who stayed behind are getting worried."

"That's why I need your help. I need you to find Agatha the Hag. Most of the creatures who were fighting with me in Demon Territory are in Kovol's cave. Agatha's the only one I know with a light bright enough to hold off the Shadow Men, if they're still there." He didn't want to tell Patches how the Shadow Men had left most of the creatures as stone statues, and others, like her father, in cold comas. Or that the creatures were all Kovol's prisoners now and couldn't escape, even if Agatha was somehow able to heal them. But he had left Agatha the note in the dirt to look for the orange rock. She would know what to do. Elliot looked back to Patches. "Ask Agatha if she'll go to that cave and see if she can help."

"Okay, but what about you?" Patches asked.

"Can you cut me down?"

"Not while you're Kovol's prisoner," she said. "But when I come back, I'll help you fight him."

"No, don't come back," Elliot said. "I'll figure things out here on my own."

As soon as Patches was gone, Elliot looked around the area, trying to figure out other ways to use his magic against Kovol. He couldn't think of any decent ideas. Even if he did know a good trick, there was always the chance that it would backfire and make things worse.

Maybe Elliot had been wrong about all the blood in his head helping him think. Thinking was actually getting pretty hard. Also, his feet were beginning to complain about not getting their fair share of blood.

Only one thought had worked its way through Elliot's brain, the one idea that might be the perfect trick against Kovol. Elliot twisted around until he found the exact spot he was looking for, then closed his eyes and made his idea happen. There was no way to tell if it would work. And it wouldn't do him much good unless he was able to get out of this rope.

He squirmed and kicked and tried to think himself thinner. But none of it worked.

Being Kovol's prisoner was starting to get old.

Chapter 20

Where Kovol Needs Deodorant

When Kovol finally returned for Elliot, he seemed to be in a worse mood than usual. At least he snorted a lot, and stomped his feet, and had this low growl that wasn't too different from the way Reed sounded on days he had to wake up extra early for school. It was no surprise to Elliot that Kovol was in a bad mood. Ever since he'd become king, Elliot had noticed that bad moods were normal for evil creatures. And if they were in good moods, it was probably because one of their evil plans was going well. So the bad mood didn't bother Elliot nearly as much as a good mood would.

"It sounds like destroying Earth is a lot tougher than you thought it would be," Elliot said. He figured that he and Kovol might as well have some conversation.

But Kovol only grunted. He paced back and forth, every so often looking up at the bright springtime sky. Maybe he was waiting for the sun to go down before he did anything really mean. Elliot understood that. He had always felt that if he were a super villain, he'd do all of his super-villain work at night too—as long as he had taken a nap in the daytime so that he didn't get tired.

Elliot wondered if Kovol had taken a nap that day. Probably not. He'd probably had more than enough naptime in the last thousand years.

"I have a question," Elliot said. "What are you planning to do after you destroy Earth? Because if you destroy my world, then you destroy yours too. What if you get bored and want some candy from the store? But there is no store because you destroyed it?" Elliot shrugged. "I'm not sure that you really thought this plan through."

"I will destroy Elliot," Kovol muttered.

"Well, yeah, I think you've made that clear," Elliot said. "But what about everything else? Maybe you haven't noticed, but Demon Territory is the ugliest, stinkiest, dirtiest place in the entire Underworld. And if you go around destroying all the nice places, you'll be stuck without a home."

"I'll destroy everything," Kovol said. "Except for one sunny island."

Elliot's ears perked up (except he was still upside down in the rope, so his ears actually perked down). "Oh, like Fiji or somewhere? My teacher went there for a trip last year."

Kovol grunted, which was probably a yes.

It gave Elliot another idea. Hiding his grin, he said, "So you don't want to destroy *everything*. Mostly just me, right?"

Again, Kovol grunted a yes.

"What about all those creatures you took prisoner inside your cave? Are you going to destroy them?"

This time Kovol spoke in sentences. "I'll rule those who serve me. Those who fight me get eaten."

Elliot thought that was a pretty lame way to rule. The Brownies didn't bow to Elliot because otherwise he would eat them. They bowed because he served them and loved them and did everything he could to make their lives better.

But to Kovol he only said, "I'm the one who got all those creatures to fight you. I'm responsible for that."

"So I must destroy Elliot," Kovol grunted again.

"Yes, I *know*. But you've already got me. So it doesn't make sense to keep all those other creatures as your prisoners."

"You're right," Kovol agreed. "I need creatures to serve me."

"So you wouldn't care if everyone you took prisoner down there went free?"

"No."

Elliot hoped that would be enough. He wasn't clear on how all the rules of magic worked, but Kovol had just said he didn't care if all the creatures he had taken prisoner went free. Was that enough to release them?

Technically speaking, Elliot was also one of the creatures that Kovol had taken prisoner. So if they were free, did that mean Elliot was free too?

There was only one way to find out. Elliot closed his eyes and tried to think of a place where he wanted to poof himself. But it wasn't an easy decision. Wherever he went, there was a chance that Kovol might follow. So he couldn't go home or to Burrowsville. And he didn't want to go to Demon Territory, where Kovol could take him prisoner again. If he got the chance, he wouldn't mind stopping the war long enough for a bathroom break. That would give him a good place to think.

Elliot was usually a pretty good thinker. But sometimes he was also a pretty slow thinker, and trying to figure out where to poof was definitely *not* a good time for him to take so long to think.

Because while Elliot's eyes were shut, Kovol decided he might as well just get rid of his prisoner once and for all. He made a twirling motion with his fingers, and Elliot started spinning with his rope. "I like my breakfast scrambled," Kovol said.

"News flash," Elliot called back. "Breakfast was hours ago! I guess you'll have to wait until morning." Except he already felt his insides scrambling. He didn't want to do this all night.

Elliot opened his eyes only long enough to figure out that he was getting dizzy really fast. Then he closed them again and tried to poof away to anywhere. It didn't matter. He'd poof to the top of Mount Everest if he had to. Or to the moon. Or, better yet, to Fiji. He thought Fiji might be nice this time of year.

But with so much blood crowding out the other thoughts in his head, and with the problem that he was now spinning like a top, Elliot couldn't form a single picture of anywhere he ought to go. In fact, he couldn't put any thought together that made sense. He started sputtering things back to Kovol like "I… you…sometimes pickles…let's dance."

He wasn't sure what that meant. Kovol didn't seem to understand it either, because he slowed Elliot's spinning long enough to say, "No more. With Elliot gone, no one rules the Underworld but Kovol!"

Kovol raised his arms above his head to strike at Elliot, releasing the most horrible armpit odor that had ever been sent into the world. A butterfly that had just flown into the area exploded as soon as it crossed the smelly vapor. When the breeze carried the odor to a fat pine tree, eight of its branches fell straight to the ground. If Kovol's armpits had smelled good, like a fresh-baked apple pie or something, Elliot still would have wanted to live. But to have that disgusting stench be the last thing he ever smelled—he could not accept that!

So he closed his eyes and made the decision just to poof out of the rope, where Kovol was aiming his curse. He wasn't sure where he'd go next, but all he cared about was getting away from that smell.

While Elliot was thinking, Kovol began building his magic. The skin on Elliot's arms prickled with static as the magic gathered between Kovol's beefy palms. It felt like a ball of invisible lightning, and when it was all gathered, Elliot knew it was coming straight for him. This was exactly what Fudd had warned him about earlier that day.

"Poof!" he ordered whatever part of his body controlled the magic. But he felt nervous about what Kovol was doing, and it was hard to concentrate, even to drop out of the rope. Elliot realized he didn't know for sure that he *could* poof away. Maybe his trick to have Kovol release all the prisoners had worked. And maybe not.

"Poof!" he said aloud. He closed his eyes and pictured himself falling onto a soft mattress pad right below him.

But the magic failed again, and whatever Kovol held between his palms was beginning to spark.

"This is the end!" Kovol said. "Now I destroy you."

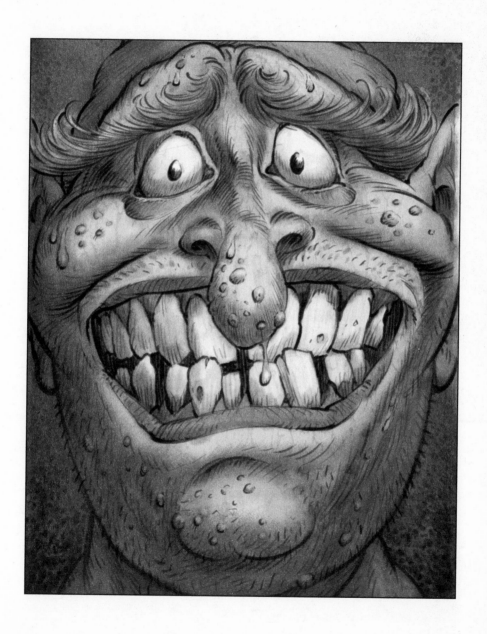

Chapter 21

Where Grissel Bows

Despite what Kovol had threatened, it wasn't the end, or at least not the end of Elliot. Because with a very loud yelp, Kovol was suddenly thrown into the air as the ground beneath him exploded. Kovol was many things—all of them bad—and this included how bad he was at flying. Kovol shot high into the air, his arms flailing and his roar echoing higher and higher into the air.

"Poof!" Elliot said again. And this time the magic worked and Elliot fell onto the ground. Unfortunately, he had forgotten to include the soft mattress this time, so his fall kind of hurt. But not as much as a ball of lightning would have, so he didn't complain.

He sat up but remained on the ground for a moment while all the blood in his body went back to where it was supposed to go. He ran his fingers through his hair and tried to figure out what might have caused that explosion. He knew only one creature who could do something like that.

"We're even now," a voice behind Elliot said.

Elliot turned, surprised to find that he was actually pleased to see Grissel standing there. Grissel had hated Elliot from the moment he heard about him on a Halloween night more than three years ago. He had tried to destroy Elliot ever since Elliot became king of the Brownies, and had refused to stop trying, even if it meant suffering the cruelest ever punishment of nothing to eat but chocolate cake…without frosting! And yet Elliot had saved his life. Now Grissel had come to repay the favor.

"How did you get here?" Elliot asked. "I thought the Shadow Men turned everyone into stone or put them in cold comas."

Grissel shrugged. "Agatha found the orange rock that was your Shapeshifter. She helped him change back, and then he explained what had happened. When the Hag transforms, she isn't nearly as pretty to a Goblin's eyes, but her light is very warm. With that light, she can heal the curse of the cold comas. She healed me first and is still healing the others."

"What about those who were turned to stone?"

Grissel shook his head. "They cannot be healed as long as the Shadow Men fly."

"Then I need you to go back and protect them," Elliot said. "Until I find a way to stop the Shadow Men, I don't want anything else to happen to our friends."

Grissel blinked at Elliot. The corners of his mouth began to splinter as if he was trying to make an expression that his face was not used to. After some serious cracks, his mouth formed something that almost looked like a smile. Then he bowed and said, "King Elliot, many of those stone creatures are my friends too. I didn't think you would care about us, but I was wrong. I will not allow harm to come to anyone in the cave until you find a way to save them."

"Thank you, Grissel," Elliot said.

"No, King Elliot," Grissel said. "Thank *you*." After a short bow, Grissel disappeared.

Elliot waited only a moment before calling for Harold. He didn't know how far away the explosion had carried Kovol, but they didn't have much time. He waited a moment, sure that the Shapeshifter must not have heard him. Then he yelled, "Harold!" again.

He had expected to see Harold arrive in his human form, but instead a mosquito popped onto Elliot's nose. If Elliot could have seen it with a magnifying glass, he would have noticed the small white patch of hair on the mosquito's head—a sign that this was his friend. But Harold the Mosquito only buzzed, "No! Leave me alone!" Then he gave Elliot a bite, because that's what mosquitoes do. And he poofed away.

Elliot itched his nose, then said, "Harold, get back here right now! I have to talk to you!"

A small spider monkey appeared in the tree above Elliot. Same white patch of hair, same Shapeshifter. "No!" the monkey howled. It looked around for a bunch of bananas, but since this was not a banana tree, it threw some pinecones at Elliot's head and poofed away again.

Elliot stood up and put his fists on his hips. "Harold! You will come here right now, or I will tell Cami that we never want to see her again."

Several seconds passed when Elliot thought even that threat wouldn't be enough to bring Harold back. Finally he poofed in front of Elliot, in his human form. But his arms were folded, and the look on his face was somewhere between upset and furious.

"Don't ask me for anything else, because I won't do it," Harold said. "You gave me one job, to keep Kovol away from Demon Territory. I didn't do that right. And then down in Kovol's cave, I should have transformed into a Hag and tried to put off enough light to chase the Shadow Men away, but I didn't do that either. All I did was turn into an orange rock. Not diamond or gold or some useful metal. Just a dumb orange rock. I don't dare to do anything else to help. I might be more dangerous to our side than Kovol."

Truthfully, that same thought had occurred to Elliot. But he hoped this time he had found something so harmless that even Harold couldn't ruin it. Elliot sighed as he stared at his friend. Who was he kidding? Nothing was too harmless to be safe from Harold.

"Just come with me, please," Elliot said, and then quickly added, "And before you tell me no again, it's something with Cami."

Harold's eyebrows lifted. "Cami?"

Elliot smiled. "Cami with Warts—I mean, Cami Wortson, the love of your life."

"I'd do anything for the love of my life," Harold said. "You know I would. But I can't risk making any more mistakes."

"Are you kidding?" Elliot said. "Do you know how many mistakes I've made since becoming king? Maybe you made a mistake by bringing Kovol back to Demon Territory, but it was really my mistake for having us go in there unprepared. Everyone makes mistakes. But my dad says that's always okay, *if* you're willing to fix them."

Harold sighed. "How do I fix this?"

"Let's go back to my house," Elliot said. "We'll poof straight to my room."

"Okay," Harold said glumly. "I just hope you know what you're doing letting me make mistakes around your family."

"Uh—" Elliot began. But it was already too late. Harold had poofed away.

Where Harold Confesses

When Elliot and Harold poofed into Elliot's bedroom, they found Cami on the floor reading a book. She jumped to her feet, startled. "Oh, you scared me!" Once her heartbeat started up again, she said, "I'll never get used to you doing that."

"I'll never get used to doing it either," Elliot said, although he had already begun to think that magic might be the perfect solution to his problem of getting to school on time. He added, "How's Reed?"

"He still thinks it was all a dream," Cami said. "After he rested for a while he felt better, but he's definitely not going back to the Quack Shack today."

Elliot hoped the Quack Shack would still exist after today. Not only because it would mean Kovol had failed in destroying the world, but also because he really liked duck burgers.

"Are there any new sinkholes?" Elliot asked. Cami shrugged. "The reporter who was covering the story fell into one and broke his leg. They can't do any more news on the sinkholes until they find another reporter who'll agree to go out there." Then she noticed Harold, who had done nothing but stare lovingly at her since he poofed in. "Who's this? Another king?"

Harold fell to his knees in front of her.

"Do you know how wonderful it is to look at you through my own eyes? How do I describe the joy of looking at you looking at me as I look back at you?"

Cami made a face and turned to Elliot. "What's he talking about?"

"Get up, Harold." With his foot, Elliot nudged the Shapeshifter in the back.

Harold started to stand up, but Cami put a hand on his shoulder and pushed him down again. "Wait a minute." She fingered the patch of white hair on Harold's head. "I've seen this before."

Harold froze, looking as guilty as if he had just been caught robbing a bank. Elliot shook his head, mad at himself for forgetting that Cami was actually a pretty smart girl.

Her eyes narrowed as she first stared at Elliot. "About four months ago, I saw this exact patch of white hair on your head for a few days. And for those days, you were acting so strangely. Sort of like—" Now she turned to Harold. "Sort of like *you* were acting just now!"

Elliot tried to look innocent. "Hmm, that's weird."

But Harold cried out, "I can't lie to the love of my life!" Now he stood, but he clasped his hands as he faced Cami. "Elliot was trapped in the Underworld, and he begged me to come up to the surface and pretend to be him."

Elliot's nose wrinkled. That wasn't the way he remembered it, although he was certain that was exactly the way Harold did.

"But how could you do all that?" Cami asked. "You don't look anything like Elliot."

Harold blew out a deep breath, and as he did, the bones and coloring of his face shifted to match Elliot's. Other than the white patch, his hair lightened to dark blond, and even his clothes changed to a simple T-shirt and jeans, exactly the same as Elliot's.

Cami let out a scream. Not a big scream or a long scream, but a very girly scream that made Elliot's toes curl.

"Change back!" he said to Harold. "Hurry!"

"Yes," Cami agreed. "This is so creepy!"

With another deep breath, Harold returned to his usual form. He said nothing more, but his eyes pled with Cami to accept him for who he was, in whatever form he might happen to be.

"You can change shapes?" she asked.

"He's a Shapeshifter," Elliot said.

"And what does he really look like?"

Elliot shrugged. "Whatever he wants."

Cami looked from Elliot to Harold and back to Elliot, and with each turn of her head, her face got redder and redder.

"Are you mad?" Elliot asked. Was it really such a big deal if a Shapeshifter had pretended to be him for a few days? So what if the only reason he and Cami were sort of friends was because Harold had been so nice to her during that time? He really didn't see what the problem was.

Cami poked Elliot in the chest. "I decided to be friends with you because you were so nice when we did the science experiment together. But that wasn't you being nice. It was him. Which means you never wanted to be my friend in the first place!"

Elliot wanted to tell her she was wrong about all of that, but she wasn't. It had never been his idea to be Cami's friend. However, now that she was, he didn't mind it so much. In fact, sometimes her friendship wasn't awful at all.

Then she turned to Harold. "Why do you keep saying I'm the love of your life?"

He smiled shyly. "Because you are the most wonderful human I've ever known. The most beautiful, the kindest, and with a voice that melts my heart."

Elliot couldn't stop himself. He gagged.

Cami's face scrunched up. "Get out!" she said to Elliot.

Elliot backed up a step. "It's my room!"

"I don't care. Get out!" Turning to Harold, she added, "If you really liked me, then you wouldn't have lied about who you are! You get out too!"

She backed both Elliot and Harold out of his room, then slammed the door on them. The door even flattened Harold's nose for a second before it popped back into place.

"Quiet up there!" Wendy hissed from downstairs. "Reed's asleep."

Harold turned to Elliot, his eyes wide. "The love of my life yelled at me."

"I guess we probably deserved it," Elliot said. "I never thought of how she'd feel about you pretending to be me."

356

Then Harold smiled. "Hey, I just realized that was our first fight. One day she and I will look back on this moment and laugh about it all."

Elliot rolled his eyes, then cracked open the door to his room. Cami still stood in the doorway with her arms crossed and eyebrows pressed low. Before she could speak, he said, "We're both sorry about what we did. And it's okay if you don't want to forgive us yet, but we really need your help."

"How?"

"Do you still have the paper-mache doll of me from when we played Capture the Flag this morning?"

"You made fun of it."

"I know. I'm sorry about that too. But I need it now."

"I already took the doll home."

"Can you go get it? And then maybe bring it to the same place in the woods where you had it this morning?" She hesitated, and he added, "You don't have to do this for me, or for Harold, but would you do it for the human race?"

Slowly, Cami nodded. "I'll do it for the human race, minus you two."

Harold smiled. "Actually, I'm not part of the human race. I'm just in that form right now."

Cami's face reddened again, but Elliot took another step forward and said, "No, that's good. Stop talking, Harold." Then he called, "Patches! I need some turnip juice." While he waited for her to come, he asked, "Are the twins home now?"

"They got home about ten minutes ago," Cami said. "Wendy's feeding them some dinner. She offered me some too, but I'm not sure it was food."

Whatever it was, as long as it could be eaten, it sounded good to Elliot. But he didn't have time to eat now.

Patches poofed in with a large bottle of turnip juice in her hands. "Here it is. Are you thirsty?"

"Not exactly." Elliot looked at Harold. "Now can you turn into a goat?"

Harold winked at Cami. "Goats are one of my better animals. I know you'll be impressed."

From the little that Elliot knew about girls, he guessed Cami wasn't likely to be impressed with Harold's changing into any farm animal. Except maybe a horse. He knew most girls liked horses.

Harold let out a deep breath, and his body immediately curved so that he stood on four hooves rather than hands and feet. White hair spread all over his body, and his face molded into that of a goat's.

"Ho-oww do you like me no-oww?" he asked Cami.

"Eww," Cami said.

Then he bleated to Elliot, "Wh-y do you ne-eed a goat?"

Elliot took the bottle from Patches and held it out to Harold. "Spit in this," he said. He wasn't sure whether Minthred's sleep recipe would work, but it was worth a try.

Harold the Goat gathered a big wad of spit in his mouth, then shot it into the bottle.

"Disgusting!" Patches cried. "No Brownie will drink that now."

"I don't want a Brownie to drink it," Elliot said, putting the lid on it again. "I have much bigger plans for this. There's just one more ingredient I need. Anyone know where I can get some earwax?"

Everyone in the room stared at one another, but no one seemed to have any earwax available at that moment.

"Can you get some here by magic?" Cami asked.

"Magic can't just create something from nowhere," Patches explained. "It has to exist somewhere first."

"We need to think of someone who would have a lot of earwax," Harold said, tapping his hoof on the floor.

"The Trolls?" Elliot suggested. "I've seen their ears, and there's got to be pounds of it in their heads."

"But Agatha told me they're all turned to stone," Patches said. "If we got any, it would be stone earwax."

They all froze when a roar boomed from the woods behind Elliot's house, rattling the windows and even shaking a few books from Elliot's bookshelf.

"What was that?" Cami whispered.

"Kovol," Elliot breathed. Kovol was looking for him.

"You've got to poof somewhere far away," Patches said. "Where Kovol won't think of looking for you."

"I can't," Elliot said. "When he couldn't find me before, he went after Reed.

358

I have to go back and face him now, or he'll look for my family. Harold, will you stay here as me to protect them, just in case?"

"What if I mess up?" Harold asked.

"You won't," Elliot said. "I know this time you won't."

"What can I do?" Cami asked. "I promised you I'd help."

"This is my fight," Elliot said. "Just get that paper-mache doll into the woods." He pointed to the jar of turnip juice and goat spit. "Keep track of this too. It's really important now."

"It's also really gross now," Patches said. Then she added, "Be safe, Elliot."

Before Kovol had finished his second roar, Elliot closed his eyes, pictured Kovol so clearly it made his knees turn to rubber, and then poofed himself there, ready for the final battle.

Chapter 23

Where the Magic Fails

Sometime last year Elliot had seen a cartoon about a kid who battled hundreds of alien invaders all by himself to save planet Earth. He had liked the movie, but that's all it was, just a story a bunch of writers had made up. Right before poofing back to the woods to face Kovol, Elliot tried to think of even one true story where a kid does battle with someone a lot stronger and wins.

He didn't know any. Not even one.

But he couldn't worry about that with Kovol. Besides, Elliot liked the idea of being the first kid ever to win against such odds. Of course, he wouldn't be able to tell everyone that he was the one who saved Earth. Maybe when he was a hundred years old and on his deathbed, he could gather his friends and family around him and say, "Did I ever tell you about the time I saved the world?" Yeah, that'd be cool. He was going to put that on his calendar for eighty-nine years from now. *If* he was still alive eighty-nine minutes from now, of course.

Elliot's plan had been to poof in quietly and make the first attack on Kovol. And it would have been a fine plan, except he maybe did too good a job in picturing Kovol and poofed in right on top of the evil Demon's head. Since Kovol was bald, Elliot slipped off his head and would have fallen all the way to the ground if he had not grabbed on to each of Kovol's long, twisted horns.

Kovol yelled and swung his head, trying to get Elliot off. Elliot would have been very happy to get off, but he couldn't let go with Kovol swinging him so hard. His body was flung around wildly in the air. Kovol got angrier and angrier, twisting his head as far to the right as he could. Elliot's body flew all the way around Kovol's head, and he accidentally kicked Kovol in the nose.

Kovol fell back in pain, and this time Elliot let go of the horns and scrambled free as fast as he could.

"So that's how you want things to be," Kovol muttered.

No. Actually, the way Elliot wanted things was for Kovol to never have woken up in the first place. Or if he did wake up, he'd have wanted Kovol not to have made such a big deal about Elliot's taking his last hair. Maybe Elliot could have politely apologized for taking the hair, and then Kovol would've said, "That's okay," and they could've played a game of Limburger soccer instead of all this.

However, none of that was going to happen.

Kovol charged for Elliot, with his bruised nose snorting and his claws out. Elliot whispered to his magic, "Block him," fully expecting a shield to come up between them. But instead, a pile of toy building blocks fell from nowhere above them, landing on Kovol like a perfectly square hailstorm. Kovol looked up to see what was happening, and the corner of a block landed straight in his eye.

"Ow, my eye!" Kovol yelped. "Why would you do that?"

Stubbornly, Elliot folded his arms. The blocks had been an accident, but this was supposed to be an ultimate battle to save the world, so he wouldn't apologize.

"That's right." Elliot tried sounding as tough as he could. "And there's more where that came from!"

Maybe that was true, maybe not. He wasn't really clear on where any of this was coming from.

Kovol huffed and ran toward Elliot again. But Elliot was getting the feel of Pixie magic now. It wasn't great magic for strength or power, but it was excellent if you were trying to trick someone.

So when Kovol started running, Elliot pictured old-fashioned roller skates on the bottom of the Demon's feet. To make it funnier, he pictured girly ones. Even pinker than a Pixie dress and with glittery hearts covering every inch of them.

The skates appeared, and with his arms flailing around, Kovol rolled right past Elliot and crashed into the trunk of a wide oak tree. Even though he knew he shouldn't, Elliot laughed. Besides, why not? Kovol's anger couldn't get any worse. He hoped.

If Kovol had been a Troll or even a Goblin, Elliot probably could have continued with magical jokes for the rest of the day. But Kovol couldn't be tricked for long. And he definitely didn't think the roller skates were nearly as funny as Elliot did. Once he kicked them off his feet, he turned and hurled back a ball of energy so fast that it threw Elliot into the air. Elliot landed with a hard thump on the ground.

Now it was Kovol's turn to laugh. Only, unlike Elliot's happy laugh over a funny joke, his was dark and mean and made Elliot think maybe he didn't want to get back up again.

Still seated, Elliot tried throwing an energy ball of his own at Kovol, but it came out more like a gentle puff of air. Kovol swatted it out of the way like he would a bothersome fly.

"Pixie magic," Elliot whispered. It wasn't about strength. It was about trickery. He had the idea to make it rain actual cats and dogs, but Kovol struck at him first, creating a sinkhole exactly where Elliot was sitting. With nothing but air suddenly beneath him, Elliot fell. He tumbled head over heels into a hole that looked bottomless. Finally he found the magic to grab on to a dangling tree root, and then he began the long climb back to the surface. Kovol stood at the top of the sinkhole with his smelly armpits raised again. He was gathering more lightning between his clawlike hands.

"Oh, no you don't!" Elliot closed his eyes to picture the edge of the sinkhole becoming a sheet of thick ice. Kovol slipped on the ice that magically formed and landed on his large Demon backside, then slid over the edge and right past Elliot into the sinkhole.

"Gotcha!" Elliot called. Then he poofed back to the surface and brushed his hands together. Carefully he peered over the edge, curious about how far into the hole Kovol had fallen.

But Kovol wasn't down there. Which means he had—

"No, I've got *you*!" From behind, Kovol grabbed Elliot around the waist and lifted him into the air.

Elliot put his hands over Kovol's and tried to pry himself free, but Kovol was a lot stronger than Elliot, even with the Pixie magic.

"I'll take your magic before eating you," Kovol said. "You'll taste better that way."

"I'll taste terrible!" Elliot said. "I haven't had a bath for three days!" He couldn't let Kovol take his magic. For that matter, he really didn't want to be eaten either.

Elliot squirmed, but it was useless. He tried to pull together enough magic to get away from Kovol, but he was being squished too tightly for the magic to work properly. Elliot felt a little frustrated by that. If he had invented magic, he would have made it so you could use it even when you were squished. Or maybe *especially* when you were squished.

Kovol pulled him back over solid ground. Elliot knew for a fact that it was solid, because Kovol dropped him on it. He tried rolling away so that he could gather some magic to defend himself, but Kovol immediately put a foot on Elliot's chest. That made it hard to do magic, which was a problem. It was even harder to breathe, which was a much bigger problem.

Standing over him now, Kovol started moving his arms, almost as if he were pulling an invisible rope out of Elliot's body. Elliot felt the magic being dragged out of him, and he held on to it with all of his strength. But strength was not one of the gifts of Pixie magic, so all Elliot had was his own determination not to let Kovol take this magic. It would only make Kovol more powerful, and it would leave Elliot completely defenseless.

Elliot swatted at the Demon's foot with his hands, but it didn't do any good and only tired him out faster. He closed his eyes, searching for enough magic left inside him to fight back. Anything. But as hard as he searched, he found nothing at all. If he couldn't figure out something soon, the last Underworld war would be over in the next few minutes.

Where Tubs Teaches Kovol

Just when Elliot thought he could hold on no longer, he heard a voice some-where in the woods behind him. "Let go of our brother!"

"No!" Elliot cried in the loudest voice he had (which at that point was little more than a whisper). That was either Kyle or Cole, one of his younger twin brothers.

A fat stream of water shot through the air, hitting Kovol squarely in the back. It knocked him off balance, and Elliot rolled out from under his foot.

Elliot sat up on his elbows. Kyle and Cole were nearby with a kinked hose they had somehow dragged all this way into the woods. Behind them were Wendy, Reed, Cami, and, for some reason, Tubs.

"What are you doing here?" Elliot asked

"I told them about you," Cami said. "I told them everything. Maybe you can't tell your secrets, but I can."

Elliot scrambled to his feet and ran over to them.

"King, huh?" Reed said, his mouth in a half smile. "How funny is that?"

"This isn't a joke," Elliot said. "You have to run away from here."

"And miss all this fun?" one of the twins said. They released another spurt of water at Kovol, knocking him back down.

"We came to help you fight," Wendy said. "When Mom and Dad are at work, they tell us to take care of each other. Well, that's what we're doing."

"They meant to be sure we all eat dinner and get our homework done," Elliot said. "Not help fight Underworld wars!"

"Yeah, yeah," Tubs said. "Duck."

Elliot ducked down, and Tubs lobbed a rock at Kovol, clonking him on the forehead and knocking him down again.

"Now's your chance," Cami said. "We got that ugly beast distracted. Now use some magic to finish him off."

"I'm not sure I have any magic left," Elliot said. "If I do, it'll take a while to charge up again." He took a deep breath. "Besides, we'll just be fighting him all day unless I can finish making that potion."

"I brought it," Cami said, holding up the bottle of turnip juice.

"Water!" the twins yelled and sprayed Kovol again, but this time he was ready. He used a shield to push the stream of water back onto Elliot's family. Kyle and Cole dropped the hose, and everyone scattered behind the nearest tree, bush, or rock where they could fit.

Elliot had chosen a thick bush off to the right. From there he saw Wendy and Reed behind nearby oak trees, dripping wet. The twins had squeezed together behind a large rock. Cami was in another bush. And...where was Tubs?

Elliot peeked out to where Tubs stood facing Kovol. In his hands was another rock.

Kovol looked confused. "You're not running," he said.

Tubs's eyes narrowed. "I know all about you, jerk. You're just another bully, a loser who tries to make himself feel better by hurting others. I know that, because I used to be a bully too."

"Nobody insults Kovol," the Demon said.

"I used to think nobody insulted me either," Tubs answered. "They do, but they say the insults behind your back. You should've heard what the kids used to say about me."

Elliot was pretty sure a lot of kids still said those things about Tubs.

But it was true—ever since Elliot had stood up to Tubs, he didn't bully people anymore.

"I'm the most powerful creature in the world!" Kovol yelled.

Tubs snorted. "If you were powerful, you wouldn't have to be mean. Elliot's the nicest kid I know, and he's more powerful than you'll ever be!"

Kovol roared. Then Tubs threw the rock at him, which bounced off his chest like a rubber ball. Kovol widened his hands for some magic.

"No!" Elliot leapt from his hiding place and dove for Tubs to knock him out of the way. However, just as before when they had played Capture the Flag, Tubs wasn't going anywhere. He was a lot thicker than Elliot, so Elliot only crashed into the side of Tubs's body and landed on the ground.

Tubs grabbed Elliot's arm and yanked him to his feet, then said, "If I don't get to bully this dork, then nobody does!" Tubs's idea of friendship, Elliot figured.

"Everyone start throwing things," Elliot yelled. "Whatever you can find!"

From their hiding places, Elliot's family and Cami threw rocks, sticks, and whatever else they had. Wendy threw a tube of her favorite lipstick. Reed threw packages of pickle relish. Cami threw some coins from her pocket. At first Elliot wasn't sure what the twins were throwing, but then he recognized them as the burned chicken nuggets from Wendy's dinner last night. He didn't blame them. If his pants pockets weren't full of holes, he'd have hidden his dinner there too. He wondered whether Wendy would be happy or angry to learn that her dinner had just been turned into a weapon. Probably a little of both.

None of the items hurt Kovol, but they distracted him. He couldn't defend against everything, so he tried just zapping the items as they got close to him.

The distraction gave Elliot a chance to run behind Kovol. He might not have any magic yet for a fight, but when he did have magic earlier he had prepared something special for a moment just like this.

Once Elliot had gotten a good head start, he yelled at Kovol, "Tubs was right. You're nothing but a bully. I'm not afraid of you, and you'll never catch me."

Then he ran. If Elliot had learned anything from his days of being bullied, it was how to run away.

Still, Kovol was catching up to him fast, and the place Elliot wanted to get to was farther away than he remembered. But every plan has a point where there's no turning back. Elliot was way, way past that point.

Kovol started sending shots of magic forward, almost like lasers. They hit the trees beside Elliot, punching huge holes through their trunks. Elliot began running in a zigzag pattern so that Kovol wouldn't know where his target would be next.

The zigzag slowed Elliot down, and Kovol was still getting closer. If he hadn't been so interested in hitting Elliot with magic, he might have figured out that he could probably grab Elliot if he reached out far enough.

Just ahead was a patch of ground with a brown haze over it. Elliot headed directly for it. He recognized the carefully laid-out leaves where he had magically marked the place where he should jump. When he reached it, he leapt forward as far as he could.

Kovol clearly didn't know the leaves were a signal to jump. He continued running forward…straight into the gripping mud…again.

"There's no gripping mud on the surface world," Kovol said, thrashing at the mud.

Elliot stopped and turned back to him. "There is now." He raised his hand to see if he had any magic to use on Kovol, but still there was nothing. He didn't think Kovol had gotten all of his magic, but he'd taken a lot of it, and he needed time to build it up again. Time was the one thing Elliot didn't have. (Well, that, and a solid gold time machine, but he wasn't thinking about that just then.)

"I can still fight you from here," Kovol growled.

"Not if you can't see me," Elliot said, already running away. "Until then, you're stuck."

Chapter
25

Where the Juice Is Shaken or Stirred

Elliot left the mud pit and ran toward his brothers and sister, who were on their way to find him. Wendy grabbed him first and closed him into a hug almost as tightly as the way Kovol had squished him before.

"Okay, okay." Elliot pushed away until he could breathe. "I'm fine."

"Hey, Elliot," Kyle said. "Me and Cole were thinking that if you're the king of these cookies—"

"Brownies."

"Yeah, Brownies. If you're the king, then what can we be?"

Cole punched a fist into the air. "We want to be your royal knights of the round table."

"I don't have a round table," Elliot said. "And I don't have any knights."

"Still, this is pretty big news," Reed said. "I thought it was exciting when I got that promotion last month at the Quack Shack, but that wasn't nearly as cool as this."

"I'm sorry I didn't tell any of you," Elliot said. "I couldn't, or else the Brownies would have gone away forever. And they needed my help."

"That's forgiven," Wendy said. "But now that we know, we want to help you. Cami said you have magic."

Elliot shrugged. "Kovol pulled

most of the magic out of me. The Brownies say that when they use their magic too much, they have to wait a while until it works again, sort of like recharging a battery. All I can hope is that I have enough magic left to charge up."

"Where's Kovol now?" Cami asked.

"Stuck in gripping mud." Elliot didn't have time to explain what gripping mud was, but his siblings didn't seem too curious. As long as Kovol was stuck, that seemed to be all they cared about.

"So send all of your Underworld friends to get him now," Reed said.

Elliot shook his head. "That won't work. Even stuck in the mud, he's still powerful enough to put up a good fight. As soon as it's dark enough, he'll call his army to help him get out. They're called Shadow Men, and they're just as scary as they sound. I don't want to fight Kovol anymore until I know I can win. It's time to end this." He looked at Cami. "Where's Harold?"

"He's still afraid to make another mistake." Cami frowned. "He said if he does, then I might not like him back. I told him nobody cares when people make mistakes. They only care when people don't try to fix them."

"So is he coming?"

Cami shrugged. "He said he'll think about it."

"Oh, good grief," Elliot said with a sigh. "Where's the turnip juice?"

She handed it to him. "Here. But you said it isn't ready yet."

"It's not. And I really don't know how to get that last ingredient." Then he remembered that his sister's food sometimes tasted a little strange. "Hey, Wendy, you don't happen to cook with earwax, do you?"

She made a face. "Ha-ha."

"No, seriously. Last week you made some cookies. I kind of thought—"

"I don't cook with earwax!"

He held up a hand. "No, I didn't think so." At least a big part of him had hoped not.

"You need earwax?" Tubs stuck his finger in his ear and pulled out a slimy clump. "I've got some."

"Thanks, Tubs," Elliot said. "But I need a lot of it for this potion to work."

"How much do you need?" Tubs reached into his pocket and pulled out a plastic sandwich bag with a huge blob of earwax inside. It was every color of gross, and so large he must have been collecting it for years.

"Disgusting!" Cami said. "How long have you had that?"

"Since I started preschool," Tubs said. "Do you like it?"

"No!" Cami and Wendy said together.

"Yes!" Kyle and Cole said at the same time.

Reed said nothing. Either he didn't have a very strong opinion on the subject of earwax collections, or else he was too grossed out to speak.

Elliot held out his hand for the earwax. "Well, I love it. Can I have it?"

Tubs pulled it closer to himself. "I dunno. I almost threw it at Kovol before, when we were all throwing things, but then I remembered how long I've been working on this collection. I can't just give it away for nothing."

"How about to save the world?" Elliot said.

"Yeah, I guess that is pretty important." Tubs thought it over. "Will they print my name in the newspaper about what a hero I am?"

"Probably not. We'll never really be able to talk about what happened here."

Wendy stepped forward. "But I'll make you some of those cookies that Elliot says tasted like earwax. A whole plate of them. And maybe they'll be helpful in getting your head to make more earwax."

Tubs smiled as if that actually made sense to him. "Yeah, I'll save the world with this bag of earwax. And who knows? Maybe I can use the next glob to save the universe!"

Elliot didn't think earwax worked that way. But at least Tubs handed him the plastic bag.

Cami knelt on the ground and opened the bottle of turnip juice. Being careful not to touch any of it, Elliot pushed the earwax out of the bag and into the bottle. It plopped to the bottom in a big clump.

"Now stir that in with a stick!" Wendy said.

"Or just shake it up," Reed said. "That's how we mix things at the Quack Shack."

While Wendy and Reed argued about whether the drink should be shaken or stirred, Elliot put the lid on and held it under his arm. He didn't think either one mattered. Minthred hadn't mixed it up, so neither would he. Besides, if he got Kovol to drink it, it was all going down in one swallow anyway.

"How's your magic doing?" Cole asked. "Is it back yet?"

"I don't think so," Elliot said.

"It had better hurry," Kyle said. "It's getting dark."

Elliot had noticed the same thing. In the woods, the trees were taller and the leaves denser, so it always felt dark earlier here than it would in Sprite's Hollow. And it definitely was getting late. At least, Elliot had felt his hungry stomach rumbling for some time.

A cool wind washed over Elliot's face. As long as the breeze was cool, that was only the weather. But any moment now the wind would shift, coming from Kovol's direction. And it would feel warm, even hot. It would be a signal that the Shadow Men had come.

"What happens now?" Reed asked.

Elliot's original plan with the potion had required the use of magic. He didn't have that option now, and he really wasn't sure how to trick Kovol into drinking the potion.

"Tell him you have this yummy drink and he can't have any of it," Cami said. "People always want things more if they know they can't have it."

This wasn't always true. One day each month, the school cafeteria had Mystery Meat Day. All the kids were pretty sure that meant the lunch ladies took the leftover meat from every other meal that month and ground it all together. And each month, the principal got first in line for lunch, then told the students they couldn't have any because it was all for him. It was his way of getting the kids to hurry into the line with him. But it never worked. As far as the kids were concerned, the only mystery with that meal was how many of them would lose their lunch before the day ended.

Despite that, Cami's suggestion was pretty good. Except for Mystery Meat Day, an idea like that usually worked.

"I'll try it," Elliot said. "But I've got to hurry. I want Kovol to drink this before he calls his army. All of you, stay here."

Chapter
26

Where Kovol Gets Jealous

Elliot returned to the patch of gripping mud where Kovol was still stuck. With mud pulling at Kovol's arms, he still folded them and frowned at Elliot. Kovol said, "The only reason I'm not attacking you now is that it will be much more fun once I'm free."

"Yeah, whatever." Elliot held out the bottle of juice. "I don't care, because I just drank some of this…um…yummy stuff. And you can't have it."

"Why would I care about that drink?" Kovol asked. "I have a much better drink, and you can't have it either."

"Why not?" Elliot asked. "I want some!" If it was good enough for a super villain, it was good enough for him. Then his eyes widened. Kovol was only using Elliot's own trick against him. Rude!

So Elliot stuck out his chest and said, "My drink made me stronger than you. I could snap you in half with my two fingers."

Kovol rolled his eyes. "You couldn't snap a twig."

"Oh, yeah?" Elliot picked up a nearby twig to prove him wrong. But he must have grabbed a really strong one, maybe one made of metal or something, because it wouldn't snap, even when he used all of his fingers. With a sigh he dropped it on the ground and broke it with his foot. "Aha!"

Kovol yawned, then pointed at a nearby tree branch. It cracked in half and almost fell right on top of Elliot's head.

"Show-off," Elliot muttered. This wasn't going so well.

He tried a different idea. "I'm sorry I pulled out your hair. I never planned to make you go bald. But if you want my opinion, it looks better now than if you tried to comb over that one hair to fool people."

"I'm not doing this because of the hair," Kovol said. "I'm doing this because I'm evil."

"I've met other evil creatures in the Underworld," Elliot said. "You're the worst, of course, but from what I've seen, if you decide that you want to change and become good, you can do that."

Kovol smacked hard at the mud, sending the message that his current life plans had nothing to do with becoming good. He would never help old ladies cross the road (unless he could eat them on the other side), or plant flowers (except maybe a prickly cactus), or do anything that a good creature would.

"Maybe you should just sit there and think about it a while longer." Elliot eyed the bottle of turnip juice. "Do you want a drink while you wait?"

"The last time I had a drink like that I fell asleep for a thousand years," Kovol said. "The great wizard Minthred tricked me."

Elliot snorted. "Oh, yeah, you were tricked by the most powerful goat-herding wizard of all time, no doubt. All right. I'll be back in a while and see if you changed your mind about the drink." He started to leave, then froze. Something in the air had changed.

He looked up at the skies, but the dimming air suddenly became as black as midnight. It wasn't that late yet. Which meant only one thing. The Shadow Men were coming. There were so many of them overhead that they had blocked out any remaining light.

Kovol sent a charge of energy straight toward Elliot. It hit the bottle of turnip juice first, throwing it high into the air where it landed somewhere far away. The remaining energy crashed into Elliot's chest, and his body hit against a tree with a hard *oomph* before sliding back to the ground.

While Elliot lay there, breathless, the Shadow Men gathered around Kovol to pull him free of the gripping mud. Since they were made of little but smoke and flame, it took all of them to lift Kovol's massive body. But when they stepped away, Kovol stood on solid ground, dripping with mud. And well rested to finish the fight.

Slowly, the entire army turned to face Elliot. Sweat from their intense heat rolled off his forehead. He had no magic to fight any one of them, much less this entire army. Yet he stood, prepared to give it his best try.

Then a small body poofed in front of him. "Stand back, Your Highness," Mr. Willimaker said. He held a long stick of bright light. "I'll protect you."

"So will I," Fudd said, appearing beside Mr. Willimaker. He wasn't facing in the correct direction, but his stick of light was held high and ready.

"You're both healed too?" Elliot said.

"Everyone in the cold comas has been healed," Fudd said. "They're only waiting in the Underworld long enough to get their light from Agatha. Then they'll come to help you too."

And sure enough, one by one more creatures poofed in. As they did, the Shadow Men backed farther and farther away. By now they knew what those sticks of light could do. And with each new creature who arrived, their chances got worse.

"Give the word and we'll attack," Mr. Willimaker said.

Elliot nodded and then called out, "Creatures of light, *we* are the strong ones, not them! Darkness can only exist where there is no light. And each of you holds in your hands the power to chase away the darkness forever. They can give you a burn, or suck warmth from your body, or even take your eyesight. But you are holding the power to destroy the darkness. We will not leave these woods until the curse is ended and Kovol remains alone. Creatures of light, attack!"

They rushed at the Shadow Men, swinging their sticks in every direction they could. With each hit, ashes fell to the ground like black snow. Kovol tried fighting in defense of his army, but everyone was moving too quickly, so he had no idea where to send his magic. From where Elliot stood, it was hard to see if anyone was winning, but so far his side definitely wasn't losing. Still, there were so many more on their side than his.

From the trees behind him, someone whispered, "Hey, this is cool. Good job, little brother."

"Reed!" Elliot hissed. "I told you to stay back."

"Yeah, we ignored that. You're the Brownie's king, not our king. So where can we get some of those sticks?"

"This is their fight," Elliot said, "but I need you to spread out and look for the bottle of turnip juice. Kovol threw it somewhere, but I don't know where or how far away."

"So your Brownies get the fun job," Reed said with a sigh. "All right, fine. We'll find that bottle."

Less than a minute after Reed left, Kovol must have had enough of the battle, because he let out a roar loud enough to shake the tops of the trees. Everyone froze. Kovol charged forward and grabbed Elliot, lifting him high into the air. "Drop the sticks, or I'll eat your king right now."

Without a moment's hesitation, the sticks clattered to the ground.

And unexpectedly, Elliot laughed. "I know the real reason you stopped the fight," he said. "You are so jealous."

"What?"

"You're jealous because all these creatures came to fight the Shadow Men. Nobody wants to fight you."

"They can't fight me, because I'm so powerful." Kovol's voice was angry, but maybe a little worried too.

"There's only one of you, and there are hundreds of Shadow Men," Elliot said. "You're only as strong as the last thing you ate for dinner. You can't even escape gripping mud without them. But they're always strong. Stronger than you. Scarier than you. More powerful than you'll ever be."

"*I* am the most powerful!" Kovol boomed. "They are my army. I cursed them to life!"

"They're not alive, so they don't die," Elliot said. "But you could. That makes *them* the most powerful creatures in the Underworld."

"I will win this war," Kovol said. "Me, and only me! And nothing is as strong as Kovol!"

Elliot tried not to smile. "There's only one way for you to be as strong as them."

Kovol might not have fallen for the turnip juice trick, but he fell for this one perfectly. Forgetting about his plans for Elliot, Kovol turned toward his army. He blew out all the air from his lungs, then began sucking it back in, tugging at the Shadow Men with his breath, just as he had pulled magic from Elliot's body. One by one the Shadow Men were dragged into his mouth, swallowed up whole. Large rings of smoke blew out of his ears, and with each eaten Shadow Man, Kovol's body grew larger and darker. He filled himself with their flames and their powers to curse. If he was bad before, then he was horrible now.

"What have you done?" Mr. Willimaker whispered to Elliot.

"We could never have beaten his entire army," Elliot said. "Kovol just made a big mistake."

"But he has all of their power now," Mr. Willimaker said. "His entire army is within one body."

"And in *only* one body. Don't worry, my friend, the best is yet to come." Elliot knew how to finish this now. He had a plan.

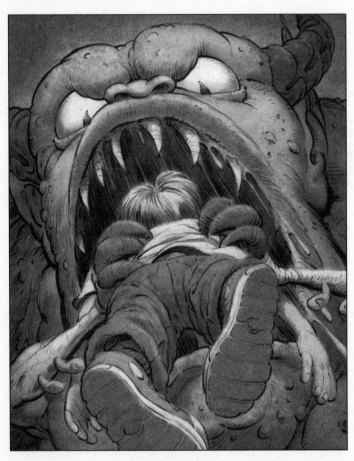

Chapter 27

Where Kovol Eats His Last Meal

Elliot ran out of the clearing and back into the woods. "Reed? Wendy? Where is everyone?"

"We can't find the bottle," Wendy said. She was with Kyle and Cole near a grove of tall trees, each of them searching as fast as they could.

"It's not over here!" Reed said with only his head poking out of a thick bush. Tubs was a little farther away, but he was still searching too, so Elliot knew neither of them had it.

"Where's Cami?" Elliot asked.

Reed pointed to his right, and Elliot went running in that direction.

"Cami?" he called.

"Over here!" she answered. "I think it's close. I can see the broken branches where it must have landed, but it rolled away somewhere."

Elliot walked toward Cami's voice until he found her, and together they followed a trail as wide as the bottle down a steep hill.

He spotted the bottle first. "There it is!" He started toward it, then something hit him in the back and he yelled in pain and fell forward.

"Elliot!" Cami screamed, running beside him.

"I'm all right," he said, holding his back. "One of Kovol's shots must've hit me."

"Are you really all right?"

"Yeah," he muttered. "It's just—that sort of hurt. A lot."

"Let me look at it."

"No way," Elliot said. "Girl germs."

"Oh, good grief. There's no such thing." Cami lifted up his shirt enough to look at his back. "Wow, I see some sort of mark there about as long as my thumb. Are you sure you're okay?"

The hit had knocked the breath out of him and stung a little at the time. He had no idea what kind of mark was on his back, but as far as he could tell, he was fine.

"Call one of your Brownies to come look at it," Cami said.

"Maybe later," he said. "Just get that bottle."

"I think I know your plan," Cami said. "I'll take care of it if you can get Kovol there."

From the top of the hill, Kovol yelled, "Show yourself, Elliot, so that I can destroy you!"

Elliot couldn't think of a better reason *not* to show himself. But he didn't want Kovol aiming that magical energy at any of his friends or family.

Elliot slowly stood, but a voice behind him called, "Okay, but which of us is Elliot?"

Elliot turned and behind him saw…himself. In Elliot's form, Harold stood in front of Cami, blocking her body with his.

Kovol sent more balls of energy down the hill, but he wasn't sure which Elliot to fight, so he wasn't aiming well. It was easier for Elliot to dodge his attacks this time, which was good because his back still stung and he was moving slowly.

As Harold blocked the balls, he declared, "Cami Wortson, you are the love of my life. Give me an order and I will obey."

"Puff us away from here!" she cried. "I've got the bottle. Puff us away."

Harold turned to her. "Uh, my love, the correct word is 'poof.'"

"Then poof us!" Cami screamed. "Hurry!"

"Ah, the love of my life nags with the sweetest voice," Harold said, although Elliot thought the expression on his face as they poofed away wasn't exactly the most loving.

Kovol roared when they disappeared, but Elliot stood, ready to face him. That hit on his back was exactly the jump-start his magic needed. He felt the energy of the Pixies again, pulsing and vibrating inside his body like a humming engine. But he didn't plan on using it. Not yet anyway.

"Are you the real Elliot or another fake one?" Kovol yelled.

"There's only one way to find out," Elliot said, already backing away. "You'll have to catch me and see for yourself."

Just as before, he ran and Kovol followed, his feet pounding into the earth behind Elliot like miniature earthquakes. Luckily, this was the very spot where he and Tubs and Cami had played Capture the Flag only that morning, and Elliot knew the area well. He only hoped Cami had done her part. He wouldn't have time to make sure, and there were no second chances.

"No more waiting," Kovol said. "When I see you, I will eat you."

"You'd better," Elliot said. "Because I'm the most powerful wizard since Minthred a thousand years ago. The only way to become as strong as me is to eat me."

"No!" Cole darted out from the bushes where they had been hiding. He ran up and kicked Kovol in the shin. "You can't eat our brother!"

"Hush!" Elliot hissed.

Then Kyle ran forward and said, "You won't even like him. Last year when Elliot and I were in a fight, I bit his finger and it tasted awful."

Kovol laughed, then picked up Kyle and tucked him under his arm. "I'll eat you next."

"No, you won't!" Elliot swerved around with the idea to do magic. He could play the trick he had used on Fidget before of "This is a stickup!" and Kyle would be free. The sticks would lift Kovol up in the air just as they had with Fidget. But he didn't know how much magic he had left or if it was strong enough to lift Kovol. There had to be another way.

Maybe he didn't need magic to trick Kovol. He remembered how he had gotten away from Tubs earlier that morning.

"Get me!" Elliot yelled. "Just me. But only if you catch me!" Then he ran back to Kovol, who dropped Kyle in his hope to grab on to Elliot. But Elliot crawled between Kovol's legs while yelling for his brother to run. Kovol leaned low to reach Elliot and then, just as Tubs had done, tumbled into a somersault. Elliot waited to be sure Kyle had gotten away, then circled around and continued his race.

The somersault only slowed Kovol for a moment before he was back on his feet running again. Elliot wasn't as far ahead as he would have wanted, but he hoped it was enough. Two steps before he reached the clearing where he and Cami had hidden their flag that morning, Elliot took a hard left turn and ducked behind a tree.

A moment later, Kovol came to the same clearing and stopped. If Elliot had wanted to hide, he was doing a terrible job. For there he was, just standing still, with no expression of worry or surprise on his face. In fact, all he had was some strange smile, as if he had a great secret.

"This is the end," Kovol said, charging forward for a final attack.

He picked up Elliot's body and crushed it like a soda can, then dropped the entire thing in his mouth.

And not two seconds later, the evil Demon fell flat on his face, sound asleep.

Chapter 28

Where Elliot Has a Scar

Cami was the first to jump from her hiding place after Kovol fell. Harold came out behind her, and she even gave him a quick kiss on his cheek, causing him to turn redder than a raspberry.

Kyle came out next and quickly got a punch in the arm from Cole, who had run after Kovol to save his twin brother.

Elliot was the last to step out from the tree. Just as he had known would ppen, Kovol had eaten the paper-mache Elliot doll in one bite. Inside that doll was a very large jar of turnip juice, goat spit, and earwax.

And Kovol was sound asleep.

Mr. Willimaker and Fudd poofed in next. Mr. Willimaker gave Elliot the lowest bow he'd ever made, and when he explained to Fudd what had happened, Fudd also bowed to Elliot. Then the other creatures who had fought the Shadow Men near the gripping mud appeared. They began cheering and dancing and singing.

Reed, Wendy, and Tubs ran in next. Wendy gave Elliot an enormous hug, and Reed patted him on the back. Tubs shoved his hands into his pockets and said, "That was pretty cool. Maybe you're not such a dork after all."

"We were so worried," Wendy said. "We saw Kovol hit you with that ball of energy and knock you over."

"It felt like he threw a bowling ball at me," Elliot said. "But other than a mark on my back, I don't think he did any damage."

"What mark?" Mr. Willimaker asked. "Let me see it."

Elliot turned and raised his shirt. "What does it look like?"

"It's a scar in the shape of a crown," Mr. Willimaker said. "Kovol tried to curse you, but whatever you were thinking about must have blocked the curse and saved your life."

"I was thinking that I didn't care what happened to me," Elliot said. "I only wanted to protect my family, and the Brownies, and the rest of the Underworld."

"That's a wizard's mark," Mr. Willimaker added. "Only the most powerful of all Underworld creatures ever get one of those."

"I'm no wizard." Then Elliot remembered that Minthred was only a goat herder. He probably never thought he deserved to be called a wizard either.

"Truly you have the heart of a king," Fudd said. "And today you saved us all."

Patches poofed in and immediately hugged Elliot's leg. "Elliot—I mean, Your Highness! I just heard the news! We'll throw a big party in Burrowsville to celebrate. We'll have everything yummy to eat there—carrot soup, cabbage pies, cauliflower cookies, all the best foods!"

"Yum," Elliot said. Even Wendy's scariest menu had never included cabbage pies.

"We'll have that party tomorrow night," Mr. Willimaker said. "Can't you see how tired the king is?"

"I am tired," Elliot agreed. "A party tomorrow would be better. Besides, we still have to figure out what to do with Kovol."

The Elf Slimy Toe Jam, or whatever his name was, stepped forward. "We have a plan for that, King Elliot. We shall create a home for him deep in the Underworld seas, where the Mermaids will keep watch over him. Even if another Shadow Man does exist, he'd never get through all that water to rescue Kovol. We feel that Kovol will sleep there forever."

Forever sounded pretty good to Elliot. He nodded his permission at the Elf, and then thanked him for Minthred's journal. "Maybe one day someone will write a book about my story too," Elliot said.

Mr. Tojam laughed. "A book about an eleven-year-old human who becomes king of the Brownies and fights an Underworld war? Who'd ever believe it?"

Elliot joined in the laughter. "Yeah, that does sound pretty crazy. Thanks for taking Kovol to the Mermaids. And thanks again for letting me see Minthred's journal."

"You saved our world," Mr. Tojam said. "Thank you, King Elliot." He bowed, then snapped his fingers, and both he and Kovol disappeared.

"Until tomorrow night, then," Fudd said. "I'd offer to poof you home, but I know you still have Pixie magic, so you can probably get yourself there better."

"I could," Elliot said. "But for tonight I'll just walk home with my family. See you tomorrow." And that was the most ordinary thing Elliot had done all day.

Chapter
29

Where Elliot Goes Home

Elliot remained pretty quiet for the rest of that night and through the next day. His parents got home sometime that morning, but nobody said anything to them about the Brownies or Kovol or the Underworld war. They had all promised Elliot they would keep his secret. And even though it wasn't much of a secret anymore, Elliot appreciated their promise.

It would take a long time for Sprite's Hollow to repair the many sinkholes throughout town, but at least there had been no new ones. All of the reporters got scientists to come on their news shows and explain that the sinkholes had been caused by a freak meteor storm several thousand light-years away. The scientists seemed to believe it, the reporters didn't seem to understand it, and everyone went on with their lives.

Elliot hadn't been the only one to notice that the sinkholes on Main Street were in the shape of his name. But then the mayor of Sprite's Hollow, Mayor George Fillat, convinced everyone that the sinkhole was in the shape of *his* name and said it was a sign that he should be reelected. His campaign slogan was immediately changed to "Protecting our town from all danger over and under the world!"

Elliot snorted when he heard that, but there wasn't much he could do about it.

That afternoon, Cami stopped by the house to check on Elliot. "You seem quiet," she said. "Everything okay?"

"Definitely," he said.

"I told Harold that I'm not the love of his life," Cami said. "I don't want to be the love of anyone's life right now, just their friend." She was quiet for a moment, then added, "Are we friends, Elliot?"

"Definitely." And in that moment, he didn't dislike her at all. Even calling her Toadface didn't seem so funny anymore.

"You want to play a game or something?" she asked. "And don't say definitely."

"Then I'll just say okay," he answered. They spent the rest of the afternoon in the backyard kicking a soccer ball around and then helping Cole and Kyle dig a hole for a new springtime mud puddle.

When it was time for the party that evening, Elliot invited his brothers and sister and Cami and Tubs to come along. The Elves would be in charge of poofing everyone down there, so he knew it would be a smooth ride.

The clearing in the center of Burrowsville was spread with tables and picnic blankets and food wherever it fit. Hundreds of creatures from every corner of the Underworld had come. Elliot recognized many of them as the creatures who had been turned to stone in Kovol's cave. With the Shadow Men gone, their curse had been lifted.

Standing near the front was Agatha, back into her usual Hag form. Elliot ran to her and wrapped his arms around her waist. "Thank you, Agatha," he said. "Nobody else but you could've healed everyone."

She patted his back. "And I knew no one but you could've saved the Underworld. Oh...oopsie."

Something wet and squishy plopped onto Elliot's head. Whatever it was, Agatha immediately picked it up and Elliot jumped back. Agatha had her hand pressed over her left eye.

"Eww!" he cried. "Did your eye just fall on my head?"

With a little pop, Agatha squeezed her eye back into place and laughed. "Don't be silly. Eyes don't just fall out." He reached up to check the top of his head for leftover eye parts, but she pushed his arm down. "I wouldn't do that. One moment, dear." She blinked, and he felt a breeze pass through his hair. "Yes, that's better now."

"What did—" Elliot stopped. "Never mind. I won't ask."

She smiled. "I am a Hag, and these words you must know. I'll always admire you, wherever you go."

Elliot grinned back at her. "Thanks, Agatha."

Mr. Willimaker ran up to Elliot. "Your Highness! Here's your crown!"

The crown was small enough that it would have fit better on Elliot's wrist than his head, but he put it on anyway. His family was given their choice of seats, and then Mr. Willimaker led Elliot up to his toadstool throne.

Fudd was already sitting beside Elliot's throne. He was facing backward and hopelessly trying to find his cup of Mushroom Surprise drink when Elliot sat down.

Gently, Elliot put a hand on Fudd's shoulder and steered him to the correct position. Then he handed Fudd his drink.

"Thank you, Your Highness," Fudd said.

Elliot picked up his own cup of Mushroom Surprise—his favorite of all Underworld foods—and clicked it against Fudd's cup. "Cheers!" he said.

"What should we toast to?" Fudd asked. "To a long reign for King Elliot, of course!"

"I think a better toast is a lifetime of happiness for all Underworld creatures," Elliot said.

"Yes, Your Highness." With that, Fudd pushed back his chair and stood. For once facing in the correct direction, he raised his cup to the crowd in front of him and said, "When Elliot was made our king, I was the last Brownie to cheer for him. So I want to be the first of all Underworld creatures to officially thank him for what he has done. In honor of Elliot Penster, king of the Brownies, may we toast to a lifetime of happiness for all creatures who helped bring peace to the Underworld. And a lifetime of happiness to the human, King Elliot, and his family and friends."

At once, the entire audience clicked their cups together and said, "To all, a lifetime of happiness."

With that, the dinner was served. Elliot ate very little of what was offered to him, in part because most of it wasn't food he really liked, but also because the only thing he really wanted to do was look over the crowd and try to memorize as many faces as he could.

When dinner was over, Mr. Willimaker nudged Elliot on the arm and asked, "Is there anything you want to say, Your Highness?"

There was. Elliot stood and the crowd went silent. "You've all said a lot of nice things about me ever since I became king," he began. "That's been really cool, but I think none of those things were true *until* I became the king. I was just an ordinary kid before. And the thing is, I'm still an ordinary kid. But I had to learn that even someone ordinary can do something extraordinary."

The creatures in the crowd looked at one another as if they wanted to clap for Elliot. But something in the way he spoke suggested he didn't want them to clap. He only wanted them to understand. So they nodded softly and waited for him to finish.

Elliot's smile widened. "When I first became king of the Brownies, they were ordinary too. But you all saw the way they fought yesterday. They might not have the strength of the Goblins, or the sneakiness of the Pixies, or the grace of the Elves. But you saw their bravery and loyalty in the fight against Kovol. They've learned to be extraordinary too." Then he looked down for a moment. "And because we both understand that, it's time for the Brownies to have a new king."

A gasp spread across the audience. Patches stood up from her seat and yelled out "No!" then ran up the aisle near him. When she got close, her father took her hand and held her back.

"You know it's time for this, and so do I." Elliot said it to everyone, but to his friends most of all. He would miss the Brownies and they would miss him, but they also deserved a ruler who could always be here in Burrowsville with them. And he was ready to just be Elliot Penster, ordinary eleven-year-old kid, again.

"What will we do without you?" Mr. Willimaker asked.

"You will be the chief royal advisor," Elliot said. "Any time the ruler of the Brownies needs help, you are the first person to talk to. No one gives better advice, and no one has served me with more loyalty."

"But what if the Brownies get into trouble again?" Patches asked. "There's no one as clever as you, Elliot."

"Sure there is. Patches, you are smarter than anyone else I've met down here. I want you to be the chief royal scholar. If there's anything the ruler needs to know, you are in charge of figuring it out."

Patches bowed low. "Yes, King Elliot."

"I'll serve the new ruler any way I can," Fudd said. "Though I know with my blindness, I won't be as much help as I want to be."

"Your blindness only helped us to see you better, how good and loyal and strong you are," Elliot said. "But it won't be a difficulty for you any longer."

Fudd shook his head. "There's only one way to heal this curse of the Shadow Men, and that's—"

"That's for a magical creature to give up his magic," Elliot said. "I still have a little of the Pixie magic left."

Fudd shook his head. "No, Your Highness. If you're ever in trouble on the surface world, that magic can save you."

"I'll never be in as much trouble as I've had down here," Elliot said. "I don't need the magic. Just my friends and family."

Tears streamed down Fudd's cheeks. "Don't do this for me, please. I'm not worth it."

Elliot put a hand on Fudd's shoulder. "You're my friend. Besides, I'm still the king. You don't get to tell me no. Patches, how do I do this?"

"Put your fingers over his eyes," she instructed.

Elliot knelt in front of Fudd and put his fingers over Fudd's eyes. The magical vibrations he had felt inside him rose from his chest and traveled out his fingers, and then they were gone.

As the magic entered his body, Fudd stumbled back and fell to the ground.

"Are you okay?" Mr. Willimaker asked.

Fudd rolled to his stomach, then pushed himself up. He put a chubby hand in front of his face and wiggled his fingers, then began laughing. "I see my hand! I can see!" He picked up a spoon and looked at himself in the reflection, "Argh! I forgot how ugly I am." He ran to Elliot, still laughing. "You are a great king, Elliot. Thank you, thank you for what you've done. But I'm sorry to take your magic."

"You didn't take it. I wanted to give it to you," Elliot said, "and to give you this too." He took the crown off his head and handed it to Fudd. "You are the king now."

Fudd shook his head. "Me? There are other Brownies who deserve it more."

"You don't become king because you deserve it. You become king because the Brownies deserve you." He raised his cup of Mushroom Surprise again. "Long live King Fudd."

The entire audience raised their cups. "Long live King Fudd," they all repeated.

Elliot smiled. "It's time for me to go home now." He walked down to his brothers and sister, let Reed punch him lightly on the arm, and then said, "We need someone to poof us there."

Several Elves stepped forward, but Fudd raised a hand. "It will be my honor to send Elliot on his last trip home from the Underworld."

"Just one minute," Elliot said. "Everyone move back." Thanks to the Mushroom Surprise, he burped out the king of all burps. Or at least the former king of all burps. It knocked over the nearest table and melted the tablecloth. "I have to admit, I will miss that," Elliot added. Then he stepped back. "Now it's time."

And with that, Elliot closed his eyes, felt the last tug in his gut, and opened his eyes back in his room. Reed sat on his bed across from Elliot.

"That was pretty cool," Reed said. "Are you okay?"

Elliot smiled. "Yeah. Everything is great."

And for the next day and the next and every day after, Elliot played and learned and laughed as any ordinary kid would. Every once in a while, though, he would stop when he smelled the very strong odor of pickles. And sometimes a pointy brown hat would peek out from behind a bush. And he would know that even though he was no longer the king, a part of him would always belong to the Brownies.

Warning: Any similarity between this story and any actual story of an eleven-year-old king of the Brownies fighting an Underworld war is, believe it or not, a really freaky coincidence. Seriously, what are the odds of that?

About the Author

Jennifer A. Nielsen lives at the base of a very tall mountain in northern Utah with her husband, three children, and a dog that won't play fetch. Although she has never fought in any Underworld Wars, she did once engage in a battle to the death with a noisy cricket that had gotten loose in her house. The battle ended in a tie and the cricket is fine. We are less sure about the condition of the house.

About the Illustrator

Gideon Kendall graduated from the Cooper Union for Science and Art with a BFA and has since been working as an artist, illustrator, animation designer, and musician in Brooklyn.